A CERTAIN DOUBT

Michael Fincham

Appin Press, UK

First Published 2012 by Appin Press an imprint of Countyvise Ltd
14 Appin Road, Birkenhead, CH41 9HH

British Library Cataloguing in Publication Data.
A catalogue record for this book is available from the British Library.

ISBN 978 1 906205 94 2

Cover design by Rob Williams. Book design by Charles McIntyre.

AUTHOR'S NOTE

This is a work of fiction though it is based on what little is known of a real person. Guilhem d'Autun existed as does his abbey and tomb in the very pretty village of St Guilhem le Desert in the Herault South West France.

I make no pretence to be a historian but have tried to the best of my ability to stick to the majority historical view of the main events that take place in the novel.

There was a Jewish colony in Narbonne at this time and it appears that they agreed to help King Pepin to drive the Saracens out of South West France. The great mosque at Cordoba was begun at about the time outlined in the book. The coronations of Charles and Carloman as kings of Francia AD768 is documented. The coronation of King Charles as Emperor by the Pope in AD800 is also well recorded. The struggles of the church in Rome at this time to regulate and unify both beliefs and liturgy are also well accepted as is the part played by King (later Emperor Charlemagne) Charles in this endeavour. Perhaps Charles could be considered the first European?

The recent discovery of an ancient Coptic text bolstering the possibility of a 'Jesus line' headlined in *The Times*, dated 20th September 2012, is an extraordinary coincidence that certainly adds to the debate surrounding the reliability of ancient scraps and writings as a foundation for belief. And it is uncannily close to the heart of Guilhem's search for certainty.

CHAPTER 1

758 AD
– The Beginning –

There were many things that seemed to be out of reach. The pommel of his father's sword, which gave off its dull metal gleam as it moved around the big rooms of the cold stone castle, attached to the formidable side of Thierry Comte d'Autun. It was much easier to get to know the sword hidden in the worn tooled leather casing than his father's face, which always seemed to loom out of a distant height, almost hidden by the lush beard which preceded it.

'Aha, they tell me you have been up to mischief again,' and there would be an absent-minded chuck under his chin. Rarely, he was rewarded with a swooping hug which always lifted him up into the roof, and then a moment of heart stopping joy when his father's eyes, warmed brown in smiles, looked straight at him.

'A good boy who will turn into a real man is always up to mischief.' A quick kiss planted firmly in the centre of his forehead followed, and then almost in the same unstoppable moment, Guilhem was back with sword hilt, scabbard and the distance that always seemed to be between him and his father.

There were many other things that were always out of reach. Big ironwork latches on the rough hewn oak doors that led to more interesting parts of the castle; especially the doors that led to winding narrow stairs that twisted dimly up into the unknown.

'Guilhem, my lord Guilhem!' The shrill voice of the serving maid assigned to him for the time being.

'Please my lord, I have told you before. That bolt is not to be drawn.'

'But why Matilde?'

'Because your mother says so.' Such an unsatisfactory answer, that barred him from all things of real interest.

Undoubtedly, wherever they led would be more interesting than the large square beamed kitchen, or the great hall with the smoke laden fire that often burned reluctantly seeping tendrils of grey smoke up the wall, leaving its black stain behind. Sometimes the reluctant fire seemed to come alive, swallowing great logs of holm oak or ash or scrub pine, in a leaping backdrop of yellow and orange. Usually, this would happen when the hall was full of strangers, and the big tables had been moved to the centre of the room for a welcome feast.

It was here, in the place where everything was always beyond reach, that much of his early youth was spent.

'My lord please, not so near the fire!' The serfs that tried to keep up with the uncertain rushing enthusiasms of this unruly child were also tasked with teaching him many of the essential rudiments of life. With the servants he was shown how to ride the small wiry ponies that were in the common use of the people. He soon learned that riding was only a small part of horsemanship. Feeding, watering, cleaning; visits to the roaring flames of the blacksmith to see the magical transformation of red-hot iron to the shaped shoe. It took a long time to be convinced that nailing these iron hoops to the hooves was not a painful ordeal for the animals.

'Blacksmith,' the little figure would ask, 'are you sure that you are not hurting Fidelius?'

'My lord, we need to do this so his hooves may not wear away. Now that would be cruel! Do you understand?'

But even after many visits, he winced when the first nail was driven. How could this shaggy animal with the big eyes stand there so placidly? Years later, he would still wince on occasion - reflex from the early years that would not leave him. Then there were bridles, halters, and stirrups to put on, adjust and remove. And these were of hemp or leather and of different designs.

When the weather changed so that the cold rains swept along the coast and the wind drove the sleet like invisible arrows, occasionally the snow would drift into the castle through all the gaps and lie in frozen crystal powder on the stairs by some of the window openings. Then he could be found by the big fire with arms locked around a log beyond the compass of his arms and longer than his height. Face red with effort, all muscles straining, the little soot covered figure would try to roll the log onto the fire to rekindle the flames from their dingy smoking embers to the orange and red that signalled real heat, and which if large enough, could transform the room from the cold winter misery.

'Please my lord, we have told you before. You are not to feed the fire. Your mother will have my hands cut off if harm should befall you.' Matilde would swoop down and set him away from danger. Even as a small boy, he felt that it was undignified to be swept up so unceremoniously.

Usually he would be spotted with an accompanying cry of alarm before he could achieve the Herculean task and would be gathered up and led, hand held firmly, to his mother's room.

Here was a place where he was nearly always allowed to go and so less interesting. There were few private rooms in the castles of the time, but the Countess Aude had the unusual privilege of a room for herself and her husband on the occasions he visited her. He was to see how rare this privacy was many times and in many places in later years.

Aude was the second daughter of Charles Martel, the most powerful Sire in France. In spite of this, she often wore an expression of slight distress, as though she was continually trying to make sense of her lot in life. It was as though the weight of her lineage had blurred her own personality. On occasions when some servant girl led him unwillingly to her chamber, she would greet Guilhem with an air of surprise, as though she could not remember exactly who he was.

'My son, are you in trouble again?' The soft clear voice would feign anger.

Then her eyes would crease in love for the wiry figure which always seemed to be in a helter skelter of inexplicable enthusiasms.

'Come, my love, give the poor slaves some peace.' And she would smile her thanks to the apprehensive wench who had brought him safely to her once more.

Aude could connect to the quick curiosity of the seven year old, and holding the dirty hand after a quick embrace, she would lead him to the table in the window and set him a practical task, such as sorting the wool skeins for the loom which occupied much of her time.

'Let me see, my young lord. These colours are all in a muddle. Help me sort them out.'

Sometimes there would be deliveries of skins, or lengths of cloth to be checked, and they would count together whether the merchants had delivered the orders correctly. In later years, this attention to the accuracy of suppliers and the necessity of constant checking would be a most valuable attribute to take to the craft of war and the success of an army on the move

His mother's room was a place where he felt safe and unchallenged, and he was often to be found making his way there at odd times of the day, to be enveloped in a smell of lavender and clean skin that was not the norm for the rest of the household. But Guilhem was not a quiet child content to watch his mother at her loom, or keeping quiet while she gave orders for the household day, or even when she had company, which was not often.

'Enough mama. Enough. I must see that my pony has been shod correctly.' A sudden squirm, and somehow he was gone, leaving behind a note of his visit in the form of a berry stain on the linen robe, or a darker smear on her neck which was never easy to remove.

In spite of the unconditional love that he found with his mother, he found that in later years she was a strangely indistinct figure that would not hold steady in his mind. She seemed to merge into the echo of lavender, as though she were trying to break through a veil. The constancy of her love seemed to hide the detail of her person from his memory.

There were people that Guilhem remembered far more easily, although not always with such quiet pleasure, such as the priest who tried to teach him the ways of the church, and the essential liturgies and prayers that a Christian son of a Count should have as the foundation of his life. Guilhem liked the church, where it was always dusk and where the huge stone blocks grew like giant legs into the even darker heights. Even when the sun shone hot outside, it seemed to lose all conviction when the hot rays tried to fight the permanent gloom. It was a strange place for a small boy to like, but there was something about the solid stone and the way that the squalling streets were suddenly shut off as he crossed the paving slabs into the dark.

He could tell that here was a place of consequence; a place where even a small boy could sense that there was meaning beyond the stone.

The problems started with the priest assigned to make sense of it all to the little boy who wandered unafraid beneath the heavy Roman arched portico and wanted to explore the bell tower and the vestry where the mysteries were. The priest smelled of rotten teeth and garlic and was a slab-like man who carried his flesh like a pork roast, and whose hands were always wet. But the real difficulty was that his words did not connect into a whole for Guilhem.

The story of the Lord Jesus riding on a donkey into the town called Jerusalem in a far away land and where, after dinner, the Roman soldiers found him and took him away and nailed him to a wooden cross, did seem to relate to the blackened leathery corpses that sometimes adorned the gibbets on the paved way at the entrance to the fortified town. A random collection of these tall crosses stood on a small rise near the small guardhouse that also doubled as a tax collection point. Provided the wind was from the west, the gagging scent of the deterrent fruit was normally wafted away from the town.

But Jesus had done good things and had even organised his own crucifixion for Guilhem's personal benefit. It was very confusing. At this point they would trail, hand in unwilling hand, down the echoing nave to stand in front of the wooden cross with a rough hewn figure twisting in a stasis of agony with real iron nails punched into the wrecked hands and feet, from which trails of blood coursed generously.

Sometimes he was taken out of the main church into the brilliant sun and across a small cloister to another building, which by contrast was lit by well spaced windows. Here he would be handed over to Father Bedier, a priest whose need for the tonsure was abrogated by the lack of hair anywhere on his head. He was a smiling man with crinkly blue eyes, carrying more weight in front than behind, whose hands were surprisingly fine and agile. He introduced the young heir to another world of light and colour, where scrolls of pale brown parchments would magically transform into tales of far lands with exotic trees and animals that wound their trails of brilliant blue and green and gold down the scroll margins. Here he was shown that the stories and prayers that he learned in the large gloomy mystery of the church were being told again and again for the use of people far away, so that the Word of God would never be lost. This was the most important work that man could do.

It was here that he first met the boy that was to change his life. For here, attending the lessons attached to the glowing scrolls, was a young boy whose name was Witiza - the son of the Comte de Maguelone. A boy of a very different mould to Guilhem. He was some three years older, and already showed many of the traits which would mark him out from the other young minor nobles of his time.

Witiza, even at the age of ten, was a presence that gave weight to the space around him. It often seemed that the air ceased to move around the grave figure, tall for his age, with a prominent forehead and an already aquiline nose. A boy who did most things well and who could learn everything first time. It was not at all clear why there should be a bond between the two young boys with such different temperaments, especially given the three year age gap which, at ten and seven, was immense. However, it soon became clear to all around that Guilhem had acquired a patron and, when needed, a protector.

The days passed between the castle and the church and the scriptorium, and the many activities that made up the training of a young noble of the time. Witiza was not always around, as his father's castle was a day's ride from the ancient town of Narbonne. In spite of the gaps in time, which sometimes could stretch over many weeks, their friendship grew steadily. Slowly, the young Witiza became a source of knowledge for the scampering Guilhem. When even Father Bedier could not hold still the impatient mind, Witiza would put an arm round him and quietly repeat the point, so that it not only became clear, but even important enough to be retained. Learning was nearly all about retention, and this tended not to be the strong point of the seven year old.

It was never clear to the observers round the two boys what the attraction was for Witiza, nor what the silent magic potion was that he possessed to quiet the restless mind and impatient body. Whatever the bond, Guilhem started to make real progress in knowledge of the scriptures and the religious life and ceremony; with history and with rudimentary mathematics for which he did seem to have a natural aptitude. Reading proved more of a hurdle, but the patience of his tutors began to be rewarded as on occasion he would ask to look at one of the many scrolls in the scriptorium and could be seen with his tousled head bent over the script forming the Latin words in slow succession.

Admittedly, the history of battles and campaigns seemed to be of much higher interest than the prayers; collects and gospels endlessly copied by the monks in the scriptorium. But there in the sunlit windows of the bare stone room, he also began his love affair with the brilliant colours and illustrations of the early illuminated manuscripts taking laborious shape before his eyes. All the colour in the world seemed to be concentrated onto the parchment in a miraculous riot of intensity.

Blues born of woad and indigo, reds ground from laque de garance, or kermes derived from the ground beetles that fed on the oak forests; gold leaf applied with meticulous exactitude to highlight the glory of the Word of God.

While there was little doubt that the true inclinations of the son of the Comte d'Autun lay in action rather than the quieter pleasures of academic excellence, nevertheless there began to emerge the structures that would shape his life. This development took place in the security of his mother's unconditional love and his father's distant, amused approval.

The surroundings of the church and monastery balanced the harsh realities of existence of the time. In the background there was always Witiza, who seemed to hold the young Guilhem more as a work in progress than just as a young friend. As time passed, it also became clear that development of the life of the younger spirit was a principal plank of their relationship.

While it had always been clear that Witiza only had one choice in the path that his life would take, which led inexorably to a life devoted to Christ and the church, there was no such predestined route for Guilhem. As the years passed, this caused strains in the friendship, but the intensity of the continuous discussions also created an unbreakable rope between them. Each discussion added a strand to the twisted fibre that sometimes stretched to near breaking, but in the act of pulling apart actually strengthened the tie. It was a strange relationship for young boys.

Of course, it was not all earnest discussion and prayer. Even the solemn Witiza could be persuaded to go hunting, or to take part in some trial of physical strength. To begin with, his was always the arrow that struck home to find the mark in the small deer, or large hare, or on occasion a particularly slow quail. At first, the wrestling challenge always ended with Guilhem on his back looking up into the fiercely concentrated face which seemed to reflect the importance of victory for a higher cause. When it hurt, which was not infrequently, Guilhem would go red in an effort not to cry, and would wriggle frustrated under the pinioning arms of the older and heavier boy. But sometimes, having been thrown yet again by some considered move of Witiza the wily, he would lie in the dust or on the sand laughing in an uncontrolled fit. This seemed to disturb Witiza more that the unintentional pain he sometimes caused. He could never understand the humour of defeat.

However, the time came when on occasion the natural speed and quicker reflexes of the younger boy brought him the occasional victory. He could not hold Witiza down for more than a flash and Witiza, wriggling frantically under this unexpected turn of events, would escape the hold protesting that his left shoulder had never touched the ground, while brushing the telltale grains of sand away. The first time it happened, he denied having been bested all the way back to the castle where they changed, washed and ate before going through the church to the scriptorium. Before entering the church, Witiza stopped and put his hand on Guilhem's shoulder.

'You were correct. It was your fall. I should not have denied you,' and without waiting for a reply, he entered the high arched portal and was lost in the gloom.

CHAPTER 2

804 AD, Gellone
– The Beginning of the End –

He was being followed. A flock of crows sprayed into the air some quarter of a day behind. Above the crows, two brown vultures wheeled patiently high in the blue. He was not really surprised. He had been under observation for much of his life, though he had wondered if taking the tonsure would at last free him. Evidently not. The man stopped; he could see it from here. Poised between the sky and the gorge, his position mirrored the point of change to another life which seemed to be the culmination of those years of marching to destinations that were never final.

He was returning to build an abbey in the service of God, and to make peace with his maker before the years took their toll. Memory took his mind to a hall far away and a crackling fire. In front of him stood the spare figure of Prior Alcuin with piercing blue eyes and expressive eyebrow, 'by the fruits of their labours ye shall know them.'

To this end, he had forsaken the trappings of life at the court. Just one month earlier, he had taken the position of an abbot of the Benedictine brotherhood, under the direction of his former friend and mentor, Bishop Benoit of Aniane. He was sure that the Bishop was responsible for his pursuers.

Last time he had looked down at his valley, it had been in the guise of a count defending his lands from a warring band of brigands, which had led him a tortuous dance through the scrub before being trapped half a day later at the end of the valley. None of them had survived. Now in the saddlebags were the rough woollen gowns of the priesthood, and under the leather campaign helmet was the bare circle of the tonsured scalp.

The horse snuffled his neck and he smelled the comfort of her grass breath and warm skin against his shoulder. Her skin rippled a fly away, and the mare's foot pawed the ground. The scent of thyme drifted up.

His horse at his side; the scent of the garrigue pleasing the air; the warmth of the mid-morning sun; the evidence of man at work in the service of his god; all seemed to be confirmation that his choice was blessed. The man flicked his nose unconsciously with the back of his hand as he always did at moments of decision. Surely this would be his final resting place, and when they saw that he was engaged in the service of God, they would finally leave him alone. He looked behind again to where the crows had betrayed his pursuers. The sky was empty, but he was sure they had not yet given up.

He turned back to the small settlement dwarfed by the vertical cliff. His martial eye quickly noted the faults in the work. The midden placed too close to the stream; the way the foundations had moved so that already the small church building was twisting out of square; the poor state of the small irrigation channels choked with weed. The defences were non-existent. Years of peace and the lack of a strong leader had left its mark. The whole area had the look of a place which was slipping slowly into self-indulgent decay.

As he looked, the corpulent figure of a monk came out of a doorway and rolled across the green to the church. His lips tightened with the displeasure of one who looks on disorder as a sin; a sin not of omission but of commission. Thirty years of campaigning at the side of Charlemagne, King of the Franks and Emperor of the west, meant that the warrior monk had been chiselled into a man who knew what was necessary for survival.

CHAPTER THREE

804 AD, Gellone
– Pursuit –

Witiza's hard bright faith of their shared youth was at least, in part, the reason that Guilhem had taken the tonsure, and that the world of sweeping political ambition that had surrounded his life had shrunk to this small valley in the foothills of the Cevenne. He rode slowly out of the stand of holm oaks and poplars and across the grass meadow glancing back at the cliff top. There was no sign of his pursuers. He rode past the rough hewn doors of the church which were hanging open revealing a glimpse of the plain wooden altar behind which hung a surprisingly fine carved and painted crucifixion of Jesus. The body twisted in agony reflected the listing frame of the building. It reminded him of the cross of his childhood in Narbonne.

He was passed the church before anyone appeared to take any notice, but then at the same time his presence seemed to seep into the consciousness of everyone. Work stopped and a curious gaze surrounded the stranger with the tinge of apprehension that strangers always brought with them, especially a stranger with such a disfigurement.

He was not recognised; nobody knew this weathered figure with the worn accoutrements and the sliced nose who was so at one with his animal. He guided the mare between the poor dwellings and the apprehensive stares to the top of the slope where the stone building backed up against the cliff. This building stood out as the one construction built with care and which exuded an air of solid harmony. The warm grey limestone blocks were well fitted and the door of thick oak planks and heavy iron fittings leant a purposeful air to the two storey construction. The windows were oblong and bigger than normal for a building of the time.

The scriptorium had been built to house the many precious manuscripts, books, and parchments that he had been bequeathed by the hermit priest Alcinus with his dying breath. Alcinus was another who had suffered the final penalty because of Guilhem's heritage, even though the sword that had killed him had been meant for Guilhem himself.

The picture of the extraordinary cave library cut into a cliff top on the edge of the sea not far from Constantinople sprang vividly to mind as Guilhem looked with pride at this centre of learning nestling in the sunlit gorge. Maybe the fine old hermit had not died in vain.

The knocking reverberated through the compact two storey building, and in a few moments a young monk stood in the bright sunlight shielding his eyes.

'Is brother Jonathen able to see an old friend?'

'He is here but....'

'Tell him that Guilhem is here.'

'Guilhem?' the monk looked enquiringly.

'That should be enough,' Guilhem said quietly.

Within a very short time there was a flurry of activity within the building. Brother Jonathen's voice clearly heard.

'Fetch wine and bread. Make a space at the table. Don't worry about that. We will return to that; call everybody. The count is here!'

A moment later the familiar elongated figure appeared in the doorway. Brown cassock hung somewhat awry and one sleeve stained with a red splash. The blue eyes deep set under strong white eyebrows. A smile which transformed the thin ascetic face lit the air around even in the midday sun. He knelt;

'It is the Seigneur ! Welcome back. It has been too many years.'

Guilhem bent over and lifted the kneeling figure,

'I am no longer your c c count.' The slight stutter which had been with him since childhood was not a result of shyness or indecision. It was rather an unkind trick of the tongue which belied his normal clarity of thought. That, and in latter years the cruel scar that disfigured a well modelled profile, were the things that occupied the first impressions of newcomers to his acquaintance. 'I have come to be your abbot.' With that he removed his leather helmet and revealed his tonsured head. Jonathen stared with an uncertain look.

'But how can that be .... What has happened... Have you fallen from favour with the Emperor?'

'It is long story brother Jonathen and we have time for it to be told.

For now I would meet your people and eat with you some of the bread and wine I heard you order.'

A long look followed that statement and brother Jonathen could see that that was all he would hear for the moment. But his lord seemed to be well and content with whatever had befallen in the past.

Jonathen led Guilhem into the shaded cool room. A stone floor and a well made table surrounded by sturdy stools, in front of which stood a disparate group of six, three of whom were monks all clad in brown of the Order of the Benedictines. Two men stood a little apart bearing the tools of their trade; the one in a flax smock, with a fleecing knife stowed in a wide leather belt and the other with a pestle and mortar which contained a brown paste which matched the colour of Jonathen's cassock.

Lastly and standing behind the little group was a young girl whose plain over dress was white with flour and indeed so were her hands and arms. All knelt as he entered the room.

There was mixture of apprehension and excitement on all the faces. Apprehension outweighed the latter on the young girl's face and so Guilhem went to her first.

'This is Giselle, daughter of Bruton the shepherd. She keeps us fed and helps to clean the Librarium in those areas we allow.'

'And w w what will your flour be turned into today Giselle,' asked Guilhem, the slight stutter seeming incongruous from their lord who carried quiet authority so naturally.

The young girl flushed with embarrassment and kept her eyes lowered.

'A pie my lord, a pie with lamb and turnip, and also onions and flavoured with...'

'That will do my child', said Jonathen kindly. 'She is a good cook my Lord,' he added, 'and looks after her father and two brothers. Her mother died two years ago.'

The introductions were soon over with Guilhem finding a suitable word for each, a skill he had learned early in his career as a soldier. If people were to follow, they should know early that each was valued as an individual for their special place in the world.

After wine had been drunk and the good bread consumed, Guilhem stretched with satisfaction, 'and now my friend let us see the work.'

With commendable discipline Brother Jonathen, suppressing his flood of questions, his greying hair flying round his head, led the way to the far end of the building after signing to all to return to their tasks.

'We have taken to making our own parchment.' He pointed to the skins stretched upon racks. The smaller goatskins hung in various stages of cure, goatskin being the more usual base for the parchments.

In another area the larger calf skins hung out on stretchers. These would form the more expensive vellums used for the books created for the courts of the regional dukes and counts. Some were destined for the great library at Aachen where the Emperor Carolus Magnus expressed his own love of learning by the continuous acquisition of books and manuscripts, although the great king was not a fluent reader himself.

'You should be making leather garments' said Guilhem with a quick appreciation for the income potential of the small workshop.

'Well,' replied Brother Jonathen, 'We do use the faulty pieces for shoes and bindings, but there is only enough to supply our small community here.' Guilhem remembered that the parchments could only be made from perfect skins. Even the smallest blemish made the piece unusable.

'We also make our own inks for the scrolls and books and brother Alsom teaches our two novices the skills of writing and illuminating our manuscripts.'

'Jonathen you have done well, and I have much to learn of your work and our dream we began all those years ago, but I must pay my respects to the priest at the church. So we will look at everything in the coming days, but before I take my leave let me see what you are working on in the scriptorium.'

Brother Jonathen led the way up to the second floor. Here the reason for the bigger windows was immediately clear, as the whole area was flooded with a light that picked up the small patches of brilliant colour from the pages, drawing the eye to the exquisite detail of each letter coming to life under the painful concentration of the scribes. Seated close to the windows the novices were working on the parchments clamped into position in front of them. Each table had an array of quills, squirrelhair brushes and a series of small pots that seemed to spill pure colour into the sunlit room.

Even the entry of the former count seemed to go unnoticed which Guilhem noted with wry approval. This was not the time to examine the work in detail, but he was drawn to the desk of the nearest scribe watching the unwavering concentration with which a luminous blue was being applied, creating a fold in a gown that swept up in to a branch of the initial letter on the page. It was a book of the gospel of Matthew written in Latin in uncial script which was the most common in the region.

'The work is being supervised by Bishop Alcuin,' said Jonathen quietly .

Guilhem nodded and walked quietly on, satisfied already that at least part of his dream of fifteen years was being fulfilled. This was a place where learning and the spread of the word of God was being undertaken with reverence and skill. Alcuin was one of the finest scholars in western Christendom and well known to Guilhem. It was the memory that had struck him earlier in the day. A prior then it was Alcuin who had helped set on this path all those years ago.

'My Lord, we were not ready. We had no word.....we...'

'It is as I wished Jonathen. I wanted to see our little dream as it really is. I have been worried that the changes that are happening across Christendom would have affected our vision. You wrote that we have lost our scholars from Cordoba and from Narbonne. Our church has made it hard for them to stay? And then there are things that even you know little of. More of that later. I can see there is much to be done. First I must see the priest and then I will call everyone together. My possessions are few as you can see so if I can rest beside you at night in the dormitory.......'

Guilhem had dined with his monks and listened to their concerns.

'Now before I take my leave this evening Brother Leo what of the work of the church?'

'My Lord abbot we work and worship and try to follow the teachings of our mother church. We try to follow the teachings as best our frailties allow. We work among the people and tell them about the ways of the Lord. Nearly all attend the service on the Sabbath and on the Holy days as our Lord Bishop and the Holy Father have laid down. We try to minister to the sick and dispense justice in the case of dispute and give the sacraments as we have been taught but....' his voice seemed to trail away, drifting on the air of doubt that had intruded on his steady flow of points ticked off in the service of the church and of God.

Guilhem sat quietly waiting. He had heard too many reports from his lieutenants on too many campaigns not to know that more would be learned from silence than any interruption.

Leo shifted uneasily and hefted his belly roofward perhaps hoping that this time it would stay aloft, his eyes darting round the little circle lit by the low yellow flickering flame that wafted animal fat, smoke and uncertain light in equal measure, seeming to echo the doubts that were suddenly crowding in on the group.

'Well as you know my Lord abbot, the people here, they are not schooled in the ways of the big cities. Many who have come to join have come down from the forests and they have brought their customs with them. Some do not want to enter into the ways of our Lord. Or perhaps I should say that they take part of our teachings, but seem to somehow change things. They do not always ....' Leo clasped his belly nervously.

'I understand, Brother Leo,' said Guillem quietly. 'I have come across these problems in many parts of our Emperor Charlemagne's realm. Many of his people are closer to the old ways than to the teachings of our Lord. For them the power of land, the influence of the trees, the significance of their special places, the sacrifice to the God of hunting or of the river is still too close to let go. It is so with the peoples across the Rhine whose lands are never ending forests and whose clothes are the skins of the bear and whose foods are mostly hunted and gathered. But we were all like them once upon a time. Our d..d..duty.' The little stutter honed their attention. The back of his hand flicked unconsciously at the gap of his missing right nostril. 'Our duty in this place is to show how the Lord has helped us to bring light into our lives, to show how we have learned to do many things better than in the old ways.'

Guilhem thanked the brothers for the meal and the prayers for their safe passage through the night. As he walked slowly back to the dormitory attached to the scriptorium, it seemed to him that though there was much to do, the tasks were within his grasp. This was a place where he could indeed make a difference to the small community. Maybe even the wild forest people wedded to the old religions could be brought to see the light. Indeed there was a great deal to be done. His hand flicked his nose.

However if the new abbot of Gellone had looked up to the cliff top that he had traversed a few hours earlier he might just have been able to see the faint outline of three horsemen in the fading light and in the gloom the glimmer of metal.

CHAPTER IV

761 AD
– The Visit –

The horn echoing over the walls of the castle announced the visit. The visitors were expected. Messengers had alerted the house of Autun some days before. News of the arrival of Guilhem's grandmother Nanthilda, the dowager queen and widow of the deposed Childerich III, spread through the castle and the family assembled at the city gates to greet her. They were accompanied by a colourful crowd of townspeople keen to get the latest news and to see if the travellers could be persuaded to part with some money in exchange for food, wine lodgings or even the comfort of a willing woman.

Nanthilda the dowager queen, a long time widow, but whose importance had not much diminished with time arrived in style surrounded by soldiers and as part of a trading group. Where possible journeys were made in groups protected by soldiers.

Bandits and warring nobles were a constant threat to travellers. She was on a state visit to see her son and daughter-in-law. In truth the visit was really to assess the progress of the young grandson Guilhem and to assess the possibility of further sons always needed to protect the line. Nanthilda had another reason wanting to make early contact with the young grandson; a reason hidden inside the layers of family ties and affairs of state and succession planning. A secret that was carried from generation to generation of her late husband's family and which in today's world could lead to the greatest penalty of all.

The small queen dressed in dark full length cotton robes and veiled from the gaze of ordinary people carried herself well on the small dappled mare, but when she was helped down by her son, Thierry, she twisted slightly and bent with age, though she impatiently brushed aside any further support. The diminutive figure slowly straightened eliminating the stiffening effects of hours in the saddle and the wear and tear of the years. In the space of a few moments, standing in the shadow of the larger than life Thierry she seemed to grow in authority and to command the hot dusty space around her. Thierry bowed and then embraced the small figure and the rest of the household led by Aude followed in paying their respects.

'My son does well? I hear the king is pleased Thierry.' The words sounded normal but little warmth accompanied them. In truth Thierry was a disappointment to the old queen. He had shown little interest in his ancient lineage and the stories that surrounded their family. Nanthilda hoped that her grandson would be different.

Then it was Guilhem's turn to kneel. The old queen quickly raised him and throwing back her veil for the first time, seized his arms, looking into his dark brown eyes for a long moment.

'You have grown well,' she said. 'Tomorrow you will come to see me and I will find out if your mind has been nourished as well as your body'.

'Yes grandmother.'

With that she gestured to Thierry to guide her through the great gates of the castle and on to her chambers where she could rest and prepare for the feast to be held later in the day in her honour.

Guilhem had met his grandmother before when he had been much younger and the little figure had made a mark even then, leaving an impression of eyes that searched deeper inside him than was comfortable even for a boy of five or six. There was also a faint odour that somehow had imprinted itself on his memory. Not exactly unpleasant but somehow foreign to his nostrils. The deepest impression had been that of age. Guilhem had never seen such a face mapped with so many folds and tributaries; but from which pleated landscape the eyes continued to ask with a fierce intelligence. Strangely the impression of age was stronger then than now in spite of the passing years.

Guilhem could not admit to himself that he was frightened of the small white haired figure who seemed to command respect so easily. On the other hand he could not say either that he was looking forward to the next day. The occasions when he felt somewhat at a loss to explain his unease were becoming fewer as the years passed but his response was still the same. The sturdy eleven year old figure trudged up the winding stone stairs to find his mother. He needed to find out what was expected of him the next day.

Aude was seated at the oblong table giving instructions to the steward about the evening festivities called in honour of Nanthilda, mother of Thierry. The wife of Childerich III was part of a long line of the kings and nobles of Neustria; a line that stretched back to Clovis and the mists of the Merovingean dynasty. The nobles that paid homage to Thierry were paying homage to his lineage as well. In addition, Aude's position as the daughter of the greatest king of recent time, Charles Martel the Hammer of the Saracens and the new dynasty that had ousted the fading Merovingians, would ensure that anyone who was on the intricate ladder of power within a day's travel of Narbonne would have hoped to have been invited. The feast would be a major event and would have to reflect the importance of the occasion.

The slight figure who seemed to carry so much less authority than her booming husband, or indeed his tiny indomitable mother, was here in her element and was issuing instructions with quiet confidence. Although she was a shadow in the public arena, she was a confident administrator in private. He waited in the familiar window embrasure until the meeting was over and the steward had bowed his way out.

'Your father has asked that you attend the feast tonight.'

Guilhem looked at her. He had never attended a large feast. His heart jumped. This was going to be a special time and to be at the feast was a coming of age for any boy. He already knew from the courtiers' gossip many of the names who would be attending. His life was changing and it was something to do with the old lady who carried such authority.

'Mother I have come to you because grandmother Nanthilda has asked to see me tomorrow. And now you say that father has asked that I am present at the feast.

Is it a s-s-special time? What should I wear? Why does my grandmother want to see me alone?'

The questions came tumbling out and his voice tailed away uncertainly.

'Come here Guilhem.' Aude started laying out the skeins of wool for sorting as she had done so many times before.

'You have not helped me with the wool for a long time now. Why is this?'

His faced flushed with embarrassment. It was true and the quiet reproof hurt. It was true that his visits to the haven of his mother's chamber had become much less frequent over the last year.

'Mother I am sorry its just that.....' Uncharacteristically the voice tailed away again. He did not know why these visits had diminished without him realising. This room always a haven from the rough and tumble of the outside world; a place which had been needed as a respite from growing up had somehow become less important over the past year.

Aude smiled in her gentle way. A smile of amusement at the evident confusion mirrored in her son's face and a smile of resignation in the knowledge that time was about to make an inevitable shift and she would be the loser.

'Guilhem there is no need to feel ashamed. You are growing up. You don't need to be by my side as you once did. Our time for this has passed but I will still love you and I will try and help you whenever you ask. Now you are in your eleventh year and you must learn about the ways of rulers and of the people. You must start to learn about our friends and our enemies. Tonight in the great hall there will be those who will appear to be your father's closest allies and those who will pay the greatest compliments to him and our household. You may be singled out for praise. Yet even here at our table there are those that wish us harm and would like nothing better than to see the downfall of our family. And then there is the church.' She sighed as though the very word had increased her burdens. Her son was growing away from her and the inevitability of loss did little to assuage the feeling of a diminished future. And she was a mother who had lost three other children in childbirth and now there seemed to be less chance of another. Not that Thierry had abandoned her bed but there had been no sign of a new child in over two years....

'The church,' she resumed as the questioning face claimed back her wondering attention,

'Even the church may not be as safe a place as you think. Not everyone holds the same beliefs as those you have grown up with under the care of Father Bedier.'

'But mother how can that be? Jesus gave us the book to follow in his footsteps and everything in the book is true. Everyone knows that.'

Aude looked at the earnest face shining with certainty. It would not be long before she would have to look up instead of down at this much loved face and with that growth would come the complications of adulthood. She was losing him and now she would have to inflict that first experience of the world as an adult where life was not so simple. But he had to learn.

'Not everyone sees the same truths even if they are reading the same words. Guilhem you will learn that there are many versions of the truth. Some people even think that the truths revealed in the writings of the word of God have already been altered to suit.....'

She hesitated. This was an idea both difficult to comprehend and dangerous to express in some quarters. The harder to say because she herself had no doubts of the truths she had grown up with where the place of God and Jesus and the hierarchy of the Church of Rome were fixed points of refuge and certainty in a world of prodigious unpredictability. Even the daughter of Charles Martel was not immune to the seeming random injustices and cruelties that surrounded the lives of rich and poor alike. After all God had taken three of her children already and here she was about to send her surviving son into the tribulations of adulthood. He was only eleven!

'To suit....It is hard to explain my dear. Let us just say that there are other beliefs that are just as important to those who hold them as the teachings of the bible, and all you have learned in the great church with Father Bedier and the others.'

'You mean like the Saracens who say that Jesus is just another prophet and that Mohammed is more important.'

'Yes something like that. Just remember that not all of us believe the same thing. More importantly remember that our Church believes that there is only one truth and that any other is wicked and should be stamped out. Whatever you hear from Nanthilda tomorrow keep to yourself and be very careful if you decide to share her knowledge with anyone. She is not an evil person but her ideas are not held by all. Go and prepare for this evening. Remember you are representing our house to the world tonight. I know we will be proud of you.'

CHAPTER V

761 AD

– Secrets –

The feast was the first step into adulthood for Guilhem. From the moment he stood by his father's side to greet the guests and receive their homage and customary presents, to the barely felt sensation of being clapped on the shoulder by his father and pushed off to bed. Time passed in a blur of excitement and confusion. Later certain moments stood out clearly and in great detail while others were lost in a profusion of sensations, smells, colours, noises, faces, and words. Above all too many words. Words accompanying faces shiny with fat and greed. Words drowned by shouts and laughter; earnest serious words; sly questioning words. Words that slipped past him before they could be caught and understood, and occasionally words that escaped in the flow of the watered wine he was drinking.

Standing next to his father under the great arched gateway to the inner keep Guilhem felt a mixture of pride and embarrassment. It was clear from the moment the first guest, the Seigneur from Capestang, knelt in homage to Thierry and offered his gift of two amphorae of wine, to the last to be welcomed at the great gate, the Comte de Maguelone, Witiza's father, with two fine horses as his gift, that this was a very special feast. The gifts lay in profusion just inside the great gate; sheep their legs tied bleating in insistent panic; pigs squealing and grunting; several carcasses of deer; heaps of skins, wolf; lynx and bear; bales of cotton from Egypt; silks and wool.

Thierry had had a word for each guest remembering a sick child; a flooded crop; a son lost at sea; a dispute over land; a safe return from a hazardous journey. Each person carefully introduced to him. Guilhem knew that the son of the Comte would be expected to remember each name and the gift they had brought.

Thierry gestured to Comte de Maguelone to precede them into the great hall and put his arm round Guilhem's shoulder.

'These people are here to show allegiance to the king Charles Martel through their acknowledgement of his representative Nanthilda and to confirm their duty to me as the king's representative in Septimania. But be careful, although they come to share our hospitality and our food they do not all wish us well.' The words echoed those of his mother earlier that day.

When they entered the great hall the ladies were already assembled to greet the guests all over again. In the centre of the line was Nanthilda, the small figure with piled up white hair which was covered by a wimple covering face and neck in purple, and a simple gown of black silk. Next to her stood Aude also with head dress and a kirtle of blue and silver embroidered damask belted at the waist reaching mid-calf. This was worn over a plain white shift of ankle length. Every guest knelt before the old lady until only Thierry and Guilhem were left.

Thierry gestured to Guilhem to follow suit. As he knelt he heard her voice seeming to carry through the movement and murmuring of the crowd although her lips appeared not to move.

'Tomorrow in the mid-morning.'

Startled he almost looked behind to see the source of the voice, but stopped the movement in time and merely bent his head in acknowedgement. As he rose he caught the merest flicker of a smile which did not reach her eyes. The old lady could see into his thoughts. Mind racing Guilhem almost forgot his place at the table until he felt his father's steering hand.

After that things moved at an increasing pace. A signal from Aude and the slaves filed in bearing jugs of wine. The feast followed in unstoppable succession: wild boar, venison haunches, chickens, oysters and fish freshly caught and a profusion of small loaves of bread. The smells of the meats piled one upon the other. Grease dripped onto faces, table and floor indiscriminately. The wine kept coming and the noise grew as tongues were eased.

At first Guilhem was silent, seated near the top of the rough trestle table between Gregorius the son of the Seigneur from Capestang whom he knew from hunting and horse fairs, and on his left a stranger. A man of darker complexion with a small trimmed beard and clothes that were of a rich smooth fabric worn looser than was the local custom. He did not speak the local Oc language but rather the French from the north which was the common language for most of Francia's nobles. Guilhem noticed that he ate sparingly and drank even less and was very neat and fastidious keeping his clothes free of the dripping fats.

This was particularly difficult because his left arm had little movement and a stick like wrist protruded from the rich brown robe ending in a bird's foot hand. Guilhem tried not to stare.

At first the stranger was quiet after having introduced himself as Adelchis an ambassador and trader.

'Yes I remember ambassador. You are from Axum which is very far away and you brought a box of herbs for my mother and silver goblets for my father.'

Adelchis looked at him with added interest and with a particularly winning smile, but said nothing further and the young lad Gregorius nudged him in the side and pointed to a guest on the other side of the table who had managed to drop a large chunk of boar onto his tunic and in trying to wipe the mess away had knocked his mug of wine over his neighbour who seemed ready to take offence at the accident. Luckily he noticed Thierry's eyes on the incident and the moment passed with cuff on the shoulder and a reach to replenish the spilt mug.

Gregorius occupied his attention for some time with a tale of a hunt in which he had starred by trapping a boar on a cliff edge and dismounting had stood his ground under the inevitable charge managing to spear the animal in the neck as it hurled itself at him and to finish the kill with his dagger. The noise of the feast bounced around the stone walls and echoed in Guilhem's head making him lose his ability to concentrate on the tale of daring and courage.

At that moment there was a loud knocking on the table, his father using the handle of his dagger to gain attention as he rose to address the guests.

'As you all know we are here to welcome my mother, Nanthilda queen to Childerich III, and through her to acknowledge the greatness of our heritage over many generations through time back to king Merovech. Our royal blood line which made our great kingdom of Francia which is now protected by our new king Pepin, former mayor of the palace.

Queen Nanthilda is here to receive homage on behalf of King Pepin so that you all can see that even the line of our dynasty has supported the election of Pepin as king, and also so that she may tell our king that we are all his loyal vassals. You will each be received by her in the upper chamber after the feast. Meanwhile I ask you all to stand and drink to the long life and prosperity of King Pepin and his council!'

The hall echoed to the scraping of the benches on the stone flags and the room stood, although Guilhem noticed that some seemed happier to rise than others.

'To King Pepin,' the shout went up and mugs of wood, pewter and silver were raised and emptied in one motion. As they settled back on the benches and more wine and beer was called for, Guilhem felt a slight pressure on his shoulder. Adelchsis lent close and his voice carried clearly through the hubub.

'You, master Guilhem, I understand will be having your own audience with the queen tomorrow. I can advise you, master Guilhem, to say little and listen with care. Your father did well in that toast to the king, don't you think? It must have been difficult for someone from the true line.' It was a voice that that carried weight without needing volume. A voice that seemed to ask questions even when none were stated. A voice that would be easily remembered.

'But how did you.....?' The question died in Guilhem's mouth. His mother's warning sounded through his tired head. Strangers may seem to be friends but may be not what they seem. Adelchis seemed to understand what was going through his mind and once again gave him a quick look of approval for his reticence .

'Do not trouble yourself young master. If God wills it we will meet again in your search for truth.' With that he made his excuses and left the table, but Guilhem noticed that he was quickly taken aside by a small group and they disappeared out into the courtyard.

With that Guilhem's interest in the proceedings faded fast. To his surprise it was his father who left the immediate throng around him and came to his side.

'You have done well my son. Adelchis thought highly of you, and now it is time for rest. You will be seeing my mother tomorrow and you will need to be fresh. There will be much to learn and many surprises and you will have to make up your own mind about what you will be told. Remember you are of the ancient line of kings.'

He clapped Guilhem on the shoulder and pushed him toward the great oak door that led up to the sleeping chamber for Guilhem and the young guests that were staying. The great oak door no longer held the mystery of a few years ago. He could open it himself now. A mystery that dissolved on one level left the opportunity for another to take root in its place.

'Perhaps it is my father who should be king,' he thought sleepily as he pulled off his boots and the fine over tunic worn for this special occasion.

CHAPTER SIX

761 AD
– The Golden Bee –

The next morning brought another fine day and he was well into his own plans to take advantage of the summer sun, which revolved around going to the shore with a small group of friends after his lesson with Father Bedier, when one of the pages brought him a message from the old queen Nanthilda.

He had totally forgotten this meeting around which so much mystery was building. He felt off balance and unprepared. Next time he would make sure that meetings were not forgotten and that if preparations were needed he would ensure that he had made them. Luckily he was given a breathing space. Some of the guests from the night before were still to pay their respects and to swear their allegiance to King Pepin.

Guilhem first went down to the kitchens where he found the kitchen slaves trying to recover from the mounds of leftover food and dishes, tureens, plates of wood and pewter and piles of goblets thrown carelessly into a huge tub. Piles of bones were heaped in one corner and the kitchen heaved and swirled in clouds of steam from boiling vats. Great tubs of hot water were being emptied into a large stone sink and dishes and pans were scrubbed, scoured and stacked.

Bones were thrown to the pack of barking, leaping and snarling dogs who knew that this would be a feast day if they could ensure more than a fair share. Guilhem picked his way through the chaotic scene grabbing a chunk of bread and a leg of chicken as he went. Out in the back courtyard he picked his way through further remnants of the feast to the well; hauling up a wooden bucket he drank from the wooden ladle attached to its side and poured the rest over his head and face. Refreshed and now wide awake, clutching his breakfast Guilhem made his way round the thick stone walls back to the main courtyard where he had greeted the guests the day before and then through the great hall and up the winding stairs which led past the bedchambers to the top of the western defensive tower. He needed time to think about the forthcoming encounter with his grandmother queen Nanthilda.

Only a sling shot away the vast expanse of the biscuit colour tiled roof of the cathedral of Saint Felix dominated the narrow streets and led the eye to the Pont Vieux which carried the great road Via Domitia across the city and on past the harbour and on to the Spanish borders and even to the land of the Saracens. This too had been built in the ancient times. Why were the ancient peoples able to achieve so much? His mind wondered over the stories he had learned. Maybe Nanthilda was as old as the buildings! What did the old lady have in store for him? He tried to go over the events of the last two days.

First the arrival of the old woman who seemed to cause unease and respect in equal measure.

Then the invitation to his first feast and a warning from his mother that not everyone who seemed to be friendly was necessarily so.

Surely the boastful Gregorius could not be part of a conspiracy, but the ambassador on his left Adelchis, who knew about his impending meeting with Nanthilda and who had made that comment about his father's speech; he was someone of whom to be careful. Although Guilhem had rather liked the stranger from Alexandria with the quick intelligence and the air of mystery.

'Your father did well with the toast. It must have been difficult for someone from the true line.'

That must have meant something but Guilhem could not see any further. The true line? Nanthilda was his father's mother. Maybe he was going to learn something about his father's family. At that moment his personal attendant and squire at arms, Arnaud, appeared anxiously at the top of the stairs.

'The queen Nanthilda is ready to see you and asked me to give you this. You are to take it with you to her chamber.' The slave handed an oblong box to Guilhem. He opened it and inside was a scroll of soft parchment. As he unrolled it Guilhem could see the colours of the illuminated edge reveal themselves. The design was comparatively simple yet complete. The left hand side of the scroll showed a long staff intertwined by clinging vines of blue and green. A bright golden bee in exquisite detail clung to a top leaf.

On the top right was the outline of an empty crown and down the right side a fantastical fish again in pale blue and green scales. There was text in the middle in a script unknown to Guilhem who could read Latin quite well and who also had an acquaintance with Greek. A list of some kind arranged in two columns.

Replacing the scroll with care he descended the winding stairs and went to the upper chamber. Nanthilda was seated in the big oak chair with the carved arms that his father often used when he was in council. She was dressed in the formal robes of the previous day having been in state session as representative of King Pepin. She beckoned him closer. Guilhem crossed the room and knelt as he had seen the others do the previous day.

'Grandmother, you wished to see me.'

She laid her hand on his head for a moment. 'Could you read it Guilhem?'

'No my Lady the script is not known to me though it did seem to be somewhat similar to some Arabic I have seen.'

'It is written in Aramaic the language of our Lord Jesus.What do you think this scroll could be?' She spoke in a low clear tone that invested her words with extra weight.

'I don't know, but p..p..perhaps the words could be a kind of list.'

'They could indeed. It is a list showing part of your family lineage. The kings that were the fathers of your fathers into the mists of time. Your family is of interest to people in many parts of the world and so this one is written in a strange tongue. It was brought from afar – from a land that lies high in the land across the sea.' She smiled and gestured for him to rise and take the chair on her left.

'And what do you think about a queen of the royal line coming to your father's court to receive homage on behalf of King Pepin?'

Guilhem felt that this was nearing the centre of the meeting. 'My grandfather Childerich. Nobody talks about him. Did he die long ago? Why was he not the king?'

Nanthilda looked at him directly.

'Now that is a very wise question from someone so young and I am going to tell you the story. My beloved husband Childerich was a man who loved the mysteries and God, perhaps too much, and so made many mistakes during his reign. These mistakes lost him the support of many of the nobles that owed him allegiance. Indeed some rebelled and refused to pay him homage. Pepin and his father before him Charles Martel, the hammer of the Arab heretics, had become very powerful in the court. Even my father-in-law king Theoderic IV depended too much on the power of the mayors of the palace. A few years ago Pepin made an alliance with many of those who defected and they took the crown from my husband Childerich and put him in a monastery where he died. Lord have mercy.' She crossed herself. 'Pepin was elected king. I have to say that for the kingdom of Francia this was a wise move, for the kingdom is now stronger and Pope Steven II in Rome has confirmed the crown in the name of Pepin the Younger seven years ago. At that time Pepin came to me and said that the kingdom would be much strengthened if the Queen of the royal line and her heirs would support him. In return for this allegiance your father Thierry would have sovereignty over the south part of Francia. The hope of our family is that the true royal line will be restored some day. Meanwhile it has been a good alliance for us and for all of Francia.'

Guilhem got up from the chair. There was too much to take in. He couldn't sit still. So many questions. 'Why did my father not tell me this before? N..n..nor my mother. She never ....'

'No Guilhem that was because I asked that this story not be told until I felt the time was right. I wanted to see my grandson and to judge what man he would become before this was told to him. Soon you will be leaving home to attend the court of Pepin and to learn to be a soldier and prince to follow in your father's place.

You had to know before you left for Pepin's court. He and his allies will want to know that they have a safe friend to succeed your father. Remember through your mother, the daughter of Charles Martel, you are cousin to Pepin's sons Carloman and Charles. Yet you should know that not all are happy that the royal line of Merovech is no longer the ruler of Francia and the line is no longer recognised by the pope. You are unique in that within you run the lines of the past and the present.'

There was a silence. Guilhem needed time. What was expected of him now? This was the first he had heard of his move to the court in the north though he had been told that his education would be continued in other places. But that had seemed to be a long way in the future. The scroll. What had the scroll to do with his family and the intrigues at the court of Pepin.

Questions. He had entered the room feeling quite grown up but suddenly he felt very young and unprotected. He was not sure that he really understood the implications of all this information. The certain ground that he stood on until now seemed to be suddenly shifting and he felt that something was expected of him. But what?

Nanthilda sat quietly waiting for the boy to make the next move. It would tell her something of the qualities that lay within the child.

'I think I understand what you have told me, my lady, but I d..d..do not know what you want me to do about it. I would like to talk to my friend Witiza.'

Nanthilda noticed the slight stutter and wondered if this was a sign of lack of confidence that could spell trouble in the future. 'You are about to leave the shelter of your home here in Narbonne. When you go to the court in Aachen you will be surrounded by the family of King Pepin and will continue your education with his sons Carloman and Charles. They will be watching to see if you can be trusted to follow in your father's footsteps. But also at the court there will be many relations you have not yet met from the old royal line. You may find that they wish to involve you in schemes against the king. Although you are still young it is important that you are aware of these things before leaving home. Yes I have heard about Witiza the son of the Count de Maguelone. A very serious and clever young man I am told. I see no harm in talking to him.'

'Thank you my lady for all you have told me. I will be careful when I go to the court of king Pepin. Who is Adelchis?'

There was a sudden stillness in the room. Nanthilda straightened her head dress unnecessarily. 'Ah yes! Adelchis. Now this is something which must never be told to anyone outside this room except those who believe as we do. Adelchis is one such. The scroll in the box was brought by him from across the ocean for he lives in that far off land. You will not understand everything that I will tell you now but the dangers of this knowledge are greater than the politics of the court. Yet the two things are linked by your heritage. Can you swear to me on the honour of our family that you will keep this secret from all those outside.'

'What about my mother and father? Everything that you tell me is known to them, is'nt it?'

'Your father knows this story but has chosen to live his life as though it is of no real importance. You will also have this choice, but I swore to my husband who told me the truth of his line in the years when the church in Rome was more,' she hesitated searching for the right word, 'flexible, that I would make sure that the sons of his sons would know the true story from me. Your mother may also have some idea of the beliefs of the Merovingian line of kings but would not agree with our truth and feels that today such knowledge is a danger to those who know it. She does not want you to follow this path.'

She tapped the box which contained the scroll. 'Here lies part of the secret of your line. But first I must have your promise that this will be our secret for ever.'

'I..I..I'm not sure that I should know. What should I do with such a secret? If my mother and father don't agree... and I am only young. What should I do?' He shifted uneasily in front of the formidable old lady, twisting one leg behind the other and yet in spite of his unease he kept his gaze on the old queen. He was showing indecision but not fear.

Nanthilda looked at the child who now revealed his true age, and yet with a wisdom beyond many of similar years. He did not leap at the attraction of a secret which was usually irresistible to young and old alike.

'Guilhem come here.' She took his hand. 'Look at me. My years are many. I do not have much time left and I do not want to reveal the whole of this secret in writing. Part of it that should carry little danger of itself is in the scroll. It is too dangerous to the holder and too easy to destroy to place the whole story on parchment. Come back this afternoon when you have had time to think. And I do not think worse of you taking time to reflect.'

With an uncharacteristic gesture she ruffled his hair and pushed him gently towards the door.

'Guilhem! Wait a moment. You should take these with you. If you decide to become part of our secret keep one close about you always and place the other in a safe place that you can find again. The bee is a symbol of your line.' With that she unfolded her palm and tipped into his outstretched hand two small golden bees exactly as the one he had seen on the scroll.

Later the same day Guilhem and Witiza were in serious conversation in the cloister behind the great old church of Saint Felix.

'Soon I will enter the church as a novice. It is something that I have known that I must do for many years. You have known it too. Although I will always be your friend I will not be with you to give help and advice as in the past years. You will soon be far away in the misty north at the court. I will be sent to the cathedral at Maguelone and I hope later to Rome to study with the great priests of the church. My life will be dedicated to the service of the church and in the spread of the true word. I know that is why I am here on earth.'

Guilhem looked at his friend with a faint unease at the intensity and certainty with which his mentor saw his life. It was this that had attracted him as a younger boy but now for the first time there seemed to be a part of life's complexities that had passed Witiza by.

'I know Witiza that we have not long to be together, but now, now I need to know what to do. Should I learn this secret that Queen Nanthilda is offering? The court of King Pepin seems to carry danger for me and my line. If people find that I know something special will it make my life at court harder?'

Witiza looked at his young friend being thrust into adulthood so early. Yet it was not so unusual in their time for the very young to take on the duties and responsibilities of adulthood. Forced by circumstance and the capricious nature of both man and the natural world, life was often a short span laden early with unexpected responsibilities.

He grasped Guilhem by the shoulder. 'You must accept the secret and the burdens that may go with it'.

'But I cannot share it even with you and so who will tell me what should be done.'

'No, if you learn something in this way you must be true to the giver of the secret. If you don't know what to do then you must keep it close until you have grown and one day you will know what must be done.'

Guilhem looked up at his friend. 'Right, meet you in an hour by the three pine trees on the dune near the beach. Someone gave me a new bow at the feast and I want to try it. I will hit the target more often than you!'

A quick grasp of Witiza's arm and he was gone. The concerned youth and suddenly the quicksilver child of earlier times.

As he ran from the room he crashed into the tall figure of his father who was not often to be found in the environs of the church unless required to attend on the holy days and religious festivals.

'Father!' He searched in the small pouch fastened about his waist. 'Look! This is what the old queen gave me.' Unfolding his hand he showed the two golden bees.

'She said not to tell anyone except our family. She said you knew the story that had to be secret. She....' Thierry put his finger to his lips and looked round. The confident air that normally accompanied him evaporated..

'So now you know too. Guilhem I'm sorry that you have to carry this knowledge with you so young.'

'But father I do not understand why our history is so secret. Why is it so important and dangerous. It's just a list of names like learning about our kings and Roman emperors and the names in the bible.'

'Guilhem I cannot tell you more than she has done. You must do what she has commanded you. I can tell you that when you are older you will be able to make a choice to pursue this knowledge as far as you can, or to put it to one side. The queen Nanthilda probably told you the choice that I made. In due time you must make your own. I must go now. I am meeting the church council about the tithes that must be set. Trust in your judgement Guilhem as your mother and I will also.'

With that he was gone into the gloom of the church and Guilhem ran for his bow.

CHAPTER SEVEN

804 AD, Gellone
– The Eyes of the Church –

Guilhem put his foot on the rough hewn block of limestone and leaned forward looking intently at the clear outlines drawn in wet sand inside the sand box. He wondered if the church would object to him instructing that the sign of the three bees be carved on the inside of the great west door. The head mason, Pierre Clergue, stood anxiously on the left side of the box which had been laid out inside the wooden church. Guilhem shook his head in irritation. Even now the family heritage clouded the mind

'It must be simple but strong. But it must also reach up so that all those who come within the walls would be able to follow the echo of their prayers toward heaven. It must be able to act as a shelter of last resort in case of attack.' His eyes followed the scale marked on the side of the box.

It would be about forty paces long and fifteen paces wide and strongly buttressed on the outside.

At the end of the box a space had been sectioned off and there were outlines of the elevations showing the low pitched roof surmounting the west door by a simple cross. A well proportioned stone-pillared door frame with two concentric arches in the revived rounded style led the visitor into the shelter of the house of the Lord. Once inside a series of strong pillars supporting rounded arches guided the eye to the altar which was raised by two shallow steps. Light would be provided by a row of narrow oblong openings along the north and south sides of the nave set high up near the top of the supporting arches.

They could act as defensive windows in the event of a siege. They would be reached by temporary wooden scaffolds which would hold the bowmen. Not ideal but enough to delay an attack thought Guilhem.

Joseph Fulrad, one of the scribes, was at a table nearby and was busy outlining some of the details of the doorway and windows on scraps of parchment. A talented draftsman, Jonathen had lent the mason the use of Joseph to help articulate some of the ideas.

'My lord abbot could the windows be made in arches like the door. Smaller of course.' A series of small arches appeared on the rough parchment high up on the exterior surrounding the deep embrasures.

They were joined by Jaques Fournier, a man of many parts, having served as a sergeant in the service of the Count of Toulouse and in the campaigns against the Saracens in Spain. Guilhem had come across his big frame on more than one occasion during the time of the wars. He had earned the reputation of steadfastness to go with his size. And even then, if he remembered aright Jacques Fournier had a deep hatred of those who denied the word of God. However by trade he was a master carpenter and had particular experience in the construction of the tall timber scaffolding that underpinned the stone arches as they were built until the lime mortars had developed the strength to support the shaped blocks.

'B..b..but that is a big improvement. It will look more like a house of God than a fortress.'

'The windows are like that in the church of St Felix, your church in Narbonne my lord abbot.' The deep voice barrelled out of the deep chest and ended with an unexpected liquid gurgle that betokened a weakness in the large strong looking man.

Guilhem instantly saw why the new design appealed so much. Indeed an echo of his childhood would be created here in his very own tribute to the lord.

'Yes. Of course. That's right Jacques. And that's how we will b..b.. build it.'

Pierre Clergue looked doubtful. He did not like Jaques who was always ready to take charge. Stone masons were the true architects.

Guilhem turned away from the table and hurried out of the church into the warm September sunshine. Three months had passed since his appearance in Gellone. A great deal had been achieved but there was so much more to be done.

He looked up at the limestone cliffs towering above his little valley. The fresh green of the early summer had given way to a darker richer colour with the occasional touch of yellow and brown on the oak and chestnut. Near at hand to the north west of the tiny hamlet a large ditch had been dug across the valley at a point where it was about five hundred paces wide. The earth had all been piled up on the south side of the ditch and was forming the raised base for a wooden palisade one and a half times the height of a man. The timber showed the white scars of wood newly cut and shaped. The fortification had reached about half way across the valley.

Through the uncompleted half he could see the corn standing proud at shoulder height with the ears already heavy. It was ready for harvest and it would be a good crop to take their little community through the winter. Further away and to the left, the stalks of the harvested wheat revealed the brown dried furrows of late summer already being encroached by bindweed, spurge and meadow saffron. That had also been a good crop. Guilhem knew that the little community somehow credited him with the successful harvest. For the time being that would do no harm. They would work harder through the coming months to make it happen again!

It was going well. The Lord appeared to be pleased with his choice of how to end his days in his service. He gathered the brown habit in his left hand to clear a thorn patch. It still didn't feel right; this all enveloping gown seemed constricting after all those years in the soldiers tunic.

But this gown of God was a small price to pay for a chance to make things right.

He was going to inspect the new latrines and the replaced midden which had been moved a hundred paces away from the settlement and well away from the stream that was their precious water source. He wondered whether he had a somehow unhealthy interest in excrement. But the importance of drains and water had been borne in on him over many campaigns. Sickness had been the cause of many a defeat and a good water supply often the reason for victory.

Guilhem circled the high thorn hedge and the woven bark fence which had built to provide a semblance of privacy. The pits had been dug deep and were framed with stout oak planks. Steven the novitiate had done a good job. He was indeed turning out to be the reliable one amongst the churchmen. He must remember to acknowledge the work.

With everything seeming to be so blessed with good fortune

Guilhem wondered why he was feeling so restless. As he turned back from his brief inspection and started the short walk to the librarium he saw Jacques standing in front of the church as if looking for someone. Guilhem raised his hand in acknowledgement. Jacques looked surprised and abruptly turned back inside the church as if remembering something.

That was it. That was the cause of his unease. He was being watched. Guilhem was certain.

Jacques Fournier had been sent by Benoit to ensure that somehow the new abbot did not turn from the true path and resurrect his foolish doubts. Guilhem felt sick. It seemed that his childhood friend Witiza had become more implacable with the years. Not only his name had changed! Certainly they had clashed on more than one occasion over his lifetime. Guilhem had hoped that taking the tonsure would allow them to resume the old relationship. This spy felt like a childhood trust betrayed.

His route to the tonsure was not that unusual. Many men who had played their part in the world chose to end their days in the service of God in the hope that their souls would be saved by the good Lord. In spite of the many hours of discussion with his old childhood friend Witiza, now bishop Benoit of Aniane, he felt that Benoit did not trust him. There was no doubt that the distrust had emanated from the rumours of his inheritance and his acceptance by the Jews of Narbonne as being of the line of David.

For bishop Benoit, Guilhem Count of Toulouse, faithful servant to the emperor Charlemagne, and his childhood friend was a special conundrum. Not only was he a member of the Merovingian dynasty around which the tales of heresy buzzed like moths in blowing candlelight, now visible and now obscured by the smoke from the tallow and the encroaching shadows, but his career as prince and soldier had even included an expedition to the edge of the known world in Africa. Their meeting in that foreign land had possibly changed the shape of Christendom. Certainly their differences had been etched deep by the events so far from Francia.

All this had been discussed into many long nights and Guilhem had again and again sworn to uphold the true church and its teachings. He had done so because he believed that the church was indeed the way to salvation.

In the end he knew that it was the Emperor's support for his lifelong friend that had ensured his entrance into the church. And yet he was still being watched.

Guilhem felt the flush of anger rising to suffuse his face. There was more evidence than this feeling of being watched.

But now he was here. Surely the last steps that had brought him to this valley with the mission he had outlined to Benoit entitled him to encouragement and support from the mother church. It seemed not. His past was going to follow him to the grave. Even his mentor and early teacher could not allow him to find the peace he searched for without the extra insurance of a spy. Maybe more than one. He scanned through the people that surrounded his project. Jonathen in the librarium; one of the first to be inspired by the first phase of the project of scholarship and the creation of the means of spreading the word and of recording and storing knowledge from all parts of the world. Jonathen of the keen mind and kind heart.

He who had been with Guilhem at the start of this vision of Gellone fifteen years ago. 'It is time to tell Jonathen something of what is happening' he thought.

Leo the priest who strove to do the best he could for the church and his flock, but was undermined by lack of belief in his own abilities.

Steven was the most able of the little group and had quickly become his right hand man in all things practical to do with the development of the community. It should not be forgotten that he was also the most educated amongst the churchmen, apart from Jonathen. There was also the Maguelone connection. Of all the others Steven fitted best in capability and background. Guilhem was reluctant to saddle him with the role of Judas. He had become fond of the ready smile and cheerful ability to get things done in a way that took the people with him, even those who started by shaking their heads and grumbling at yet another unreasonable task. Yet Guilhem knew that the most unlikely person could well be part of this watching brief.

It still didn't make sense. What was Benoit afraid of? Was he afraid that Guilhem would be the mainspring of a new heresy starting in this remote corner of Francia. That he would start such a blasphemy surrounded by churchmen and undertake the building of a monastery at the same time. To what end? Surely this was not the way that such things started?

His hand flicked against the missing right nostril and traced the scar that gave his face such a forbidding appearance. He would take Jonathen into his confidence and see if he could help.

Turning the big iron latch he entered the librarium and went upstairs. Jonathen was at the far end of the room leaning over the desk of one of the novice scribes. They appeared to be discussing the accuracy of the text being copied. This was a common problem in the life of a scribe. Difficulties arose in deciphering the text being copied and sometimes although the text was clear it was wrong in fact.

Any changes were important decisions. If the texts were biblical, proposed changes would have to be approved by the sponsoring bishop. In this way, over the years and copies of copies, the words took on a life of their own subject to constant reinterpretation.

Guilhem waited patiently at the top of the stairs. Finally Jonathen raised his head and saw his abbot. From a distance the disfigurement was more noticeable than when closer to and gave his face an angry cast. Jonathen saw the quick tilt of his head indicating that he should join him downstairs. Laying his arm briefly on the novice's shoulders in encouragement he followed Guilhem down and saw his shape in the doorway heading outside. He followed.

'Brother Jonathen I need to show you something,' Guilhem began abruptly, 'I suspect that Jaques Fournier and maybe others are spying on me and reporting to Bishop Benoit.'

'Why do you think that my lord abbot?' The tall ascetic figure looked down on the angrily pacing man.

'Its partly instinct. After years of court intrigues you get to know when s..s..someone seems to be unduly interested. And he's always around even when subjects other than the building are being discussed. Just now he was watching me as I went to inspect the work on the latrines – good work by the way – there was no need for him to be there and the way he turned away when he saw that I'd noticed him. There's something going on. I feel that I have to keep proving to Benoit that I really am here to serve God and the church. And there is something else.

Something more tangible. My cell is being searched.'

There was a pause as they paced down the winding path that edged the stream as it ran away from the site of the new church. Building was starting here too as the villagers became used to the idea that something important was really happening and that their income had a more solid foundation. Although his mind was elsewhere Guilhem noted that he would have to ensure that the stream was not polluted as the village extended away from the new drainage arrangements.

'Well?'

'I don't think it's you, my lord,' said Jonathen.

'There's n..n..no-one else he could be watching', said Guilhem rather irritated at having to expound the self-evident truth.

'It's not really you. It's more likely it is some kind of tangible evidence they seek. May I assume this is all something to do with the story of your heritage?'

'What evidence?' Even as he spoke Guilhem knew that Jonathen was partially right. The church wanted to find the hard evidence that kept the Merovingian heresy alive, but they thought that he could be the route which led them to that evidence.

They arrived at the door to the abbot's cell.

'My chest in here is searched often. After my suspicions were aroused I set traps to see if it has been opened. There is a tiny pebble I place under the hasp. If you lift the hasp it will fall. Let us see...'

Quickly Guilhem entered the small room and went straight to the large oak chest ranged against the wall. The two tonsured heads bent close, Jonathen's flying circle of white contrasting with the disciplined brown hair streaked with grey of the abbot.

'Look!' Guilhem held a very small black stone in his hand which he had gathered from the floor.

'Again today! Surely they must realise that I would not keep anything important here. It's too easy to...'

'My lord abbot, you forget. This is your private room. It is a sacrilege that is being committed here. Not many would dare. Even fewer without the command of a senior man of the church,' Jonathen continued excitedly,

'They don't know what they are looking for. They feel that your long association with Gellone and the library and your experiment of bringing the Saracen and the Jewish scholars here may be hiding something,' the words tumbled out in a rush that was often Jonathen's way.

'They feel that somewhere in our collection of manuscripts and books you will have hidden at least a clue to the secret of your family and that you will lead them to it. It's true is'nt it? There is something here that even I do not know about.' A short pause then Jonathen's anger burst out. 'And YOU are angry because of a lack of trust!'

Jonathen looked away as the silence from Guilhem confirmed his guess.

'My lord abbot you put all our work here at risk. Even when we came here first the church would have wanted to destroy any evidence that supported these mad stories that surround your ancestors. Then we might just have suffered a rebuke for keeping such material. But today Rome seems more frightened than ever of any story that deviates from the line of the true church. Today everything we have worked for could be burned and all of us working here for so long could be cast out of the mercy of Christ. You have not acted as a friend to me or the church my lord abbot.'

'You are right to be angry,' replied Guilhem to this outburst, 'but this tale that I carry with me and the small pieces of evidence that I have found over my life time are not mine to give to any power that would destroy them. All my life I have had to live with this certain doubt. Could I serve the church and yet keep such information as I have secret as I was sworn to do from childhood. I c..c..can tell you Jonathen that the tale of my ancestors has many gaps. Such evidence as I have seen may persuade some who have seen it that the road to salvation is not through the gospel stories we have learned. Even if....' His voice tailed away.

Jonathen's reaction could alter the rest of his life and his dream of Gellone and the abbey being his route to salvation. In fact the intensity with which Benoit would react might even see him joining his Lord on a cross.

'The evidence is in those manuscripts and books you sent from Byzantium in that script that no-one can read?' The tone was questioning but there was no real question being asked.

'Not from Byzantium. At least not that I know my friend. But it is true there is something hidden. I was given something to protect when in Rome. I was told Aramaic,' murmured Guilhem, 'the tongue of our Lord Jesus. Evidence? Yes some may say so.'

CHAPTER EIGHT

AD 761
– A Different Truth –

Guilhem had three months to keep the secret from Witiza and from everyone else for that matter. He had taken Witiza's advice and returned to the upper room to see his grandmother once again.

'Here is a copy of the scroll I showed you this morning,' the old woman seemed pleased that she could share this secret with him. 'Beside each name in the strange script you will see there is a name in Latin. These are the names of some of your forefathers over many generations. Let us see how quickly you can learn, Guilhem.'

'But why is this a secret? Many people must know our history and the names of my father's fathers.'

'It is true that some know these names, but even here there is dispute in some cases as time can warp the truth. Some may have an interest in showing that this is not the true line.'

Guilhem was not really satisfied but he had a good memory and the desire to win the approval of his grandmother stifled further questions. He bent to the task with the old lady testing his memory as he went.

'Very good, Guilhem,' the old lady released a quiet sigh of satisfaction at a task accomplished as though a burden was being shared.

'You have a good mind. One day you will be shown the remainder of your history and asked to commit all to memory. There will be surprises along the way, my son. Do you know that your father is called king by the Jews of the town?'

The question and sudden change of subject startled Guilhem just as he was basking under his grandmother's praise.

'Yes I have heard it said, but I did not think it important.'

'I will not say more. But I repeat that there are those around us all that would be very unhappy to learn that you have been given the opportunity to follow a different path. Such knowledge could put you in danger. That is why you must keep this secret. It is a test Guilhem, to find if you are worthy of the whole story. Or whether others will have to take this secret down the ages till the time is right to tell the world a new truth.'

Later that day his father told him that it would soon be time for the next phase of his education and that in return for his oath of fealty to Pepin, Nanthilda had told him that the court was willing for Guilhem to attend with the sons of Pepin and a number of other sons of the nobles who were loyal to the throne. This would mean going to the court at Aachen on the borders of the kingdom and leaving his family and friends. What happened at the court and how he behaved would determine his future. Thierry hugged him close and whispered that he knew they would all be proud of him.

Although Thierry must have known of the subject of his meeting with Nanthilda not a word was spoken. Guilhem was experiencing the first burdens of secrecy that would become part of his life in so many ways.

Guilhem waited for the secret to escape. For the first few days after his meeting with Nanthilda he could feel himself swelling with the importance of this thing hidden inside. Then gradually in the face of apparent indifference the swelling dissipated and with a feeling of some disappointment life returned to normal. All the people important to him knew that something special had happened in the upper room where Nanthilda held court. Yet nobody said anything to him. Nobody even asked him what had happened that morning. Surely they could see that he was carrying this burden which was so important. The problem was that Guilhem himself did not really understand why the knowledge he had gained could have such significance. He would love to have talked to someone, especially Witiza. However even Witiza did not refer to the secret and gradually Guilhem came to accept that nothing was going to change in the near future.

Although Thierry maintained a presence in the castle in the centre of the city much of the administration and control of trade was in the hands of the Jews. In a unique arrangement Pepin the Short had ceded virtual control of Narbonne and parts of the surrounding areas to the Jews. They collected the taxes and the duties on the harbour trade. This last was an important source of wealth as Narbonne was a major port through which goods passed on the way to the north and even into

Spain.

The reason for such a treaty, unique in all of Christendom, where the Jews were regarded with suspicion and sometimes dislike because of their refusal to acknowledge the truth that lay with the Lord Jesus, was rooted in recent history. Close to the time of Guilhem's birth and for many years previous the Saracens had continually attacked Narbonne and the surrounding areas with the objective of seizing control of the valuable trade routes. In 750AD Pepin had inflicted a heavy defeat on the Saracen general Ambassa but he was only able to complete the victory with the aid of troops provided by the Jewish settlers in Narbonne of whom there were over five thousand. In recompense for this act of support Pepin made an agreement with the Jews that allowed them an unusual degree of autonomy.

Jews were not unusual figures to Guilhem and his Frank friends growing up in the shadow of the castle. There were three synagogues and many of the trading posts were owned by the Jewish community. Although a common sight in their strange black robes and skull caps there was little contact between the Jews and Christians. Guilhem had already learned why the Jews could not be friends with the Christians as part of his religious instruction. The foul breathed Father Teissiere was particularly vehement in his dismissal of these barbarians who did not love Christ.

On the other hand the two communities lived quite peacefully side by side mixing where necessary, but not intermingled.

Some four weeks before he was due to leave Narbonne for the forests of the cold north, Guilhem was at work in the scriptorium trying to master the uncial script. The late summer sun was streaming in through the open windows providing perfect light for the task of painstakingly copying the letters. This writing did not come easily to him.

He was pleased when Father Bedier guided his hand to the faint ruled line within which these letters with a life of their own were meant to stay. Hunched over the wavering lines, brow furrowed in fierce concentration, his tongue curled over his upper lip the wiry figure struggled to make the quill obey. Why was it so much easier to direct the point of his sword or whirl the slingshot to its target?

'Stop now Guilhem. I want you to go down to the port and deliver this letter to the Rabbi of the synagogue which lies behind the trading post on the left side. Do you know the place?'

'Yes Father. But there are many priests at the synagogue and I have never met any of them.'

'This one is expecting you. His name is Caiaphas. This note is only to prove that you are the son of Thierry. This Rabbi is well known to your father as he is in charge of collecting the taxes at the harbour. A portion of these are remitted to the Count as part of the tithes of the kingdom. He will ask you to drink something with him and you should accept. He is a very learned man and has agreed to share some of this learning with you. It is not often that Christians and Jews have the opportunity to learn from one another. Many of my colleagues here in the church would not agree with what I am doing. But this is a time when you can learn much that is unexpected. Indeed not long ago you were called on to learn something,' he paused, 'unusual.'

Instantly Guilhem knew Father Bedier was thinking of his secret. 'But how.....?' Father Bedier shook his head.

'Now you will be asked to learn about something else that you know nothing of. You will have to make up your own mind about what my friend Rabbi Caiaphas has to say. We have tried to teach you to think for yourself as well learn the skills useful for a courtier at the side of a king. All I ask is that you show courtesy to this wise man and make no instant judgements on what he has to say. Keep your mind and ears open but speak with care and consideration for those that are different. May the wisdom of God guide you and give me grace that I am doing right by you.'

Narbonne called Narbo Martius by the Roman general who had founded the city had already grown prosperous by reason of its harbour and its Mediterranean trade. It had added importance because it had been an important military staging post along the Via Domitia which linked Rome with Spain. The city was a mixture of the ages with some of the grand Roman villas still in use, often side by side with recent buildings of wattle and thatch. Some of the streets were paved with stone but most of the lanes wriggled their dusty way past markets, churches, small open spaces, hovels, inns, all in apparent disarray thrown up in the moment of need. The city stank less than most others of the era, a fact that Guilhem was only to appreciate in later life as he travelled widely. This was because the Romans of ancient times had installed a very effective drainage system which still ran under the city and was to a greater or lesser effect still functional, although many of the more recent dwellings did not make use of this great feat of engineering.

The main port of Narbonne was some three sesterces from the city although there was an ancient canal through the swamp and reed beds of the bay of Bages that connected the outer port and the city. Another feat of engineering from the time of the giants of the past.

Unexpectedly released from the confines of ink and parchment Guilhem called for his squire at arms; horses were saddled, grasping the bay's mane he vaulted easily into the saddle with the careless grace of the young, and they rode out of the castle gate into the noise and bustle of the busy city. Vendors selling wine from the great amphorae which stood on their metal rings; piles of onions, beans, large sagging bags of wheat and barley, chickens clucking and screeching, ducks huddled down, motionless in the hubub awaiting their fate with apparent indifference. Caged birds, linnets, larks, and the occasional splash of brilliant red and green –parrots from Africa with their tall black turbaned merchants standing impassively until interest was shown when a huge white toothed smile would greet the unwary shopper. Many a parrot would not survive for long after purchase!

The young boy threaded his way through the confusion with the ease of use and the confidence of the young. Mostly the way cleared for the two horsemen as if the inference of importance filtered subconsciously to the throngs of people. Soon they were trotting across the Pont Vieux their hooves clattering along the paved section. They were quickly out of the city and moved past smallholdings mostly growing the vegetables that fed the city markets. Here the paving showed more signs of deterioration with great holes appearing where the stone base had been shifted and worn by the heavy cart traffic of the centuries.

This was the first thing that had happened that was out of the ordinary since his meeting with Nanthilda. He felt a sense of excitement mixed with apprehension. Nobody knew of this little excursion down to the port. By itself it would arouse little interest. It was well known that the port exercised a fascination for the young heir as it did for most of the boys of his age. Here the world came to Narbonne, still one of the two or three greatest ports on the Mediterranean.

But going to visit a Jewish priest of the synagogue at his age and alone, that would excite a great deal of interest. Guilhem thought for a moment. He had not told his squire at arms the reason for their sudden visit to the port and it was not for Arnaud to question such a decision. The lad was new to the post. Guilhem decided to go to the synagogue alone. They would take station by one of the stalls on the quay and he would tell Arnaud that he had to visit a merchant and would leave him well provided with wine and cheese. He trotted slightly faster now that he had made a decision with which he was pleased.

The late summer sun was hot, ensuring the final ripening of the vines that ran up the hillsides on their right hand. On the left the bay of Bages appeared, a shallow saltwater lagoon that was connected to the sea by the canal that was famous in the kingdom of Septimania and the source of so much wealth in the region. The outer port Nouvelles lay at the mouth of the canal. A perfect haven from the rough seas and strong winds that were a feature of this part of the coast. Such a breeze was in evidence as they rode along past the rafts of water birds that came to feed in the richly stocked waters.

They were soon at the harbour with its small group of buildings ranged along the quays. In effect Port Nouvelles was a suburb of Narbonne separated by the canal. Here the bigger ships leaned their way across the deep blue sea cutting through the white capped waves, their big patched lateen sails of rust coloured canvas full bellied in the wind. Then the calls from the sailing master would ring out against the wind; the big sail would start its broken winged collapse as the ropes strained to hold its descent; sail stowed, boom lowered, the great oars would sprout from the ports and the slaves would bring the laden vessel alongside. Shouts and curses from the ship's officers always accompanied the last few cable lengths. More often than not there would be the crack of the long rope whips across the sweating, straining backs already scarred by many such arrivals and departures.

The smaller craft having completed the port formalities and paid their dues could row the remaining distance to the heart of the city. The larger vessels would start the back breaking task of loading and unloading. As many as twenty ships could be alongside at any one time. It seemed as though all the nations of the world met at this small point. Black from Africa, brown from the Arabian gulf, swarthy Greeks and pale skinned Venetians; mixed colours and tongues in a never ending kaleidoscope of swirling movement along the harbourside. The inns and taverns were rarely short of business. Indeed much trade was conducted at the tables of these establishments which could offer wine, ale, food, and often women for the delight of those who travelled far from their own hearths and womenfolk.

Guilhem swung down off his horse and led it through the swirling crowds. Arnaud was close behind. He made for a tavern slightly set back from the main quayside and which had a small stable in the rear. They were quickly settled at a table which gave the best view to the end of the quay which had the deepest water and the largest ships. Arnaud who had not been often to the port was instantly entranced.

'Stay for a time Arnaud. I have to find some special leathers for the boots the shoemaker is making for my trip to the north. I won't be long.'

'But master I am to be at your side at all times. The sergeant told me I should never leave you alone.'

Guilhem pointed to a stall about fifty paces distant behind which was a large warehouse. Great hides hung over poles outside.

'I'll be in there. It may take some time to find the right qualities and the leatherseller is a hard bargainer. Stay. Order another cup of wine if you like. I won't be far away.'

With that assuming there was no more to discuss Guilhem turned and walked off. Soon he had disappeared inside the dark door. Walking quickly through the warehouse he called the merchant.

'Master Bertrand, I think you remember me. Could you lay out some skins that are right for making strong boots that will resist the cold and snow of the winter in the north. I am bid to the king's court shortly'

An order from the Count's son! That was prestige enough to set the merchant bustling away.

'Choose carefully. I have another errand to fulfil. I w..w..will return shortly.'

With that Guilhem continued through the warehouse and into the bright sunshine at the rear. Wasting no time he cut through a narrow alley and came out on a small rise that led away from the harbour. Across a small square stood the trading post which was run by the Jews and next to it stood the synagogue. It was a plain building of sandstone with heavy oak double doors. Although there was constant traffic of long robed Jews in and out of the trading post, the synagogue sat neglected in the sun and there was no movement around it. He would definitely attract attention if he tried the great front doors. Was there a side entrance or a dwelling place behind?

He walked as casually as he could across the square trying to appear uninterested in the synagogue itself. As he did so an elongated figure with flapping black robes and generous greying beard that was doing its best to engulf the face on which it sprouted detached itself from the trading post and disappeared up the side of the synagogue. Guilhem hesitated and then deciding that this was as good a lead as he had, he followed. A narrow alley led up the side of the sandstone walls. There was no-one in sight. Feeling distinctly nervous, he pressed on along the blank wall and suddenly there was a small recess set back with an iron bound door with a small window set with heavy iron bars. The door was open. He stepped into the black shadow feeling the chill of a room which had never seen the sun and which was permeated with the faint smell of incense. His eyes tried to accustom themselves to the gloom and eventually he began to make out a larger space beyond the entry.

'The son of Thierry Theoderic and Aude, pupil of the Christian brother Bedier, and friend of Witiza from Maguelone.' The voice surrounded him but did not locate the speaker. Guilhem felt as though he was suddenly naked in front of this voice and yet he was not exactly frightened. There was no threat in the voice; more the feeling of a smile.

'You have a letter from Father Bedier.' Guilhem nodded and immediately felt foolish. A nod could not be seen in the gloom. Now he felt like a child again and the excitement of this secret visit seeped away. He felt young and disadvantaged by this voice in the dark which knew so much about him. If he spoke his own voice would waver and he didn't want to show his inexperience and nervousness to this assured stranger. He stepped forward into the larger space holding out the letter in front.

'Lost your tongue young man.' The voice materialised right beside him and he felt the letter being taken firmly.

'Are you the priest Caiaphas?' Finally the words came, bursting out, too challenging.

'And if I were not?' the question was left hanging as he began to make out the figure beside him.

This was not at all as he had imagined the meeting. He was being made to feel a child again and a stupid one at that.

'If you were not, I should ask you where I could find him. And for my l..l..letter back,' he added hastily.

'Would you indeed,' the voice carried laughter in it now, but there was no mockery. And with that Guilhem began to regain his confidence. Perhaps this visit would be alright after all.

'Follow me young Guilhem Theoderic,' and they went through a big space which looked like the nave of a church, and on past a large carved wooden screen and through another small doorway, Caiaphas bending to avoid hitting his head and suddenly they were in the light again. A small bare room with high desks in front of a window and a plain table with benches on either side revealed itself to Guilhem's blinking gaze.

'You will take a cordial with me?' The tall figure preceded by the beard hurried about the room and in a moment they were seated with a clay jug containing camomile cordial and two rough cut wooden mugs. Suddenly thirsty Guilhem drank deeply and was refilled. There was a short pause while they looked each other over.

Dark eyes divided by a large curved bony nose looked at Guilhem with a kindly glint. The bushy greying beard contrasted with almost white hair which had been cut short and on which rested the improbable skull cap.

'How does it stay on?' Guilhem sat up, once again wrong footed by this stranger from a different land and with a different God.

Caiaphas removed the cap carefully and placed it on the table. Guilhem could immediately see the copper clip which had held it in place.

'We call the cap a kippah and the clip is known as a kippah clip.'

'But why do you wear them?'

'Because we believe that we are always in the presence of God and that this is a small way to show respect.'

'But we believe in God and we do not wear kippahs'

'So are you right and we wrong to show our respect in this way?'

'I think that we must be...' Guilhem paused. He didn't want to offend this man from a strange land with even stranger customs. Especially as on the brief acquaintance so far he did not seem so very different from many of the priests in the church at home.

'I think that if the Holy Book said something about it then ...'

The older man swept up the cap and replaced it with the automatic gesture borne of daily custom.

'Ah yes! The Holy Book. We have arrived at the matter of letters sooner than I expected with one so young. Wait a moment.'

With that he rose and hurried back into the large hall, and quickly reappeared carrying a number of leather tooled boxes some of which were inlaid with gold to outline the script. Guilhem was immediately reminded of the scroll box which Nanthilda had given him to examine.

'These boxes contain parts of our holy books. These five scrolls we call the Torah. The first is called Genesis. Or it would be if we wrote in the Latin tongue.'

'B b but our first...'

'Is also named the book of Genesis,' Caiaphas finished the sentence for the confused youth. He carefully unrolled one of the scrolls. I am sorry that you cannot see how closely your Holy Book and mine resemble each other but this is written in our Hebrew language. You will have to trust me.'

Guilhem had no doubts. The Jewish Rabbi was an easier man to trust than some of the priests that surrounded him at home; especially Father Teissiere of the foul breath.

'But why then, if this is so, did you kill the son of God?'

The simple direct question hung in the air, carrying with it eight hundred years of conflict. Only the young could ask such a question without causing upheaval and dispute. Even then it would depend on the wisdom of those present. Even from the young such a question could cause pain and distress. Caiaphas breathed deeply realising that the whole point of the meeting would depend on how he reacted to the ingrained Christian view and the simple conviction expressed by Guilhem.

'I believe your grandfather Childerich king of the Franks died in a monastery and your grandmother Nanthilda acknowledged the man who deposed him as king.'

Guilhem was totally thrown off track by the sudden change of subject.

'I th..th..think that is so but what has that ...'

'Hear me out young prince.' The older man rubbed his forehead wearily. This question of Jesus hung over every Jew especially those who lived far away from the holy land. It sapped the energies of his people and was so often the cause of their persecutions and destruction. Even here in the haven of Septimania it was never far away.

'Your grandmother made such a decision to save her family from more death and loss of all their lands. But there were many in the court who wanted her to resist and to fight for the right of her husband's family to rule as they had for many a hundred years. She gave in to tyranny. Was it right? Maybe you should be king of all the Franks.'

Guilhem felt a shock run through him. This was a thought that had never been expressed. Neither his father nor mother had ever mentioned this possibility.

Suddenly he understood more clearly the dangers that lay ahead at the court. Life was becoming more complex in a short space of time. Could he cope with all these new ideas that were being thrown at him and make the right decisions?

'In the holy land all those years ago our priests made a decision to help the Roman conquerors that ruled our land to catch a rebel who was causing trouble in our land. At that time few in Palestine believed that Jesus was the son of God. We thought then that he was man like us all and our books tell us that today.' He tapped the pile of scrolls in front of him.

Instinctively Caiaphas understood that these new thoughts were becoming difficult for Guilhem to cope with.

'You are not here to argue for your faith Guilhem, and nor am I for mine,' he grasped the young boy's shoulder. 'Father Bedier sent you here so that you could see that there are many beliefs held with equal conviction by many peoples of the world. And that there may be many roads to the truth.'

'Can there be many truths Rabbi Caiaphas?'

'I do not know Guilhem. But I believe that we should allow people here on earth to find their own paths to God and in the end he will be a fair judge of our mistakes if there are such. Let me just say that our scholars have also traced your line back to before the time of the prophet Jesus. For this reason we pay homage to your father and his descendants.'

He rose indicating the meeting was at an end. Guilhem also realised that Arnaud would be raising the alarm if he didn't appear.

'You are wise beyond your years,' said Caiaphas, 'do not let the pressures of the world narrow your mind to one path. The world has many truths to show you yet, if you are open to them. Come back to see me when you can. We Jews share our history with you and there is much that we can learn together.'

Guilhem sped out of the small side door. 'King!' He wanted to shout, 'I could be king!'

His excited rush carried him into the leatherseller's warehouse through the rear door. He stopped in a narrow space between the hanging hides, the strong smell of rough cured leathers thickening the air.

'But that's the problem. I could be king and so Pepin must keep me close. And the secret of my family; where does that fit? Can there be many truths? They keep telling me to be careful when I am at the court of the king. There must be more, much more to find out........'

Which was exactly the lesson that Father Bedier hoped the young seigneur would learn.

CHAPTER NINE

804 AD, Aniane
– The Hunter –

Bishop Benoit paced restlessly in the small cloister at Aniane listening to the messenger. The messenger, burnt dark by many years in the sun, still covered in the dust of travel on the cart from Gellone, made little skipping rushes as he struggled to keep up with the ungainly strides. He was anxious because he had nothing of note to report and the bishop was of uncertain temper. Gesticulating eagerly he assured Benoit that the abbot was under constant surveillance and had given no cause for suspicion. He had received no special visitors or parcels except a ceremonial gift from the Emperor himself, and that he had received in a formal ceremony in front of all the congregation including Fournier.

'And what was this gift from our Emperor,' Benoit interrupted to show interest although he knew this could have nothing to do with his own quest to exorcise the trail of heresy with which he knew Guilhem was in some way connected.

'It was part of the holy cross my Lord. A splinter of the very true cross,' he held his hands out to demonstrate the size which was about the length of a man's finger.

Anger flashed across the pale face. 'Your lord abbot is indeed in favour with our Emperor. That is a gift which we would envy were we to be subject to such emotions.' He knew the ironic tone was quite lost on the anxious skipping figure still making his ineffectual rushes to keep up. God he found these little people so boring!

'And no letter from Fournier or more useful message,' the way 'useful' was spat out at the dusty figure heralded a storm. Benoit held himself in check with difficulty.

'Go. The kitchen will find you food and drink. Wait, take this,' and he threw a small coin at the anxious man who disappeared in a trice through the arch at the far side of the cloister. Benoit allowed himself a moment of self congratulation for having displayed such Christian control. This was something that had become harder as the years passed.

Although his zeal in the service of the church had not abated through the years, the grey icy eyes and hollow cheeks betrayed a lack of peace with his lot, as though his faith was burning him from the inside and leaving him stranded with a life which was not the source of nourishment that he had been promised. The church had proved to be a hard taskmaster and always seemed to have an endless supply of tasks that had no end, such as stamping out heresies which sprouted like weeds.

The thoughts brought him back to the problem of Guilhem. This would have to be handled very carefully. The Emperor Charlemagne had as much influence in the ways of the church as the Pope himself. After all it was the Pope who had created the title for Charles in recognition of the services done for Rome over the years and the many campaigns fought on his behalf. The first Emperor of the west was anointed in the basilica of St Peter by Pope Leo III himself to create a balance of power between Constantinople and Francia, and to reward Charlemagne for his defence of Christendom against the Avar pagans in 796 and his later defence of the church against a rebellion in Rome itself.

He had stood side by side with Guilhem in his role as Count of Toulouse, Lord of Septimania and the second most important general of Charlemagne's armies. In many of the campaigns Guilhem had fought beside the greatest man of his time as one of his most trusted lieutenants.

There was nothing proved against his childhood friend. In fact he was sure that here was a man worthy of the Lord and a true follower of the church. It was not often that a man as powerful as the Count of Toulouse would renounce the world and turn to God. The abbey at Gellone would be a success and bring wealth and power to Aniane as a daughter estate, which was why he had finally given Guilhem his blessing and laid his hands on him so that he could rise as abbot of Gellone.

However that was not the only reason he had agreed to support his friend in his search for a peaceful end to his life. Benoit felt that Guilhem would lead him to the evidence that upheld the heresy attached to his family and their supporters. Even if Guilhem himself did not believe in these devilish tales, there was something that held him back from handing over whatever it was and declaring openly that his family served only one master on earth and one Lord in death, the true Christ.

Was that enough to make him a heretic in the eyes of his temporal lord Charlemagne? Benoit thought not. Proving heresy for something not done was much harder than showing a sin of commission.

It was very frustrating. He would have to wait until Guilhem decided to pass on the secret and move it to the next protectors. Surely he could not die without ensuring that at least some sympathisers had a means to perpetuate the knowledge so important to them. And he had to be doubly careful. Guilhem had watched while his colleague had burned a document rather than let it fall into Guilhem's hands. There was just the remotest chance that that had been a terrible, terrible mistake.

He looked across the small cloister gathering the autumn sun with its warm sandstone pillars each topped with a stone crown of leaves from which sprung the rhythmic arches which in turn provided the walkway for prayer and meditation. In the centre a simple stone bowl held the clear waters of life which trickled over the edge and into an oblong pond.

Herbs grew in squares separated by paths of crushed stone. Simple peaceful perfection so at odds with the whirling frustrations in the mind of the bishop.

'Perhaps there's a way to force him to move this treasure!' Benoit stopped as the thought struck home.

'Perhaps if he thought that someone was narrowing the search, he would move it to a place of safety and then....'

Before he left the peaceful cloister to write a message to Fournier he wondered how it was that Guilhem had established so close a protector in Charlemagne when his very name posed so obvious a threat to the new line of kings.

CHAPTER TEN

766 AD
– Related by Blood –

A heavy mist icicled the fur fringe of their hoods. Thick snow underfoot drew the colour from the winter dawn. Breath drawn out of frozen lips died in the phantom laden air and joined one grey to another as it faded into the silence. The small group waited like dead stumps melded to the trunks of the birch, beech and pine of the forest. The king's men had learned the hard way that the forest craft of the tribes was well known as the difference between success and failure and now they had set the ambush in their style.

The prince Charles breathed into Guilhem's ear, 'I can't feel my feet!'

'Think my spear is frozen to my glove!' Guilhem murmured in reply.

A muffled crunch, followed by the squeak of dry snow. In an instant, the discomfort of the wait melted in the flow of adrenaline. Another crunching step, and the labouring grunt of someone under heavy load. Nobody must move until the raiders were in sight and the signal given. Then the first shape loomed suddenly close. Closer than Guilhem expected. Still no move from Charles. Another shape came into view, in harness like a plough horse, pulling a heavy-laden sled. Behind the sled in the swirling mist, two figures were bent under their own loads pushing the sled up the slight incline.

Guilhem felt a tap on his shoulder. He forced his freezing feet into motion on the unfamiliar snowshoes. Two steps, three, four; still no reaction from the ghostly group around the sled. Then the raider's leader turned, mouth agape, and a warning shout still in his head as a spear quivered its silent journey into the side of his neck.

Guilhem bent and knifed the bindings of the clumsy snow shoes from his feet. Hoping the snow was hard enough to bear his weight, he ran the last few paces and launched himself at the nearest burdened figure, sword glimmering in the pale light.

The first shriek lost itself in the deadening snow. Dark eyes staring; futile arm raised. It was a girl! A captured slave. Hardly pausing, Guilhem sliced through her binding to the sled. A slight smile of reassurance and he was past her, running across the snow to join the fight as the raiders' rearguard straggled into view.

Charles was already in the thick of it. His tall figure easily recognised, the two handed sword whirling its figures in the air. The heavy clash of iron on iron deadened in the swirling mists. Guilhem saw him drop to one knee and his heart stopped. The Enger raider yelled in triumph. His sword delivered the horizontal death cut at Charles' neck. But protecting his head from the second attacker with raised shield, Charles rolled under the slashing sword and delivered a fatal thrust under the unguarded side. The triumphal shout turned into a choked wheeze and the snow turned red. The second raider saw that Charles' sword was useless, buried in the gaping wound of his comrade, and planting his foot on the sword arm, rushed in for the kill. But Charles was not a champion fighter without cause and his right leg swept the oncoming feet from under the Enger raider, his own shield arm deflecting the blow. Freeing his sword, he rolled to his feet as Guilhem arrived. Seeing he was outnumbered, the Enger fled.

The two men stood panting over the dying man at their feet. A small movement triggered Guilhem's attention and with a warning cry, he flung himself down on the dying man's dagger thrust aimed between Charles' legs, feeling the sear on his left side as he dived. Charles pushed him aside and finished the raider with a slash across the throat.

Guilhem rose to his feet and staggered. 'It's nothing. I don't feel anything. G..g..go, help the others.'

'It's deeper than you think. Sit. Take this. Press it on the wound.' Charles gave him a handful of snow. 'I'll be back.'

The small glade was spotted with swaying figures, most engaged in individual hand to hand battles. The snow blooming with crimson and pink flowers and the strange strangled sounds of battles fading into the dead winter forest.

Eventually it was over. Although evenly matched in numbers, the Enger raiders lost heart and melted back into the snow forest leaving their wounded and dead. The sled piled high with captured booty was abandoned with two captured slave girls.

Guilhem was still sitting where Charles had left him. He was feeling giddy, and the cold was beginning to penetrate the fur layers, not helped by the snow pack he was trying to hold against his side.

Charles called two of the soldiers and they carried him to the sled where he joined two other wounded men. Having stripped the bodies of anything useful, the patrol started back to the frontier settlement which had been subjected to the Enger attack. Although treaties had been signed, such raids were commonplace. It was never clear whether they were sanctioned by the warlord or not. The complicated system of barbarian vassalships and the existence of outlaw robbers meant that blame could easily be avoided.

The Prince kept close alongside the sled anxiously looking at Guilhem's whitening face.

'Cousin, you saved my life. It will not be forgotten.'

'Seigneur, where that dagger was going I saved the heirs to the kingdom.' A pale smile crossed Guilhem's face as he slipped into unconsciousness.

The room wobbled uncertainly into view. The roof timbers blurred and doubled as his eyes struggled to focus. It was hot under the heavy layers of bearskins. Dry. His tongue sought for moisture and encountered cracked lips. He tried to raise his head and the timbers darkened and crashed toward him. Then he felt an arm behind his neck and the trickle of cold water between his lips. Dark eyes smiled at him as an arm cradled his neck, her lips slightly parted with concentration as she held the wooden beaker to him. How red they were with white teeth glimpsed. Every detail of the girl seemed so important, so alive, so clear compared with the room around. He concentrated on every movement and felt her moving, the softness of her breasts, as she struggled to hold him up.

Suddenly he was awash in sensation and desire made him hard. The unexpected feeling made him blush and he turned his head away, spilling some of the precious water. That was when he saw the old Queen Nanthilda seated not far away, next a smouldering fire and gazing at him intently. The effect of sudden lust evaporated as quickly as it had arrived. He was properly awake now and the room stabilised around him.

'You will be well now,' said the old lady. She rose slowly, using the chair as support. 'Change the dressing as I showed you,' she addressed the young girl, 'And remember to use the salve from this pot.'

She pointed as she left the room, her stick thumping heavily on the wood floor. 'I will return young Guilhem. We have things to discuss and I will want to know if you have remembered your lesson that we shared in Narbonne.'

The young girl busied herself with tearing some linen strips and then, pulling the heavy skin cover back, she pulled his shift up leaving him naked to her unconcerned gaze and pointed at the bandage that lay across his stomach. Guilhem realised that she must have seen him naked and defenceless many times before. He realised with embarrassment that she and others must have cleaned him and washed him as he lay like a baby.

'How long have I....?' It did not sound like his voice at all.

She shook her head. Suddenly his memory clicked and the face of the rescued slave girl behind the sled and his nurse became one. She probably could not understand either of the tongues of Francia. She would be a captured slave from one of the Saxon forest tribes, but not from the Enger. Maybe it was preferable to be a slave in the house of the Prince of Francia than taken by a rival tribe or robber gang.

The young girl moved with easy grace around the room, the coarse wool gown tied at the waist giving occasional glimpses of the figure underneath. Taking the new strips of linen, she moistened them in water and then took the salve and pasted it to the strips with a practised hand. Then she approached the bed and helped him to lean against the soft feather pillows. Making a face to indicate that this would hurt, she began to unwrap the existing bindings. As she reached the torn flesh, he gasped at the sudden pain. But there was little fresh blood and the ragged tear had begun its crusted healing. She smiled at him and nodded while quickly replacing the old with new bindings plastered with ointment. Evidently it was going well.

Guilhem tried again by signing sleeping and waking to find out how many days he had been out of action. Suddenly understanding, she mimicked his pattern five times. No wonder he felt weak and light headed.

At that moment there was noise outside the door, and Guilhem could hear the high clear voice of Charles as he entered. The high pitch of the voice was always an unexpected contrast to the big bony frame and large square head framed with luxuriant reddish beard that curled about his face.

'So my friend, you live and so, thanks to you, do I!' Lifting a heavy oak stool effortlessly, he placed it by the bed and sat astride in one fluid move. He leaned forward. At eighteen he already had the easy manner of a leader and a man not subject to doubt.

'We taught them a lesson. They didn't expect any pursuit in winter. But I judge they will be back. We lost three men and they seven. And we nearly lost you my friend. You must not get into this bad habit of throwing yourself on daggers,' he laughed. Charles was a man of optimistic temperament.

'Not good enough my lord. They are many in that trackless forest they call home. We cannot keep the borders if we lose one man to two of theirs.'

'You are right, my friend, but for now I must give thanks to the good Lord that he placed you by my side. And I shall reward you well. First you shall have Visna,' he pointed to the nurse who had knelt as soon as he had entered the room, 'and then we must find you a command post away from the court. I know you have just saved my life, but the advisers to my father, King Pepin, say that you are a threat to our throne and there are those who want to see the family of Meroveus restored through you. How do you answer?'

It had come at last. This was what he had been warned about. It had not come through the hidden innuendoes of slippery courtiers, or even a message left in the night by an invisible malcontent. It was Charles himself, a man easy to respect and an obvious leader who had challenged him to make an open promise of support.

'Things are as they are my p..p..prince. However royal my blood, my family relinquished the crown to your family. My father gave King Martel his allegiance and confirmed his allegiance to your father, and I will do the same. And it is t..t..true also that we are related by blood.'

The stammer which had been with him since childhood did its best to belie the sincerity of his words.

'No more needs to be said. Get well in the care of the Lord and in the arms of Visna here and do not try too much too soon!' He winked and was gone.

It was three days later, when he was out of his bed and trying to pen a letter to his mother with a worn quill, ink that had more lumps than a cow's udder, and parchment that was being reused once too often, that the Dowager Queen returned to his room.

'So you have confirmed your allegiance to these mayors of the palace. These usurpers of your line!' The figure leaning on her stick had not even waited for a greeting. It was strange how much power came from the twisted figure bent with age.

'As you did also, my queen,' answered Guilhem, bowing as he did so.

'Charles says you are a good soldier with a wise head on young shoulders. You saved his life. He trusts you. One day you could take back what is yours.'

Guilhem looked at her with questioning eyes. Was she really encouraging an act of treason?

'There are some, perhaps many, that would follow you as a prince of the blood.'

'He asked me directly Madame. I gave my word as a Christian and as a son of my father that I would be loyal. I do not think we should talk further on this subject.'

The little figure swathed in black with a white wimple head-dress gave a sigh. The bright eyes looked at him keenly. 'Bring the chair closer to the fire. These days I am always cold. My blood runs slow. My time is nearly done.' She raised her hand to forestall any protest as she sank onto the chair and held her gnarled hand to garner the extra heat.

Moving the chair reminded him sharply that the wound in his side was not yet healed. He winced as he dragged it to the fire. His grandmother took no heed.

'It is good that you have answered so. To take the easy route of temptation for power would put you in danger all your life. The prince Charles has greatness within him and you will do well to serve him.

Your greater task is to preserve your family. The girl, Visna, is she with child yet?'

Guilhem blushed, the heat spilling through the roots of his head. He had barely lost his virginity with Visna and the old lady, as usual, seemed to know his most intimate moves. Visna was still there kneeling at the side of the room. He hoped that her slowly improving grasp of the language had not gone so far. After all it was only two nights ago.....

'Babies!' he thought. It had never even entered his mind. 'No. Of c..c..course not. At least I don't think.....' His voice trailed into silence.

'I am not a fool,' the old Queen went on. 'Neither you or even she can know yet,' she paused, 'but I wanted to remind you that your heritage carries with it responsibility for future generations, as well as obligations to the past. The scroll, you remember the scroll and the names we learned together? Tell me the names.'

That summer seemed so distant, yet in sharp focus as the warm summer breeze with its hint of sea salt ruffled his hair on the tower overlooking the beige tiled roof of the great church of St Felix. He could feel the vellum in his hand as he had unrolled the strange scroll with the tree winding its green leaved way round the plain wooden staff, and the monster fish on the other side, and the vivid golden bee. He could visualise the meaningless script in its perfect columns and the feeling that something important was about to happen. He could also remember the feeling of disappointment when he left Nanthilda. It was as though he had almost discovered something of great moment, but that its true significance had been kept from him

'The names we learned together, you and I. Let us see if your memory serves us well my child.'

Guilhem let the time come to him. The upper room with the carved chair usually reserved for his father. The heavy oak table and the narrow defensive windows that let in just enough light which lay in strips across the floor of stone and rush matting. The sound of the old lady's voice repeating the strange names, which were only lent weight by the insistence of her conviction. Once, her bony hand had struck like a viper, and he felt his jaw seize with surprising strength as she forced him to meet her gaze.

'Chlodwig II, not Chilperic,' she had whispered at one point. 'It has to be right. If it is to be true, it has to be right!'

'Clovis, Childeric, Meroveus, Clodion, Faramund, Frotmund, Boaz, Titurai.' The names came out as a roll call of the gods with no sign of a stammer.

'Yes, yes. It was so. And who was Faramund married to? Who was his queen?' The old voice broke the spell and as the vision of the room faded so did his memory.

'You must carry the line in your mind. It must be complete. Here!' She thrust a scroll into his hand. 'This is the whole history from David King of the Jews right down to your father. The list is transcribed to Latin. Fix it truly in your mind and then burn it. Now is the time to make sure it cannot be lost while you live. Now, while you recover from your wounds.'

'When I was a child I learned because I was a child and you were the Queen of old, my lady. But now I must understand what I am learning and why. If this is a list of my forefathers, why does it carry danger and secrecy with it?'

'Send your slave away, Guilhem. She may not understand our tongue, but there are many who would give much to learn the secrets of your line.'

Guilhem went to the still kneeling Visna and raised her gently. Making signs of drink and food, he gestured for her to leave.

'You are a child of the church in Rome. You believe in Jesus, the Son of God, who died for us all on the cross. You believe in the Bible and the writings of the apostles.' It was not a question and Guilhem merely sat in silence. Lack of contradiction was acceptance enough.

'Some of us believe that the Bible does not contain the whole truth and that there are writings from the time of our Lord that tell another tale. We think that from the earliest days the truth was subject to the prejudices and politics of man, and that Paul and Peter were already selecting the truth in their own image. Do you think there can be more than one truth?'

'I think that....' There were too many questions in his mind. He could feel that this was a moment on which his future might turn. He felt too uninformed, too ignorant to answer questions of this weight. The vision of the old Jew Caiaphas unrolling the ancient scrolls flashed into his mind. 'Do not narrow your mind. There can be many truths.'

'I think that people believe in their own truths and they do not always agree.'

The old lady's face lit up and she leant across the fire and took his hands in hers. 'Father Bedier said that you could carry the burden and were wise beyond your years. This you have already learned. The Jews believe that our Lord was a prophet, but not the Saviour. The Saracens believe that Jesus was a prophet, but he did not die on the cross, and also that he was a prophet among many. The church in Rome believe that there is only their truth as a route to salvation, and it is a fact that this route is certainly becoming a way to great power and wealth in this world. I am not so sure about the next...' She cackled almost to herself, revealing an almost toothless mouth.

'Guilhem, do you know why your father was chosen to be the ruler of Septimania under King Pepin?'

'Because the Prince's father, Pepin, had taken the kingdom of Francia away from my grandfather, and this was a way to keep my father's loyalty.'

'That is a wise and political answer and it contains within it some of the truth.' The old lady looked up at him with respect from her huddled position against the fire.

'Why do you think the Jews of Narbonne have so readily accepted him as the King's representative?' There was no reply to this question, and yet it was true that of all the areas that owed allegiance to King Pepin, Septimania was amongst the most peaceful.

Nanthilda continued. 'It is because of your lineage. They too believe that your family has a special place in the history of the Jewish peoples. When your knowledge of your line is complete, Guilhem, you will learn that there are many who see your family as sons of David. The very David who slew Goliath and was king of the Jews.' She paused to gain breath. She tired easily these days.

'But we are not Jews!' The idea was not tenable. It fought against everything that he had learned in the monastery at Narbonne. Then he remembered Father Bedier whose eyes were full of faith in the goodness of man and of God and who had sent him on a mission to see the Rabbi Caiaphas.

'We are n..n..not Jews,' he repeated, somewhat less definitively, his stammer coming to the fore under the shock of this strange news. His feet seemed to sink into the fresh rush matting as though the floor had shifted. It felt as though a keystone had moved and made unsteady the certainties that had been his life. It was as though the weaknesses caused by the wound were infecting his mind. He leaned against the table.

'Guilhem, think of the ages that have passed since David of the Old Testament was king. So many years; so many generations; so many mysteries of the past. Yet it is true to say that some scholars of the Jewish faith understand that the line of Merovech carries with it the true blood. For that reason they accepted our family to be their ruler in Septimania.'

'Why are you telling me all this now? Who else knows this story about us? Does the King and Prince Charles believe this about us?' The questions came tumbling out.

'This story is not widely known, Guilhem. Further, of those that have heard it, few believe that there is any truth to be seen in these wild tales. The old King Charles Martel merely took advantage of a myth held by those Jews who had helped drive the Saracen from the lands of southern Francia.'

The Dowager Queen paused. The folds in her ancient face deepened. Her voice combined resignation with insistence.

'I have not long left to live. Soon I will find the truth in the next world. Will my beliefs condemn me to the eternal fire? Who can know? But my task in this life is to pass to you what I have learned and believe to be true. You may choose to ignore it as your father and mother have done. As our Lord said, sometimes truth is seen through a glass darkly. It is not always easy to choose the right way.' She drew breath. 'Guilhem, we believe that your family is one of a select few, chosen to seek the truth and to preserve it for all time. We believe that your line lives on with a special purpose, and that through your heritage a better way to God will be revealed.'

Guilhem let the words wash over him. They seemed to come from a great distance. In his mind, he knew that he should feel that something momentous was happening, but he could feel nothing. He was numbed.

Eventually someone spoke. It was he. 'This truth,' the word came out louder than he expected but he found control difficult. 'This truth;

how can it hold against the wisdom and teachings of our church? How can it help me? How can this help anything? It will cause t..t..trouble and even bloodshed. What do you expect me to do with this story?'

'Only you can decide what to do, Guilhem. I can tell you that there are other hidden strands of a different truth to that taught by Rome that even I am not aware of. They will carry the story in secret till a time has come when it is safe to discuss such things. The last thing I have to say is that there is evidence for this truth. Evidence that has been well hidden, and some of which is in far distant lands. There are many keys needed to unlock the truths we hold, if one day you should want to follow the path of your line. Maybe, if God wishes, he will send you to discover what you can. Maybe it will be your task to tell the world another story. Maybe you will choose to forget this day.'

'But how will I know? Who can I talk to? What could I do?' The questions flooded out.

'You can talk to no-one here. You can do nothing till the time comes. Till then, live your life as you have. Be loyal to the Prince and the kingdom in this life, as far your beliefs will let you. Soon you will find a way to discover more, if you so wish. And now I must go and let that wench Visna speed your recovery.' Laughing to herself, the old lady heaved herself painfully from the chair and hobbled to the door.

'Farewell my son. I do not think we will meet again. I leave for the palace at Aachen tomorrow. Be true to yourself and all will be well.' She paused at the door. 'If you want to learn more, and there is more that even I do not know, remember the merchant ambassador from Alexandria, Adelchis, and also the old Jew, Caiaphas.'

Guilhem felt as though the world had left him alone, surrounded by people who could never help to share this burden. People who would want to kill this lie and him with it. He felt that he should pray for guidance, but suddenly he was uncertain. Was the God of the Jews the same God that he had been taught about over the years? Who would listen to his prayers now?

Suddenly he was very tired.

CHAPTER ELEVEN

805 AD, Gellone
– Moving the Evidence –

It was nearing the end of winter. Heavy rains had turned the track into a ploughed mess of dung and mud. Four oxen pulled the laden sled up the winding slope with stubborn, mute incomprehension. The drover curled his long whip against the uncomplaining flanks of the lead ox. A keen wind from the north drove needles of icy rain under his cowl searching for the few remaining dry patches. His boots stuck and sucked at the mud gaining great clods every few steps. Another load of stone for the abbey church inched its painful way to the plateau of Gellone.

Jacques Fournier watched its slow progress up the hill from the shelter of the guard hut let into the west wall of the completed stockade. The slow advance with its air of inevitable progress echoed the measured rise of the great church. Buildings were built at the pace the good Lord allowed. There was little point in trying to hurry the process. The whip made little difference to the pace of the oxen. A mason could only cut and shape the great blocks at a certain speed. Everything had its allotted time except for the wishes of Bishop Benoit and the discovery of….. what exactly? That was one problem; he didn't know what he was looking for. He didn't know what form this proof of heresy would take. So far the attempts he had made to panic the abbot into moving the mystery items seemed to have failed. He had even suggested to the mason Pierre Clergue that the work on the church could be speeded up if they used the already dressed blocks from the scriptorium. This had resulted in a confrontation with Brother Jonathen who had suggested that the construction of one building to the glory of God at the expense of another would do little to guarantee his place in the hierarchy of saints!

The abbot had supported this view and so the scriptorium had remained untouched. In fact its work was increasing and new scholars had joined the little group. Now there was a further cause for suspicion for they were not all of the faith of our Lord. Jews from Narbonne and the Holy Land and a Saracen who said he came from Cordoba in Spain and another from a land called Ethiope, wherever that was. How could heathens be allowed to work on the holy books?

Meanwhile he was no further forward. The bishop had sent a monk Bertrand into the little community who was an expert in the form of the Gregorian chant and was also a cellerer of proven ability. He seemed to be a pious enough sort with a quick wit, short legs and a short temper to match. Abbot Guilhem had taken to him although at this stage his skills as a cellerer were hardly needed. But even this addition had produced no result. At least if they did find something in the library of scrolls and books he would be able to read it. Fournier had no skills in that direction.

It was at that point that the idea came to him. An idea that would surely flush out any secrets that the blessed abbot was concealing. The answer was fire. Not a fire to destroy the librarium; that would destroy the evidence that Bishop Benoit was so determined to find, but a small fire that would maybe destroy a number of manuscripts that were being worked on.

'Foul weather to be hauling rock, my friend!' He hailed the drover with a smile, 'You have made good time. Over there by the east window. Then get yourself by the fire.' The deep voice barrelled out of his chest ending in the familiar wheeze.

'Thank you sir, thank you,' the drover glanced from under the soaked cowl that shrouded his face. Jacques was not known for greetings or compliments. Perhaps his woman had been particularly inventive the previous night.

Three nights later the fire was discovered by the night guard who was actually making the rounds assigned to him in spite of the continuous rain. Jonathen was first on the scene followed by Bertrand the newest of the monks to join the little community. Hands made clumsy by the cold and rain fumbled at the great iron lock while they could see the flickering orange light of the fire that threatened to destroy a lifetime's work. Finally the door burst open and they rushed into the large room that acted as workshop and kitchen. The flames were reaching up the wall to the left of the fireplace and already working along a wide shelf on which were laid the partially completed works of the day. Jonathen rushed at the shelf and oblivious to the danger swept the burning vellum sheets to the floor and started stamping on the burning scraps. Bertrand found a large container of water and tipped it across the floor to cut off the flames. Suddenly Guilhem appeared in the door already armed with a large brush of wet hazel twigs. With this he swept along the line of fire breaking it into smaller flickering embers.

'Throw your cloaks on the flames. Do not let the flames spread to the librarium!' he shouted. Finally containers of water started to arrive, organised by the night watchman, and within a few moments the remaining flickers of orange and yellow were tamed and the sooty group were stamping the remaining sparks into oblivion.

'Good work everyone. It could have b..b..been much, much worse. Jonathen you will take charge here. Where is the night watchman?'

'Here my lord abbot. I was on my...'

'No, no, be not afraid my friend. But for you this could have been much worse. And this not a night to be out. Your vigilance will be rewarded.' Guilhem searched for the name. 'Simon isn't it? Simon you have done well. Come and see me in the morning.'

Memory worked its magic and the night watchman retired full of the pride of recognition and as if praise itself was all the reward he sought.

Although the hour was late all the members of the scriptorium had arrived on the sooty scene. Jonathen quickly had them organised into small teams. One to concentrate on cleaning and clearing; one to sift through the parchments and partially completed books to identify the damage. Guilhem himself took part in the clearing team, his hazel brush still in hand. Bertrand seemed most anxious to help and Guilhem found him at his side more than once.

With a gesture he prevented the eager hands from throwing more water on the scene and the brushes and cloths from wiping the fire traces away. For a few minutes he wandered around the room checking the limits of the fire spread and then gradually circling back to the fireplace which must have been the source of the accident. He paid particular attention to the leg of a table on which a pile of half finished manuscripts had been placed, and which had burned most fiercely. The table and this pile of parchment seemed to be the place from which the fire had spread.

He beckoned to Jonathen. 'Can you see how embers from the fire, assuming there were some not properly extinguished, could have travelled three paces and spread to this table?'

The tall bony figure took in the scene and then wiping his hand wearily across his forehead shook his head slowly. A black soot mark followed his hand and even his flying halo of white hair lost its customary defiance.

'You think someone set this fire. If so this is not against our work here my lord abbot. This was done as a warning to you.'

'Not a warning. More to provoke a reaction I think. I place Jacques Fournier and his friends behind this attack. They took a risk. Fires do not often do what they are told.'

'My lord abbot, I do not think you can continue to risk nearly twenty years of work to protect your secret. Somehow you must show them that they are wrong. You will have to move it or them.'

'But that is exactly what they hope for Jonathen. They hope that in moving it I will give them an opportunity to seize it. If I can prove that Jacques is behind this then he can be imprisoned or executed. That would stop them.'

'They will send another my lord. You have no right to put the work of God in front of your precious secrets. You have taken your own vows. How can you seek salvation by your good work here in our valley when at the same time you put us and our work at risk. We are not part of this problem my lord. Your duty is to remove the danger from us.' Jonathen stopped. Perhaps he had gone too far. This was his abbot and he had a duty to him as well.

'Of course you are right my friend,' Guilhem spoke wearily. A weariness that did not just belong to a disturbed night and anxiety about the possible losses. This was the weariness of a burden carried through the years. A burden that he had never sought but that he supposed was his particular cross. Here at the end of his life he still felt his duty was to protect the mystery of the golden bee, or at least that part of it that had been revealed to him. Yet he would not be the cause of some great upheaval to the mother church either. He had hoped so much that the move into the church would allow the secrets to rest till another age when man had learned more about the will of the good Lord.

'I need time brother Jonathen. I will come up with a plan to leave our work of learning safe and yet to keep my promises.'

Three days later spring had made one of its sudden shifts from wolf to lamb. High white clouds puffed their way across the soft blue of the early year sky. In the sheltered valley the new grass had taken that shade of unreal emerald, and blackthorn showed white clusters in among the trees and scrub of the limestone cliffs. Brother Adalung walked with his enthusiastic lean beside Guilhem as they made a tour of the early season preparations for the sowing and planting. The path hugged the side of the valley to leave the maximum area for planting. Beside them two figures in long sleeved smocks had started to plough with the aid of a team of oxen heavily yoked in pairs with a long thick plaited hemp rope attached to the eye of the plough. The normal wool cowl head-dresses had been cast aside in the unexpected warmth of the spring sun and sweat was already shining on their foreheads.

Adalung called out a greeting to the ploughman bent over the strong oak handles used to guide the heavy iron shear that was cutting into the still heavy sod. 'Pierre, may God give strength to your arm and make your furrows straight!' Pierre Maury lifted his thick gloved hand in acknowledgement for a brief moment, and returned to the crucial task of keeping the shear straight and at the right depth. Too deep and the seed would not flourish till too late. Too shallow and the birds would demolish the crop before it showed. A lazy crack of the whip held by Pierre's son-in-law Raymond brought a snort from the lead pair and the plough lurched forward accompanied by a grunt from Pierre. This was a job that needed experience, strength and concentration.

On past the ploughing team they walked up the valley to where it bent round to the left. The stream called Alesse burbled and chuckled its crystal way back toward the settlement. As they rounded the limestone outcrop the valley widened out again into a bowl completely surrounded by cliffs and steep mountainsides. A flock of sheep was grazing peacefully in the idyllic scene. Lambs were making those confused skittering runs of the new born as they lost and found their source of food. The sheep standing unconcerned amidst the bleating cacophony certain that their own young would attach themselves to the right teat. A young shepherd boy gazed over the scene with his dog lying in the shade beside him.

It had been a good lambing season and so far the wolves had not made many inroads into the flock. Guilhem saw the square of wicker hurdles where one side had been opened for daylight grazing. When dusk fell two more shepherds would come up to drive the herd into the shelter; the open side would be closed for the night and watch would be kept. The circle of cliffs kept man at bay but wolves and wild boar and lynx were a different matter.

Guilhem had not just come to the end of the settlement for a stroll in the sun, though it was his habit to inspect all corners of his small domain on a regular basis.

He wanted a private talk with young Phillipe Baille who had exhibited a heightened sense of restless exploration and had given his parents anxious moments when he had disappeared from time to time for two or three days before returning with the unconcern of the young for the anxieties of the old. His employment as shepherd had been chosen by Adalung to try and instil a sense of responsibility into the young lad. At least he was here and had not wandered off leaving his flock to the mercies of the wild.

Guilhem suddenly felt overwhelmed by a sense of God's blessing on the little settlement.

'I think we should g..g..g..give thanks for God's grace and care for us Brother Adalung. We should pray.'

'Yes my lord abbot but let me introduce young Phillipe and check on the sheep so that he is not frightened by our appearance. See he has not yet seen us. How many?'

Adalung called to the young lad. Phillipe jerked to attention. He had not noticed the approach of the two men. When he saw Guilhem he reddened as if caught in some reprehensible act and his eyes were immediately hooked by the disfiguring scar on his abbot's face. Quickly he demonstrated the count with his hands and fingers. There were forty seven. This apparently accorded with the priest's reckoning. 'Well done. You have not lost any as yet. You have food enough?'

'Yes thank you sir. There has been no trouble and I have never left my....'

'Its alright lad. We have not come to find fault.' Adalung gave a practised gaze over the scene.

'The lord abbot would like us to give thanks for our blessings on this place. Kneel here beside me for a moment.'

The little group knelt in the warm spring sun and Guilhem asked for God's blessing on their little community.

'I think all is well here my lord abbot. We can return on the other side of the stream and see how it goes with vegetables that are being planted out,' said Adalung after the short prayer was concluded.

'You carry on my friend,' said Guilhem, 'I will stay here with young Phillipe awhile and make my own way back.'

He sat on a rock beside Phillipe and watched the monk stride purposefully off jumping the little stream as he went. He glanced at the nervous figure beside him. A lad who had never been this close to his lord abbot and who could not stop his gaze returning to the spoiled face 'Court nez', they called him. The story was that this was the mark of a Saracen sword and close up there was no reason to think otherwise. In a way it made him seem more like one of them. He began to relax.

Phillipe thought about this abbot who they were told had been a famous count, but then there were few abbots who carried the marks of war so maybe it was so. But why would anyone give up all those horses and nobles and gold and great armies. His mind began to dizzy at the possibilities.

Guilhem sat quietly beside the black haired lad. About fifteen or so he guessed.

The soldier's eye noted the worn sandals and broken ties which had been mended many times. The wool smock was not that clean either and had a hole under the left arm. A large fading bruise was visible on his left arm and a swelling over the eye.

'How did you get those Phillipe?' the young lad knew what he meant.

'Fight. A sort of fight, my lord.'

'Did you win?' Guilhem asked with a smile in his eyes. 'Did you win?'

'Can't win. Never can win,' Phillipe mumbled looking down and seeming more embarrassed than the little exchange warranted. Guilhem suddenly understood, or thought he did.

'Your father?' The question hung in the air. The young lad nodded ashamed.

'Your father Hugo who is a strong man with a spade and quick with his fist, and who is helping us build our church?' The boy nodded again but said nothing.

'Well I understand young Phillipe that you know these hills and forests better than most.' Phillipe was startled by the change of subject. 'I would like to know if there is a way out over there.' Guilhem pointed to the steep hills and cliffs that surrounded them.

'The forest people have a way. If they wanted to they could come that way but it is hard to find.'

'But you know how they do it, don't you Ph Ph Phillipe? Could you take me at night? Could you find the way for me if I wanted to go that way?'

'Perhaps I could my lord, but it is a hard way with much climbing.'

*   *   *   *   *   *   *

Eight days later as spring had somersaulted back to winter and a March wind roared through the gorge de l'Herault, an attack was launched on the lower outpost that guarded the road to the village. It was that time before dawn when the spirit sinks and takes the body with it. The guard found himself in the embrace of something much rougher than the rounded arm of the shepherd's daughter Lisette of which he had been dreaming. A hairy forearm across his throat strangled any thought of sound and the faint prick of iron in the side of his neck stilled any idea of throwing his assailant.

'The lord abbot will not be pleased, my friend. Be silent.' A quiet confident voice whispered in his ear. The guard nodded assent.

'Now let's see if there are any defences at all. Blow the alarm.' The guard looked at the bandit in surprise. Was this some trick that would give his attacker an excuse to plunge the dagger into his neck? The bandit nodded encouragingly.

'We will not harm you. We will leave that to the abbot,' he grinned; the light from the brazier barely showing the white of his teeth. The guard reached for the horn slung on a hook close by and trying to still his fearful stomach blew the alarm. In moments the defences, some two hundred paces behind the outpost, were being manned and the noise of booted feet could be heard among the shouts of the sergeant at arms. At that, several more figures appeared out of the dark and with loud yells they charged the second defences. Throwing spears thudded into the woodwork and rope ladders were slung over the stockade.

As instructed and rehearsed many times by Guilhem all the able bodied men of the little village were responding in a mad clatter of clogs and boots and the clash of iron as they raced to take up their positions inside the barricade. Among them was the burly figure of Jaques Fournier gasping his way to the second gate.

The only exceptions were the monks and priests who had been instructed to barricade the librarium and close the shutters from the inside. Among these was the new monk Bertrand from Montpellier, who kept a watch to see if the abbot or his henchman brother Jonathen were paying any special attention to part of the librarium stock. It took him quite some time in the confusion to realise that the abbot was not among the group now safely barricaded in the stone building.

Far from the clash of arms and the shouts of the aggressors two figures, neither of which were dressed as monks, were climbing a tortuous path up the mountain to the west. Light was streaking the ragged cloud that raced low over the mountains as the two men struggled up the last climb. Guilhem had found the going particularly hard and struggled to keep up with Phillipe's nimble feet through the thorn and bramble and treacherous footing of loose earth and rolling pebbles. Finally the climb levelled out and revealed a small glade in the dawn light.

'You have done well Phillipe. You will be henceforth the special guide to the abbot of Gellone when I return. Take these,' and he gave two small gold coins to Phillipe. 'You will have to be well dressed and have strong boots as my guide, and tell your father of your new post. He will not harm you again.'

With a grunt that betrayed the protesting body he heaved himself into the saddle of his faithful mare which had been taken up to the mountain top and tethered there the day before by the young shepherd. A prince's conical helmet of finest iron, inlaid with gold hid the tonsure. Just above the nose guard the perfect outline of a bee glinted in the dawn light. A leather satchel containing three scroll boxes was slung over his shoulder, and round his waist his sword in its wooden scabbard covered with fine leather inlaid with bronze and silver.

Behind him and far below the cliff top in the village of Gellone little harm had been done by the surprise assault arranged by Guilhem's own men as a test of their defences. Everyone agreed that valuable lessons had been learned.

CHAPTER TWELVE

768 AD

– Captured –

The mountains of Septimania which bordered the Spanish March in the South West corner of the vassal kingdom stretched in front of the armed troop. Leather creaked and harness jingled in early summer sun. Light flashed and danced off the polished helmets and lance tips. Guilhem was particularly conscious of his own helmet made of the finest iron and inlaid in gold with his family crest. Given to him by Charles before they had left the court in the north, it had the latest nose guard and side pieces to protect the ears. After they had left the court Guilhem had had the troop armourer fix one of his golden bees to the forehead just above the nose piece. It had yet to be tested in battle.

Heraldic banners fluttered at the head of the troop. Thirty horsemen were about the business of the King Pepin under the command of the king's eldest son Carloman.

Early that morning they had left Narbonne where Guilhem had spent a short time with his parents. It had been an unsatisfactory and disappointing experience. For Guilhem life had passed as a river rushes to the sea gathering strength and breadth as it goes. A child had left and a man had returned. But there had been another tributary where time had taken its unforgiving toll, especially of his father Thierry, whose rich deep voice still carried its jovial authority but whose face behind the now grey beard had thinned and his skin had added a yellow tinge to the weathered tan. He now walked with a pronounced limp and it was clear that pain was a constant visitor which put the jovial tone at odds with his appearance.

Aude had done better physically and in the time since his last visit had added weight to the slender figure of his childhood memory. She spent much time at her devotions and although she met him with her smile of love, it was not long before her thoughts seemed to be elsewhere and inward. She did not to want to engage with life with the same quiet determination of earlier years. Neither parent had seemed able to engage with the young adult who had ridden into the courtyard with the king's son Carloman after so many years at the court. It was as though they had been stolen from him by sickness and religion. Guilhem was hurt by this almost accidental estrangement and hoped to do more to show he was still the son who loved them when he returned from this short expedition.

Guilhem had wanted to talk to his father about his grandmother who had died shortly after the memorable meeting at the frontier post where she had helped to save his life with her knowledge of herbs and medicine. She had also left him with a burden which shifted in and out of his mind with varying intensity, but would never quite allow him to forget what he had been told and more importantly what he had not been told. This feeling of tasks left undone he had carried totally alone. There was no one he knew with whom such matters could be discussed.

He had also wanted to know about the Jewish story of their family heritage which had seemed less and less likely as the days and seasons passed. At one with his horse in the morning sun his mind ran back over the unsatisfactory meeting with his father the night before.

'I hear good things about you from the court, Guilhem. We are all proud of you. Promoted to Constable already. A good sign; a very good sign.' A slight grimace crossed his face as he sank into the big oak chair in the upper hall.

'Father did you know that grandmother Nanthilda helped nurse me when I was wounded the winter before the last?'

'Of course I remember it well because King Pepin sent a full report on the cause of your wound and the efficacy of Nanthilda's salve! He is very aware that you saved Prince Charles. His messages have made it plain that provided you remain true to your vassal's oath you will fill my shoes here well, my son. It may be sooner than you think. The doctors, even the Jewish ones cannot tell me what ails me and I am not as strong as once I was.'

'Indeed father you have lost weight and I can see that your leg is causing much pain. I pray that it may pass. That you are not well makes it more important that you tell me what I should know.'

'What can I tell you Guilhem. You are my only son. Our position is strong at court. You will inherit our lands and if the Jews agree, you will be their next king here in Septimania.' Thierry shifted with discomfort. Perhaps he knew the next question.

'If the Jews agree?' Guilhem repeated in a questioning tone. 'Why should they agree to one overlord rather than another? They must owe allegiance to the king anyway.'

'Ah! I see that your grandmother told you her stories. Guilhem I have never been much interested in the stories of long ago. When I was young the old king Charles Martel took the throne and put my father in a monastery. I never saw him again. Our history seemed to be more of a danger to me and mine than a benefit. My mother queen Nanthilda took steps to protect us all and since then I have followed her advice. But she always believed in the special role of our family that has been passed down the ages and told to her by my father Childerich and his father Theoderic IV. You should know that her own family has royal roots to the kings of the Visigoths. She believed in the power of the blood lines.'

'Yes father, this I know but I do not understand why the Jews find that we have a right to rule them. Does our Holy Church agree that we are Jews also? Do you believe that we belong to such a line?'

'I am not a man of books and scrolls Guilhem. I understand that a chief Rabbi of the time when the Saracen ruled Narbonne only a few years past, sent a message that if the King Martel would send a son of David to be their king in Septimania they would swear allegiance to such a man and through him to the King Charles Martel. The message said that such a man was already an heir to the throne through the line of Meroveus.'

'Did King Martel believe them? Surely he could not take such a risk? He had just put your father in a monastery!'

'Your grandmother Nanthilda persuaded him. And so we are here! I do not know anything of the truth of the belief of the Jews, but they have been loyal to us and the king,' he paused, 'and have been very diligent in paying their taxes.' A smile crossed Thierry's face. 'A king can believe much when the taxes are paid without trouble.'

'But father surely....'

Thierry held up his hand. 'I have nothing more to say on this matter

Guilhem. When the time is right you will have to decide if you want to learn more. One last word, I can tell you that the church does not believe these claims and it thinks that they are a danger to their teachings.'

The Saracens were the reason they were headed to the newly conquered March that stretched over the natural boundary provided by the Pyranees and included the small city of Gerona. The treaty signed by the Caliph Abd al-Rahman was not being kept. It was necessary to deliver yet another reminder. Guilhem, now second in command under the leadership of Prince Caroloman, would pick up more forces as they travelled through the newly regained territories from the Counts and the Ingenuii, the free farmers, who had been granted lands as vassals to his father Thierry, Compte d'Autun.

'The problem was,' Guilhem thought as they trotted quietly along the Via Domitia, 'there were as yet not many settlements from which to gather troops.' He hoped that there would be enough to extract yet another promise of obedience from the Caliph. It was never certain that lands newly granted to those loyal to Thierry would still be loyal. It was not unknown for loyalties to be transferred, even to the Saracen, in return for some short term advantage. His father had already mounted two such excursions in the past three years. It was hoped that with the authority coming directly from the court of Pepin this expedition would be more effective.

The little troop rode slowly down the Via Domitia with the Mediteranean blue coming in and out of sight as the Roman road took its straight path through the low hills and scrub ignoring for the most part the vagaries of the coastline. Occasional tracks would lead off to the right and sometimes there were glimpses of small villages seeking the protection of a rise in the terrain, or the ruins of a stone bastide which had been sacked once too often for it to be rebuilt. This was an area that had been disputed between the old Visigoth rulers, the newer Franks and the Saracen invaders for the last sixty years. A kind of peace was now in place and the free farmers were now beginning to reclaim the land and make it productive once again.

Guilhem became aware of a horseman pulling up close beside him. The only other helmet inlaid with gold and silver told him it was Carloman, the king's son.

'This is your territory,' a slight emphasis on the 'your' in a way that managed to tell Guilhem that his territory was actually the king's land and he should not forget it. Carloman was different in every way to his younger brother Charles. He was dark skinned with black hair that did not take to the long fashion of the kings of the age. Heavy eyebrows and a nose with a slight hook gave him a permanently lowering expression while the full lipped mouth expressed permanent distaste. Carloman's outward expression unfortunately echoed the spirit of the man behind it. Guilhem neither liked nor trusted him and the prince was aware of it and so used any opportunity to provoke Guilhem to an indiscretion. Guilhem with his new promotion to Constable had been sent as second in command of the expedition because of his family's knowledge of the area and their closer connections to the feudal lords of the south west. King Pepin was also aware that the Count Thierry d'Autun was not the man he had been and this was a way to show that the new generation was there if needed. In this way it was hoped to raise sufficient troops to show the Saracen Caliph Abd-al- Rahman that breaking the treaties in future would result in a total loss of Catalonia.

'This is your territory,' repeated Carloman, 'I am told that the lord of Cabestany has a thriving village two hours south of here. Would he not provide us with men and provisions? Especially since the king's son is here?' As usual Carloman left no opportunity to remind Guilhem and others of his status.

Guilhem knew that the lord of Cabestany was a loyal vassal to his father. In fact he had already sent word to Guilhem that he was preparing a troop and supplies for this expedition. However he suspected that if Carloman thought that it was easy to raise such a troop he would ask for more.

'Seigneur, before Cabestany we will come to Perpignan. I suggest that we send the sergeants ahead to recruit from the townspeople and I have already sent ahead to the Bishop Theobald to hold a service of blessing on our expedition. The lord of Cabestany is invited and I know that he will support our cause.'

Carloman looked at him frustrated by the deft way that Guilhem had avoided provocation and at the same time had demonstrated his talent for organization. It appeared that his father had been right to confirm his promotion to Constable at such a young age.

'Very well Constable Guilhem. We shall rely on you to provide the numbers necessary and the supplies.'

The matter of numbers had been the subject of much discussion with Thierry before they had left Narbonne. They had to have sufficient numbers to punish raiders who had broken the truce, but they should not appear to be an invading army. They had settled on about a hundred and fifty to two hundred men at arms which should include at least fifty cavalry.

'There will be the numbers we have agreed, sire,' said Guilhem, hoping that his messages to Perpignan, Capestany, Collioure, Tautavel and Perthus had been received and acted upon. The march frontier towns and villages continually fighting their own battles, often among themselves as well as the Saracen, could not be relied upon.

The day was well advanced when the troop rode slowly into the main square of Perpignan in front of the church of Saint Jean le Vieux. This was one of the older churches in the region and had been attacked by the Saracens on more than one occasion. Nevertheless it stood with quiet resolution in the warm afternoon sun confident in the faith that had brought it into being. The faces of the apostles carved into the Roman arch above the west door looked solemnly at the scene of apparent chaos as the numbers in the square increased. Quickly a market formed around the growing group of the peasant conscripts. The air filled with the smell of roasting chicken. In a corner of the square a large spit was being erected and a fire started for a mutton roast. Vendors appeared carrying baskets of cherries and dried figs. There was always money to be made from war.

A messenger approached Carloman and whispered to him, pointing to the church.

'Sire, the bishop Theobald would like to hold a short service to bless our expedition and to pray for your safe return.'

'Tell the bishop we are pleased to attend him in the church and we will bring all the leaders who have provided men to receive the blessing of God on our enterprise.'

'Seigneur Carloman, do you think we could ask the bishop to pray for all who join us, not just the leaders? I think the courage and strength of each would be helped if they felt that God was on their side.'

Carloman looked at Guilhem somewhat sourly. 'I see my brother Charles has left his mark on you. That's just the kind of thought he would have had. Very well see to it that the blessing is given to all who join us.'

It was noon the following day when the first scout rode back to the column which was wending its way through the foothills of the Pyranees surrounded on all sides by the increasing density of oak, chestnut, and beech. Above them the still snow covered peaks cut the bright blue sky.

'Seigneur Carloman, smoke rises from the direction of Perthus.' The horse bucked and skittered on the Roman paving, flanks heaving and sides shining with sweat. The scout struggled to control his horse and his own excitement.

'Is it a signal or are they under attack soldier?'

'My sergeant thinks it is an attack sire.'

'Very well, Constable Guilhem call the guide and see if there is a trail that would allow a small group to cut off their retreat. I will lead the main body of men and try and prevent further destruction.'

Guilhem was taken aback by this sudden show of decisiveness but could find no better alternative to the plan and so found himself leading a group of thirty men on foot up a steepsided mountain track. The guide was confident that he could cut across the shoulder of the mountain and come down behind the column of smoke that was still sending its message of death and destruction into the otherwise clear sky. The track started by following a crystal clear mountain stream but in a very short time the forest had closed around and over them, shutting out all sound apart from the rush and burble of water and the laboured breaths of men being pushed to their limits. Talk ceased.

Ash and holly started to appear as they climbed. As the underbrush grew damper and the leaves dripped on the sweating band, the trees grew taller, slimmer and straighter as they sought the light in the narrow canyon.

Ability and custom started to separate the quick from the slow and the group began to string out. Guilhem called a halt. While the men drank from the stream Guilhem consulted the guide and the troop leader Paulus, a lean faced dark eyed man whose profession was war. The short pause over, Paulus selected ten of the most agile and accustomed to the mountain paths. They were led by a man equipped with chain mail, sword and short spear that were credentials enough. He claimed knowledge of the mountains and his eyes moved constantly while he was being briefed seeming to assess with some intelligence what was required. Guilhem was not sure that he was to be trusted but they had few true men of war in the little group.

Their task was to reach the road that was the most likely route of retreat of the Saracen raiders, and to find the most suitable spot for an ambush. Two lean longlegged bowmen from the count's trained army were stationed at the rear of the remainder to ensure that stragglers did not become deserters. Guilhem was acutely aware of the disparate nature of the men under his command. Perhaps ten of the troop were what passed for professional men of war. The remainder were a collection of men gathered by their seigneur and pushed into service.

The track became steeper and left the bank of the little rushing stream. Brambles reached out across the path and wet bracken hid the path. Moss and lichen coated the rocks causing the odd gasping curse as a foot slipped and ankles turned or knees were grazed.

Suddenly the trees thinned and rock thrust its way to the surface. Tussocky grass began to take over. Sparrows, and blackbirds called their warnings and fluttered in and out of the scrub. Grasshoppers fled in clouds churned into the air by the advancing band. Guilhem signalled a stop. He waited for Paulus to appear at his side.

They were too exposed. No sight of the advance group either. But the navigation had been excellent. They could see the Via Domitia cutting its way through the valley floor. Over the shoulder of the mountain to their right there were now two columns of smoke drifting their message of destruction into the clear sky. The smoke had billowed and thinned in places. Guilhem and Paulus paused to allow the troop to catch up.

'I don't like it,' said Guilhem. 'There should be some sign of our scouts.'

Paulus took his time allowing his eyes to become accustomed to the landscape with its rolling hillside and small dips in the terrain leading down to the distant road. The terrain seemed eerily empty. Skylarks beat against the wind; their high pitched calls battling the breeze.

'They could be round the shoulder of the hill. Down there where that valley makes a fold,' he pointed off to the right. 'But they should have left someone to signal us.'

Guilhem looked round at the group now assembled awaiting further orders. Twenty men. Half in tunics of the poorest wool and even that holed and worn. A few in some form of padded armour mostly ripped and leaking the stuffing. Five soldiers of fortune in chain mail tunics and helms of iron. All carried short spears. Twelve swords and five bowmen. The Saracen raiders would be a much stronger fighting force than this unwilling band, but not many of the enemy should yet be this far away from the plumes of smoke.

'Paulus, take one of the soldiers. Keep about one hundred paces ahead. We will follow that fold in the hillside. Stop when you reach the road.'

Guilhem formed the troop into a line allowing five paces between each. The remaining armed men were placed at even intervals along the line. Signalling the way forward he adjusted his helmet and led his troop in the footsteps of Paulus down the hill. The fold they followed deepened and began to twist. Great boulders partially blocked their path. It became harder to keep Paulus in sight.

It was the flash of sun on metal that made him jump to his left, raise his shield, and shout a warning as the first spears struck. Hidden amongst the rocks above the narrow defile the Saracen had the advantage but it was not overwhelming. The spacing between his men meant that only two were badly hurt in the first assault. The remainder crouched behind the nearest cover and waited. Further down the little ravine Guilhem saw Paulus and his soldier dodging from rock to rock trying to get back to the main group.

He signalled to Paulus pointing up. Another spear glanced off the rock beside his shoulder. As he moved he saw that Paulus had understood and was climbing up the side of the path behind the attackers. Now the Saracens had to expose themselves as they scrambled awkwardly over the rocks trying to reach the path below. Taking the lead Guilhem launched his own throwing spear at the nearest white tunic that was sprawled over a large rock three paces away. It struck home and the figure grunted and flailed his arms trying to keep a grip as his life left him. The death gave his men courage and with disparate shouts they tried to take the attack to their ambushers. But now the lack of fighting skill quickly showed as many spears missed easy targets. Guilhem drew his sword and hurled himself forward against two Saracens who had reached the level ground. Swords clashed; jewelled fingers caught the light; eyes exchanged daggers; mouths gasped open; spinning slashing blades filled the narrow space.

The second Saracen in front of Guilhem staggered and sank to one knee looking at the spear protruding through his right thigh. Paulus had struck. But the fight was slowly being won by the trained soldiers his group faced. It was at this moment that Guilhem registered a huge blow on the back of his helmet. The fight lost focus. The light turned dark and a sharp pain in his leg lead his senses away from any ability to control his body.

*　　*　　*　　*　　*　　*　　*

Aware of its passing but with little ability to take an interest in any particulars of time, Guilhem knew that he had been given drafts of strange tasting liquids; that he had lain on a cart of some kind; that his head ached, and that dark and light had succeeded each other with some mysterious force of its own.

CHAPTER THIRTEEN

768 AD

– A Land Beyond –

Nihal al-Sawba folded the fine cotton sheet back to the waist of the sleeping man. By now she knew every detail of the figure that had lain in her care for two days. The face held her gaze as always. Dark brown hair with some hint of red; thick and now lustrous after the washings he had received at her instructions and carried out by the palace servants under the doctors supervision. She had not been impressed by the cleanliness of this live body that had been entrusted to her.

'A king, or at least a prince,' she had been told by her father Vizier Ibn Abjar, 'and probably worth a great deal of ransom money.'

'He might be an infidel prince but certainly not washed as any man of her own race. At least that had been remedied on the orders of the physician,' she thought and her nose wrinkled slightly.

Her gaze followed the contour of an oversized nose though finely made. Heavy eyebrows and defined cheekbones. Even in repose the face had no comfort of flesh in it. Rough stubble underlined a firm mouth over a cleft chin. The teeth were good except one missing on the left upper jaw. She had seen the teeth as they had tried to give him food and drink of which he had taken some in spite of his state of torpor. The blow on the head which still showed as a swelling, combined with the drugs given to keep him quiet on the journey to Cordoba were still in his system.

Nihal continued her inventory. She still had not seen the eyes of the stranger which had so far remained closed, but the flat planes of the chest and lean muscled arms showed a man in good condition and well used to the hardship of war. The scar below the forth rib ran its roughened dark pink over his side and down the back as confirmation. 'But not to the hardship of keeping clean', she smiled to herself. She beckoned the servant to the bed and together they rolled back the sheet to the bottom of the bed. The prince had been clothed in loose fitting pants. Together they rolled him onto his right side giving a clear view of the left leg which had a thick bandage below the knee. Sometime in the melee a kanjar had delivered a deep cut. Efficiently they dressed the wound which seemed to be healing well.

It was time the young prince regained his senses. Nihal wondered whether she should call the court physician again. Her father would not be pleased if ill befell the young hostage. Time to try to get him to drink again. The two young women rearranged the sheet and placed pillows to raise him to an easier position. As they moved him his head rolled to one side and his eyes fluttered open.

'Visna,' more muttered words followed but they were not intelligible to the two women. The eyes closed again. They were a dark brown.

Nihal beckoned to the slave girl who attended her. It would not be fitting for the stranger to wake in the presence of women. Her father had told her to fetch him as soon as the hostage showed signs of life.

*　　*　　*　　*　　*　　*　　*　　*　　*

It was the smell that he noticed first as his mind swam up through layers of confusion. He thought he was in Visna's arms but the smell was not her familiar scent. The smell was more pervasive, and unknown. It had the effect of adding to the confusion. His eyes opened unwillingly. His sight was clear, but he found it hard to understand why he was looking at a dark robed figure with a rounded bearded face and a black turban with a jewelled pin. The last time he had seen anyone alike were Arab sailors near his childhood home......

'Arab !' The mind began its work of sorting time and place and events. Standing behind the seated figure was another man in a belted tunic and wide fitting pants. His hand on the hilt of a short curved sword. The guard.

'Seigneur, you have understanding of your position?' The voice ended in a question. The man in the turban was speaking an accented Latin.

Guilhem looked at him trying to decide if advantage could be obtained by deception. He nodded, and immediately felt a pain thump across his forehead. He winced and groaned.

'You sustained some wounds. A blow to your head and a cut to your leg. But our physicians have said that all will be well. You have a strong constitution and our medicines are powerful. You have been brought to Cordoba to the palace of the vizier of Cordoba. I am the vizier Ibn Abjar. First something to eat and drink? We have tried to feed you but our drugs have made it difficult. It is important that you regain your strength. Later we will talk. My daughter and a slave have been caring for you and I will call them. I am sorry they do not speak your tongue but Nihal has some Latin.'

His head ached as he struggled to disentangle the occasional gutteral sound that twisted the words out of true. Guilhem suddenly felt how dry his mouth was, but he was not hungry.

'Thank you. Something to drink please,' he found that the sound of his voice was strange and rasping. 'The smell, please what is it?' For some reason it seemed to be vital that he find out the source of the strange scent that insistently pervaded the room.

'The smell?' The voice was questioning as though some insult had been implied. 'Ah! The smell. Scent is an important part of our culture. I don't really notice it any more. This is very rare. It comes from the belly of a very big fish. I think the name is ambergris. Our doctors say it helps recovery of the sick'

Guilhem lay back exhausted already by the short exchange. Slowly his surroundings began to take shape. The room was large and cool. The pillars that supported graceful arches caught his attention. They were slender, six sided and banded with small mosaics in brilliant blues, greens and gold. The whole effect made him wonder if the drugs were still active. It was another world and made his own seem crude and heavy minded. He struggled to sit upright. His head throbbed its protest again.

The door opened and two women entered. The first dressed in a long blue gown of some fine cloth. It had heavy embroidered bands in gold and silver thread down the front with a thin rope like belt of worked leather. She wore a simple mantle and a light veil covered her face to the eyes.

'Seigneur, I am Nihal and this is my servant Maria. We have been looking after you since you arrived two days ago. I am sorry about the drugs. They have been too heavily employed. Beside which you couldn't go anywhere with that leg, could you?'

The voice was pitched in a low register. The Latin was softly accented. She had more than 'some' Latin. It was fluent and with a wider vocabulary than his own. Once more Guilhem felt at a disadvantage.

'Let us see if we can help that head and assuage your thirst. Try this.' She beckoned to the servant to approach; she placed an elegant jug on the floor beside the low bed and poured some liquid into a worked silver goblet. Again everything was of the finest craftmanship.

'This is made from honey, cardamom, cinnamon, clove and the long pepper. Try.' Guilhem took a deep draught of the sweet liquid. It swept through him lifting his spirit and clearing his head. He lay back. Already the movement seemed to cause less pain.

'Rest a moment and then drink just water. You will recover quickly.' The brown eyes smiled at him over the veil which did little to hide a small well shaped mouth that seemed ready for laughter and a nose a little too long for perfection.

'Now seigneur Guilhem son of Count Thierry d'Autun and prince of the line of David in the eyes of the Jews of Narbonne, I hope you will soon be able to enjoy your time with us. My father says that it could be many days.'

Guilhem looked at her astonished. How had they got all this information from an unconscious prisoner. Indeed this was some kind of magical race. He would have to be very careful.

As Nihal was leaving she turned in the doorway, 'I hope you will not miss Visna too much during your stay.' The laugh teased with a subtle innuendo.

The next day Guilhem was feeling much recovered and had eaten voraciously everything that had been put before him, even though there were flavours that sat strangely on his tongue. He had been given clothes in the Arab style made of the finest cotton. He had been told to be careful in movement because the wound in his leg was not fully healed. He had been shown the place of the privy and had noted that the system owed much to the Roman ways of building. The door to his room was not locked, but in truth there was little distance that he could walk.

Soon after the meal had been cleared away by Maria the door

opened and the vizier appeared with the guard and another assistant who carried a leather bag. Ibn Abjar motioned to the table set by the window which looked out to an inner courtyard where vines twined over trellises and made shaded areas for sitting. Palm trees defined the corners and in the middle a shallow pool reflected the colour of blue mosaic.

'Does it please you?' he gestured to the garden.

'It is very different from my country,' said Guilhem cautiously, not wanting to betray his feelings that he had been transported into a superior world. 'But I find it is a delight to the eye. We do not see much purpose in decoration unless in praise of God.'

The vizier seemed taken aback for a moment, then he smiled and opened the bag and produced Guilhem's helmet. He laid it carefully in the centre of the table.

'Or in praise of rank? I think this work of great skill also saved your life.'

For a moment they looked together at the gleaming headpiece marred by a large dent in the back of the conical head.

'This and the leader of your advance scouts told us everything about you. Unfortunately he had to be persuaded and he did not survive our conversation. Anyway he knew nothing of this,' Ibn Abjar pointed to the golden bee still in place on the helmet. 'But our scholars do know something of this symbol and so you have become of great interest to my master Caliph Abd-al Rahman.'

CHAPTER FOURTEEN

805 AD, Gellone
– Saving the Thread –

The first feeling was one of exhilaration as his faithful mare broke into a canter tossing her head as though she realised that this was not to be the sedate trot of a respected abbot, but a harkening back to times of adventure and battle. The rose tint of dawn painted its way across the horizon underlining the dark grey above it. The helmet felt heavy and rubbed at his bare tonsured scalp. It had never felt that way before. It had accompanied him in triumph and in adversity. It had saved his life more than once. Yet the little golden bee centred in the middle of his forehead had shaped his life almost more than anything. Even though he had turned away from the story it had tried to tell him, it was still forcing this ride at dawn. This little insect still had the power to cause empires to fall and the nascent foundations of mother church to heave and shift.

Yet he could not find it within himself to destroy the thread of possibility. Even if he did, this weave of man's story might weaken but it would not break. There were still threads extant that he knew nothing of, but that he held one of the stronger he had no doubt.

His hand flicked his damaged nose and he urged the mare on. Time was short. He had to deliver the scrolls he had rescued from Gellone. Paul should already be in possession of a more important piece of the story that had been sent from Rome to the hermit who lived on the wild tops behind the strange stone cropped bowl that looked as though a giant hand had stamped out a ragged depression in the earth's crust.

It was called the Cirque du Moureze and had been occupied by man since before time, and was now the dwelling of a few of the forest people who did not want to become part of the settled communities further down the valley. This could be tricky. He needed their permission to go through the bowl because the entrance was very narrow and easily defended. The other way to reach the hermit would take too long.

He slowed the horse to walking pace as the narrow track wound its way to the narrow entrance guarded by towering rocks carved by wind and rain into mythical shapes of man and beast. Where the rocks leaned in to close the sky, at above the height of a spear's throw, a narrow rope and plank bridge spanned the gap. The entrance appeared to be deserted but Guilhem knew that there would be watchers posted and that his approach had been seen some time ago. He heaved his left leg over the mare's back and grunted with the discomfort in his hip as he dismounted heavily. Suddenly he was weary. It had been a long night and his body was reminding him that the resilience of the past was subject to the passage of time.

He waited. Should he take off the helmet which had rubbed a sore patch on the bare scalp? He decided the watchers would be confused by any such change. The March wind tugged at his undershirt and found a way through his collar. It was light now but the clouds scudded heavy bellied above the Cirque.

Detaching itself from the rockface at the side of the narrow entrance a figure appeared uncannily close to him. Not for the first time Guilhem wondered at the ability of the wild people to meld with their background. It didn't take many generations of farming to lose that ability. He held his ground.

'I am the watcher of our village.' The accent was thick but it was Oc of a sort. 'What do you want of us?'

'There is a holy man who lives alone up there,' Guilhem pointed at the escarpment behind the bowl. 'I need to meet him quickly. If you would grant me passage across your land it would save much time.' The watcher looked at him from a tangle of hair and beard, but with sharp clear eyes. He was not interested in the problem of time. He was assessing the risk posed by the stranger wearing the warrior helmet with the strange markings and the golden bee.

'You mean the man they call Paul who lives alone in the way of the forest people. He is a man with strange customs but he does not try to change our ways and he has helped our sick. Will he want to see you? He does not like the company of men.'

'I think he will be glad to see me,' said Guilhem quietly.

There was a pause. Then suddenly he was surrounded by a group of the forest people all smiling and offering hard bread and water.

The watcher looked at him again from top to toe. It appeared that he had passed the scrutiny. The man stepped aside and Guilhem led his horse under the rope bridge and into the limestone bowl where the fantastical shapes seemed to crowd in on him like ghost warriors from the time of giants. Small grass patches hid among the boulders and a few goats cropped at the grass and thorn. Bushes and scrub oak found what purchase they could on the steep hillsides and little paths wound their way through the bewildering maze. Guilhem pointed to his horse and then to the far rim of the bowl and looked at the watcher who had been joined by two others and a young lad who seemed familiar. They all shook their heads. He would have to go on foot.

'Could you look after my horse and see that she gets water? And is there one who could show me the quickest route to the hermit?'

'This is Arnaud who says that he saw you when you first came to the valley. He will take you.' So saying the watcher pushed the young lad forward and as the dark eyes gazed up at him Guilhem wondered how many of these secretive people had watched his arrival

A short time later Arnaud and Guilhem were scrambling up the steep cliff at the far side of the Cirque du Moureze and Guilhem was feeling that his conversion to God's work had left his legs in a weaker state than before. For the second time in a day and night he was being led up a steep climb by younger legs than his and the pace was telling. But speed was important because he would have to deliver his scrolls to the safe keeping of Paul and then reappear in the valley of Gellone before too many questions were asked. Even so he would have to come up with a good explanation of his disappearance. That would have to wait.

'Slower,' he gasped as Arnaud's busy legs threatened to disappear in the brush ahead. 'I need a rest.'

'We are near the top,' said Arnaud leaping nimbly back to where Guilhem had found a rock to catch his breath and ease the burning in his thighs. 'And then his house is not far along the top.'

Moments later they scrambled over the cliff top and set off southwards along the escarpment. The clouds bellied their way across their path and spots of rain began to fall. It was going to be a wet walk. Suddenly Arnaud stopped and gestured to Guilhem to stay. His young ears had picked up a sound. He crouched and disappeared off the path into the scrub that surrounded them. Guilhem moved to shelter under a beech tree as the rain started to fall with more purpose. Then Arnaud appeared at his side without a sound.

'The house is near but there are two men at the doorway. They are soldiers,' he gestured trying to tell Guilhem that they wore armour and helmets like him. 'They have spears,' he made a throwing gesture and then touched Guilhem's sword to show that they were fully armed.

This was bad. What on earth could cause armed men to be sent to Paul the hermit ?

'The man with the long beard?' Arnaud shrugged and shook his head.

Maybe they had not been sent, but were bandits who thought the old man had something worth stealing. But then they wouldn't be hanging around outside the poor hut. Guilhem felt that whatever part they were playing it was unlikely to help Paul or his own mission.

Could he ask the young lad to act as a distraction while he approached the hut from the rear? Quietly he explained to the boy what he wanted. A smile broke out all over his face. This would be really fun. 'Even if they chase me they will never catch me up here!'

They separated and Arnaud strolled off through the rain down the main path which led to the front of the hut. Guilhem ducking beneath the branches that whipped their wet leaves in his face dodged his way to the rear of the stone and thatch dwelling that was the hermit's home. The wall loomed out of the rain in front of him. He waited for a moment but could only hear the sound of the wind moaning its way through a gap in the stones. Then he heard the higher pitch of Arnaud's voice.

'I'm hungry. Give me some of your meat and I will bring you honey to sweeten your bread.'

'Get off with you. You little beggar. We have business here and we don't need you around. Get off or you'll find this spear up your ass!'

The wind moaned in Guilhem's ear as he placed his head next the rough stone wall. That was not wind! He reached up and lifted a corner of the thatch and peered into the darkness of the cramped space. He did'nt need light. The hermit hung from the rafters in the shape of an x. His feet had been nailed apart to heavy wood logs. His hands tied to the rafters. Naked he hung in the slow red flow of his ebbing life. White bone showing on his right shoulder where the flesh had been flayed from his back. His long beard had been ripped from one side of his face and the remainder hung matted in the blood on his chest. The body lived yet as Guilhem followed the tortured heave of the chest. Anger threw his thoughts to the wind and rain. He must gather them back.

He would have to kill the guards, but he needed to take them one at a time. He crept forward and looked round the corner of the hut. One of the soldiers had gone a little way off and Guilhem could see the small figure of Arnaud taunting him. Waiting no longer, his hand brushed the damaged nose as he made the decision to attack the soldier nearest him. Drawing his sword as he ran he was upon the unhappy man just as he turned towards him. Keeping low Guilhem slashed at the shield that was instinctively raised forcing the defence across and to the right. Staying down, his next blow went under the soldier's guard and deep into his knee. The man howled; dropped his spear and fell writhing. The shout alerted the second soldier who came at full pelt but then seeing the helmet paused, knowing that he was facing a trained adversary even if he looked old. The hesitation gave Guilhem a moment to wrench the shield from the fallen soldier's arm. As he straightened a spear quivered its way through the rain. He had time to deflect it, making sure it did not embed in the wood and leather. An embedded spear would render the shield useless. The second soldier grinned as he took in the scarred face of his adversary and the stiffened gait. Guilhem backed off a step or two to encourage the rush. The chopping sword crashed onto the raised shield. The shock numbed his arm. Old instincts took over as he stepped up to the enemy with a straight thrust. But the man twisted to allow the sword to miss. Swords clashed again and again. A long fight would go the soldier's way as Guilhem felt his unaccustomed arms begin to ache under the onslaught. Parrying another chopping stroke he lowered his shield as though exhausted. With a yell of triumph his confident adversary slashed at his neck. Guilhem caught the expected blow with his own sword and slid the blade to the hilt of his adversary. This brought them face to face. Eyes gleamed across the shimmering iron. Then instead of stepping away Guilhem turned across his opponent planting his left leg behind him. An elbow to his chest caused him to stumble back his shield thrown up trying to regain balance. Keeping his turn going Guilhem cut at the unguarded neck. It was a death blow. Chest heaving he turned back to the hut.   Arnaud was standing in front of the other wounded soldier with a rock in each hand. He need not have worried. The man was looking in frightened disbelief at the blood that was flowing from behind his knee. His face had already lost colour. Guilhem wanted him alive.

'See if you can f f find some cloth in the hut to bind the wound.' Then he remembered the sight that would greet the young lad in the hut. 'No. Wait a moment I'll go. You get water from the well over there.'

Guilhem entered the hut trying not to look at the remnants of a man that hung so still on his cross. The sound of breath heaving its battle against death filled his ears. It was so quiet in the small space.

'I do not know if you can hear me Paul,' he said as he searched the hut, 'but I will pray for your soul. First I must find out why this was done.'

Finding an old but clean linen shift he ran back outside. Saying nothing he poured water over the damaged leg and then bound the gaping slash with strips twisting them tight with a stick till the flow had almost stopped.

He handed Arnaud a spear. 'Give this bastard water to drink. I need him alive but if he tries to move stop him with this.'

Arnaud was speechless as though the events had left his mind unable to process what had happened, but he was able to follow the instructions. He grabbed the spear and nodding took station just out of reach of the fallen man.

Guilhem re-entered the hut and taking a deep breath began the gruesome task of cutting the hermit down. Some movements brought a faint groan. There seemed little point in drawing the nails from the tortured feet. That could wait till after death. Finally he had the racked body lying on straw. He fetched water checking that Arnaud was still in charge. Kneeling by the old man he began trying to moisten the cracked lips and clean the worst of the blood from the features twisted in pain. Finally having done as much as possible he drew breath and began the ritual of prayers for the dying.

'I commend the soul of this thy servant into your hands..'

'No!' The word rasped its way into the near dark of the hut.

Guilhem had his own breath seized from him in shock. This wrecked hulk of flesh could still speak!

'It is I Guilhem abbot of Gellone, my friend.'

'The abbot?' The voice quavered against the wind and rain outside.

'It is I Guilhem who was king of the Jews in Narbonne and Count of Toulouse.

I came because I know you are a messenger of the hidden faith. Things that belong to that story are in my keeping and are in danger of falling into the hands of the mother church. I sent you a parchment from Rome some years ago. The man of prayer Grimald told me that you thought as he did. Do you remember?'

'Grimald does he still live? Have you the sign of the true way?' The voice incredibly seemed to be gaining strength.

'I have the golden b..b..bee on my helmet.' So saying Guilhem took off the helmet and held it close to the one good eye that was now open with a fierce intensity as though it was trying to see through the pain to the truth. He held a wrecked finger to the helmet and moved it over the shape of the bee.

'You can see I am on my way to God. I cannot help you, abbot of Gellone but there are others...' The voice wavered and the breaths came harder.

'In the roof there is a place.... they did this.... the church did this. Do not use their words over me. Oh Lord! You have sent me an abbot with a bee on his bonnet.' A smile ghosted through his eyes. The neck arched up as though stretching for air and then fell back to the side. There was silence in the small space.

It took time to find the space carved into a thick oak beam and covered with a perfect lid. Inside was the scroll in poor condition. Nevertheless Guilhem could see the vine curling its way up the right side till it entwined with a crude outline of a fish. It was the map scroll from Rome. On the reverse there were four names written on the flimsy parchment; Razes Rhedae Peret Usclas. Three of the names were known to Guilhem. Razes and Usclas were names of villages in the Languedoc. Usclas being the nearest by far. Razes was also the family name of the Count whose fiefdom was in the foothills of the Pyrenees and which included Rhedae. The name Peret meant nothing to him but he could guess that it might be associated with Usclas. For this small scrap Paul the hermit had given his life, or so it seemed. His mind racing and his feelings in turmoil Guilhem had to act. His left hand brushed his nose as he went out into the wet.

Arnaud was standing four paces from the soldier who was sitting sullenly where he had been left. Both were soaked in the cold persistent rain. Guilhem wanted confirmation as to who had sent these two on their merciless mission. Although he felt he knew the answer already. The 'church' could really only mean one source in this region.

'Who sent you to do this?' He pointed to the hut without taking his eyes from the resigned face. The soldier spat into the ground. He knew he had not long to live whether he spoke or not. This man with the helmet would finish him before he left.

'If you speak I will send our young friend here to fetch help. They will take you to their village. Maybe with care you will recover. At least you will have time to repent this......' Anger stopped him.

The soldier looked up. Was there really a lifeline? Maybe telling this man would help his cause when he met his end. Although the priest who sent them had told them both that this was a mission in the service of the Lord Jesus.

'We were sent by the bishop your honour. The bishop Benoit.'

'Did he speak to you himself?'

'No your honour. A priest from the big church at Maguelone met us and gave us gold. There would be more if we returned with the parchment. He said he was speaking for the bishop.'

A short time later Guilhem was on his way having persuaded Arnaud to accompany him back to the cirque with instructions for the burial of Paul, the dead soldier and the care of this wounded murderer. Arnaud could not understand the latter and Guilhem could only say that care of one's enemies was one of the instructions from God. He could see that the young boy thought little of this doctrine.

They set off together; Guilhem to find his horse and Arnaud to fetch the rescue party. The young boy soon disappeared ahead. Guilhem felt truly weary as he trudged back through the lessening rain.

As he walked his mind began the whirl of contradictions which had so often accompanied his struggles to find certainty in the true faith.

He contrasted the ideal of the abbey taking shape stone by stone, a place where men could devote their lives to prayer and learning, with the events just concluded. Two men had died because the church was so afraid of a challenge to its version of the truth.

As he plodded on through the mist that had taken the place of the rain, Guilhem thought that there were few men who had been so close to all the religions of the age as he had. It was as though God had given him every opportunity to test the story of his heritage against the beliefs of others.

And yet at the age of fifty-four, having renounced the world to hear the word of God in time to save his soul, he was still being tested.

As he reached the rim of the Cirque du Moureze he met the return party still led by Arnaud who had the inexhaustible energy of youth.

They stopped. 'Arnaud you were brave and strong. Here take this as a token of my thanks.' Guilhem gave him a rough edged silver denier patterned with Celtic leaves and with a cross in the centre. These coins were still rare but the fame of the Emperor gave them special value. A smile lit up the dirty face and the small group disappeared into the mist on their tasks of burial and rescue.

Although speed was important Guilhem was exhausted and decided on a short rest before trying to find Peret at Usclas. He was given a bowl of thin rabbit stew and pieces of bread. Lying down with his saddle under his head Guilhem fell into a restless sleep. When he woke the skies had cleared and an afternoon sun provided welcome warmth and had gone some way to dry out his wet clothes.

Thanking the small group of the forest people who had stocked his bags with food and water he forced his stiffened limbs into the saddle and rode off in the direction of Usclas. Whatever the church might say he was driven by the need to ensure that the bee could pollinate the minds of future carriers of its tale. If false it surely would wither of its own accord, but he would not accept the right of the church to extinguish this version of the story of Christ.

Peret turned out to be a free farmer. He lived in a low roofed thatched farmhouse that was built of stone. He was a large man, a full hand taller than Guilhem, with light blue eyes that looked down at him from a face deeply lined and marked by the pox. The large frame revealed a pronounced limp as he led the way indoors and he was supported by a sturdy stick.

'My lord abbot, what a surprise!' Yet his demeanor betrayed no evidence of fluster. He knelt with difficulty to receive the blessing. 'Fastrada! Wine and bread for our lord abbot.' The voice was deep and resonant. Guilhem liked him immediately. This was helpful as so much depended on him now.

'I presume my lord that the knowledge has been traced and it is in some peril?'

'Ah, my friend,' said Guilhem, 'you must have b..b..been expecting me?' The questions hung for a beat.

Then a bellow of laughter. 'I have been to Gellone my lord. I have learned much about you. There is much respect for your work and love for the abbot there. They said you were hard to surprise.'

'I think I can say the same for you my friend! Yes there is danger to some manuscripts that I would prefer to keep in our hands. And you should know that the hermit Paul was killed to try and make ...'

'No!' The stick crashed on the stone hearth. 'He was a good man. Did no harm to any. Did they get....'

Guilhem delved into his bag and held up the scrolls while shaking his head.

'And Peret, justice has already been done.' There was a pause, 'well no, not justice but some measure of retribution, at least in human eyes...'

Peret raised his deep bronzed face to Guilhem, 'so it not for nothing they call you court nez, the warrior monk, my lord.'

So it was arranged that Peret should dispatch the scrolls to friends in various places. Two of the boxes contained only copies of the scripture.

'If one of these were intercepted....' murmured Guilhem.

A great smile spread across the pain lined face. 'Indeed my lord. Indeed, such... an unfortunate occurrence might happen. I understand completely.'

The two gazes met in harmony. Both faces wreathed in smiles.

'I must get back to the abbey. Thank you.'

'Before you leave my lord. One question, if I may be allowed...'

Guilhem waited and then nodded.

'How can you serve the church and yet protect this knowledge?

Especially if you carry the line.'

Guilhem looked at this stranger who had asked him what no man had asked so directly.

'I believe it is what God asks of me.'

CHAPTER FIFTEEN

768 AD
– Love and Heritage –

It was when she lifted her veil that he fell in love. Although the veil had been a token of modest concealment it was so delicate it had done little to hide the mouth with a hint of sensuality, the lower lip just a little fuller than the upper. Or the way that a smile transformed the naturally solemn face when he struggled to remember a strange custom. Nevertheless it created a barrier which somehow precluded the idea of love. It was in the third week of his captivity when she came into the small room where he was seated at a low table with the Imman Hisham ibn Malik, scrolls spread out on the carved cedar table inlaid with mother of pearl.

She noticed his look immediately. 'Seigneur, my father says that you are now a trusted guest of our house and concealment from strangers is no longer necessary.'

'I am happy that your father regards me as guest rather than a prisoner. I am even happier that I may now see the b..b..beauty of his daughter more clearly, but I presume that this privilege does not extend to my return home.'

Nihal blinked with the surprise of the open compliment and coloured slightly.

Her laugh showed that she had quickly recovered from her confusion. 'I am sorry my lord but another of our strange customs is that hostages are not released till payment is made.' She pointed to the Imman, 'Hisham here will show you that there are many ways that payment may be made.'

'We have not touched on that yet my lady, but our friend is showing great interest in our teachings and is a quick learner, but he is a learner not without questions which may show wisdom beyond his years.' It was Guilhem's turn to look away in modest confusion. When she turned to leave the room lost a little of its colour and Guilhem was aware of absence in a way that he had never felt before. Hisham watched him gather his thoughts and made a mental note to warn the Vizier that his prize might be taking a more personal interest in his daughter than was wise. Possibly this was a weakness that could be exploited to the advantage of the true faith. It would be a good time to explain to the young captive something of the position of women in the Ummayadh culture and in particular that of Nihal.

'Your honour I have noticed your interest in the daughter of my master the vizier. Perhaps you have wondered that she is not yet married? You should know that in our culture women are not the slaves of men. They may own property and also have some discretion over the question of marriage.'

'I am a captive in your household. I could not begin to have any thoughts about her, save that she has shown such a delicate kindness to me in my situation... and it is true that I take pleasure in her presence.' Guilhem struggled to keep his words on an even keel. He felt embarrassment at having his feelings so easily exposed. Youth was not an acceptable excuse for transparency of this kind.

'Nevertheless you should be aware that even in our culture Nihal has shown a special independence and she has reached an age where the question of marriage has become....', he paused, 'more problematic. However she has shown great interest in the politics of our position here in Spain and less in the traditional path of marriage and motherhood.

'Enough of that. I think we should return to the topic of the day your honour. Perhaps you could repeat to me what you have learned so far of our faith and then we may discuss questions that you may have.'

'"There is no God but God. Muhammed is the messenger of God.' That is your fundamental prayer to be said five times daily. There is only one God; one creator and s..s..sustainer of life. He is the sole judge of our actions. You also believe in Satan as the force for evil so the actions of man can be either good or evil.

All the true prophets are descended from Abraham and are messengers of the one true God. The most important of these is Muhammed whose teachings you follow and who died only eighty years ago.'

He paused. The Imman leaned forward. 'And so your questions are.....?'

'My question is how did we reach this place of enmity between Jew and Christian and followers of Islam when all our beliefs stem from the same roots? What can be so important about the differences that we must die for them?'

'Indeed my young soldier that is a question worth asking. Of course there are fundamental differences between us and the Christian and between the Jew and both of us. Would Allah approve of our ways of defending our differences? That is indeed a question. But first you may ask whether it is beliefs that draw blood or is it lust for land and riches that we clothe in the name of religion. However that may be, wise men should try to understand that our differing faiths may indeed lead to battles in the pure name of belief.'

'But as I understand it all of these religions say that we should not kill. So why is it that our churches, mosques and synagogues support the idea of d..d..death to preserve our faith?'

The Imman looked at the young face flushed now in the thrill of discourse and in the belief of the young that there were simple answers to simple questions.

'That, your honour is another excellent question and I am not wise enough to give an answer that will satisfy you. But I can say that where man tries to interpret the wishes of God he makes many errors. It is in the nature of man to believe that the errors of others are more serious than his own. In that way we are led to take actions which seem to contradict the will of Allah.'

'It sounds to me that that is where Satan finds his way to add to the store of evil here on earth,' said Guilhem. The Imman could find no reply.

Late summer turned to autumn as the days cooled and the rains turned the streets from dust to mud. However for Guilhem this was a time transformed by love. The rain might run down the back of his neck; his boots might cake with mud; his clothes might cling and the colours run; but the weather totally failed to affect the source of his happiness.

The days passed in a blur. In the mornings he normally spent time with the Imman learning more about the tenets of Islam and the current political currents and shifting allegiances that moved inside the newly expanded Arab empires. In the afternoons he was often with Nihal in the markets or undergoing instruction in the customs of the household. They were never alone but it was clear that his love was returned.

But even when opportunity afforded a moment to speak unheard, but never unwatched, the subject of their feelings was never mentioned. It was as if they both knew that to speak would break the spell because this was a love that could never flourish.

They could have chosen to seek other ways to pass the time of Guilhem's captivity and both knew that every moment spent together would make the final parting harder. But the currents within each were too strong to allow an instant to be missed so the little things wound themselves deep into his very core. The accented Latin like a waterfall; the hesitant step whenever she entered a room where he might be; the way her black hair fell covering her face when she bent to pick a flower.

Sometimes the Vizier would send for Guilhem and invite him to go hunting. The forested hills around Cordoba were the home to boar, deer, lynx, and mountain lions. The hunts were well organised and gave opportunity to display skills with spear and arrow.

At other times he was invited to attend meetings with the masons and carpenters who were in charge of the building of the great mosque. Although Guilhem could not understand the discourse, which was always in Arabic, he learned much about the skills of the crafts involved. Under the orders of Abd al-Rahman the mosque was being constructed on the site of a Christian church. Already the small cupola was in place and underneath a shady forest of red and white striped columns were being erected. Some of these were being fashioned from new stone blocks brought by the ubiquitous slaves from the Sierra mountains. Others were adapted from the original Roman temple remains or reshaped from the Christian church. The varying heights were dealt with by the simple expedient of constructing bases of differing thickness. The forest of pillars seemed designed to disorientate the worshipper and there was no altar to focus the attention. He learned from Hisham that since Allah was everywhere it was limiting his presence to focus attention in one direction only! Guilhem wondered at the skill with which all these varying elements were put together to create such harmony.

Three months passed and Guilhem wondered that still no

messenger had come from his father or from the court of Pepin. He was sure that the prince Charles would have argued strongly for the ransom to be paid. It was about this time that he began to realise that there was another plan afoot.

The Vizier Ibn Abjar began to attend some of the lessons with Hisham and the subject of the significance of the little golden bee was mentioned. At first obliquely and in passing, but as the days passed it became obvious that this little symbol was of great interest to his hosts.

'How did you come to be in possession of this little golden bee?'

'My grandmother gave it to me. She said it was a symbol of our family.'

'Why do you show it on your helmet now?'

'It is a link to my family heritage.'

'Is it not dangerous for you to display this sign so openly?'

'No. On the contrary. I have sworn allegiance to King Pepin and his successors and wear this symbol of my family to show that I am proud of my heritage, but that I will not betray the trust of the king.'

'Has no-one from your church shown interest in your crest?'

This was an example of many conversations that centred round Guilhem's lineage.

It was at this time that Guilhem learned that all was not as it seemed with his Arab hosts. There were serious divisions within the Arab world that the shared love of Allah did not bridge. It was Nihal who first talked about their problems as they reclined one warm afternoon in a courtyard which had just been added to the palace. Each addition was more elaborate than the last and this was no exception. In the north corner a fountain set in a wide marble bowl carved intricately with vines and flowers sent its cooling water higher than a man. The spray was caught in a series of shell like saucers each set lower than the other as the stream wound across the marble space in little waterfalls. Some planted with water lilies that vied with the marble perfection of the carved.

'My father is worried that we may no longer receive our supplies from the East. The spice caravan has not arrived this month.'

'But anything could have happened. It could have b..b..been attacked by the wild tribes or...'

Nihal smiled at the little stutter which always made her heart leap.

'Of course that is possible but we think it is more likely that the court in Bagdad is showing us that there are ways they can still control us. Seigneur Guilhem you should know that the Caliph thinks that you may be able to have some role in changing our position.'

'Your father has hinted something of the same but I cannot understand what can be so special about me. But you are of the same people and the same faith. Why should you be punished?'

Nihal looked at him for a moment. 'I think this is something you should ask Hisham.' Her eyes turned to the running water and a shadow passed across her face. 'I have to go now.' With a lithe movement she rose from the couch and disappeared under the arcade leaving the hint of jasmine in the air and the insistent plashing of the fountains. As usual the space lost its glow when she left.

In recent days their discourse had become more frequently interrupted by her sudden disappearances.

The next day Guilhem found himself seated on a frisky bay horse dressed in the finest Arab style with the wide pants pleated and gathered at the ankle. His tunic was of blue brocade and he wore his helmet which had been totally restored as new by the vizier's craftsmen. He was flanked by Hisham and Ibn Abjar. They were at the west gates of the city. He had not been told why they were waiting and what was in store for him, but it was clear that something important was afoot.

A cloud of dust heralded the arrival of a band of horsemen. As they drew nearer it was evident that this was a party of senior rank. The banner bearer carried the crescent of Islam. In the centre of the band of about thirty horsemen a small figure in green and gold on a black Arab of exquisite proportions immediately took the eye. Emeralds and rubies on turbans, helmets and swords glinted in the slanting rays of the late year sun.

Dark eyes gleamed and the colours of the rainbow swirled about them as the troop handled their mounts with nonchalant ease and ended in a perfect circle around the waiting trio. The dust cloud swirled and settled. The vizier and the Imman dismounted and knelt. Guilhem wondered whether to follow but decided to stay in the saddle. His horse sidled and kicked up in unease at being surrounded. The small man in green motioned to the two kneeling to rise.

'So the constable has pride, but perhaps is as yet too young to know when to show it.'

'I do not kneel to the show of power but only to those who have the rank to command my obedience or the behaviour to earn my respect.'

Just then his horse reared suddenly and bucked and his saddle slid off its back and he found himself sitting beside the vizier in the dust blushing with rage.

The group roared with laughter and a man in green lifted his head with the point of his sword. Guilhem looked into the black eyes but they revealed nothing. He felt a tap on his shoulder and one of the newcomers hung the cinch in front of him. It had been cleanly cut and explained why his saddle had parted company with his bay. He breathed deeply trying to keep his anger under control. There was silence apart from the creak of leather and the shuffle of horses' hooves in the dust.

'I am Abd al-Rahman the caliph of Spain and son of the Ummayad house of the true followers of the prophet. You are my prisoner.'

It was the first time since his capture that the word prisoner had been used directly to him. All the days of learning, love, cool scents, silks and colours contracted into the word and this moment in the dust of Cordoba. It was the reality of his situation. Guilhem had no doubt that the little man in green silks and jewelled turban knew the effect this initial meeting would have on him. He paused, thought for a moment and removed his helmet placing it in the dust in front of him and then he knelt.

'I kneel to the ruler of Spain but not because of my s..s..s situation as your prisoner. My life is in your hands sire.' The stammer a fraction more pronounced.

In an instant the caliph leapt from his horse and landed lightly beside him. He bent and lifted Guilhem.

'Well spoken young sir. You have courage and wisdom for one so young. I hope that we can become friends and indeed allies. You look surprised but you can never tell what the future may hold. Please forgive my introduction. Now I would like to show you the palace I am making outside the walls of this city. I have named it Madinas al-Zahra. You will marvel at the skill of my craftsmen.' The little speech heralded a sudden mood change and with a chuckle he signalled that Guilhem be boosted onto his horse bareback. He watched a moment to see if the young prisoner was discomforted by the additional demand of keeping his dignity with no saddle. Guilhem betrayed no unease at this turn of events and gained immediate control of the bay. The Caliph vaulted nimbly onto his own black Arab.

They rode through groves of olives, the grey silver of their leaves tossing in the breeze. Then came fields of beans, peas, aubergines and wheat stubble where the harvest had been completed. The vines were heavy laden; the purple fruits bowing to the ground. Slaves in simple linen smocks bent to the task of harvest. Although quite late in the year the sun shone out of a cloudless sky. Further on the rich shiny green leaves of orange groves reflected the light. At intervals great wheels powered by donkeys, scooped their buckets of never ending water from the fast flowing streams sometimes directly into the irrigation channels; sometimes into the buckets of another, smaller wheel set at right angles to the first thus extending the intricate system and spreading its rich bounty even further. Here was one great source of Arab wealth and Guilhem marvelled at the skill with which the wide valley had been cultivated. Water was used to create wealth, to cleanse the body and in the ever present trickling fountains and palace pools, to cool the soul. His own people had much to learn.

Of course it could not work in a land which spent as much time in destruction as in trying to feed its people. A system like this required peace and stability. Slaves were an essential part of the system. Guilhem had learned that few miscreants sat their sentences out in the harsh stone cells. Most were put to work to help the smallholders as well as the big landowners. Cheap labour allowed the delicate flower of civilisation and art to flourish.

They did not travel far. The slope of the road showed that they had entered the foothills of the mountains that rose out of the plain not far from the city. Great terraces had been created to form level areas cut into the hillside. On the third tier a series of exquisite slender minarets topped a long battlemented wall which was supported by graceful horseshoe arches in the red and white bands that were a signature of the local architecture. The palace gleamed pale cream and white in the sun. The caliph had brought ashlar stone and the whitest marble from afar to create this shimmering mirage.

Guilhem reined in his horse and sat trying to absorb the implications of the necessary and evidently available resources that this construction demonstrated.

He tried hard not betray his astonishment at the scene and stared impassively at the extraordinary creation.

Power was being demonstrated in front of him as long mule trains plodded their way out of the distance laden with the big unfinished blocks. Near at hand over fifty camels heaved and snorted their way across the chaotic scene dragging piles of finished stone and marble under the direction of master masons.

The caliph let Guilhem absorb the scene for a few moments. 'I am bringing six thousand blocks of stone a day from the quarries in the mountains. My camel masters have over four hundred animals to help in transport and construction, and we have nearly four thousand slaves engaged on this project. This will be a palace within an administrative compound and religious schools for our immans and when the mosque is built I will have fulfilled my dream to make a unique place for man and for God. This is not a palace for fighting and for defence. This is a palace for the mind to grow and for beauty to be made for the glory of the one God.' He paused and looked at Guilhem to see what effect he was having. He gave the young captive credit for his control.

The ever present dust drifted across the band of horsemen as Guilhem sat in stunned silence at the extent of the power and wealth that was being shown. With a little high pitched giggle of satisfaction the caliph waved across the scene.

'We will show you more later, but now if we go to the west side there is a portion of the palace finished. We can take some refreshment and talk.'

'Surely it must be one of the marvels of the world. You and your people have a great vision sire.'

The caliph looked at Guilhem with interest. He had not expected a barbarian to understand what was being achieved in this corner of Spain. This and the city and the mosque were all part of a vision of a new world and a new order of man. But he might need the help of this young barbarian to allow him to fulfil his dream.

'It will be. It will be, when we have finished. But then we may never finish. So much to do. Insh'Allah we will be allowed to finish so that men may see what can be done with his help.'

Dismounting, Abd al-Rahman led the small group under the main archway through to a large paved courtyard which was still under construction. The fine dust of sawn marble blocks filled the air. Slaves hammered and sawed. Camels swayed and spat pulling the great sleds laden with the cut blocks. Overseers shouted and cursed. Occasionally the crack of a curling whip cut the air onto the back of an unlucky slave. Guilhem noticed that the slaves were of all colours and races with a predominance of negroes.

Ignoring the apparent chaos the caliph led them to the far end of the colonnade and into a room already completed and furnished with low tables of black ebony, silk cushions and fine wool carpets.

'First we must wash. Then we will take some refreshement and we will talk. We have much to talk about, you and I, young Guilhem, constable to King Charles.' The last words given a little emphasis to show that even recent promotions were known.

A neighbouring room revealed a small tiled room for washing. Large clay pots held warm water and soaps and scents. Even an unfinished building provided the means to clean and cool the traveller. 'We are a different people' thought Guilhem as he sluiced the dust way.

'You are wondering why there has been no word from your father, or indeed from King Pepin?' The small figure with the smooth rich olive skin looked up at Guilhem when he re-entered the room. Restless energy betrayed itself in the quick sentences and darting movements with which his hands dealt with an orange or cut slivers of roast partridge which had been placed before them. This was a man whose age was difficult to fathom, but who had shown Guilhem in half a day that his powers were extensive; his wealth great and his culture and knowledge considerable.

'You need not worry. The king himself has replied to our ransom demand. Prince Charles has sent a personal envoy who still awaits our reply. It seems that you are much regarded by your sovereign.'

'You have asked too big a sum?'

The caliph chuckled in his high pitched tone which seemed to contradict all that was expected from a man of power. 'Perhaps, perhaps so but that is not the reason you are still our guest. At least not the sole reason.'

'But custom demands that if the demands can be settled then the hostage should be returned to his p..p..people safely and with reasonable haste.'

'It is so young master, but we needed you to get to know us and our customs and beliefs. We believe that you can be a bridge between our peoples and so help us both.' Abd al-Rahman looked across the low table to Ibn Abjar the vizier of Cordoba.

They were now only three in the room. Faintly the shouts of the overseers and the clunk of mallet on chisel drifted along with dust motes through the arched windows. They had come to the point.

Guilhem stayed silent. There would be more to come.

'You love my daughter Nihal.' The vizier spoke in a low tone.

Her name dropped into the cool air and time missed a beat. Guilhem felt a thump in his heart which seemed to catch and falter. His ears rang with shock. This would be the lever to prize from him acceptance of the plan whatever that was. He wanted to take action; to draw his sword and cut through the confusion. But of course, he carried no sword. He tried to remain impassive.

'And I believe she returns your affection,' Ibn Abjar sighed. 'It is not what I would have wished but for the sake of our people perhaps something can be arranged....she is willing to lead an unconventional life to help our cause. I think you know that Nihal is different from other women....' He let the words drift.

'I do not think my king would approve such a match sir. But I thank you for kindness. I am not worthy of so great an honour.' Guilhem forced the words out as his emotions surged. In the act of rejection his love seemed even stronger. But this was not a possible match.

Abd-al Rahman interrupted, 'The Arab people do not act as one nation. We are split much like you and your Byzantine enemies in the east. We in Spain are from the house of Umayadd but we have been driven from our inheritance by the Abbasids led by caliph al-Mansur. His brother Abu-Abbas al-Safah massacred our people nearly twenty years ago now. And much like the Christian infidels we have our theological differences.' The small figure with the soft skin exchanged his soft exterior for iron indignation as he spoke. 'I want to lead my people back to our home and claim our rightful inheritance. Besides those pigs do not hold to the true teachings of the prophet.'

'Perhaps the constable feels the same about the insult to his own family.' It was the voice of the vizier.

Guilhem felt his anger beginning to stir again. He knew that he was being manipulated by very clever adversaries but he was too young to hold his feelings in check.

'What I feel about my family is no concern of yours, seigneur caliph. I have sworn allegiance to King Pepin as did my father. I do not feel wronged by the decisions of my family.'

'But if we can show that it not only your family that has been disinherited but that the church in Rome has deceived all your people and put the souls of your peoples in jeopardy, surely you should at least look at the evidence.' The words wound their way into his mind uncovering thoughts that had been buried.

'What if........?' the thought came unbidden, 'Maybe it is my RIGHT to be king.'

The caliph took up the reins again. The little figure all glittering green silk and gold had taken on an air of the reasonable philosopher enquiring after truth.

Abd al-Rahman rose quickly from the couch and went to a side table where they had laid their travel cloaks, hats, helmets and swords. He picked up Guilhem's helmet and touched the golden bee. 'But we know that there are those of your people who believe in a different story to that of the Church of Rome. After all Guilhem Constable of Toulouse and of the house of David of Judea this is what some of your own family believes. Remember your grandmother the old queen Nanthilda.'

'My lord it may be as you say, but my belief is in the one true Church of Rome. That is the church of my k..k..king and my people. It is true that there are other stories about our faith and of our family, but I have never paid much attention and know little of them. I am only a soldier and such things as I have heard do not bear the stamp of truth'

The caliph and the vizier exchanged glances and Ibn Abjar took up the lead.

'We were not sure how much you knew of your family heritage

but there has been intensive study by our Immans into the lives of all the prophets and indeed some of the followers of the prophet Jesus In particular we have been interested in the work of the apostle Mark because he founded your church in Alexandria. Even now his remains lie in a Christian church there. Although we conquered Alexandria a hundred and fify years ago we have allowed your churches to continue. It is our way. In some areas we have even worked with Jewish scholars to find the truth.' He reached into his tunic and brought out an oblong box made of ebony. It had the patina of age and the surface was cracked and crazed. 'Please look at the contents young constable before turning away. Our scholars say that these writings are very old. The writings are in Coptic. And here is a translation which we have had made by our scholars. Of course you may have our work checked by whomever you choose. We only ask that you look and learn. You may decide to do nothing. It will be your choice. The box and its contents are yours to keep. When you return to your people you may want to show it to your scholars and priests.'

Guilhem held up his hand. 'I am sure that there are many versions of the truth, but I see no way that anything revealed by your scholars could result in my changing my allegiances and my beliefs.'

The vizier, tall lean and bearded stretched out his hand holding the translation, 'If you are seeker of the truth, at least take time to read our work. It would please Nihal if we were able to remain friends with at least some common purpose.'

Her name hung in the air and Guilhem's hand stretched out involuntarily.

'We will leave you to reflect,' said Abd al- Rahman, the surprisingly full lips parted in a smile revealing perfect white teeth. There was no humour in the smile.

Later having been escorted back to Cordoba Guilhem sat alone in his room looking at the ancient ebony box as though, unopened it would reveal the secret of life. But the contents of the box were disappointing. It contained two clay tablets that seemed to have been cut from a larger tablet. Each had a distinctive edge as though it was designed to fit into a bigger piece. The scroll consisted of very ancient pieces of papyrus which had been carefully glued onto a newer scroll. Each ancient scrap was covered in well formed letters that created part sentences and in some cases broken words. These were in the strange script that they had told him was Coptic. The translations hinted at much but said nothing that would turn his life upside down.

I am Mark now of Alexandria. I have been entrusted with one of four mess... that .... The word is being received and even in the desert places as far away as Axum in the mountain fasntesses do our people bring the word I have instructed that should the safe keep..... in the future these precious messages should be take...to the safest places for future generations.

He stared dispiritedly at the papyrus his gaze going back and forth between the translation and the scraps of text. Then he noticed it. Faint, almost worn to nothing the outline of a bee appeared on one of the clay fragments and then 'AXUM after Alexandr.. ,' These words were in Latin. Once noticed it gained in strength. He looked away almost hoping that it would vanish. But it was still there. The outline of a bee spoke across the years to the young soldier sitting captive in a strange land.

Yet there was nothing to prove that the clay tablet and the parchment scraps were connected though it was clear that his arab captors thought there was a significant clue in putting them together.

The implications were that there was some kind of message that concerned his family line and which was of importance to the wider world. Something that the Caliph and his scholars thought would cause enough upheaval to change the political map. But what could be of such significance that made it important that he, Guilhem, should be the one to uncover the mystery? And where exactly was Axum?

CHAPTER SIXTEEN

805 AD, Aniane
– Heresy or Heritage –

The ebony box lay empty on a high dusty shelf above the carefully catalogued rows of bound books and other boxes filled with scrolls and parchment fragments. It was the only box that fulfilled no purpose in the dark stone walled library. It was kept as a reminder.

The bishop of Aniane looked up at the box and waited until the wave of pain went through its cycle, starting with low discomfort like the distant rumble of thunder to the apogee of jagged lightening, which left him shocked, breathless and grateful for the reprieve that followed. It was becoming more frequent. His always pale skin had taken on a yellow tinge and the high cheek-bones were too prominent.

'Oh Lord be merciful at my end and give me a sign that my life has been spent fruitfully in your service. That I have done as you commanded and will rest in all eternity at your side.'

The box sat mute on its high dusty shelf. Its emptiness echoed the hollowness that was filling an increasing space inside his soul. The harder he worked to rid the world of the errors of its ways the bigger the space became. The more he fasted and prayed the fainter the light of the Lord became. If only his prayers could be answered in the way they used to be in his youth. When each line of the gospel confirmed self-evident truths so clearly, and each hour of disputation was bathed in the knowledge that it was man's task, blessed by the Lord, to ensure that the Word was fulfilled by the behaviour of man.

The abbot of Gellone had vanished. Benoit did not doubt that he would re-appear to his flock the red brown hair now almost buried in grey, the lopsided smile made grotesque by the scar but still with the ability to connect with all his people within the church and without.

He would explain his absence with a jest, 'Pierre, you didn't bury your plough in the mud after all that rain.' And to the watchman who had failed, 'Jesse, I can see we'll have to provide a young wench to keep you awake,' and so on. Effortlessly he would ensure that the lessons were learned and that the village people were set onto their new tasks, and that the building of the abbey would continue apace. He would probably even call a special service of thanksgiving that the community had not been subject to a real calamity. No-one would question his absence except his own spies, Jacques Fournier and the priest Bertrand. It was they who had sent the message with the news of the fake attack and Guilhem's disappearance.

Moreover he would conduct that service with a clear conscience and in the untroubled faith of a good man. The trouble was that he was a good man! Except.....except.... Benoit's gaze went back to the black ebony box. Guilhem had brought that box to him forty years ago after he had been ransomed by his father and King Pepin from the Caliph Abd al-Rahman.

The contents of that empty box had provided the irritating grain of sand that had changed an accepting faith in Christ's true word to a mission to root out all sources of heresy. And even now at the age of fifty-nine with his strength failing God was testing his endurance once again. He would not fail this last test!

He had never wanted the Count of Toulouse to become an abbot in the true church. It had been the Emperor Charles and Pope Leo III who had been determined that Guilhem's wishes should be fulfilled.

CHAPTER SEVENTEEN

768 AD
– The Coronation of Charles –

They came for him at dawn in the cool autumn morning. At first he thought that it was a surprise hunt for his pleasure, but then the guards came and packed his few belongings and his clothes. His armour, helmet and sword were all returned, the gestures indicating that they should be worn. He looked at the ebony box. For a moment he thought, 'if I leave it behind it will lose its power to wind its story into my life. It will lie shut, mute and eventually forgotten.' Then he seized it angrily and stuffed it into his saddle bag. In the courtyard the horses were waiting, snorting and shaking their great heads and rattling the stone floor with impatient hooves. The vizier and the Imman were there.

'Fate has changed our plans Constable Guilhem. News has come that King Pepin has died. The coronation of Charles and Carloman will be held in ten days and Charles has asked that you be released to be part of this ceremony. Our Caliph has graciously granted his request and the matter of the ransom has been...' a pause, 'settled! We hope that your stay with us has not been too irksome and we wish you the blessing of Allah in your life, and that you will not carry enmity in your heart. Perhaps there can be peace between us now that you have new rulers. Please convey our hopes to your new king.' The vizier bowed and then stepped forward and embraced the surprised Guilhem.

'If I am unfortunate enough to be captured again in my life I could only hope that my captors are as g..g..gracious as you have been, my lord vizier. I have learned much from you and your people, especially Imman Hisham Ibn Malik and your daughter Nihal. If you think it appropriate p..p..please tell her that I am sorry that our paths have parted in this way.' Guilhem found his stammer betraying his emotion.

The bearded Imman stepped forward, 'take this young master, as a token of our affection and respect. It was the will of Allah that I was able to learn that the infidel are not all barbarians,' he smiled as he handed a small box covered in mother of pearl to Guilhem. 'Open it later when you have reached your destination. It may be of some small help in your search to do the will of Allah.'

Guilhem vaulted into the saddle of his favourite bay which had been brought for him. Briefly it crossed his mind that at some stage he would have to relinquish this spirited friend. His eyes strayed up to the shuttered windows of the women's quarters and just then it seemed as though one opened slightly but there was only absence in the dark space.

As the little troop galloped away through the fields of hemp, beans, onions and vines the emptiness in his heart drained the richness from the land. Even the rays of the early sun glinting on the great water wheels already creaking into their diurnal round failed to attract his interest. They splashed through the crossing of the Guadalquivir river and on to the Sierra de Negura mountains. Even here there were vestiges of the great road built by the Romans. The Via Domitia led them across the valley following the river. The sun was past its zenith as they came up over a rise leading into a river gorge.

On the banks of the river a small group on horseback awaited them. Guilhem's first reaction was to put hand to sword but his troop did not pause and soon greetings were being shouted as they drew near. A figure on horseback detached itself from the group. It was the caliph.

'Ah it is my friend the constable Guilhem d'Autun. No, no! No need for formalities,' as Guilhem made to dismount to pay his respects: the recent lesson clear in his mind. 'As you can see we are on a hunting trip, and when I heard you were to pass this way...' his voice stopped, but there was no hesitation, more an implication of purpose.

'I wished to say farewell and to make a gift of my horse with which I see you have become as one.'

'My lord Caliph I am very grateful for so generous a..'

'No do not thank me young constable. We are pleased to release you at such a time for Francia. Your people will need young men of character and intelligence, and we will need someone who has some understanding of the Arab people to guide the two kings. When kingdoms are split there is danger for their own subjects and for their neighbours. Come let us walk a little while the meal is being prepared.'

'My lord Abd-Rahman you are very gracious, but I am only a young noble among many in the court. The new King Charles will have many more weighty advisers than me.'

They swung easily off their steeds and began walking through the tussocky grass. Guilhem eased the helmet from his head, wiping his forehead wet from perspiration. The Caliph pointed at the helmet subject of so much discussion since his time in captivity.

'But none that could place his throne in such danger. The box I gave you at Madinas. Did you bring it, or leave it?' The question seemed to have no connection with the gesture to the helmet.

'My lord I have it with me, though I am not sure why.'

'You have seen the symbol on the clay. That is why you could not leave it, young Guilhem. If you choose to trace the story of the bee you may be driven to change your world.'

Guilhem looked at the small authoritative figure with astonishment. Even if his heritage proved to be as the Jews thought, he could see no real reason that the world would rock because of it.

'Think kindly of us Constable Guilhem d'Autun. Remember this time. One day we may meet in other circumstances and I will call in your debt. Meanwhile I have one last thing for you to remember from your sojourn with the infidel Arab. Although he smiled as he said the words, the smile did not reach his eyes.

'When you go to Alexandria, make sure that you visit Adelchis the trader from Ethiopia. He is a man of many parts.'

'But why should I go to Alexandria my lord Abd-Rahman? My king will need me at home.'

'Constable my prediction is that you will follow the path of your heritage. It is so said in the stars.'

The little figure laughed, genuinely this time, 'It is true your king will need you. By the way, beware Carloman. He is a weak man in a strong position.'

With that they returned to feast off a young deer spit roasted and rough wine from wooden cups. Soon after the Caliph and his party rode off.

It was quite clear that the meeting had had no element of chance.

*   *   *   *   *   *   *   *   *

The coronations took place at Noyon and Soissons on the 9th October 768 which was the feast day of St Denis, the patron saint of the Franks. Charles was crowned at Noyon, Carloman at Soissons, all as choreographed by the deceased King Pepin.

Guilhem had hardly time to prepare for the great occasion before he found himself standing in the nave of the abbey church witnessing the blessing of the bishop being administered to the new king. The crown, a simple gold circle was placed on Charles' head by the new mayor of the palace, who bowed and knelt in obedience to his new sovereign. Then followed the most important part of the ceremony as the dukes, tribal kings and churchmen lined up to swear fealty to the newly crowned monarch.

The great grey stone abbey church with its thick grey stone pillars and heavy arches. Small windows high up in the nave cast their dull light on the noble occasion. The nave was full with slowly shifting masses of dark brown robes-mostly men of the church- and the variegated fur cloaks of the tribal leaders from the northern forests. Occasionally fine cloaks in blue or red or deep purple would strike the eye. Even gold or silver threaded brocades occasionally caught the faded light and threw their ostentatious display at any who would look. Guiilhem looked up at the east window and the great plain cross that drew the eye to the symbol of the one true God.

Indeed a contrast to the delicate red and white columns and white marble of the great mosque which led the eye in no direction because Allah was everywhere.

Yet in an undefinable way he felt more content with the familiar orientation of the unadorned church and the cross that hung over the altar as a reminder of the sacrifice that had been made for him and for all. Could 'all' include Nihal? Suddenly the scent of jasmine invaded his nostrils and he was overtaken by a feeling of loss.

A young page worming his way through the crowd brought him back to the present in time to see one eyed Wermold duke of Thuringia resplendent in brocaded linens with a great black bear skin across his broad shoulders kneel and give his pledge. Two tribal leaders wild bearded from the sea-stormed coast of Brittany, Luidgard and Gersvind, in sheepskin cloaks also came and knelt in homage. This was unusual as the coastal tribes had paid little heed to the incursions of the Franks, or before them the Visigoths. The two tribes were at war and their leaders had only come to Noyon to solicit aid from Charles, each against the other. This turned out to be one of Guilhem's first tasks for his new king.

Tassilo of Bavaria, resplendent in turquoise silk and a very fine wool coat decorated with gold thread came to show his wealth. He was a short man and nearly drowned in his own splendour. Then came the bishops and abbots of Saint Gall, Mainz, Metz, Peranne and Aachen. Counts and dukes of minor jurisdictions followed. Although time had been short many had travelled great distances to ensure that their loyalty, real or otherwise, was noted by the new king.

Guilhem scanned the crowded scene to find his father at the ceremony. He was nowhere to be seen and he began to worry that sickness had kept him away. It was then a court administrator, a monk from St Gall, tried to explain how King Pepin had divided his kingdom according to Frankish law. Central Francia, Aquitaine and the south including Septimania was to be ruled by Carloman. Charles had been allocated all the lands along the North sea coast and down the eastern borders as far as Italy. His father and the Jewish leaders were presumably at Soissons!

Guilhem was trying to understand the implications of this strange division when he saw him. Although ten years had passed there was no doubt in his mind. The tall spare figure with a hawkish nose, neat grey beard and dressed in grey and brown full length robes of wool and silk was Adelchis the trader: the very same who had been mentioned by Caliph Abd-Rahman as he had been released.

Before he could assimilate the coincidence he found himself in front of his new sovereign. He knelt, 'I swear by Almighty God that I shall be a true and faithful servant and obedient to the commands of my true sovereign king Charles. So before God and this congregation I pledge my fealty.'

'And so you should cousin constable Guilhem d'Autun. It cost me and your father a pretty sum for your release I might say.' He felt himself lifted and the tall figure embraced him so taking the sting out of his greeting. The blue eyes were shining in genuine pleasure at seeing his old friend. 'We thought we had lost you there for a time. Caught by the wily Arab! Still Carloman did little better and his force was beaten back. Or so he tells us.'

The short exchange told Guilhem two things instantly. The reason that Carloman's force had not diverted the attack on his scouting troop was now clear. It was equally clear that relations between the brother kings were not good.

'We have much to talk about Guilhem, but it will have to be after the feast. Attend my court at noon to-morrow. Meanwhile speak to those damn Celts from Brittany, Luidgard and Gersvind, the ones that look like sheep blown in by a storm. See if you can get an idea what will settle their quarrel, and don't commit me to sending any troops!'

The rest of the day and most of the night passed in a blur of reunions and eating and drinking. Four months in the cultured captivity and contemplative quiet of vizier Ibn Abjar had not prepared Guilhem for the excesses of Frankish celebrations. By early evening his head was spinning with combination of rough wine and copious drafts of weak ale flavoured with yarrow and cinnamon. Each friend from Narbonne and the court at Aachen necessitated another slap on the back, a ferocious welcome hug, followed by a full mug.

Father Bedier of the kind eyes and wise council who had provided the basis of his education so that now he was one of few nobles who could read and write was there. The pork, like Father Thessiere, whose breath had not improved and whose mouth was now completely lacking in teeth, insisted on a close up encounter that made his stomach churn. Witiza was there, tall dark and austere standing apart from the displays of human weakness and excess that sprawled across the abbey buildings and into the town of Noyon. Nobles and captains from the court at Aachen, who tried to drag from him instant judgements on the barbarian Arabs and their customs and beliefs.

Before things disintegrated too far he found himself outside the refectory on his return from the overflowing stinking latrines. He wondered whether he could find a corner to escape the rumbustious crowd, or whether Charles would consider that a discourtesy to the new king. As he stood in the cool air trying to order his sensations he became aware of a figure standing in the shadow of the buttress next to him.

'Did my friend the Caliph Abd-al-Rahman treat you well constable

Guilhem?'

The voice came out of the dark carrying a light ironic tone as though it already knew the answer. Guilhem knew instantly that this was Adelchis of his boyhood feast, and who even then appeared to have knowledge of his future before he himself. The slight figure came out of the shadows and inclined his head in greeting.

'Ambassador! I was t..t..treated with great...' Guilhem hesitated further. The question crystallised a feeling that had not yet found a coherent thought to express it.

'With great consideration, and now you ask I think I was being prepared. For what I am not certain.'

'Seigneur Guilhem, if you choose to see it my friend, your life has been a preparation. But you have to find the task yourself and decide at each stage if this is a road you want to take. You have the box and the texts?'

'I have them.' Suddenly Guilhem felt very weary. It was though all the little mysteries of his life were congregating in this doorway and trying to force a recognition of some life plan that he must undertake. He did not feel ready.

'We can only provide the opportunities young constable. I am here for two more days. If you would like to meet......' he let the words trail into the shadows. 'It is not an easy road to follow my friend.' Adelchis lifted his left arm with his right so the bird's foot fingers were in the light. 'Although I am a man of many tongues I have no country. Sacrifices may be required.' And with that oracular declaration the slight, proud figure that seemed to be so certain of his place in the world revealed a longing for a different life.

The next day dawned clear, bright and with an early hint of winter in the crisp air. Most of the royal party and the guests were however far from clear or bright as they grunted, belched and farted their way to wakefulness from whatever corner on the floors of the abbey, castle, unwilling host, that they found themselves. Nearly all heads ached with excess, clergy and lay people alike.

Guilhem found that he was in much better shape than most having escaped the worst of the late drinking and having a quiet clean house at the far side of Noyon to lay his head. This happy circumstance was entirely due to his squire Arnaud with whom he had been joyfully reunited the day before. He decided to find the two Celts from Brittany and to see them separately. He sent Arnaud in search of the two and gave differing times for each to meet him.

Luidgard attended the summons with little grace, a worse headache and a muttering resentment at being palmed off with the young constable from Narbonne, wherever that was. He had hoped for an audience with Charles himself. He brought with him a young cleric who tried to bridge the gap between the wild Celtic patois and the standard Oil of the court. He sat surly, dark and resentful while Guilhem tried to get at the substance of the dispute between the tribes. He was of the tribe of the Osismii which lived on the edge of the great sea and whose lineage was descended from the great gods who had moved the stones of the earth.

'Seigneur he says that those,' the young shy cleric looked at Luidgard questioningly and received an impatient nod, 'pigs, the Veneti, have been hunting on their side of the river for three seasons. This summer they even cultivated beans and onions on his land. He says they did not get to eat any because he attacked them and took their crop. A few were killed.'

'How many were killed?' asked Guilhem, trying to get an idea of the size of the raid. Liudgard held up both hands with fingers splayed and then one hand more.

Fifteen dead must have been the result of a substantial raid. 'Ask Chief Luidgard how long the boundary has been made by that river?'

'Since his father defeated the pigs maybe forty summers ago.'

'How was the agreement n..n..noted? Was it written in the records of the Civitate of Rennes?'

Luidgard shrugged his shoulders with irritation. 'He says that his father told him that it was so and until three summers ago the pigs had not dirtied the land with their presence. He wants the king to send soldiers to teach the Veneti a lesson.'

Guilhem felt that there was little more to be learned from the surly Luidgard and so sent him on his way with expressions of the king's concern and said that they would meet again shortly.

Gersvind was very different. He came alone and spoke passable

Oil dialect. A big man, all belly and bluster with spindrift hair grey, blown across his face. Unkempt with holes in the coarse wool tunic and broken straps to shoes, he was preceded by a booming voice and jovial chuckles. Guilhem noted that his eyes, blue and bloodshot, took in his surroundings surreptitiously.

'Constable there is one river that has been our boundary since my father's father but lower down it divides into two streams. In between there is good land. We cleared it and planted our crops. Those son of robbers stole our crops and attacked our people.' A dirty calloused hand rubbed the round belly and he belched loudly. His grin showed a few blackened teeth. 'The king's wine was plentiful last night.'

'Why was the land only planted recently?'

'Because they said it was theirs, but I went to the abbey where the magistrate had put the paper many years before. I asked the clerk to come and look at the land. He told me that between the rivers was shown to be the land of the Veniti so we took it.'

'You consulted with Luidgard before planting?' Guilhem knew the answer before asking.

'No point, seigneur, they would deny it.'

Guilhem knew that disputes of this kind were the common currency of life in Francia. Agreements were made and broken with the regularity of the seasons. In this case his instincts said that the fat chieftain sitting grubbily in front of him had probably bribed the magistrate's clerk to agree to the change. This would be difficult to prove and the accuracy of the boundaries could always be questioned. He sighed impatiently. There was so much more important news to share with Charles and he needed to see Witiza and father Bedier before the court celebrations finished.

'I will not advise the king to send soldiers to fight on one side or the other.'

Gersvind held up his dirty hand, 'But, seigneur, our land is poor; their's is rich. Our need is greater if we are to feed our people.'

'It seems to me Chief Gersvind that the land is as it was for many years. If your land is p..p..poorer now it is because of poor husbandry. I will advise the king to send a magistrate and clerk to meet with you and Luidgard on the place which is disputed. Both tribes will abide by their decision and we will mark the boundary clearly this time.'

'But if you....'

'No ifs. This is what I will advise. You can of course keep fighting. In that way your tribe will be lessened and you will have less need of food.' Guilhem glanced up at the burly figure to what effect this ruthless logic would have.

Gervind decided to give up. Maybe he could bribe this new clerk. Bowing with difficulty the fat chief left. It was nearly the time to see Charles face to face. Guilhem hoped that they might even have some time alone.

The constable then returned to the stone house that Arnaud had made their headquarters.

The youth was still shy in manner, though the awkward gangly frame had filled out. Unruly blond hair topped the fair skinned face now suffused with colour as he groomed the beautiful Arab bay. The horse had his unstinting admiration. A toss of the fine head and a quiet snuffle greeted Guilhem when the horse saw him.

'I need a name for him Arnaud. Don't spoil him now!'

He went into the house and retrieved the ebony box given to him by the vizier. He wanted to show Charles the contents. In the small mother of pearl box, given by the caliph, and fixed to a velvet lining had been a golden bee to match the one on his helmet.

CHAPTER EIGHTEEN

768 AD

– Conspiracies –

'Cousin Guilhem, my young constable!' The new king unfolded himself from the low wooden bench, his presence filling the room as always, and in three large strides lifted Guilhem before his bended knee could touch the floor. Strong arms enfolded him and his face was pressed against the curly russet hair. 'I am so glad to see you back safe and I hope sound. You know Witiza of course. He has been telling of his time in Rome.'

Witiza had risen as Guilhem entered the reception hall which had been commandeered as a temporary state room for the king. He stood tall and thin even in his monks robes, smiling but contained, not to be swept up in unseemly enthusiasm at being reunited with his childhood playmate. He held out both arms, already in the manner of a priest bestowing a blessing.

'Seigneur we thank God for your safe return from the hands of the heathen Saracen. Were you made to suffer?'

'Far from it. I was treated as befits the son of a noble and a friend of the prince Charles. They seem to know quite a bit about us. But it is g..g..good to be back and see you sire; and you Witiza. I have learned much and there is much to report. Heathen they may be, but savages they are not. We could learn a lot from the Saracen my lord.'

Witiza's face darkened, 'I cannot believe the good Lord has blessed those unbelievers, but maybe your capture was arranged by God so as to help his people. In Rome there is a desire to ensure that the Christian faith is unified. That way we may be stronger in defending ourselves against these heathens. My lord king Charles agrees with Rome that we must be united and root out all heresies that contradict the one true Church. There is already a small group close to the Pope whose role it is to ensure the purity of our beliefs.' His look was directed at Guilhem as though he knew that he was involved in such wayward leanings.

This was a new concept to Guilhem who had only secular things in mind when he spoke of learning from the Arab people. In fact the idea that God had somehow arranged his adventure for their sake seemed absurd. But he could see that Witiza was in earnest. He did not want to belittle his old friend and protector.

'Never mind that now. It is good that you are safely returned,' Witiza's arm swept widely to include them all in his joy. 'With your permission my lord I will leave to prepare for Nones, and I will give thanks to the Lord for this happy time.'

In the time that they had been apart Witiza had adopted a declamatory style that verged upon the pompous. Then the severe face with its defined cheekbones lightened and was transformed by a brilliant smile. Guilhem recognised the Witiza of his childhood for the first time as he was leaving.

'He is a good man and tries his best to serve God. A bit heavy sometimes perhaps?' The high clear voice of the king had a smile in the sound. 'And now you must tell me all about Abd al-Rahman. Does he still have his eye on Septimania? But before we settle to the important things, how did you get on with our wild Celts?'

'I think you should call them to see you both together, sire. Remind them that they only yesterday swore their allegiance to you and t..t..tell them you will send a judge from Rennes to mark the boundary and that they will have to abide by his ruling. No soldiers my lord.'

'Excellent. So it shall be!' The blue eyes shone with anticipation at the prospect of hearing Guilhem's tale.

By the time he had finished Guilhem realised that the young russet headed giant of a man, now his king, also possessed a keen and questioning mind. He wanted to know more than the possibility of temporal danger from the Arab nation. He was intrigued that at least some spoke Latin. He wanted to know how they appeared to know about the relationships at the court of King Pepin. 'We know nothing of their court or their people.' He wanted to know about the books and manuscripts; the role of religion in their lives, and asked many questions of their use of water to create the wealth that had so impressed Guilhem. Eventually he had wrung Guilhem dry.

'There is something more, my friend?' The clear blue eyes looked searchingly at the wiry figure. The strong dark skinned face, the nose a little large with a hint of Semitic hook, and the square cleft chin, had taken on an air of uncertainty. Finally Guilhem drew a small square ebony box from his tunic.

'As I was leaving they gave me this sire.' He placed it reluctantly on the table between them.

'Do you want me to open it?' The question was gentle as though the concerns of kingship had been scaled down to meet the need of a single subject; the young man hesitating in front of him.

'If my king will give me leave I would like to go to North Africa. The reasons are partly contained within this box.' He rushed on. 'As you have heard my lord, Abd-Rahman hinted at some s..s..sort of alliance with us that would help him regain his lands from the Abbasids in Bagdad. It appears that there is ancient history of my family that might give us reasons to support him.'

The young king looked at his friend and subject, evidently torn by a need to seek the roots of his heritage and his duty to the king. Charles pushed the little box back towards Guilhem.

'I do not think I need to open this, constable Guilhem d'Autun. I think you must follow your heart, but I will have to ask you to delay your travels for a time. I need someone to represent me at the court of Carloman. I must keep the lines of communication open. You know that we do not always see eye to eye, and now that our father's kingdom is divided I fear that our enemies may find a way to separate us further.

'One thing more before you leave, cousin Guilhem: your father rules over the Jews of Septimania with little trouble. I am aware that this is at least in part because they believe that your Merovingian heritage gives you a right to rule them. You should always remember that I am a son of the church of Rome. I believe in our lord Jesus Christ and in the teachings that have been handed down by the holy fathers. I will not be part of any heresy against our Lord.'

'I understand my lord king. I will prepare to journey to Soissons and join the court of Carloman. I know you will release me when the time is right. I will remain your true servant, sire.' Guilhem knelt. Charles touched his shoulder and then he made for the door. As he was leaving he looked back and grinned.

'There is a nice surprise at Soissons. Your dwelling has been made ready and you will not be all alone.' The room seemed the duller for his absence.

The journey to Soissons was uneventful. Even the bandits were taking time off for the coronations and most of the warring Seigneurs were at one court or the other. Soissons was a town that looked as though it had tried to become a city and failed. The guard gate was a solid stone construction with Roman arch and guard towers. Outside the gate the usual huddle of mud and wattle dwellings begged for acceptance. A fortified wall and ditch stretched to the north, but Guilhem could see that part of the defences had been knocked down and the stone blocks lay in neglected heaps. Roman influence was clear as Guilhem and his small troop trotted through the impressive guard gate and clattered along stone paved streets, the sound of hooves echoing back and forth between the grand buildings. The senate house stood heavy, set in grey stone and much of the forum remained, yet it was clear that some of the paving had been cannibalised for buildings of unequal quality. Here and there vanished altogether and rutted mud slowed their progress. Mansions with imposing frontages and pillared porticoes were scattered about trying to proclaim a greatness that was no longer justifiable. The gaps between the great houses were filled with small timber framed houses whose heavy straw and hemp roofs weighed them back into the mud. They crowded any spare space like rotten teeth as though the town was gradually giving up the struggle for greatness. But evidently the city still benefited in part from the old Roman drainage system because the air was mostly sweet.

The scout Guilhem had sent to announce his arrival to Carloman had delivered the message and had found their billet in one of the prosperous merchant houses with stables and courtyard. The house was built part of stone and part heavy oak timbers. The merchant and small family greeted them with reluctant civility. They had had no choice but to accept the orders of the king and make these strangers welcome.

'Signeur Guilhem!' A rush of arms and sweet lips pressed against his, before he could put name to face. Her smell all apple and hay told him who it was. Visna the slave girl who had been gifted by Charles and who had nursed him back to health by the simple expedient of sharing her eager body with him. This was Charles' surprise. It seemed a lifetime ago since he had seen her. He held her high, feet kicking, to let her know that her unconventional welcome would not be punished. Yet even as he held her to the sky feeling the movement of her soft breasts beneath his fingers, it was Nihal's face that filled the sky.

His first task was to present himself to King Carloman.

'So King Charles has sent his favourite constable to keep an eye on his brother.' The tone mocking and dismissive took up where they had left off half a year ago. 'You must be a favourite. I understand that the ransom was... considerable. He suggested that I should contribute since you were under my command when you got yourself captured. I ignored the request of course. Oh go on, get up Guilhem.'

Guilhem rose from his knees, already knowing that this was going to be a posting that would bring little pleasure. The difference in style between the two courts was already evident in the richness of the robes in front him and the ostentatious display of gold and silver plate on the tables. Serfs stood around the room ready to satisfy the slightest whim.

'My lord king your brother sends kind greetings and hopes that together both kingdoms will flourish.'

'He does, does he. That will ensure our mutual happiness I'm, sure.'

A sycophantic murmur greeted this sally. The dark face lost its habitual sullen outlook for a moment.

'And how are you after your ordeal at the hands of Abd- Rahman? Still got your balls? I suppose you must have since your voice has'nt changed.' Outright laughter spluttered from the surrounding courtiers.

The routine of the new court was quickly established. As the days shortened hunting in the mornings became the pastime of all those who could ride. Although Carloman's sallies at Guilhem's expense did not cease they lessened in frequency as Guilhem became adept at not rising to the bait and providing cheap amusement for the dark faced king.

In the afternoons the king dealt with the affairs of state; received petitions; resolved disputes, and most constantly the reckoning of taxes. Carloman did not read or write but he was quick witted with an excellent memory. The reeves and bailiffs were held to account and all matters of note were recorded by the scribes for future reference.

It became clear that the court would not move before spring. This was unlike Charles who had already started to tour his kingdom. He had far to travel as his lands were partly on the periphery to the North, West, and mostly East of Carloman's inheritance. They knew his movements because his messengers were frequent visitors to Carloman's court, and they came from all parts of his kingdom; Aquitania; Gascony; and the Saxony borders of Thuringia and the sea edge of Austrasia.

Winter drew its dark cloak around the town. The forests seemed to encroach on the cleared fields as the frost-blackened branches striped the grey skies with their emaciated patterns. The rain was cold and persistent. Mud bubbled up from the broken paving and squelched its way into every household. The smell of damp wool and unwashed bodies filled smoke filled interiors. Animals were driven to shelter and added to the feeling of overcrowding with a cacophony of grunts, squeals and the lowing of cattle. Mostly this meant taking over the ground floors of the serf's dwellings. Their excrement added to the running mud in the streets. The sound of the wolf packs drew closer to the inhabited spaces; hunger overcoming their natural fear of man.

Sometimes the winter gloom was broken with a clear spell of bright days when the sun streamed its horizontal rays in red and gold and pricked the silver frost into fields of sparkling white.

The week of Christmas was one such period and the brightening sun reminded the quarrelsome and tetchy inhabitants that their ordeal would come to an end. It was hanging red in the late day sky, just after they had returned from a successful day's hunting when a small troop was seen approaching over the low rise to the west of the town. Guilhem reined in his bay which had been named Apollo by Arnaud. The fine head shook impatiently and the horse snorted. It was time for the stable and a bucket of oats.

The troop approached and resolved into its constituent parts. About twenty horsemen fully armed with hauberks and helmets and dressed in the livery of Carloman's guard surrounded five unarmed horsemen dressed in richly brocaded durra'a with the typical wide sleeves and pleated trousers of the Arab. An embassy from the Saracens under official safe conduct from Carloman was visiting the winter capital two days before Christmas. This was indeed a very unusual event. And Guilhem had not been warned, although his return from captivity was so recent.

Suddenly he thought 'maybe these are Arabs from the Abbasid dynasty. Maybe like the three wise kings they have travelled across the world to see Carloman.' It was then that the familiar face of Hisham ibn Malik came into focus. His patient teacher in the ways of Islam had come out of the westering sun.

The Caliph of Spain evidently was not relying on the young constable alone to further his dream of splitting the Frankish kingdom. Even the impassive Hisham had the grace to look somewhat discomforted.

CHAPTER NINETEEN

806 AD, Gellone
– Conscience –

The guttering light from the tall candle sconces reflected their feeble light from the tonsured scalp. Guilhem knelt in front of the altar. He did not sleep much these days. Partly because of the attempts on his life which had so far not caused even a wound. God was looking after his servant!

There was still sand enough to run before he would lead the monks at matins. The small hours crowded their bleak shadows around the flickering light.

'For our struggle is not against enemies of blood and flesh, but against rulers, against the authorities, against the cosmic powers of this present darkness, against the spiritual forces of evil in the heavenly places.' The words of St Paul to the Ephesians seemed so right. Surely he was engaged in just that battle against the forces that would strip away his right to determine evil from good.

The old leg wound ached as the cold stone crept through the woollen gown. He gazed down at the little golden bee he had place on the altar step. 'Oh Lord guide me in the paths of righteousness. Send me a sign that my secret too is part of your plan for I cannot betray it. Am I therefore evil in your eyes? Have I sinned more than most because I am a priest in your church and yet still..... ? Give me certainty that I am carrying out your will. Or let my enemies discover me and punish me here on earth.'

The gold glinted in the flickering light. Had it moved? That indeed would be a miracle. Guilhem smiled sadly; he was getting old. He gathered the little emblem into the folds of his gown. The good Lord had not answered tonight, but He would when the time was right. He heaved himself to his feet just as the cantor brother Steven came down the stairs from the dormitory. Steven, of short stature and long on considered thought, had proved to be a good leader within and without the monastery. His job in church was to lead the liturgical chants which he had taken over from Bertrand who had just vanished one day soon after the horrible death of the hermit Paul and the moving of the scrolls.

'Father,' Steven knelt and Guilhem made the sign of the cross and lifted the priest to his feet. 'You are up early Father, as always. The good Lord needs his servants to be strong in his service. And you need your sleep. You look tired and troubled.'

'Thank you Brother Steven for your concern, but I think it is the Lord's will that I spend more time in prayer. There are things he needs to say to me. Now which will be the psalm that you will lead us in today? I would like Number Fifty if you are in agreement.'

So it was that the matins service began with the Gregorian chant;
'Have mercy on me. O God
According to your steadfast love;
According to your abundant mercy
Blot out my transgressions.
Purge me with hyssop, and I shall be clean'

The sound of prayer filled the vaulted space. Each phrase ran into the dying echo of the line before till the petition reached into the heart of every stone, and drifted away into the cool dark of the spring night.

The ritual of the service worked its magic on Guilhem's troubled musings. He took time to enjoy the feeling of solidity provided by the new church. It had turned out to be just as he had imagined when he had leaned over the sand box with Pierre Clergue and Jaques Fournier. Jaques was very sick now and lay coughing his life away in the infirmary. He must visit him after Prime. Only the church and the dormitory were complete. There were many years of work ahead till the abbey would have all its buildings of solid stone, but they were coping well with the problems of living with the chaos of a building site. His thoughts wondered over a number of the tasks and problems that the new day would bring.

'Deceiving words are in their hearts, and thus they have spoken....'

The words penetrated his distracted musings and reminded him of the cause of his unease. All that he had achieved in the service of the Lord; was that to be set at nothing in His eyes because of the small nugget of gold that nestled so insistently against his heart?

Later that day before Sext, the midday service, the abbot made his way down the slope to the infirmary.

'So this is what is meant by the breath of life', thought Guilhem as he entered the small infirmary which had been placed on the far side of the stream, well away from the noise of the building work. Great rasping gasps filled the air as he approached the bed. In sickness Jaques was still a big man and the blanket swelled as the failing bellows forced air through the thickening tissues. His face was pale and beaded with sweat. Brown eyes opaque with pain stared from large hollows as he fought his lonely battle. This was not a man ready to go quietly to meet his Maker.

He heaved himself upright against the straw stuffed bolster and tried to smile.

'Not much of me left my lord abbot. Thank you for your visit to your poor carcass of a builder.' He took Guilhem's hand and kissed the ring. 'Have they set the foundations right for the cellarium and the calefactory. They must set them right so the dormitory above will be level...'

The abbot interrupted the flow of words which had left the heaving hulk stranded a breath behind. 'Now Jaques you know that Pierre Clergue is a very competent mason. You have worked together for over three years and I know he comes every morning to see you before starting work. The work is going well. Maybe not so quickly as when you are there to drive them on, but you may be proud of what has been done.'

Another great breath heaved its way to seek the precious air and Jaques eyes closed with the effort. Guilhem rose. 'No father don't go. Not yet. I would like you to hear my confession. I have not long left and you must....' The deep voice struggled and became indistinct.

'I am not sure that it would be right for me to hear your confession my son,' Guilhem held a wooden mug of water to the dying man's lips. 'I will send brother Adalung that he may hear you and comfort you with the love of God.'

'No father, no! It must be you. There are things that you only must know and it is only I that can tell you.'

Guilhem looked at panic stricken eyes that pleaded between breaths. He was not sure whether this was just the fear of death that he saw, or whether there was some other reason that Jaques wanted him to hear what would probably be his last confession. It was not too much to ask, though it was unusual for the abbot to hear confession of lay people.

'Very well Jaques I will come to you after Nones and hear your words so that our Lord may forgive your sins and we will pray together.'

Jonathen Anais and brother Steven were waiting outside the infirmary and fell into step beside him. 'It is time for you to inspect our work in the scriptorium my lord abbot. It has been many weeks and you promised to come to us every month.' Jonathen said reproachfully.

'And there is a new copy of psalm thirty three that is ready for me so that soon we may add a new prayer to our services my lord. So if I may I would like to come with you to see the new work. I think the scrolls supervised by brother Jonathen have been exceptionally fine in the last few months.' Steven's short legs scampered along as he tried to keep up with the long striding pair beside him.

So Guilhem found himself in the long upper room that he had first inspected those few years past when he had returned to Gellone to build the abbey. Two lay brothers and two monks were hard at work in the light filled room. Ladder racks held sheets of stretched vellum and parchment that were in the last stages of preparation. A faint smell of drying skins leant the air its unique mix of animal and theology. Each desk they passed added its odour dependent on the inks contained in the horn or bladder inkwells. Madder roots being crushed and ground added a plant smell to its dark reds while the woad kept in dried compressed balls only released its odour when being reconstituted with water to provide the most common blue, the brilliance of lapis lazuli being too expensive for most works.

The abbot's mood lifted as it always did when confronted seeing man hard at work in the service of knowledge and God.

At the far end of the scriptorium an easel stood in front of the open window allowing the light to fall on the completed page. It had already been attached to its wooden bearer and was awaiting inspection. 'Rejoice in the...' The opening words leapt from the page. Brother Alsom had created the capital 'R' in dark red and in the hollow of the top of the letter a small crowd of saints held their rejoicing faces to the sun and to God. It was a work of art in one letter. Alsom stood nervously beside the finished parchment.

Guilhem looked at the work with instinctive appreciation. He had never lost his love of the written word, and yet such work always gave him pause. How many lives had been changed by such works of skill and patience? Yet they were still subject to man's choice and interpretation. The shape of the world had been often changed by the choice of this parchment over that. Was the word more worthy of belief because it had been written? A sudden memory intruded. A memory of flaring torches deep underground and the grating of heavy stone slowly revealing the pale protective leather cover of other parchments. His own life had been ruled by the importance placed on such scraps from another time.

Steven turned to Alsom after a pause and then partly to cover his abbot's distraction embraced the anxious scribe.

'It is beautiful. And so clear! I will be able to see all the words even in the dim light of the church. We are all grateful brother Alsom.'

'You have d..d..done well brother,' Guilhem added his approval and Alsom beamed. In truth it was seldom that his work was criticised, but that was because Jonathen had often seen the faults early on and the reworking had been done before being displayed.

'I know your next question my lord abbot,' said Jonathen as they walked slowly back down the passage between the desks. Guilhem passing comment and encouragement as they went. 'I have looked again to see if we can accommodate our friends from Narbonne and Cordoba, but truly my lord there is not space. You have commanded that the dormitory wing be finished before other work in stone. I do not think we should accommodate our Jewish and Arab scholars in a wooden building.' As usual with Jonathen the words came tumbling out as though to forestall any argument.

Both monks were aware that it was an integral part of the abbot's dream to restart the multi faith school of learning that had flourished for a few years before his return to Gellone.

'No my friend, you are right, but we could move the workshop for the cleaning and the curing of the skins to a building down by the stream and below the village so that the water is not spoiled.'

Steven and Jonathen looked at each other. The abbot was right. It was a simple solution. Why had they not thought it out for themselves?

Was there a reluctance to risk implementing the abbot's dream that hindered their ability to solve the simplest problem.

'Yes my friends, you are right. There is discomfort in this idea. Not all the bishops are in agreement. Indeed the papal nuncio Deacon Mathew told me that if he heard that this 'mad idea' of mine were implemented he would write to Rome.

But Charlemagne the Emperor by the Holy father's own anointing is very excited by the idea. He sees that by learning together we may go some way to curing the emnity that sets Jew and Saracen and Christian in conflicts that surely cannot be the will of God.'

'Very well my lord abbot I will send messages to Ubada Rushd in Barcelona and to Rabbi Ezekial in Narbonne. They are waiting for our call and we must prepare a Christian welcome for them.' Jonathen waved his arm to include the village and its surroundings, 'but not all of our community will be happy to show our faith to non-believers in a good light. Of course we had such scholars here a few years ago. Those were good times....'

Steven changed the subject. 'My lord abbot, how long ago was the last attack on your person?'

'My friends I thought we had agreed that we had no n..n..need to bring this matter up again. The good Lord has let me live to this time so he must have a task for me to fulfil. Maybe it is the founding of our school!' His face lit up with joy at the thought.

Steven ploughed on. 'I bring up the question Father Guilhem because I think it's some six months since the bandits attacked your train en route to Maguelone. Three soldiers and two serfs were killed and...'

Guilhem held up his hand, 'and four months before that there was the ambush on the way to bless the new church at Roujon, and before that the rock fall... I pray that it is the will of God that I live so that I may fulfil his plan. But why are you raising this again now? I will not hide from my task in spreading the Gospel and ministering to our community.'

Jonathen interrupted, 'My lord Abbot, it is because of our love for you that we remain concerned. We have never proved who is responsible for these attacks although we have our suspicions.'

'Brother Jonathen, Jaques has asked me to hear his confession after Nones today. He has been sick for many months and has not long to live. I do not think it is a c..c..coincidence that there have been no attacks whilst he has been so sick. Maybe this will be the end...'

Steven said, 'My lord, you know that is unlikely. It cannot be Jaques alone who is responsible. Brother Jonathen has told me that you know why you are the subject of such unholy behaviour, though he has not told me the reason. If the cause is not dead with Jaques, surely those who give the orders will send another in his place.' His voice was deepened by concern and in his normal way the quiet logic made its point.

'You may be right Steven, but the Lord has protected me so far and I must trust in him. I believe that He wishes us to succeed in this place. What will be will be.'

Later that day Guilhem returned to the infirmary as promised, to see the weakening Jaques. The infirmarian was at his bedside trying to ease his discomfort. The rattling breaths fought their way for the little air they could drag into the congested lungs. The faint smell of houndsbene like mild mint filled the air as the infirmarian tried to get the struggling Jaques to swallow the cordial.

'Before all things and above all things care must be taken of the sick.' The words of Saint Benedict came to Guilhem as he watched the dying struggle.

Jaques caught sight of him and waved the attendant monk away impatiently. The monk shook his head as he rose from his knees and quietly gathered his bowls and phials.

'I am ready to hear you my son,' said Guilhem as he sat on the wooden stool and made the sign of the cross over Jaques Fournier.

'Thank you father, though you may not thank me for the knowledge I will give you. Yet I cannot rest until I have told the secrets in my heart. At first I believed that it was right to root out all heresies as the bishop Benoit of Aniane told us. Yet as my time here has passed and I have seen the good that this community has done and the true faith that monks...' His breath laboured and a terrible cough racked the failing frame. Guilhem waited patiently and then held Jaques head for a sip of the cordial. There was a pause as the breathing became steadier.

'I am here my son. T..t..take your time.'

'Time is short, father. Something I cannot take too much of now!' Even so a grin appeared on the drawn features, 'by the way how did you get that slash to the face? That scar used to be in my eyes when I planned my attacks on you. Because it was me father. It was me that started the fire in the library on that cold spring night. I don't really see the scar anymore. But somehow it helped to keep it front of me when I paid the bandits to attack you and when...'

Guilhem interrupted. 'Peace Jaques. Conserve your strength. It may ease your pain if I tell you that from an early time after you joined us I knew that you had been sent to do me harm. You watched me too closely! And as for the good bishop, he is acting according to his beliefs. We must all follow our conscience and hope that we are guided by the good Lord.'

A look of relief spread across the drawn face. 'You are a good man, my lord abbot. But there is one thing more. There is another spy in your community my lord.'

'Thank you my son. You need say no more. At the end of all things we will be judged as to our actions if they be right or wrong. And now we will pray together.'

'Thank you father.' A pause as he fought for breath, and then a grin. 'It is a hell of a scar though!'

CHAPTER TWENTY

772 AD
– The Beginning of the Quest –

Guilhem was carrying with him the small ebony box that contained the papyrus fragments and the golden bees. He also had translations of the papyrus scroll which scholars had confirmed as being in Coptic script – the disjointed message from Mark (the original he had decided to leave in the sworn care of father Bedier in Narbonne); a letter from King Charles to the Caliph of Alexandria and under the half decking, clothes, armour and gifts to ease his path into the uncertain desert. He also carried with him doubt. He stared uncertainly at the hissing bubbling water as it caressed the hull. He was not used to doubt, except in this one issue that ghosted his life, but now he wondered about this journey that lay before him. What was it that was driving him to follow the nebulous hints about his past? Why did he feel that he HAD to make this journey? Was he betraying the trust of the king?

The galley heeled gently in the soft breeze as the full bellied lateen sail pushed them steadily towards Alexandria. It was Guilhem's first sea voyage and he was glad that the fates had been kind with fair winds and calm seas. After three weeks at sea interspersed with brief coastal stops as they had journeyed down the west coast of Italia; never far from the land, it still seemed a somewhat unnatural form of travel to him. His sea legs had not yet given him the confidence he would have liked. And now they had left the toe of Italia on the way to Alexandria. Land was had been out of sight for three days now.

Five years had passed since Hisham Ibn Malik had paid his unexpected visit to the court of Carloman, and only now was he able to follow the trail of the golden bees; the ancient parchments and the mysterious city of Axum.

Five years of fractious peace between the two kings underpinned by continuous intrigue had been brought to a sudden end by the unexpected death of Carloman. The bloody flux had done its cruel work in five days and within a few weeks Charles had seized his opportunity.

The combination of a well armed force and judicious distribution of lands where needed, had the necessary oaths of fealty sworn by the majority of Dukes, Counts and Seigneurs in a short time. Charles had become king of the largest kingdom in Europe.

'You have served me well cousin Guilhem. There is much to do to strengthen the power of our Lord in our lands and to protect our people from the barbarians on our borders. And I would like to have you by my side, but I am mindful of a promise given to you some years ago. Do you still want to travel to North Africa?'

The boat heeled a degree further and Guilhem clutched the transom rail.

'It was an unnatural mode of travel when the ground moved of its own accord!'

Guilhem decided that he would avoid the sea in future.

'Yes sire if you will grant permission I would like to go.'

So it was that he carried messages to the Caliph of Alexandria and had been given questions to ask of Adelchis, the ambassador trader, that King Charles did not want to commit to paper.

'Land ho! And two galleys off the port bow captain.'

'Ready oars and wait!' A rumble of clattering wood sounded from below as the slaves lifted the long heavy oars off the rest position into the cradles of twisted coir rope and pushed the oars through the portholes. The long whip of the slavemaster cracked its message of urgency beneath Guilhem's feet. He looked at the captain. The caliph's navy, traders or pirates that was the question!

'Bear away to port helmsman!' If the galleys altered course they were probably pirates. The faint hiss of the sea and the creak of the mast as the large triangular sail swung wider; time stopped as all eyes strained to catch the first tell tale sign of the galley hulls foreshortening as they turned in pursuit.

'All clear sir.' The lookout called down to the deck and the tension eased away into the wind.

'Pharos dead ahead!' the lookout called again.

Guilhem ran as best he could over the slanting deck dodging the bales of skins and racks of amphorae that filled every space. There, over the horizon ahead, he could see a flashing star. So this was the mirror of the Pharos lighthouse, one of the wonders of the world! The slender column grew out of the sea topped by its flashing message. Then came the octagonal middle structure supporting the impossibly tall finger reaching to the sky.

Then finally the square squat fort that supported the whole. Guilhem felt crushed as they sailed under the lee of this extraordinary edifice. At close quarters even the blocks of stone that supported the whole structure seemed to have been hewn and moved by giants.

The lateen sail came rumbling down as they sailed to the east of the hepastadion, the Greek causeway that linked Pharos to the mainland and formed the windward side of the huge harbour that lay within its sheltering arm. The slaves bent to their task as the captain searched for a birth on the harbour pier. They had reached Alexandria; the first leg of his journey accomplished.

CHAPTER TWENTY ONE

772AD

– The Quest –

In the ante chamber the first thing that Guilhem saw was the smile and the characteristically tilted head of Adelchis, now with a black beard in which a few grey hairs could be seen.

'So it is the good Constable Guilhem d'Autun safely across the sea. You are welcome my friend,' the urbane voice with its hint of mockery greeted him as he grasped Guilhem's shoulder with his one good arm.

'Safe enough, safe enough. Though I must say that my days on the moving waters d..d..did not accustom me to the motion. I am glad to be on land again. All goes well with you, Adelchis, in the intricate patterns you weave across the nations?'

Adelchis smiled again in appreciation of Guilhem's acknowledgement of his mysterious skills.

'It is well so far, but I should tell you my friend that I have awaited your visit for many years. We have truths to find that.....' His ambassadorial caution cut across his unusual enthusiasm, 'could be of some significance.' He held his hand up to forestall the barrage of questions that would follow such a claim. 'But first we must pay our respects to Caliph Wasim Abd al Haqq and you must deliver your message from King Charles.'

Guilhem looked at him, astonished as usual at his encyclopaedic knowledge of court business.

'Don't worry my friend, the king sent separate messengers to me about your visit. I did not steal his letters.' He chuckled happily at Guilhem's consternation. Adelchis was a man that enjoyed the intrigue of mystery and even more the power of knowledge. He took Guilhem's arm, 'I am sure, my friend, that you do not need reminding but you should remember that our Arab friends here are not the same as those of your captivity those years ago. Here we are in the presence of a man appointed by the Abbasid dynasty in Bagdad.'

'I understand, or at least I think I have some understanding sir. Do they know of the consistent representations by Abd al Rahman to the court of Carloman?'

'Maybe, maybe not but you should proceed with caution seigneur Guilhem.'

They were walking the short distance to the Caliph's palace which was situated inside the ancient temple grounds of Seraphis. Away from the crowded bustling souks Alexandria was a city constructed on a scale suitable for gods and goddesses. There were large spaces between the heavy set buildings hewn from huge sandstone blocks, and something foreign to his eye about the scale and weight of the temples, amphitheatres, forums and administrative buildings set in their formal courts and gardens. Time and successive conquests had meant that these were no longer in good condition. Once again it seemed as though a golden age had past and the works of the ancient giants were drifting inexorably to a crumbling disorder. Dust eddied underfoot and drifted into the heat. Alexandria even smelt different. Guilhem breathed in the scent.

'Its betelnut and cardoman. They use it in everything.'

'There are no arches!' Exclaimed Guilhem as he realised why the buildings seemed to weigh so heavily into the sandy soil.

Adelchis looked at his companion with appreciation. He liked the evidence of an observant eye and an enquiring mind.

'You are right, my friend. Neither the Greeks who built most of this,' he waved his good arm in an encompassing gesture, 'nor the Egyptians who were first in this land understood the power of the arch.'

They turned into another square and found themselves at the foot of a giant staircase that lead up to a roofless portico. The sandstone columns were blackened with soot.

'Before we meet the Caliph, I want to show you this.'

They climbed the blackened steps and looked through the wreckage into the roofless interior strewn with shattered stone and broken columns. Marble floors had heaved and twisted in response to the intense heat. Wreckage stretched into the distance. What was so hated that necessitated this amount of determination to eliminate it?

'This was the library at Alexandria, or at least a greater part of it,' Adelchis spoke quietly and there were tears in his eyes.

'Why?'

'Fear I think. Fear that somewhere in the greatest collection of knowledge in the world something might show that the prophet was mistaken. And distrust. If knowledge had not been gathered in the name of the prophet it should be available to contaminate us. It is said that when the Muslims attacked Alexandria about one hundred years ago the Caliph Omar instructed that the library be burned because 'the contents will either contradict the Koran so they are heresy, or they will confirm it so they are superfluous." He paused and the tone was weary, 'perhaps something else; I don't really know. But I thought you should see it. Here you can see that knowledge can be dangerous. Beware Guilhem, beware!'

'Why especially me Adelchis? Am I at special risk?'

'The danger of knowledge young constable. The danger of knowledge - whether real or perceived. My people believe that something special was brought here a long time ago. When this was destroyed,' Adelchis' good arm swept through the blackened ruins, 'when this store of knowledge was obliterated, somethings were saved. One in particular...'

'Was taken to Axum,' interrupted Guilhem.

'Indeed. So you have made the conection seigneur Guilhem.'

'But I still do not understand why this mystery can can be of such moment. More writings for the scholars to dispute?'

'Sometimes, my young friend, just sometimes knowledge can change the course of history. Perhaps this is one of those times so not all was lost!' There was a sudden change of tone as though Adelchis was determined to show that there was always hope. They turned to go back through the hall of wrecked columns. It was then that Guilhem caught a movement of a white robe behind the pillar on his left side. He grabbed Adelchis and felt him flinch from the contact on his withered arm. He put his hand to his lips and motioned with his hand so that he led them behind a broken wall. A long dagger had appeared in Adelchis's good right hand.

'How many?' he whispered.

Guilhem shook his head. He drew his own sword.

Adelchis said, 'I know this place well. There are steps over there. Narrow. They would have to follow one by one.'

Guilhem nodded, bent down and picked up a handful of rubble. Carefully he lobbed two or three bits away from the direction of the stairs. A pause. Then a faint scuff and a glimpse of two figures.

'Now!' he whispered.

Bending low they dodged between the blackened pillars. He turned as they reached the top of the wrecked stairway. His ruse had only given them a step or two. The first of the assassins threw his knife. As Guilhem pushed Adelchis and twisted low, it clattered into the stone lintel. The stairwell was too narrow for swordplay. Guilhem, chest heaving stared into the eyes of his attacker only two steps away. Two more figures loomed over his shoulder. A slight grin told Guilhem that the man was enjoying his task. A movement behind the first attacker.

'Down! Knife!'

They stumbled backwards down the stairs as the second knife whistled at Guilhem. He flinched, but the flying blade hit his own raised sword. Then they were at the bottom of the stairs and out into the courtyard where people sauntered by immersed in the business of the day. The attackers melted back into the gloom of the stairway.

They stood looking at each other in the bright sunlight. A grin spread across Adelchis face. 'Beware, Guilhem beware! I had no idea it would be so soon.' Laughter born of relief spread across his whole body. It was the first time Guilhem had seen this man devoid of his mask to the world.

'But who? Why? I know nothing that could possibly be of danger to anyone.' A pause, 'do I?' he asked doubtfully.

'Maybe it's because of who you are, not what you know. Or maybe they think you know something.'

'But who are 'they'? And why must it be me they were after? Surely you too may have enemies.'

'Oh yes! I have enemies my young friend, but I have made my home here for over ten years and have never been attacked in this way. No, we can assume that someone has an interest in stopping you. Who knows where we are headed and why you wanted to make this journey?'

Guilhem thought over the few weeks of preparation for his journey. The king knew where he was headed after Alexandria. Also one or two members of the court knew of his trade mission this far and so it could be assumed that the church...... It was possible that even the Ummayad of Spain knew. Of all of them only the Saracen court of Abd al Rahman would guess of his mission into the deep desert.

'And they want me to make this trip,' he mused aloud, 'and you; you know,' he turned to Adelchis, 'only you and Abd al Rahman could know that we have another quest and you both want me to go. Even I am not sure why I am travelling into the unknown and yet there is s..s..something that drives me to follow this uncertain path that has shadowed me all my life.'

'Very well seigneur Guilhem, let's not worry further for the moment. Now we must present your letters to the Caliph and seek his seals of safe conduct. I have been to the desert before and so this is not so strange a request. I have trade there. As for you I suggest that it is curiosity and adventure and the possibility of trade that draws you to the desert.'

Two weeks later they were part of a caravan that wound its way along the great river of the Nile towards Wadi Halfa. Guilhem's own world had shrunk into insignificance in face of the wonders with which he had been faced. The giant pyramids at Giza had been followed by the enormous temples at Luxor and in between the palaces and gardens and statues that spread alongside the sluggish rich brown waters. Great fields of cotton and corn and barley bowed their laden heads to the ever present sun. It seemed to him that some race of gods had landed here to show man what could be done. And then they had deserted their creation. For it was clear that nothing approaching the scale of the past had been attempted for hundreds of years.

South of Aswan, their caravan much diminished, they left the banks of the great river and struck south and east into the dry dun desert. In the distance faint purple shapes hinted at mountains ahead. Overhead the sun bleached blue from the sky and burned the early morning shadows into the yellow grit and took away any hope of comfort. In the noon of the day they usually pitched tents for a time to allow the sun to spend some of its power before resuming their plodding journey till night when the temperature fell abruptly. The guides were kind to Guilhem who was the only desert novice. They showed him how to wear the burnoose to protect his head and shoulders; how the robes should be tied to allow such air as there was to flow; and how to dig a small depression in the sand so that he lay on cooler ground. He was a quick learner and soon became a favourite with many of them with his curiosity about their lives, and his natural ability with both camels and horses. Most they liked him because he never grumbled or asked for special consideration as the guest traveller.

Adelchis left him to himself as much as possible, intervening only when sign language or other attempts at communication ran into the sands of incomprehension. Arabic was the common language for most. Coptic was common also and many local tribal dialects which the guides and soldiers talked among themselves.

On the fourth night away from the river Guilhem could not sleep and so he rose from the rolled blankets, and taking one with him as a shield from the cold night air, he walked a little distance away from the camp fire and muted sounds of animal and man. He found a good place to settle with a rock at his back and sat for a while listening to the faintest rustle of the sand grains shifting in the night. Soon the cobalt sky with its myriad cities of shifting lights drew his thoughts out, up and away from the immediate questions about his mission. His mind tried to grapple with ever bigger questions. What did God want of him? Why had man allowed the knowledge of the giants of the past to slip into decay and loss? But even as these great questions came into his mind he found that the answers slipped out of reach and followed his gaze to the numberless stars, becoming more tenuous, the harder he tried.

'It is time we talked....' Guilhem bolted upright, heart pounding. The voice was so close. Anyone could have attacked him alone in the.... 'It's alright it's only me, Adelchis. And yes you were certainly off guard. Alone too!'

'My God! What a shock,' he tried to calm his beating heart. 'That's a real lesson. But why are you up?'

'Because seigneur Guilhem I too was not in the mood for sleep and we have only five days more before we reach Axum. I thought we should talk now in the calm of the night. I may be able to prepare you in some way for the discoveries we may make.'

'It may be the calm of the night, but there's no calm in me after that shock Adelchis!'

Guilhem rose easily to his feet and walked a few paces breathing deeply. 'Very well, that's better. I may be able to concentrate now.'

He sat down again and looked at Adelchis the mysterious trader that been in and out of his life since the age of eleven.

'You may be wondering my friend at my interest in your journey to the heart of Ethiopia?' There was an even rise in tone that implied that Guilhem would have considered this. 'You should know first that I am a Christian. My people are Copts and our roots are in Ethiopia, especially the ancient city of Axum. We were a great people with power and riches living in faith and blessed by the son of God. We believe much the same as your church of Rome though we have been called heretics by some after the council of Nicea nearly three hundred years ago.'

Although Adelchis maintained his controlled diplomatic voice there was an air of suppressed excitement in the way his body leaned forward. His good hand rubbed his withered arm as though it ached.

'Since then we have been isolated here on the edge of Christendom between the Arabs and the tracts of unknown Africa. Actually our Arab conquerors have been fair to us. Apart from the 'Gezya' tax which is imposed on all those who do not follow the prophet Mohammed, we are left alone.' His tone of increasing bitterness changed, 'actually Mohammed married a Copt, Maria, that's why they leave us alone. Not many Christians know that!' A wry laugh faded into the cool night air.

'I'm sorry Adelchis, but I still don't understand how all this ties in with me and my heritage. All my life people have hinted at some great mystery that lies in my family history. S..s..something that I should unearth to change my life and maybe the life of others. I don't understand the hints and mysteries such as this,' Guilhem pulled the small ebony box from his robe. 'Do you know what is in here? You seem to know more than me about so much of all this.' His voice rose with the years of exasperation finally bubbling to the surface.

Adelchis grabbed his arm, looking round as though afraid they might have been overheard. 'Peace, my friend. I will try and get to the point, but you must understand that in all this we do not yet deal in certainties. I think it is God's will that we are here together on this adventure, but we must be patient until we find....' His voice tailed away.

'There you are again! Find what?' Guilhem hissed in frustration. 'Everytime I think something is to be revealed a curtain is pulled down and I'm left again wondering what the hell I am doing in the middle of this desert,' he paused, 'though the stars are a wonderful mystery in themselves aren't they.'

'I don't want to tell what you may find Guilhem, because it is important that you are the one who makes sense of it and maybe there will be nothing of great note after all. Nothing is certain. Especially nothing is certain in the causes of belief! Now before we try to sleep I will tell you some other things about our Christian doctrines. First, who wrote the Gospels?'

Guilhem looked at him as though the question contained some unexplained theological trick. 'What is wrong if I say Matthew, M..M.. Mark, Luke and John? I am sure you are going to tell me I'm wrong!'

Adelchis smiled at the caution displayed by this young soldier who answered as though the sands might shift under his words.

'As far as you go that is right. At least that is what the holy fathers and learned philosophers have told us. Did you know that these are only four among many writings left by the early Christian fathers? Have you heard of or seen the writings of Thomas, Philip, even Mary, and others?' he looked at Guilhem, 'No? Well worry not my young friend because neither have most of Christendom! But they exist and I have seen some of these writings. The Gospels we know today were chosen by great Christians of the past; in fact largely by scholars such as Iraneus of Lyon and Athanasius of Alexandria. At least you should know that what we are taught today has been the subject of much dispute since the death of our Lord Jesus.

'I think that is enough for tonight. Let's see if we can get some sleep now. Another early start beckons. And yes, I do know what is in the small ebony box!' In this last he was only partially correct.

In the morning the sky was heavy with a thick yellow grey overcast. The air moved uneasily round them, hot and clammy. The guides delayed the start and kept climbing to the top of the nearest dune and looking anxiously westward. Then Guilhem heard the shout, 'Khamsin! Khamsin!' the camp stirred into action. One of the guides who had taken Guilhem under his wing pushed him into the lea of the small hill and demonstrated that he should dig out a hole in the sand and with aid of the tent skins make a small shelter. He sensed the urgency all round him as the animals were also brought into the shelter of the slope and securely tethered and he found small shelters springing up around him. He set to copying the nearest one, but still did not understand what they were to shelter from. Suddenly Adelchis was at his side.

'Come with me. You should see this. It will help you understand the desert.' His normally urbane tone was staccato. They climbed up the steep slope to join the chief guide and the sergeant of the armed troop that had accompanied them all the way from Alexandria. As they reached the top the air seemed to suck the breath from them. About two thousand paces in front of them a black cloud tinged with yellow reared into the sky blotting out the sun.

'That is a khamsin, a desert sandstorm. It may last an hour or a day. Only God knows. Take your...'

'Look! Look there to the left. Horses and camels!' It was true; fading in and out of the wall of sand a group of about seven camels and horses were fleeing the storm. Dwarfed by the towering wall of sand they didn't look real as their bright red and white robes streamed behind them.

'They'll be alright if they can make it to us, but those horses will need shelter to survive.'

'It looks like a boy in front. What is a child doing out here?'

By this time the tiny grains of sand were beginning to whip into Guilhem's face. The fleeing group was only a hundred paces away by now. They would just make it. The guide and sergeant waved them over the brow of the hill pointing to the camp below. As they swept passed and struggled to control the panicking animals down the steep slope, Guilhem felt that somehow he recognised the boy.

Adelchis gripped his arm, 'Let's go. In a few moments you won't be able to see more than three steps in front of you.'

They stumbled back down the sheltering slope. A roar of a thousand waves stole their senses and the stinging sands pricked and needled at any exposed part. Head bent Guilhem crashed into the slight figure just outside his tiny shelter. He grabbed the boy's arm and dragged him down into the confined space. The slight figure resisted for a moment and then they found themselves huddled out of the screaming wind. The boy unwound his burnoose and looked up at Guilhem. His heart leaped and stopped. He was looking into the laughing eyes of Nihal.

'I never thought I would see you.....'

'I thought I would never see....'

The words simultaneously uttered were swept away by the howl of the storm.

CHAPTER TWENTY TWO

772 AD
– The Quest Continues –

The wind hollowed out speech as the sand pricked and stung even in the shelter of the makeshift tent. Guilhem held her head in both hands; eyes locked on each other awash with absence and with a combination of disbelief and joy. The years apart contracted into that moment of realisation that their unspoken love had not altered. Guilhem drew her head towards his lips but at the last moment Nihal placed the palm of her hand on his mouth shaking her head but still laughing. The touch explained her avoidance. Guilhem could feel the invisible coating of sand on her skin. The fine dust had made a natural barrier. Instead he drew her down till they lay side by side looking into each other's eyes, questions building in the echoing thunder of the storm. Nihal's eyes filled with tears that left wandering tracks in the fine dust on her cheeks. Time stopped.

Later they realised that the khamsin had passed. An eerie silence filled the makeshift bivouac and then the sounds of surrounding activity began to penetrate their world. Every sound seemed muffled as though their ears were still buffeted by the tearing winds. The coating of fine new sand shifted underfoot and scoured colour from objects making them insubstantial.

Although there were so many questions; so many declarations; so many decisions, indeed a confusion of the unknown, this was not the time to resolve anything. Quickly they joined the checks on animals and people and began preparations for striking camp and resuming the journey.

The air had been cleared by the khamsin and the hot breeze held no hint of moisture. Now the discomfort was in the fine sand that had found its way beneath their clothes and into all the crevices of the body. It chafed and rubbed and as the temperature rose it brought with it a longing for the splash and cool of water and a means of washing the storm away. But the desert gave no hint of relenting as the caravan plodded its way through the unending wasteland. Although it seemed trackless to Guilhem the guides showed no hesitation in their choice of direction as they wound their way through the low hills and wadis. Eventually they stopped for the noon break and the temporary depressions in the sand were made to find the minimal relief below the burning surface. Guilhem noticed more activity than usual among the guides and two pairs of soldiers were sent back over the track that they had just traversed. But in the excitement of at last being able to talk to Nihal he soon forgot about them.

'Guilhem, son of the Count d'Autun, I am so happy to see you,' the words were strangely formal considering they had just spent hours in each other's arms, albeit chastely and in near total silence.

'Such absence as we have had makes words difficult...'

'That is so but.....,' interrupted Guilhem.

Nihal held her hand up, 'it is not right for me to interrupt you Guilhem but before we speak of what is in our hearts there is something I must say. I am here because of you but not because of us. I have been sent as an emissary to help my people. I am here to carry the truth of your discoveries back to my people and in the hope that our feelings for each other may ensure that nothing is hidden.'

'I understand nothing of which you speak Nihal. I am here t..t..to find the truth of my past and to resolve the mystery in which this has been shrouded since I was a boy. I do not think the forces of the world would have much interest in a personal quest.'

Nihal's heart jumped at the stutter which had always tugged at her heart and nearly unbuckled the words which could not then be spoken in their time in Cordoba.

'I know that the Jews in Narbonne have an interest in my heritage though why it is so important I don't really understand. But who else can find any thing of interest in this ancient story, yet it is true that many have hinted that there is something that I could uncover that...that could change the world. Even your caliph Abd al-Rahman suggested as much but.. ...' His voice tailed away stifled by emotion and he reached out to take her hand. To tell the truth he was disappointed. The last thing he wanted to talk about was his heritage and the unexplainable interest the world persisted in showing in it. He wanted to talk about love and longing and how they came to be together in this merciless desert after so many years. Most of all he wanted to take her in his arms and kiss the dust away from the lips that still showed so red through the desert sand. His eyes traced every feature; the thick full eyebrows; the deepset eyes with their shades of brown; the amber skin blushed rose under the dust.

'If you stare any more I will disappear,' she had started to laugh, 'besides such a stare does not belong to the manners of a courtly noble.'

He remembered the sudden mood changes amongst the palms and lilies beside the pools of the inner courtyard. The way she trod the delicate path between acknowledgement of their deepening feelings, and the way she lightened the mood brushing back the heavy fall of hair and looking up from under the tilted head at him with such obvious flirtation that he had to laugh.

'Yes I know this is not what we want to talk about. But before we say what we have to say my love, there are things you must know. For instance one of the reasons my father agreed that I should make this journey is that I come from a Christian family on my mother's side. My great grandmother was a Copt from Axum. She was related to Maria, the very same who married Mohammed!'

'There are Christians in your family!' Guilhem was astonished as she knew he would be. His mind was racing. Would this make the possibility of a union between them any easier?

'There were Christians in my family,' she corrected him gently. She could read his hopes and didn't want them to be raised. 'We lost touch many years ago when my grandmother married the chamberlain at the Abbasid embassy in Axum. Later my people, the Abbasids were driven away from Africa by the Ummayad rulers. So now we are in Spain.'

'But now we are here. Here t..t..together in a foreign land .....'

'If I come to you in the night so that we may be as one, you should know that the fact that we have broken many taboos may not change our futures. Even my father knows that if I found you in the wide desert that I may return to him.. changed.' She looked away blushing. She held up her hand to forestall him, 'but he is prepared to make this sacrifice if I can bring back to him knowledge that could change our world. And I have decided that you are more to me than anything so we must seize our opportunity here in this far away place. It may be that we will be allowed to be together in a different future.'

'Nihal this is madness. I cannot dishonour you for some mad dream that people around us have. What can I discover that could change the world?'

'I don't know either my love, but I know that some feel that a new story discovered by a son of the house of David could be so important as to change the balance of powers between Arabs and the West, and between kings and princes in the West.'

'I am a noble in the service of King Charles. I am here only because all my life there have been hints that the truth of my heritage has some importance bigger that one man's life. But I do not know if I want to be the unwitting cause of some catastrophe that I have no control over. I could turn back now.' Guilhem scrambled to his feet angrily.

At that moment the sergeant in charge of the guards came up to them and gestured for Guilhem to follow him.

'Go Guilhem, go! We need time,' and she smiled through eyes filled with tears.

The guard led him over the rise behind which they had taken shelter. Beside a large rock Adelchis stood looking back over the way they had just come. He was listening intently to one of the guides. 'This man is telling me that we are being followed seigneur Guilhem, and he asking whether we want try and capture them or at least frighten them away.'

'Does he know how many?'

Adelchis asked the guide who seemed quite voluble in answer to a simple question. Guilhem guessed that this probably meant that they were uncertain, and so it proved. Apparently there were some four desert Arabs about two or three sesterces behind but he sensed that they might be the vanguard of a bigger troop.

'What and when is our next stop? How many days before Axum?' The questions came easily and decisively. Guilhem was on firm ground when it came to matters of war.

'He says tonight we will reach the oasis of Mai Agam. We should stay there for two nights to rest the horses and to water all the animals. Axum is about three days journey after that.'

'Right. I suggest we do nothing till we reach the oasis tonight. If there is a sizeable s..s..settlement there it is unlikely that there will be a direct attack. It is more likely that they would try something in between the oasis and Axum. We will use the rest to see if we can find out more about our shy friends. Do you agree?' Guilhem looked for confirmation to Adelchis, who nodded his agreement.

The oasis of Mai Agam proved to be a settlement that balanced uneasily between prosperity and poverty, surrounded by defensive walls of mud brick. Date palms waved over the cooling springs and scrub bushes of thorn and acacia provided welcome green to the traveller's eye which had felt starved by the unrelenting shades of brown desert terrain. The party was made welcome by the local chieftain Dejazamach Hailu, a man of considerable girth, few teeth, and one badly scarred eye which was milky and sightless. His attitude to the strangers was considerably improved by Adelchis' silky charms and two jewelled daggers which indicated that the travellers were prepared to pay their way. Guilhem did not trust him.

Guilhem, Adelchis and Nihal were given separate tents of reasonable size hung with brocaded silks. Thick carpets were strewn about the floors. Closer inspection revealed that the luxurious appointments had been well used; the silks were torn and ragged and many of the carpets threadbare in places. Nevertheless it was a touch of welcome luxury after the days of desert travel. Soon great tubs of hot water had been prepared and each of them luxuriated in the scented water feeling the sense of renewal as skin sloughed off the layers of dust, sand and sweat.

A traditional feast followed, but Guilhem tasted little and waited for the formalities to end with impatience. Nihal was not allowed to take part in the feast with the men and had been provided for separately with the other women. Eventually he felt that it would not be discourteous to leave the festivities and rose quietly to walk back between the palms and the trickling steam to his tent.

The scent of jasmine told him that she was waiting for him. He pulled off his boots in the outer space and then pushed the hanging curtains aside. The light from one dim oil lamp glinted on the thick black hair hanging to the waist of the kneeling figure. A gown of turquoise silk glistened in the dim light. She put her fingers to her lips and held out her arms. Guilhem could hardly breathe as he folded her close burying his face in her neck, his lips and tongue absorbing the smooth texture and scented warmth. His hands moved over her breasts and gently unfolded the silk till the dark tipped shapes were bare to his touch. His lips followed his hands and he felt her quiver as he kissed. She was still kneeling but now he nudged her gently down his mouth never leaving the expectant skin as it wove a pleasure trail over her body. He felt the wiry touch of her secret hair on his chin and paused. This might be something too strange for one new to love.

Time was lost in pleasure; then suddenly he felt her thighs tighten and she thrust her sex hard against his mouth. There was a loud exhalation caught and then softening in a dying breath.

They lay lost in the moment. It seemed impossible that it should be so right after so long a time. Nihal was not finished. To his surprise he found himself being raised and fiercely kissed. Then he was on his back and she had taken control, riding astride him she pulled off his remaining clothes and took his straining sex in firm hands. It was his turn to shudder as she guided him into her urgent body. A hot warmth surrounded each part of him as she slowly lowered herself.

'This way you do not have to worry about hurting me,' she breathed in his ear as she crouched over him. Finally she accepted his full length and for a moment they lay motionless. But it was too much for Guilhem and he gave an involuntary cry as he released himself deep into her.

'Was this as it should be my love?'

'I don't think there can be any 'should' between us my princess. It was as it could be only b..b..between us.' They lay quietly for a time. Then Nihal made as if to rise, 'I think I should be in my tent when morning comes, my constable from Francia!'

'You may be right. We cannot break too many conventions too soon, but I don't want you to go just yet. I feel that the night may not be over for us. I don't trust that chieftain Hailu. You can go at dawn.'

Guilhem rose from the cushioned bed and went to the chest that had accompanied him from Francia. Opening it he took out his sword and dagger. Unsheathing the sword he positioned it over the scabbard. If the scabbard moved it would scrape against the sword making a grating sound. Then he pulled some silk threads from the hangings and tied one end to the scabbard. He led the other end to the back of the tent and pushed it through making sure there was sufficient length on the other side. Pulling on the wide legged pants he went outside and tied the silk thread across the thorn bushes which grew behind the tent.

'Now we can sleep my love.'

Nihal was looking at him wide eyed. 'I could not sleep now my love, if I drank a cup of opiate.'

Guilhem blew out the lamp and pulled her down into the warmth of the bed. 'Let us see if happiness can bring rest. I am probably worrying about nothing, but I am thinking of those who were following us for the last two or three days.' With her back to him they lay under the skins absorbing warmth from each other's contented bodies. It was not long before the regular breaths of sleep could have been heard by an onlooker.

It was in the coldest hours of the night that Guilhem awoke. For a moment he wondered if the slight chill creeping round his neck had woken him. He lay still. There it was again; a slight scraping sound as the scabbard was dragged from beneath the sword. In one lithe movement he rose to his knees and stroked Nihal's cheek. She woke wide eyed to find a firm hand across her mouth. Instantly comprehending the situation she nodded. Taking the sword Guilhem rolled silently across the tent floor to the back wall. He waited. For a time there was silence. Then a soft tearing sound came about an arm's length in front of his straining eyes. Then a shape dimly visible as it snaked under the torn tent skin. When he was half through Guilhem pounced. One foot pinned the outstretched arm to the floor. Both hands seized the head of the unsuspecting assassin. With a grunt he pulled sharply upwards and twisted sharply to the right. A gasp of disbelief and a slight snap; the man lay dead half in and half out of the tent.

'I'm sorry but I'll have to search him. You don't have to watch. Just go back behind the hangings.' He looked up anxiously to see the effect this sudden turn of events had had. She stood hand covering her mouth and then shook her head.

'If two of us do it we will save time.'

'Thank you. If you think you can bear it. Perhaps you could light the lamp my love. It's all over now. There won't be any further attacks tonight if he does'nt return they'll know he failed and we are awake, but I need to find out what I can about this unfortunate before I take him outside.'

With a heave Guilhem dragged the rest of the body inside the tent and with the light of the lamp they set about a thorough search.

It was Nihal who made the first discovery. On the inside of the wide belt a narrow pouch had been sewn and in it was a small silver cross and a few coins. Guilhem took the cross and examined the coins. They were minted in Rome, but that by itself proved nothing. Such coins had found their way across the world. He put the coins back in the pouch. A few moments later he made the second find. Taped high up on the inside of the dead man's thigh was a new minted gold coin. Such gold was rare outside the exchanges of kings and nobles. Guilhem guessed that it would worth about a year's wages for a freeman soldier. It bore the head of the new pope Steven IV.

A Christian faction had an interest in preventing Guilhem from reaching his goal.

CHAPTER TWENTY THREE

806 AD, Gellone
– The Heresy Hunters –

J onathen Anais was taking his morning walk after prime before going to work with his beloved scrolls in the librarium. These days the long stride was a little shorter and a stout chestnut crook eased the pain in his right hip.

It was a few weeks after Jacques Fournier had gasped his last painful breath. There had been no further attacks on the lord abbot but Jonathen was still worried. The small group of fanatical bishops, deacons and priests that had been charged with ensuring the purity of the 'one true way' would not let the death of one of their number stop their determination to serve God by rooting out heresy in all its forms.

He was a troubled man taken out of the comfort of his scrolls and parchments and inks and tossed into the maelstrom of church politics by his love for abbot Guilhem. Since the fire in the library three years ago he had learned much about his former count; the wiry campaigner with the slashed nose and slight stutter that ran so counter to his decisive leadership. He knew that Guilhem had been the reluctant recipient of some form of secret to do with his family heritage. And he knew that the Church had decided that this secret represented a threat to their attempts to unify Christendom. He also knew that the abbot was a man who served God with devotion and executed his pastorship with humility and love.

A small blue butterfly with tiny black spots on the upper side of the wing caught his eye. Its wings opened and shut shyly as it balanced on a yellow dandelion flower. Jonathen caught his breath at this little miracle of nature. Each time he was taken unawares at the strength of his response to the wonders enacted daily around him. He crossed himself and gave thanks that the good Lord had led him to this valley and to the man who had enabled him to devote his life to the beauty of the written word and man's search for knowledge.

Intrigue and violence were foreign to his nature, which was why this backwater of learning hidden in the folds of the Cevenne hills had become so precious to him. And now there would be the opportunity to expand his knowledge once again with the imminent arrival of Rabbi Ezekiel, which translated as 'God strengthens', so he had learned, and the Imman from Cordoba Mawhab al-Qurtabi which meaning as yet he did not know. He remembered with pleasure the heated discussions that had been part of daily life when the Imman Ben Abdul Hassein and Rabbi Ephrahim had brought their learning and new books to study. Now once again there would be new scrolls to explore, new puzzles to unravel, and new arguments to refute. New insights to be gained to the glory of God. Surely all this treasure would not be put at risk by a few fanatics in Rome?

Guilhem had always said that the attacks were designed to frighten rather than kill. The real objective was to discover the evidence that supported the heresy. He paused in the warm June sun. The sun concentrated on the bald patch created by his tonsure. It was strange how different people showed their respect to God in such diverse ways. The Jewish and Arab scholars would always have their head covered and he was being burned by God's sun!

As was often the case with Jonathen his thoughts flew in and out of his head in a somewhat chaotic pattern that was echoed by the uncontrolled halo of white hair that circled the tonsure. It took the written word to concentrate the fine mind that lay beneath the untidy exterior.

'Good morning father,' Pierre Maury's voice shook him out of his reverie, 'God willing it will be another fine crop this year.' Pierre was speaking from a spot some six paces inside the boundary of the wheat field. The dark craggy face glistening with sweat surveyed his handiwork with well earned satisfaction. A rare smile invited approbation.

'You have earned the thanks of all the village Pierre. You and your son-in-law have worked tirelessly and we have been rewarded with three years of fine yields.' The large calloused hands gripped the long hoe and the grizzled head bobbed with satisfaction. 'Not all seem to understand the work that goes to make a good crop father. You have to keep at it all the time. Even now these tares suck goodness from the soil.'

The wheat stalks nearly shoulder high swayed in acknowledgement.

They were at the point where green turns to gold and the seed heads were not yet heavy.

'Now that father Steven, he understands what it takes. And you father and of course the lord abbot,' he added hastily. 'Mind you father Steven seems to be lost for a friend outside the church now that Jacques has gone, God rest his soul.'

Jonathen's stance stiffened with the shock of revelation. 'Father Steven and Jacques, they were often together?'

'Yes. Many noted that they were close. We thought they must have much to discuss about the building. Seemed to like each other's company. Separate like if you know what I mean.'

'Thank you Pierre. Continue God's work and bless you. Bless you,' he repeated as he hurried away back to the chapter house. He was sure he knew the identity of the other spy in the camp and Guilhem must be told.

He entered the settlement through the open gate which pierced the completed heavy earth embankment along the western side and which now spanned the narrow valley. Chickens clucked and scratched; tethered goats added their nasal complaints to the continuous sound of hammering sawing and chiselling which had become the norm in the life of Gellone.

Guilhem was seated at a table with the Sacrist and the Prior Leo, formerly the priest in charge. Leo had changed under the leadership and encouragement of the abbot. He was still a big man, but now his weight carried authority. Now he could read fluently, and even write although as yet that was still a laborious and slow business. Jonathen stopped as he remembered that the monk responsible for that progress was brother Steven, who had devoted much time and patient love to help Leo's education.

'Could there be more to it than that? Was Steven recruiting another ally determined to undermine Guilhem by finding the secret and denounce him as a heretic?' He stood waiting for the abbot to acknowledge him, his mind racing as the possibilities ran their confused patterns.

Eventually the business was done and Guilhem smiled his welcome to his favourite brother. Even after all this time the smile seemed to emphasise the cruel disfigurement to the abbot's face while at the same illuminating the gentle faith that drove him.

'Come, come brother Jonathen. Sit down. You look anxious. Has something happened in the library?'

'No, no my lord abbot. All is well. The preparations are advanced to receive the Rabbi and the Imman. No it concerns you. I think I have discovered the...' Jonathen stopped in mid flow. The consequences of the accusation overshadowed his excitement. After all, what real proof did he have to condemn Steven in this way. 'That is, my lord, that is I think I may know who... but I am not sure .. yet it would seem probable that it is so . And if it is so then you should....' His voice tailed away in confusion.

'You think you know the identity of the other traitor within our settlement who is ordered to uncover my heresy.' Guilhem's voice was calm, almost unconcerned. 'Don't look so surprised my friend. Only this subject could cause so much consternation. You are going to tell me that you suspect brother Steven?' The voice raised slightly to allow the possibility of error, but certainty was the major note.

Jonathen sat down with a thump of surprise. 'But if you know why have you allowed him to stay?'

'Firstly I don't know, my friend. I strongly suspect. Secondly it is easier to keep an eye on the one you know. If Bishop Aniane lives long enough he will send another to replace Jacques and surely he will contact Steven.' Guilhem heaved a sigh. 'I am getting tired Jonathen. All my life I have served the Emperor well and with him the interests of the church. Still they will not leave me alone. All because of an accident of birth.'

'But my lord you have never given them that that they seek.' His tone was gentle and concerned. This was a man who he had regarded for most of his life as an exemplar. It pained brother Jonathen to see this good man in such distress.

'If you had seen what I have seen you would know that there is no certainty in it. But yes, even so there is something within me that will not let this thing go. Even if I have no belief in it yet I must p..p..preserve the story for other generations. Besides this Jonathen, there are other tendrils of this vine. When I am gone the mystery will remain. Do you not think that it is God himself who is guiding me in this way? Every day I pray for a sign as to whether I am right or wrong.

But enough of my troubles. We must do what we must. Are the rooms prepared for our visitors? I am so looking forward to seeing what may come of this interchange.'

'Your troubles are our pain my lord. I will pray that you may be given peace in the name of our Lord.'

Guilhem rose and placed his hand silently on the kneeling figure in front of him. As he did so the shape of the kneeling priest in the tomb of the church of St Mary of Axum came unbidden into his mind. The moment would never leave him.

CHAPTER TWENTY THREE

773 AD
– The Kingdom At The Top Of The World –

In the fabled land of Sheba every rock was once a loaf of bread. There it had rained gold and silver and pearls for eight days and nights. Being so blessed the land blossomed with palaces and temples and riches of every sort. The land was fertile so hunger was banished. At the centre of this blessed land was the city of Axum and it was to this city that Adelchis was now leading Count Guilhem d'Autun, Nihal and the remainder of the caravan that accompanied them from the oasis.

The Lord God had protected this land from the merely curious and those who would come to take its wealth by raising it to the sky where it lay nearer to heaven.

The caravan had been climbing for more than three days. Vertiginous rock faces funnelled the searing heat into the narrow gorges making the reds and purples and greys of the basalt and tufa rocks waver in the heat. The track was seldom wider than two camels and more often riders were forced to dismount to lead the laden beasts along narrow ledges which hung on the rock face daring the intruders to violate the sacred land.

On occasion a rushing river alongside the path would hurl itself out of the barren rock, shades of emerald and foaming silver pearls. This signalled a time for a pause to water the animals and to bask in the sudden cool of the mist.

Once or twice a guide would stop and point upwards. There would seem to be nothing but rock cutting its jagged shapes to the sky, but with signs and encouragement to look harder an oryx with its graceful curved horns could be seen motionless, part of the rock face.

When it was possible Adelchis, Nihal and Guilhem spent time together. Adelchis tried to educate them in the ways of his strange homeland. It was important that they did not upset the king and the court, but equally important that the church hierarchy believed that their mission was blessed by God and that Guilhem was indeed the one who carried the true blood.

'As you will see God is close to us as we are closer to Him, The blessed Mary chose this land to found her church. We feel we are the protectors of the true faith.' He pointed to the dizzying ranks of jagged rocks whose steeples pierced the narrow sky.

'And we are hewn from the mountains. Isolation has made us wary. Rome finds us difficult to reach. Even the followers of Mohammed have dashed themselves upon our iron lances in vain. Our men are either soldiers or priests and monks. We do not feel that we need the teachings of others. I am not representative of my people, my friends, I am weakened by the soft sea airs and the excesses of the lowland rulers.' He smiled and rubbed his withered arm, but it was not clear that he was joking.

Although it was difficult to be alone sometimes Guilhem would sign to Nihal and they would fall some way behind. In between the history lessons from Adelchis; the exigencies of the route; and the need not to slow the progress of the caravan they exchanged the stories of their lives.

On one occasion Nihal seized Guilhem's reins and led them to a secluded curve on the river bank. They sat on rock cooling their feet in the rushing stream. A flash of black and white hurtled across the bubbling torrent. Suddenly the pied kingfisher was flicking its tail for balance on a boulder just out of reach. It looked at them with one jet eye; cocked its head at the rushing water and was gone, emerging in instant triumph, the tail of a small silver fish protruding from the outsize beak.

Nihal clapped her hands in delight. She took Guilhem's hand. 'So was I such an easy catch as that my prince?'

Then an instant mood change as she continued her story.

'When I refused the third suitor that my father had brought to me, he became desperate and said I was bringing shame on his household. This happened just before they brought the dirty wounded infidel into my care.' Her eyes shone with mischief. Guilhem refused to rise to the bait. Their night together had not loosened the bonds between them, but he had already learned not always to respond to the teasing challenges. In fact the enforced abstinence of the trek stoked the fire of their love.

'I know Guilhem. I know what you need to know.' She leaned closer to him till their thighs touched. 'You want to know if I have known a man before you. You cannot understand how a virgin could have behaved as I did.' Her eyes looked sideways at him. Even for a woman who had been given independence from the norm and who had learned the secrets of a courtesan ambassador to be used in the service of her people, this was difficult.

'When my father understood that I would not lead the life of a married woman he sought permission from the caliph that I be trained to be of service to my people. I was trained in many things including how to give pleasure; how to read speech from a distance; how to read in six different scripts; how to pretend and how to lie with conviction and many many other....... I can never marry Guilhem, not even an infidel.' She put her fingers to her lips and then laid them gently over his mouth. 'You were the first to benefit from my training, and my feelings for you are not false, but one day I will have to leave you and we will have to live our lives as our princes order us.'

The river flowed on ignoring the choking feeling of his distress. Surely there must be another way. They were bound by love but constrained by circumstance and custom. In a way they knew each other because of his heritage but even that would not allow them to be together. This ancient story was ruling their lives; and yet it was because of the golden bee that he had taken her into his arms and tasted her sweetness.

'I know I do not understand everything you are saying Nihal, but we are here in this wild country. Who can stop us m..m..marrying here so far away from our other lives?'

'So you would leave your king to live in the desert with this wild woman? Think Guilhem. It cannot be.'

At that moment in the deep gorge in the mountain wilderness that surrounded them Guilhem knew that this treasure that had been given would also be taken.

The next day Adelchis told them that the climb through the mountains of Adwa would finish that morning and that they would be met by the king's guard and escorted to their quarters in Axum.

'It would be politic to put on a show my friends. Remember Guilhem you are here with letters from the great King Charles, and you madame I suspect may have some message from the Caliph of Spain?'

This was said with the knowing tone of the career diplomat.

'Even you Adelchis whose web may reach from the place of the rising sun to the western edge of the world will have to be content with 'suspect'.' Nihal spoke with straightened back. Adelchis acknowledged the rebuke with a minimal bow and left them.

So it was that as they topped the last rise and rode into the rolling plain of the land of Sheba Guilhem was attired in full armour. The morning sun glinted from the polished helmet and the finely made chain mail hauberk moulded his shoulders like cloth.

Nihal in a durra'a tunic in turquoise silk beaded with pearls and pleated wide fitting pants, was fully veiled with shear white cotton. Modestly impenetrable from a distance; close up the dark eyes, the full lipped mouth, and challenging nose were clearly visible. She was both a conundrum and a presence to be reckoned with.

Adelchis kept his satisfaction to himself. His charges would make the right initial impression. He noted the rank of official sent to greet them. The chamberlain to the king led some hundred warriors all in perfect white bishts. They were mounted on a hundred pitch-black horses. A hundred lances flashed and flickered the sunlight back to the travellers. A hundred banners fluttered from the lances, each with the royal crest. The central saturnine figure whose black kufiya was threaded with blue and gold, separated from the phalanx and rode to meet them. Guilhem, glancing back at Nihal for encouragement, nudged his brown Arab forward which neighed in protest and skittered sideways.

The chamberlain, dark cadaverous face with high cheek bones, waited impassively till Guilhem brought the stallion under control.

'King Abuna Yemata Selassie bids you welcome and what is his is yours also save that belonging to the Lord God.' Suddenly his eyes stilled. His speech faltered. Staring at Guilhem he swung off his horse and standing on the dusty track he yielded precedence and bowed low. A surprised murmur followed from his troop.

'Dismount. Lay your hands on him and raise him. Kiss him on both cheeks. You may speak Latin.' The low tone came from Adelchis who appeared at his side without a sound.

Guilhem did as he was told and the king's chamberlain His Excellence Habtu Gabre was soon all smiles which revealed black gaps in his teeth which added to the impression of being welcomed by a talking skull.

He noticed however that that the phalanx of white robed officials and soldiers folded them into their midst in such a way that it was not entirely clear whether they were guests or prisoners.

CHAPTER TWENTY FIVE

773 AD
– Before the Storm –

Time stood still on the roof the world. And the rising and setting of the sun did not stir the great king Abuna Yemata Selassie into response. No doubt this was the effect of the nearness to God, but Guilhem wondered if his own Seignieur King Charles would understand. The days passed.

'It was the bee on your helmet that caused such consternation. A part of our church regards the bee as a sacred symbol. There is a story that in time a leader will come to lay his claim before God. This leader will carry the sign of the bee and will earn the right to see the sacred texts.'

Adelchis had hoped that this would speed the permission of the bishop and the abbot but the days turned to weeks and there was no sign that the permission to see the sacred texts would be forthcoming.

One day he took Guilhem aside making it clear that he wanted time alone with him. 'I think my friend that the time will soon come when you will be permitted to seek that which your heritage allows. I have decided that you should know our interest in your quest. In short the beliefs that are carried by our church are not all the same that the Romans try to enforce. It is possible that your discoveries may help us to break the Roman yolk. Yet our own elders would not let us open the secret place unless in the presence of the one foretold who bears the blood.'

'But how can it be that a soldier from Francia can hold the key to the beliefs of your people here in the remote mountains of Africa?' Guilhem was bewildered and angry. So much expectation and so little understanding on his part. Could such confusion be part of God's plan for him?

'To that my friend I have no answer but I have followed your progress over the years in the hope that your finds may help my nation, and maybe bring all men closer to truth.'

Guilhem found the waiting particularly hard. He was not a man given to contemplation. He was happiest when circumstances required action. And now he had been given many hours when he was forced to confront his life and his reasons for being in this remote outpost of the known world. This thread that tied his existence here on earth to the roll call of the names his grandmother had made him learn all those years ago seemed to have a power at odds with his penchant for current action. Was he actually here because of the lure of unspecified power that his mysterious heritage constantly hinted should be his by right?

Then there was Nihal. How could she be part of God's plan for him? Yet she too was here because of his supposed connections to the house of David. In this her people also saw an opportunity to change the course of history. Their love was an accident and she would not allow it to change their fate. The thoughts whirled round his head like a swarm of bees. He needed something to happen to simplify life.

Axum was a city in constant ebb and flow. On most days a haze of dust on the horizons in any direction would herald the entrance of yet another camel train. Saffron, salt, silk, mustard, pepper, raw cotton, tusks of elephant, leather cured and uncured, wheat, sorghum, pots, beads, jewels, armour, and slaves criss-crossed the wide unpaved streets. Out of the dust came a never ending hubub of goats bleating, camels roaring protests, the cries of vendors, the beat of drums and the clang of blacksmiths hammering, straightening and bending armour, swords, spears and horseshoes. Overlaying this bewildering frenzy of moneymaking and infusing the haze were the smells of cardamom, hemp, betelnut, pepper and dung.

At the centre of this extraordinary never-ending market sat the king and his palace officials quietly collecting taxes on the movement of goods. This had resulted in great houses and palaces being built just off the main thoroughfares. Behind walls of mud brick and guarded gates the air cleared, the sounds drifted into the background and the music of fountains in great formal gardens transported the visitor to another world.

It was in such a residence that Guilhem and Nihal had been housed. Each had been allocated a wing of a large mansion on a road on the northern outskirts of the city.

Their favourite place was a tiny courtyard that led from Nihal's quarters. The stonework that surrounded it was rough and coarse compared with fine marbles of Cordoba. But the stones had toned their colours to the warmth of the sun, and a small erratic fountain gurgled and bubbled in a corner. Here the sounds of the world could not reach them and they seized hours greedily wrapping their bodies round each other till a sheen of sweat would cover them and they would roll apart exhausted but not sated.

At other times they would lie silent just staring into each other's eyes hands exchanging fingers and hearts full. He would trace the outline of her nose, just too big for perfection and breathe the hint of jasmine that came and went like a shadow. But even in times of laughter, nearly always initiated by Nihal, there was the shadow of impending fateful separation which added intensity to every moment.

'No not today. Are you happy that there will be no heir this time?' Her time had come when she declined sex averting her eyes and her characteristic way of pressing her fingers to her own lips before using the hand to create a barrier.

'I...' He checked, startled by the mixed emotions that coursed through him.

'Would you stay? Even if we could not marry. If you would stay with me then I would be happy that you were with child.'

'Guilhem, I can never stay. But there is no child. But I have thought about the possibility. If that were to be the only part of you I can take with me, it would be your most precious gift.'

He folded her close, unable to speak. He knew at least part of the sacrifice that Nihal was proposing.

At this time she was even happier to be desired and to see that Guilhem was not like so many men who could find no use for women when sex was not allowed. In fact he became even more possessive and tender when she declined his advances. This just increased her love for him which she showed by finding ever more outlandish ways to make him laugh.

It seemed as though time stood still when they were cocooned in the little courtyard, but the life outside did insistently intrude. There were trade arrangements to make; arms for spices; wine for slaves; pots for cotton and silk. The death's head figure of the chamberlain became a frequent visitor along with merchants and other government officials. Habtu Gabre was a tall lean figure with a ready smile that clashed with the gap toothed mouth and skull like appearance. He was a man of considerable education and could write in Amharic, Latin, Ge'ez, Jewish and even Amaraic. He spoke these and other languages and was an invaluable guide to both Nihal and Guilhem.

'Today we will hunt for lion,' Habtu announced after they had been in Axum for about six weeks. 'Today we will go for two, maybe three days and the king will come with us!'

'The king, but we have not yet been g..g..granted an audience with his majesty,' said Guilhem.

'It has been... difficult to arrange Count Guilhem. There have been many discussions about your request. The church has had reservations about your presence here. I should say that the king will take a special interest in you during this time.' He turned to Nihal, 'I am afraid the lady will not be allowed to accompany us.'

'It must be as his majesty wishes. Please tell him that I am disappointed not to be granted the favour of his acquaintance.' Her anger was concealed beneath the formal response but Habtu was clearly aware of it.

'If things go well on the hunt you will be invited to attend his majesty and to meet the queen and his children.' Nihal's stance softened somewhat although it was clear that her audience was dependent on Guilhem making the right impression.

The hunting party left at dawn the next day. They were to rendezvous with the king and his entourage later in the day. As they trotted out past the baths of the queen of Sheba in that early time when the end of night is marked by the absence of light, they passed a group of horsemen trotting purposefully into the city.

'Their errand must be urgent.' Guilhem commented to Habtu as they passed in the gloom.

'God guide their steps,' replied Habtu and smiled so that the white and black of his teeth showed in the gloom.

Guilhem gave the chance encounter no further thought. The dawn at this hour was more the lack of night and it was cold. The absence of shape around them echoed the feeling in Guilhem's heart. He realised that if this was the start of a procedure that would lead him to the sacred tomb, it was also a signal that his time with Nihal would be coming to an end. Once again his life was being driven by forces that he did not understand. There was still time to ride away but this would not bring him a life with his love, and furthermore deep inside he knew that he could not turn away from his destiny.

A hibiscus red strip to the east lay improbably under a layer of black and the sky overhead started to fade the stars into morning. The day of the hunt had begun.

Acacias spread their feathery tops in the growing light. Eucalyptus trees peeled and wept for more water. The grass was tall, scratchy and pale brown. The plain stretched into the morning light broken by the purple of a mountain range. As the light grew, another range of higher mountains appeared. It was an endless folded land cut deep by vertiginous gorges at the bottom of which streams and rivers rushed or meandered. Sometimes sandstone yellow rock charged out of the ground and twisted itself into buttresses and spires and rock chimneys laced with grey and red. Thorn scrub bordered the path in dense patches. A hooded vulture with its fleshy red dewlapped neck and vivid white patches scrolled lazily in circles above them. Nearer there was the 'chatter' of the bulbul bird its red throat working at its song.

In the middle distance a troop of baboons rose out of the scrub and lolloped away to safety. Everything was strange to Guilhem's eye and he realised that in this isolated corner of the world truth might be rooted in a different landscape of the mind.

Suddenly the terrain changed and they rode down a twisting path to a much lusher landscape fed by two or three streams. Tall acacias shaded the valley. Thorn gave way to dense leaf and vines climbed the ironwood trees. In the middle of a clearing stood a large tent, around which preparations for the hunt were being made. In front of the tent stood a large man in wide fitting brown pants with a broad leather belt. Attached to the belt were three curved hunting knives. A loose heavy silk shirt of a darker shade covered most of the heavy torso. A gold chain hung round his neck and a thin circlet of gold topped the craggy bearded face of King Abuna Yemata Selassie. And by his side was Adelchis.

'Your majesty.' Guilhem knelt in front of the imposing figure.

'Rise up. Rise up! I am happy to greet the emissary of the great king Charles of whom I have heard much.' He leaned forward and assisted Guilhem to his feet. He stared down into Guilhem's eyes.

'This great king; is he as tall as me?' He gestured with his hand indicating height from the ground.

Guilhem paused as if trying to remember the height of his friend and lord.

'No, your majesty, I think you are the greater by a hands width.' The lie flowed smoothly as he placed his hand under the outstretched palm of the negus Selassie.

A slight pause, then a loud bellow of laughter. The king spoke to his courtiers in their language and they all laughed and clapped. Then he turned back to Guilhem. 'It is well that the negus of Ethiopia cannot be overshadowed by such a king no matter how great.'

Adelchis dipped his head in acknowledgement of a game well played, and rubbed his withered arm reflectively.

'Come eat. Tella to drink!' The barley brewed beer was light and cool. A bowl of meat stew with pieces of injera bread was placed in front of him.

'Eat. You will need your strength today. It is antelope meat and very good,' the urbane voice of Adelchis murmured in his ear.

The negus sat on a log and patted the ground beside him for Guilhem. Status was important for this negus who lived so close to God. They exchanged pleasantries while the negus took measure of the young stranger. Then his attention was diverted by a huntsman.

'Where have you been?' Asked Guilhem looking back and up at Adelchis who was still standing.

'Arranging,' came the cryptic reply, 'if you gain the approval of the negus, especially if you kill a lion, things will move swiftly. Don't drink too much of that beer. You will need a cool head!'

'You have never hunted the great beast before?' The negus asked.

'Never, Sire.' Abuna Yemata Selassie looked at him from foot to head and back. 'You have speed and quickness of eye. You have endurance but you do not have great strength. If you have courage and God is kind you will triumph. If not....'

Soon after this exchange the king disappeared into the tent and re-emerged in a simple brown cotton robe with the same hunting belt and the three daggers. The crown had gone. He carried two spears, of different lengths, one that reached to his shoulders and a throwing spear. A slave gave Guilhem two spears of similar lengths.

A group of black slaves led by a very young warrior set off ahead of them and quickly disappeared into the bush.

'Lion have been seen not too far off. The slaves will beat the bush. The lion will run towards us. If there is a female we will let her live. When the male attacks you will kill him and we will have a great feast.' The great king of Ethiopia grinned and clapped Guilhem across the shoulders.

'Don't worry my friend. When we reach the place where we must wait I will show you how it is done. There will be only the two of us and we have to be like brothers and act together.'

For the first time Guilhem was apprehensive. He had thought there would be a group of hunters who would make sure that the great negus would not come to harm and that to some extent he would be protected as well. Now it seemed that this whole expedition was more of a rite of passage that would in some way prove his fitness to see the hidden treasures. Once again he was being led by the circumstances of birth to a fate over which he had no control.

The bush and trees gave way to open grassland whch rolled away to the purple mountains that always bound the vistas in the land so near to God. Occasional great twisted tree trunks of enormous girth towered out of tall grass like ruined castles. Their improbable canopies spread like roots to the sky.

'You have not seen these great trees before, my friend.' The negus stopped and followed Guilhem's gaze to the nearest of the huge trunks. 'These trees are called baobab and are very valuable to the animals and to the people who live in the forest. They provide food from their leaves. We mix the powdered leaves with sorghum porridge. It is very good for strength and well being. Colour dye is also made and the fibre can make ropes. Look at the birds in the top. Many nest there. And inside the trunk it carries water all the year round. This is truly a tree of life.'

'Your land is full of wonders Sire. To our eye everything is strange.

There is much to learn, but we know little of your country. Yet you are close to our Lord Jesus and we share much in our beliefs. It is.....'

'We are protected by our mountains. Now there is also the barrier of Islam which makes it difficult to travel. I believe it is God's will that we are left alone so that we may preserve the true word.' The negus stopped in mid-sentence and pointed to a distant rise in the grasslands. Three specks in the blue sky lazily circled. 'There! We are in luck Count Guilhem. I think those vultures are circling a kill made by our prey. There are lions there. Come we must go before they move on. We do not know how old the kill is, but the vultures are low.'

The muscular figure strode ahead through the tall grass. Guilhem followed and behind him came a group of court officials and bearers. The afternoon sun sucked energy from the air as they strode across the plain passing the occasional baobab which released flocks of green lovebirds and black headed siskins. In the grass rail birds with russet breasts scuttled out from under their feet.

Eventually the striding figure paused, glanced behind to ensure the presence of Guilhem, took a long draught from the leather water pouch he carried and motioned Guilhen to follow his example.

The circling vultures were much closer now and the sun was half way to its western horizon.

'We must wait down wind of their resting place. I will search for a game trail then we will wait in the shelter of rocks or trees. Keep careful watch. You will have little time. The king of beasts is large and fast but he blends with his background. It is easy to miss his attack before it is too late. When he charges try to make him turn. Then use the throwing spear. Unless you are very accurate it will not kill the great beast. He will attack again. When he leaps upon you his belly is exposed. Your second spear, like this...' he crouched, planting the spear in the ground, then thrusting up at the imagined leaping beast. 'After that...' Selassie shrugged. 'You will need your sword or dagger,' He gripped the handle in his belt. 'Lastly remember his paws are as dangerous as his teeth.' He turned his back and slipped off the cotton tunic. Great welts of scarred flesh ran diagonally down his back.

'Now, here is a good place. We must be silent. If I am right he should come from that direction,' he pointed to a vestigal gap in the waving grass. 'You will have the first strike. If you miss I will try to attack him and protect you.' The great king took Guilhem's arm and gripped his elbow. Guilhem returned the clasp as they looked at each other.

'You have fear. That is good!' The king smiled.

They settled down by the faint bush trail. The sun cast its shadows. The great white backed vultures cruised unconcernedly in gentle circles, their wings stiff against the wind, awaiting their turn. Time passed and the tension eased from Guilhem's muscles. Then a coughing grunt came from the tall grass. Selassie gripped Guilhem's arm and pointed. Guilhem stared at the gently waving grass. He could see nothing until he realised that he was staring straight into the eye of the king of beasts. Immediately the shape of its face grew out of the dun coloured grass until it was impossible to see anything else. Selassie pinched his arm hard; he knew the paralysing effect of proximity to such an animal.

The great beast slowly emerged from the cover of the tall grass. Keeping low to the ground the maned head looked cautiously round the clearing. Muscles rippled under the shoulders. The tail whisked slowly from side to side. Somehow Guilhem knew that he would be the next meal. He looked round at Selassie. There was no-one there!

A loud roar filled the space and the lion launched his attack. 'Make him turn if you can' Guilhem remembered and galvanized into action he sprang out of his crouch and screamed. Even as he did so he thought how feeble a sound it was, but the great beast was unused to confrontation and stopped in a cloud of dust about ten paces away. It crouched and started to circle to its left. Its flank was exposed. Guilhem hurled the throwing spear and it buried itself deep in the powerful shoulder. Too far back for a kill. Another roar; the lion tried to bite the spear and then turned back to Guilhem and hardly pausing sprang straight at him. His leap was weakened by the first spear and barely cleared the rolling figure of the young man from Francia, as the long spear found its mark in the heaving chest. The king of beasts subsided onto the shaft driving it deeper. Another choking roar but quieter; he scrabbled at the dry earth. Guilhem drew his sword and waited. The king of beasts struggled to get his feet but his strength had gone. He rolled onto his side; the great head raised a last time as death took hold and his eyes lost light. Guilhem, his thighs shaking, wanted to wet himself.

CHAPTER TWENTY SIX

773 AD
– The Discovery –

They came for him in the early hours of the night. It was raining. A steady emptying of the invisible night sky that promised no relief. He had left the warm breath of Nihal's skin and the familiar hint of jasmine for this unrelenting world of water, cold and discomfort.

Five horsemen plodded through the unrelenting rain each sheltered by long leather coats greased against the water. The group consisted of constable Guilhem, son of the Count D'Autun, Adelchis ambassador to the world and puller of strings, and Habtu Gabre chamberlain and right hand man to the negus of Ethiopia, plus two armed nobles who escorted them in the downpour. Guilhem was soon immersed in his own thoughts hunching his shoulders against the elements.

When he had returned from the lion hunt something had subtly changed between him and Nihal. There was a tenderness mixed with the passion that drew their bodies together. She would hold his face close to hers as though drawing every line in through her dark eyes in case he vanished before her. Always a woman of mood now she swung more unpredictably between passion and tenderness. Sometimes she would be almost detached; asking him when he was going to see the hidden scrolls as though that had become the most important thing between them. At other times she would put her hands to his lips as he was about tell of important trade agreements, or gossip from the court. Then standing close so his mind swam in her scent she would lead his hand beneath her robe to find her sex warm and ready.

His mind leapt to the extraordinary meeting with the Patriarch of the Coptic church. Abba Wolde – Mikhael who sat with quiet certainty of his place in the world – a corporal solidity at odds with the spirituality of his position. A simple brown cotton robe denoted his priestly calling but was devoid of rank save for the large embossed silver cross that hung from his neck. Guilhem had knelt and the Patriarch laid his hands gently on his head, pausing for longer than usual. Then making the sign of the cross he indicated a place on the bench beside him.

'Count Guilhem d'Autun, why are you here?' The voice was low but very clear.

Guilhem looked for the first time into the eyes of the man who could decide the fate of his quest. With a shock he realised they were blue and the ruddy countenance seemed shockingly foreign in the land of dark skins and aquiline features.

'Because I am drawn here my lord.'

'You want to change the world?' A slight inflection turned the statement to a question.

'I want to serve God in the path he has chosen for me and to serve my king as he has entrusted me.'

'And if they are not the same.....'

Guilhem paused. He realised that this was the question that had not faced him as he had travelled across the world to this strange outpost on the edge of the unknown Africas.

'And if they are not the same I will pray for guidance, and seek advice from those around me. If the path is clear I will follow it.'

The blue eyes flickered. 'The path that God sets for you may not be easy my son. Yet you are said to be of the House of David. Tell me how the line falls to you after our Lord Jesus.'

A picture of the old dowager queen Nantilda came between Guilhem and the calm enquiring face of the head of the church. This was the test for which he had been prepared since childhood.

'Jesus the Christ, Joseph the Rama, Josue, Aminabad, Castellors, Manael, Titurel, Boaz Anfortas, Frotmund, Faramund, Clodion, Meroveus...' He paused and the names rolled out of the mysteries of history and faded into the high ceilings.

The Patriarch held up his hand. 'You have been well schooled my son. There are very few who can recite the roll. You bear yourself well. But you do not realise what convulsions may be released across the world as a result of what you may find. Legend has it that scrolls were brought by Mark to Alexandria soon after the time of our Lord. From there they were brought to Axum when Islam spread its tentacles into Egypt nearly two hundred years ago. The abbot of Salama was made to swear that they would be hidden untouched till a scion of the house of

David should come bearing a key and knowledge of his heritage. No one has seen them since.'

Guilhem looked directly at the round face with the blue eyes which looked at him with a mixture of resignation and apprehension.

'You can refuse permission my lord patriarch.'

'I am bound by ties as intangible as the thread that led you here. If you have the key that fits, our Lord means that the world should see what has lain hidden for so many years. I pray that it may be to the benefit of mankind and not run counter to the teachings of our church.' The tone of voice betrayed some further meaning which Guilhem could not interpret.

'And I, that I may be strong enough to bear what burden may be given to me to bear my lord Patriarch.'

The Patriarch rose slowly as though carrying a great weight.

'Go with strength and the blessing of God and return in peace my son. I think the Lord has chosen his vessel well.'

Guilhem knelt and Abba Wolde-Mikhael made the sign of the cross over him. With no further word he turned and slowly left the room. The blessing left Guilhem feeling even more uneasy.

The burden that had been with him since the meeting with his grandmother queen Nantilda bore down on the young soldier from Septimania. It was bigger now. Much bigger.

The rain poured unceasingly on the silent group as they rode in the black dawn.

CHAPTER TWENTY SEVEN

807 AD
– The Church Eternal –

It was as though the heavens had decided to wash the world clean of all sin. The large party had been in the saddle since daybreak, although to tell the truth daybreak was only a supposition in the gloom. The rain reminded Guilhem of that journey at the top of the world thirty-four years ago. Now the abbot of Gellone was on his way to pay his respects at the funeral of his bishop and he still carried the burden with him.

Witiza later Benoit Bishop of Aniane had finally given his restless soul to God. Guilhem had found it difficult to grieve for his old childhood friend. In fact the first reaction had been one of relief and a lightening of the load that Benoit's persistent harassment would be finally over.

'Remember my lord, it is the church that searches out heresy not just one man.' It had been Jonathen who spoke

'It is so brother Jonathen, yet bishop Benoit was the one who was convinced that I carried a secret that could harm the church. Surely now he is gone they will have more important recusants to chase.'

As they plodded steadily onward the sky began to lighten and the rain eased doubtfully into an intermittent mist. Eventually the sun worked its daily magic and sucked the cloud away into a blue sky. His spirits lifted with the cloud. The balance of right and wrong seemd to tilt decisively in his favour, even if Jonathen was right and the church continued to harass him.

'I have never been to Maguelone.' Jonathen appeared coinciding with the thought of him, pulling his grey up beside Guilhem. 'I hear it is a great church and a fitting place for the bishop to be laid to rest.'

'It is so and it is also his home. The Count of Maguelone was his father. I hear that Charles has sent emissaries from Aachen, and Rome too has sent men of the church.'

'Do you not fear further attempts to prize your secret from you, or to silence you forever?' Jonathen had lowered his voice as far as he was able. His excitable nature was not always coincidental with quiet discretion. He looked anxiously at the man he held so dear, running his spare hand through the grey hair that had been subdued by the rain.

'I am what I am. I cannot change course now Jonathen. We have almost completed the vision that we both had all those years ago. I am sure that Gellone will flourish under your guidance should something happen to me. Now we must prepare our thoughts for the day ahead and pray for the soul of the bishop.'

It was obvious that no more would be said so Jonathen fell back and left Guilhem to his thoughts.

The gently rolling plain stretched out ahead as they left the escarpment of the Cevennes behind and headed towards the small settlement of Montpellier.

Two days later the party rode through the vines and along the edge of a marsh that bordered the sea. The church could be seen well before the coast. It stood massively brooding in the sun as though trying to prepare the mourners for the grim reality of death. Inside, the nave was full of spectral figures in brown and black robes relieved by the weak light filtering down from the high windows, reflecting a sea of tonsured scalps.

The archbishop of Septimania stood at the lectern to read the epistle;

'For our struggle is not against enemies of blood and flesh, but against the rulers, against the authorities, against the cosmic powers of this present darkness, against the spiritual forces of evil in the heavenly places. Therefore take up the whole armour of God.......'

The power of Saint Paul was present with them in the dark confines of the church. Guilhem reflected that his old friend had indeed become consumed by the battle against the imagined forces of evil. Perhaps he had lost sight of the messages of love and redemption that the Christ had also brought to the world.

The abbot of Gellone shifted to ease the pain in his hip and his hand flicked his damaged face as he realised that his Christian duty called him to pray for the soul of his old friend, rather than to muse on his weaknesses.

'O God, you are my God, I seek you,
My soul thirsts for you
My flesh faints for you,
As in a dry and weary land where there is no water.'

The chant was taken up by the whole assembly; the words as familiar as the breath in their hearts. God would surely find a place in heaven for such a man.

It was then that Guilhem noticed the group of churchmen congregated at the far end of the nave near the altar. They were distinguished by the trimmings of rich fur on their robes and the weight of the chains of office they carried. The delegation from Rome had come, as promised, to bid farewell to the bishop of Aniane.

As the congregation oozed out of the west door one of the group detached himself and took Guilhem by the arm.

'The archbishop Clement would like to commend you on your efforts at Gellone and especially on your work to foster learning and understanding of the faiths of all the nations.'

'Please tell his Lordship that I am flattered that my work has come to the notice of Rome.'

'He would like to learn more. Maybe there should be such a school in Rome. You could attend him after vespers in the chapter house?' A slight inflection made it a question yet it was not a request.

Guilhem suddenly felt uneasy. From what he knew of Rome there were many doubters about the path he was taking with its ecumenical bias. He nodded and dipped his head in acknowledgement. The back of his hand brushed his disfigured face as he turned away. His eyes scanned the milling crowd looking for the light grey halo that would identify Jonathen. There! He spotted the flailing arm that signalled an impassioned discussion. Mind you with Jonathen there was seldom any other kind.

'We should pay our respects to Bishop Benoit,' and firmly grasping Jonathen's arm he steered him to the far side of the church. Benoit lay in state fully clad in his robes of office. The heavy stone sides of the sarcophagus seemed to constrict the figure. The severe hollow cheeked face slept in death in the space carved like a halo for the head, but there was no peace in the expression.

'You were right. The fall was good.'

The unexpected apology sounded across the years and Guilhem saw the youth, straight backed in the conciousness of conscience satisfied, disappear into the darkened arch of the church of Saint Felix in Narbonne. So much had been lost between the mentor of his youth and the persecutor of his old age.

The grizzled figure of the old campaigner stood companionably beside the thin ascetic priest who topped him by a hand's width, each lost in his own thoughts in the presence of death.

'The delegation from Rome want to see me later. They say it is to talk about our work at Gellone. But I feel that our friend here may be pursuing me from his grave. If I am gone for too long send for Peter the Deacon. He is the Emperor's man here and does not take kindly to the encroaching power of Rome.'

'This is not like you my lord – to take heed of danger in such a way. There is more than a suspicion I fancy.' The tall figure looked anxiously at his friend.

'There is nothing certain my friend, just a feeling that Benoit would not let me go. And I am not ready yet to face my maker. There is still much to be done to finish the monastery and to give a firm foundation to our work of learning at the school.'

As dusk fell Guilhem faced Archbishop Clement and two other clerics across a plain table. Clement was a small man, thin lipped and a way of hesitating in mid-question.

'So you hope to further the word of God,' pause, 'by contact with those of other faiths who seek to destroy those who believe in the Lord Jesus?'

'I think the Lord our God intends that we should be able to find what is good in all men, and that we should be open to knowledge from all peoples. In discussion men of learning may bring us closer.'

'Ah! 'Court Nez,' they call you that do they not, I think there is danger in what you are undertaking. There is a risk that our own beliefs may be contaminated,' hesitation, 'by the false trails left by those who do not believe in the one true God?'

'Surely my lord archbishop God would help the seekers after truth to c..c..come to the right decisions in his name.' Guilhem's stammer was a little more pronounced than usual. 'After all is it not true that the beliefs of Judaea, of Islam, and of the f..f..followers of Christ all stem from Abraham?'

'But we are but men and can easily be led astray.... would you not agree?' The voice was more gentle than ever; the lips in a tighter line.

'My lord I have learned in my life that there are good men of all faiths who hold to their truths as we do ours. Knowledge should not be an enemy. Surely God will help those who....' 'Could it be that you hope these 'researches' will lead to proof that you and your line hold a key to a different truth?' The question came from the bearded priest on Clement's left. It was the first time he had spoken.

Guilhem realised that his worst fears had come to pass. This was the point of the meeting. Now he was to be put to the real test.

The bearded one spoke again. 'It is true, is it not, that you have always hidden some matters from the eyes of the holy church? '

'I took the tonsure. I swore to be true to God and to the holy mother church. To the best of my ability I follow the teachings of Rome and our Lord Jesus Christ. I did all these things in the belief that God called me to do this in his name. I .....'

'Enough! All this may be so. Yet there is this thing you hide from mother church. Our beloved friend Benoit of Aniane tried for many years to get you to reveal what secret heresy you may be concealing under the pretence of service to God. This is the work of the devil indeed!'

'I have never betrayed the....'

'Keeping the secret to yourself is betrayal enough.' The bearded priest got to his feet. 'We have been patient for too long.' He turned to archbishop Clement. 'It is time to test the body in the hope that the devil may be driven out. Take him down.'

Guilhem had time only to wonder how the nameless priest seemed to have suddenly taken charge before he was seized and dragged to a large cellar. A heavy blow to the back of his head mingled the darkness of the room with a spinning falling sensation. As he lost grasp of his surroundings, he thought he heard the mocking tones of his persecutor.

'King of the Jews they call him here. Let him suffer so then!'

Pain dragged him back to consciousness. It spun hot ropes across his shoulders. It screamed panic in his straining lungs which struggled for air. And a different kind of dull ache stretched every sinew in his legs. His mind wondered through this maize of agony trying to make sense of it. Then he realised he was stretched on a cross in the shape of an 'x'! As far as he could judge he had not been nailed to the cross from which he hung in the dark, but tied to it. Attached to his feet a weight of some kind added to the pain designed to stretch his body into submission.

Guilhem felt the strand of stubborn resistance which had been integral to his life being shredded to insignificance. All that remained was existence and a longing for relief. Mists swirled as he rose and sank on the edge of consciousness. Then the memory of another misty void over which he had hung in fierce exultation pushed the pain into the background. This was a void he would embrace. The good God would claim him before the narrow wall of compromise built into his life could be battered down by pain or retraction.

'Oh God take this thy servant......'

At that moment the doors were flung open and a crowd of men carrying blazing torches rushed into the room. They came to a ragged stop as the spectacle of the crucified man revealed itself in the uncertain light.

'Take the weight from his feet. But slowly, very slowly.'

Guilhem did not recognise the voice of his rescuer but had time to wonder if he still wanted to live before he fainted.

CHAPTER TWENTY EIGHT

773 AD

– The Word of God –

The path narrowed and their guides motioned them to dismount. The horses were left behind and the path steepened and narrowed as it twisted up into the steady rain. Occasional small rocks shifted underfoot and disappeared into the mist on their left. Guilhem sensed that the void into which such stones disappeared soundlessly was one that he would prefer not to see. No one spoke. Laboured breaths and the faint skitter of stone deadened by the mist and rain were the only sounds on that desolate rock face.

The group came to an unsteady halt at a place where the path widened by two or three handwidths. Set in the rock wall was a stout wooden stake about one and a half times the height of a man. The leader took the stake and looking up into a bulging overhang, he pushed hard with an upward motion. It thudded with a hollow sound onto a wood trap door set above them. Three times it sounded. They waited. The rain eased slightly and a wind tugged fitfully at the sodden men, bundling the mists into ragged shapes that teased the eye with glimpses of cliff face and vertiginous falls of red, ochre and grey before closing the vista again.

Guilhem saw a rough hewn ladder directly in front of them attached to the rock face, but the trap door was to the right, out over the swirling void. Somehow one would have to leave the comparative security of the ladder and risk a fall to invisible depths. His legs suddenly lost strength.

Then the sound of iron bolts being drawn across the trap door. A bearded face, weathered and dominated by nose and eyes peered through the gap. A slight nod as though they were expected, but no word of greeting. Two thick ropes dropped through the door; each looped as a stirrup. Such was the entry to the sacred monastery of Abba Salama.

The ladder was climbed by each man in turn. When they reached four rungs from the top the rope was swung towards them. Guilhem watched as the two warriors grabbed the swinging ropes and stepped into the stirrups in one lithe fearless movement. As each man balanced on the rope he was pulled up by a kind of winch which swung the swaying lift out over the dizzying abyss. Indeed thought Guilhem as he readied himself to grab the swaying ropes this was a place that must protect a great secret.

Was it to be that his fate and even the fate of the world could depend on the strength of his grip as he swung out over the misty void? Before stepping onto the rope stirrup he felt again for the box containing the translation of the words of St Mark, the two golden bees and the broken clay tablets that was always next to his skin. Then as he swung out, his hands white on the rough ropes a sudden exhilaration swept through his whole body. At last he would resolve the mystery that had dogged him for so long. Maybe it was his destiny to find a new truth.

Strong hands helped him up through the trap door and he was surrounded by white robed monks from the monastery. He found hmself in a small cave that protected the access to the sacred place. As he looked towards the cave entrance it suddenly brightened and he stepped out into a shaft of brilliant sunlight. The clouds were rolling away and pale washed blue sky chased the remaining gloom into the distance. Guilhem looked behind to see Adelchis emerging through the door holding both ropes together with his one good arm. For him the danger had been even greater.

'They say that the Lord protects all pilgrims of good faith.' He grinned happily at Guilhem's concerned look.

'And those not of good faith?'

Adelchis turned to one of the priests and asked; then turning back to Guilhem he translated, 'he says that they do not count and are not counted!'

They laughed together. Such belief was strong indeed.

The inaccessible plateau stretched in rolling plains around them. Wheat fields just turning from green shook their stalks clear of the heavy rains to welcome the warming sun. Fruit trees stood in orderly rows and small vegetable patches, tomatoes, beans and onions completed the picture of land well worked. Nearby low grass thatched huts stood around a large compound which was strangely devoid of activity.

A low muffled boom reverberated from the ground somewhere

under their feet. This was followed by another. It was impossible to locate the direction of the sound. As their party assembled at the entrance to the cave – as far as Guilhem could tell all had survived the test of good faith – the booming sound took on a regular beat. Two monks led the way through the compound toward a low- lying rocky outcrop. There the path took a slow descent between rough hewn walls that had been carved out of solid rock. As soon as they entered the defile the sound grew in intensity and each stroke of the drum echoed round the group as they hurried towards its source.

'The kebbero announces the beginning of the climax to the service which we will attend,' explained Adelchis as they hurried down the slope, the rock walls hemming them in as they went deeper.

'But where is the church?' Guilhem tried not to shout above the now insistent reverberations of the deep toned strokes of the hidden instrument.

Adelchis smiled and motioned with his good arm in an, 'all will be revealed' gesture.

Suddenly they came out of the narrow defile into a space in which another vertical rock wall towered into the small patch of blue above. The surface was indented but there was nevertheless a discernible layered pattern to the chisel marks in the hard tufa. As his eyes became used to the light Guilhem could see a row of windows carved high up in the rocky face. There were no joints in this man-made cliff. They turned right and walked about forty paces before they came to a right-angled corner which led to an imposing entrance. Guilhem suddenly realised that he was standing in front of a great west door to a church.

In front of the curved arch carved out of the solid rock a larger space had been forced out of the recalcitrant stone. As they looked up the rising sun just caught the squat tower that rose above the door. They were looking at a church that had been hewn blow by blow from solid rock so that it lay hidden below ground level. There lay before them a testament of the power of belief and an ability to withstand hardship that was beyond comprehension.

The boom of the kebbero drew them into the dark interior which had been hollowed out to form the nave. The early light through the high windows dimly revealed the interior showing a space a little smaller than the church of Saint Felix in Narbonne. Smoky torches flickered their smelly light all around and the close air was filled with an unfamiliar incense. The monks stood crowded against the rocky walls, while down the centre of the nave two rows of white robed priests faced each other. Each held a prayer stick and they swayed slightly to the quickening beat of the kebbero which at close quarters drove thought out and forced movement through the vibrating rock into the feet. Even Guilhem felt himself caught by the strange rhythms and his head began to swim through the thick wall of sound and the smell of foreign incense. Suddenly one of the priests broke ranks and leaped into the space between the priestly rows. Whirling and stamping his unshod feet onto the hard rock floor he seemed to float weightless down the aisle and back faster and faster as the prayer sticks joined the kebbala in a wall of sound. Then he fell prostrate in front of the senior priest who had stood motionless in front of the altar. Silence.

The congregation knelt and Guilhem recognised the incongruous white face of Abba Wolde-Mikhael the Archbishop of the Coptic church. The sign of the cross and a benediction rang out. The fallen priest was helped to his feet and the service was over.

Adelchis held Guilhem and motioned him to stay as the church emptied. In the uncertain light he could make out two black robed figures kneeling at the side of the altar. Even at a distance and in poor light Guilhem knew that they were not local priests.

Like black crows they emerged from the gloom. It was the long ungainly stride that Guilhem recognised first and then the cadaverous figure of Witiza stood before him.

'It can't be!'

'You are not seeing spirits Constable Guilhem.' The deep voice and slow enunciation bridged the years. They clasped each other's shoulders and examined each other's faces. It was Witiza's grey eyes that dipped away first.

'I must introduce my colleague from Rome, Deacon Josephus.' The shorter figure dipped his head in acknowledgement and made a praying gesture with his hands together.

'I am honoured to meet you Constable Guilhem. Witiza has spoken of you from time to time during our stay in Rome.'

'Josephus is here because he is an expert in ancient texts in many scripts.'

'But we do not.......'

'My friend ever since that day in Narbonne when you told me a little of your grandmother's secret I have made it the church's business to find out as much as possible. It has been very difficult. Those who would lead you away from Rome are adept at false trails and evidence is hard to find.'

Guilhem interrupted. 'But even I have no idea what we may find, or even if I will be allowed to see whatever is meant to be here. Whatever it is surely cannot be of such importance to Rome as to send you here just for this!'

'On the contrary Guilhem we think you may be an unwitting innocent in causing untold harm to the mother church just at the time when we are making headway in establishing one path to God through the church of Saint Peter in Rome.' The deep sonorous voice accompanied the sweeping gesture that included the church in which they stood. 'You have seen here the danger of which we speak,' the deep voice lowered, 'what we have just witnessed does not follow the path we have set for all those who follow Christ.' Witiza's eyes blazed with disgust.

'The archbishop has refused us entry to the crypt wherein lies the Tabot which may contain the treasure you seek.' The thin voice was that of Josephus, dry and precise and full of disapproval.

'Witiza you must believe me. I wish no harm to the church. His majesty Charles supports your efforts to have one true church and I am his servant.'

'It is innocents such as you my friend who can turn the world upside down. I have to tell you Guilhem that we cannot allow that to happen.'

Guilhem searched his face for the boy who had guided his hand to form his first letters; who had wrestled on the warm sands and who had been his protector. But the boy had turned into this implacable man whose heart now faced in a different direction.

'We hope that you will persuade the Archbishop to let us see the evidence, if such there is, so that the church may be able to give an opinion as to both content and truthfulness.'

'Ah! Truth there is a word to conjure with, my friends. Guilhem, the Archbishop would like you to wait on him in the sacristy. No, no don't worry with introductions. I have met your friends from Rome at the king's palace.' They were the urbane tones of Adelchis springing from over his left shoulder. As ever in place to influence events.

Archbishop Abba Wolde-Mikhael sat in a carved ironwood chair, his robes of brown and white unobtrusive; the silver cross about his neck. He held another tall cross of wood with a gold inlaid design depicting a delicate vine climbing the long arm of the cross. Guilhem was immediately reminded of the scroll the old dowager queen had shown him all those years ago. He knelt; the Archbishop placed a solid hand on his head. A comforting warmth spread through his body as though the hand possessed some strange power of reassurance.

'Rise my son. Before we go to the Tabot to see what the good Lord may have to reveal to you, and indeed all of us, there are things I want you to know. As you can tell I am not a native of this country. Many years ago I was sent by Pope Zachery to be a bridge between Rome and this far off place. I was drawn by the fierceness and purity of the faith I found here. There may be errors of doctrine of which the Holy Father may not approve but I believe that there are compensating strengths in this land which should be left to flourish. I wanted you to see the service and to meet some of holy people so that you may have some understanding of our people before we visit the holy place.

Rome wants to mould us as one. The priest Witiza and the Deacon Josephus are here to make sure that any new knowledge that may be revealed cannot be used to weaken the temporal or spiritual power located in that far off place. But even mother Church may make errors, at least so I think. From what I have seen and learned from our friends here you may well be the one sent by the good Lord to reveal his wishes and you should know that there are different hopes and fears that will accompany you to the Tabot.'

There was something about this speech that made Guilhem feel uneasy yet again.

He looked at the men standing in the small room. The chamberlain Habre Gelassie with his skull like features; Adelchis the ambassador whose purpose in following this thread of history was as yet not fully revealed in spite of their talk in the desert; the abbot of Abba Salama and two other holy men of his monastery.

'Son of David, you are welcome to this monastery and to this church hewn from the rock by our faith, tempered by privation, strengthened by suffering and rewarded by prayer. We put ourselves to the test every day as our Lord Jesus was tested. I have heard well of you and that you bring with you tokens of your right to be here.' The words were in perfect Latin and came from the abbot of Abba Salama. 'I am Abba Gabre-Hiwot and have been abbot here for twenty years. It is my destiny to say who may be allowed into the holy Tabot for so it is written.'

The young soldier from Narbonne looked at the expectant faces that filled the room. All eyes were on him. At that moment his mind cleared and the burden of expectation lifted as though there was a guide to carry him through the task which had been set for him by history.

He took the small box from inside his gown and set it on the table in front of Abba Wolde-Mikhael. He opened it and took out the two golden bees, the small parchment and the broken tablets.

'These have been given to me. Some have come via Islam through the Caliph Abd al Rahman. The parchment is a translation of a letter that purported to be in the hand of St Mark. The original remains hidden in Francia. Some have come from my grandmother Queen Nanthilda who also gave me knowledge of my heritage which links my line to the house of David.' He turned to the abbot Gabre-Hiwot. 'It is your destiny to give or withhold permission. It is mine to stand before you. I am a servant of my fate.'

The small group leaned forward imperceptibly to see the small objects laid before them.

'Ah!' The abbot sighed quietly, 'those who are the servant of events cannot resolve themselves of responsibility for the effect of those events. Tell me Constable Guilhem what did you think of the gate to our community here on the high plateau?'

The sudden change of subject took Guilhem by surprise, but he guessed that the question was not to be taken lightly.

'I think when a man comes to this place my lord abbot, he must put his trust in God.'

'It is so,' the abbot smiled a smile of such joy that his face seemed filled with love for everyone around him. 'That moment when you swing over the abyss; it gives me such pleasure! Let us go!'

The Tabot (a small wooden chest that represented the ark of the covenant) stood on a rock plinth in a small low roofed cave hacked out below the altar. In places the walls ran with moisture filling the air with heavy damp. Three torches spluttered their smoky light in the tiny space. The side of the rock plinth had been carved to show Abraham, his arm raised to smite his son. A hand was reaching from the sky to forestall the fateful blow.

'There! Such faith in the Lord.' The murmur came from the Abbot. 'Now let us see if you bear the key.'

The silence was complete apart from the guttering torches. The dark pressed down outside the circle of flickering light. There was palpable tension in the tiny chamber.

'You see the depression at the end of the hand of God. Yes, there...' Guilhem bent down to examine the carving closely and at the end of the outstretched hand there appeared in the dim light the unmistakable outline of a bee. He fumbled for the golden bee in his pouch. It felt warm and heavy in his hand as he placed it in the waiting niche. It fitted perfectly. He pressed it into the rock so it would not fall and suddenly at the foot of the plinth there was a low rumble and a perfectly made rock tray slid out in front of them.

An intake of breath in the heavy air. In the tray lay a long leather bag. It was badly discoloured and cracked. The bag lay on a clay tablet of which one corner had been broken. Guilhem took the fractured piece from his box and carefully fitted it to the broken corner. The little group stood motionless, frozen in expectation. He pushed it slowly into position. There was a muted gasp as the piece fitted perfectly. After so many years the piece was whole again.

'My son it would seem you are the one but the contents may be much damaged. Damaged!' he repeated, 'the fates may have another trick in store for us.' This time it was the archbishop.

It was left to Guilhem to carry the damaged bag back up to the sacristy. He laid it carefully on the table. At a nod from the abbot one of the priests stepped forward to try and extract the contents from the damaged leather.

Gradually the outside of a scroll emerged from its ancient resting place. It was indeed badly damaged. Black mildew spotted the delicate parchment and spread its spores in uneven blotches across the emerging script.

With infinite patience the two monks bent to their task, weighting the edges of the unfolding goatskin. In places the fragile story cracked and tore. In others the damp had done its work masking whole areas of the unfolding blocks of square shaped letters or signs. The letters were spaced in short lines and slowly unfolded in two columns. There was no decoration to relieve the eye only the destructive patterns of mould stains. The marks were not Greek or Arabic or Latin. The script seemed to have been made in haste as it did not have the controlled rhythm and careful spacing of many documents he had seen. The parchment unfolded along the whole length of the table; another was brought to support its overflowing length. Apart from occasional murmurs of distress as another spoilt area was revealed there was silence as the work continued.

Guilhem had stepped back from the table as he observed the intense concentration of these men of learning. The writing meant nothing to him so he was able to watch and reflect. He took time to watch the reactions of the silent group. Habtu Gabre standing motionless as a post, his skeletal thin frame emphasised by the brocaded durra'a of purple with the insignia of Chamberlain over his heart. Guilhem noticed that he too was looking at the assembled group. Their eyes met and passed. The abbot, his rounded figure bouncing with agitation, as he tried to get close to the unfolding script. He seemed to have some understanding of the words that revealed themselves intermittantly through the black of the mould. His face mirrored his excitement and despair as the words from another age flickered in and out of sense.

The two scholars were bent over the unfolding parchment revealing only their tonsured pates to his gaze. The last two were Adelchis and the patriarch Abba Wolde-Mikhail. Adelchis maintained his usual air of prior knowledge as though this was an event of some interest which would only come to fruition through his good offices. The patriach clutching his staff tightly and stroking the silver cross had taken station in the doorway and seemed undecided whether the documents or the people should bear the weight of scrutiny. In the end the unfolding script won.

Guilhem realised that the archbishop too could translate the phrases as they revealed their tantalising glimpses of a message from the past. But his eyes flickered round the room as though he was trying to assess if anyone there had some ulterior motive for being there. Guilhem himself was the focus of many of his questioning glances. Tension grew as the scholars bent to their task.

'Its Aramaic script.' The younger of the monks broke the silence.

'Could it be a summary....?' It was the Archbishop Abba Wolde-Mikhael but he was interrupted. 'Look, there is a small box.' The young monk held it high for all to see.

'It appears to be covered in wax.' The box disappeared from Guilhem's sight as the monks carefully broke the wax seal.

Then, 'my lord archbishop there is a separate scroll inside, much shorter and in a different hand and in good condition,' the young scholar held the parchment high for everyone to see.

'Is it clear enough to translate for us? It is a miracle that it is so preserved.' This time it was abbot Abba Gabre- Hiwot.

'The young monk started to tremble as he absorbed the implications of the words he was translating. His high domed forehead glistened with sweat.

'M..m..my lord archbishop...' his words tailed away and left the small assembly in a tense silence.

'I think, my lord, our friend is trying to say that we are looking at the words of our Saviour written in his own hand.' The suave tones of Adelchis filled every corner of the small room. He was not rubbing his withered arm.

A shaft of sunlight fell on the manuscript and illuminated the dust motes dancing weightlessly in the silent room.

CHAPTER TWENTY NINE

773AD

– Absence –

But the next morning it had disappeared. After Adedchis' stunning announcement Abba Wolde-Mikhail had gathered the scroll and reverently re-rolled it. He had placed it in an iron bound ironwood chest which he had carefully locked. Then he had called the stunned group to pray for guidance and wisdom and had suggested that those who could read the scripts assemble the next morning to start the work of translation. Everyone had been sworn to secrecy until they could understand the import of the discovery. But the next morning the chest was empty while the larger damaged scroll lay on the table as they had left it. A monk had been placed to guard the door to the sacristy through the night. He swore that no one had entered the room. Every member of the monastery had been searched as had all the guests.

It was two days before Guilhem was able to return to the mansion in Axum. It was empty. All traces of Nihal had disappeared, except one. Even the scent of jasmine which had subtly dusted the rooms with her presence had vanished. On the bed lay a small scroll, tied and sealed.

As he opened it her scent drifted up from the papyrus. His eyes filled as he struggled to make out the words.

There are tears in my heart for the pain you will feel. There is such fear that I may not have the strength to face the world without you by my side. The sleeping prince they brought to Cordoba changed my life but the world would never allow us to live in peace. You are following your destiny and I must follow mine. You brought such joy.

Inch'Allah we will find such again,

Nihal daughter of Ibn Abjar

Vizier to the Caliph of Spain

He carried with him into the echoing rooms another scroll which Adelchis had given him just before he had left the monastery of Abba Salama and swung out over the deep gorge through the trap door on his dizzying exit.

'This is the best I could do Constable Guilhem. There was so little time. It is from memory and there was some damage so there are gaps. But it may help...' and he had clasped the young soldier to him with his strong right arm.

His mind full of Nihal, Guilhem reluctantly unrolled the scroll and stared at the words that made little sense as they clashed with Nihal's farewell and his own turmoil. Then gradually their import began to sink in. He was looking at Adelchis' attempted translation of Jesus' short message to the world apparently written in his own hand – and this from only a few moments sight;

FOR THOSE WITH EARS TO HEAR

Those who would follow me to my father's mansion may xxxxxxx the teachings of the Son of Man. If ye abide in me and my words abide in you ye shall be saved. Many things I have spoken to you but it may be that the generations have corrupted xxxx

Therefore I have caused to be written down such teachxxxx in the xxxxxxxxxx. This short letter from my hand accompanies it to its resting place. I have commixxxxxx xxxxxx

In this way the word of the Loxx xxxxxxx down the generations till the end of time.

I call you not my servants but I have called you friends as are all xxxx who believ xxx. When the time comes for me to join my father in heaven the Word will be sent North, xxxxxxxxx, West to xxxxxxxx in safety for future generations so that the 'Word' shall not die. This will go to Alexandria with my family as I fear that neith xxxxxxxxx the Romans will let those who believe on me, xxxxxx them live in peace..

xxxxx and the Writings I have caused to xxxx be not afraid. There xxxxxxxxxx have found the truth again and it is the will of my Father. Amen

And underneath Adelchis had added 'sorry this is the best my memory would allow. The decision is yours Constable Guilhem'

Guilhem stared in disbelief. This copy made by Adelchis would never be believed by the world. It was not clear how much of the large scroll so disfigured could be deciphered. It was as though they had found something that might change the world, only for the treasure to be snatched away.

In such a short time his world had been shaken and he had lost both the hope of a definite solution to the hints that had lain as an undercurrent to his life, and the love that had brought such joy.

And all this had not really made clear what his roll was supposed to be. Even if the word 'family' indicated that Jesus of Nazareth had married and had even had children there was no prophesy that showed that the Merovingian line was destined to find the writings and to use them to change the teachings of the church. Surely the scholars through the ages could not be so wrong? How could it be proved that this was not the work of some mischief-maker? But then which writings were to be believed... could even the Gospels be false? His mind whirled in confusion. These were not problems that he could solve. 'I am not a theologian, but have I been led to this place for some other purpose?

Or had evil triumphed in this far off corner of the world and the Devil himself stolen the treasure?' Guilhem realised that he had never felt so tired and alone in his life. He wondered back to the empty bedroom and sat on the piled skins hoping for a sense of Nihal that might have permeated the bedding in the way that she had entered his heart, but the bedding had been changed and there was only absence.

It was dark when he awoke. It took some moments for him to recall his position as his hand had reached for the soft curve of her hip and he had drawn the first breath of the day as usual to inhale her scent. The empty space keened through his heart and for a moment he found it difficult to breathe. Slowly anger replaced the ache in his heart.

Then he realised that the events of the last few days, already starting to take the quality of a dream, could not be left to drift away. He had been given a key to a treasure of extraordinary significance and it had been stolen, not just from him, but from mankind. He would have to find it again. Action would help to heal the pain.

Habtu Gabre had returned to Axum to report the extraordinary events to his king. then he came to Guilhem, alone in his house.

'There was one strange thing – the monk Asgedum – the guard that Abba Gabre-Hiwot chose to keep watch over the sacristy that night – he complained of feeling sleepy all the next day. But he swore he had never shut his eyes during the night. Otherwise we cannot explain how the scroll disappeared. Maybe the Lord God himself took it back!'

'What happened to b..b..brother Witiza and deacon Josephus?'

'The next morning they were asked to leave. The abbot said we should not speak to them of these events. There was much protest at their treatment and I personally searched all their belongings before they left. That caused a big upset I can tell you. A monk gave them food in the small cave by the entrance and I sent soldiers with them.'

'I suppose,' said Guilhem thoughtfully, 'they are returning to Rome.'

'Indeed, indeed. They are in a great hurry to report to the Holy Father about their unspeakable treatment by these savages of Ethiopia.' His skeletal face creased into a wide smile and his teeth were revealed in all their glory.

'These things have happened to us before Constable Guilhem, yet we are as you see us. Different. But we serve the Lord in our way.'

It was suddenly clear that the only people with reason to hide the truth were those who served Rome. Somehow Witiza and Josephus were on their way and it was more than possible they had stolen the momentous script. A frail remnant that even now might change the world. He would have to stop them. After all it was his!

'Can I c..c..catch them or are they too far ahead?'

'The Negus sent them with guides to the oasis of Mai Agam. It's the one where all the caravans rest between Alexandria and Axum, but they are two days ahead.' He paused. 'There is a way that cuts two days journey but it is very hard and dangerous.' Habre Gabtu looked at the young soldier of whom he had grown very fond over the weeks since that first meeting on horseback when he had seen the golden bee in Guilhem's helmet. 'We'll go together! It will be an adventure! We have to travel light. Your baggage will have to follow.' His eyes shone with excitement. Maybe there would be a fight. Habtu came from a warrior family and it had been some time since he had had the opportunity to display his prowess.

'I have to get permission from the Negus, but he will grant it I am certain.'

By dawn the next day Guilhem, Habtu and two guides were clinging like flies to the near vertical rock face that plunged headlong to the narrow ribbon of white water far below. Although the air was still cold, sweat ran into Guilhem's eyes, the salt stinging and blurring his vision as he clung to the handholds. The guides flitted easily from step to step like mountain goats, gesturing, encouraging and always smiling.

Habtu Gabre translated, 'your left foot... there. There is a handhold, up, up yes there!' His teeth shone in the early dawn but even he was finding the descent hard. 'Another hour. There is a resting pl...' there was a scrabbling of small stones as the ledge crumbled. In a flash one of the guides was there supporting Habtu's weight for a moment and then placing the foot on a firmer footing.

'I had been told of this route but never taken it. Now I understand why we were always discouraged.'

Chests heaving they eventually reached the resting place. The guides signalled that they should take off their packs and drink from the leather pouches. Guilhem surveyed his hands, already bleeding from the sharp edged tufa. He poured a little water over them. One of the guides looked pityingly at him and shaking his head he squatted beside Guilhem and tearing strips of cotton from his headdress he bound his hands.

'This is Bisrat. And over there is his cousin Ras Gugsa. They have a small farm down there.' Habtu pointed down towards the river and through the impenetrable chaos of jagged rocks and twisted spires. The river still seemed along way away and Guilhem could not conceive of ground there that would constitute a farm.

The sky visible as a narrow strip far above them turned to burnished blue though the sun could not yet reach them in the narrow defile. The tumbling roar of the torrent below drifted up to the resting group. But in a few moments the guides were pulling them to their feet. They pointed to the sky and spoke to Habtu.

'They say that we must make time now. When the sun comes overhead the heat will force us to take shelter.' Guilhem's thighs were already aching from the descent, but he forced himself upright and they set off again.

Night was falling as they tumbled exhausted out of the narrow gorge and onto the flat desert plain.

'Their farm is about two hours walk. We can make camp and rest or go on. There are horses we can buy at the farm. Well my friend?' Habtu looked at Guilhem with some concern. The descent had left the young noble limping and hollow eyed.

'We need to catch them before the oasis.' Guilhem's voice rasped in his dry throat.

Anger still burned in Guilhem and deadened the effects of pain and thirst. He had come to this far-off place expecting to find a resolution to the questions that had rumbled in the background of his consciousness for so long. Like a firefly glowing in the dark he had been given a glimpse and then it was snatched away before he could make sense of it. Now it was gone and with it the one person who should have been at his side.

A great white moon shone in the cold sky. The eerie light cast short black shadows on the desert sand as they trudged wearily into the barren silver sea.

The next dawn found Habtu Gabre and Guilhem already an hour into their pursuit. The short rest had worked wonders and this time they were on horseback. Although unable to carry full armour for their descent the previous day, Guilhem had his hauberk, his sword, and his helmet. He was back in his element, a soldier again and taking action.

'My friend I would advise you to remove the helmet. When the sun is risen the reflection may be seen from far off. They have four experienced guards with them and we need to get close before they know there are pursuers. Besides our turbans are much cooler.'

The time passed and the relentless sun burned the shadows away bleaching the colour from the thorn brush and turning the sand into a never ending plain of grey. Occasionally a rocky outcrop would thrust its bleak shape onto the horizon as though guarding the emptiness from the unwelcome invasion.

Habtu reined in his mount and swung lithely to the sand. He pointed to barely visible traces. 'They are not far ahead. If we go quickly we may catch them before nightfall.'

For once the rule of hiding from the sun during the day was broken and it was as the sun turned the sand to gold and the rocks were touched with pink that Habtu signalled a stop. He gave the reins to Guilhem and loped into the setting sun seemingly unwearied by the heat and the long ride. Guilhem dismounted and waited in the gathering shadows. He felt night draw the heat from the air and there was till no sign of Habtu. He was just beginning to worry about his protracted absence when he materialised by his side, teeth gleaming in the dusk. He squatted in the easy manner of the desert traveller.

'They are making camp a little way ahead. They have posted guards-two at a time. What do you plan to do now?'

'Get the scroll back – if they have it,' Guilhem paused. He realised that he had no real plan. Was he prepared to kill to recover the Jesus script?

'The scroll belongs to your people as much as to me. I have been the agent of its recovery but I would like to hear the wisdom of the patriarch and the abbot as to how we should use this find.'

A great smile spread across the dark skull-like face. Habtu Gabre came close and put his arms on Guilhem's shoulders. 'That is well my friend. The abbot Abba Gabre-Hiwot told me that you were a man to be trusted. The mark of the Lord was upon you. If it had been otherwise I would have had to kill you!'

Guilhem looked at him feeling the weight of the long strong arms on his shoulders. Then he smiled in return feeling the burnt skin on his reddened face cracking in the gloom. 'How good it is to be among friends,' he murmured. 'So we will try to leave the Roman priests unharmed, but we must recover the scroll. Let them take the news to Rome. Without evidence Rome cannot act.'

'We will have to take the guards first. If you can provide a small distraction...' Gabre let the words tail away. Guilhem nodded. He knew what was required. Hobbling the horses they set off into the darkening desert. It was not long before Gabre dropped to the ground. He waited for Guilhem to catch up and they crawled up a slight slope. About fifteen paces away the shape of a man gradually emerged from the gloom. He was seated on a rock; the shape of a spear gleamed in the night.

Habtu Gabre teeth glinting in the dark - he was enjoying this moment – made circular motions. Guilhem nodded and the spare figure melted away. Guilhem waited, then scraped his boot across the sand disturbing some pebbles so they rolled down the slope. The guard was alert. He looked towards the sound and stood searching the night. Guilhem threw two pebbles to the right of his own position and the guard crouched, coming forward; then he hesitated and called into the night. Another figure appeared beside him and both approached Guilhem's position. At that moment a shadow errupted from the desert sand behind them. Guilhem stood in full view and launched his spear at one guard while the other was taken across the neck by Gabre. The broken bodies buckled into the ground. Two gone; but Guilhem thought that the call from the first guard could have alerted the others.

As they came over the sand dune the campfire flickered its welcome into the night. Four figures were standing in its light. The guards had drawn their curved swords. Firelight tinged the edges of each drawn blade.

'Witiza! It is Guilhem and Habtu Gabre. We have come to claim that which you have taken from a sacred place. The scroll is not yours to take!'

'If this is indeed the word of our Lord it belongs to Rome. To the descendants of Saint Peter.' It was the voice of the Deacon Josephus, high pitched and quavering under the mixture of fear and the import of the moment. They didn't even bother to pretend they had not stolen the scroll.

'I have been given a part in its finding. It has lain in the monastery of Abba Salama for hundreds of years. This was the will of God. Its f..f..future should be decided by those who found it and by those who guarded it for so long.'

'Well may you stammer young Guilhem,' the deep voice of Witiza rang across the desert. 'We are servants of the church and it is your duty to obey the church.'

'But not mine!' The accented Latin of Habtu Gabre interrupted. 'In the name of the Negus, Abuna Yemata Selassie I command you to return that which you have stolen.'

'I will burn it rather than give it up.' The small stout figure of the Deacon stepped close to the fire and held his hand over the flames. In it a rolled scroll could clearly be seen.

'You must swear by our Lord to let us take this holy message to the father Pope Steven. When the pain becomes....' He gasped his voice pitched higher in agony, 'I will let it go so it cannot fall into your evil hands. Quick make your decision. I cannot hold!'

Time froze; the stars whirled across the cold night sky. The sickly smell of burning flesh rotted the air. It was the guard nearest to Josephus who suddenly whirled and dived at the outstretched hand.

Too late! Josephus plunged both hand and scroll into the flames. A brief flare accompanied the howl of agony as Josephus reeled back from the flames bent over his smouldering hand. The smell of flesh remained in the nostrils of the paralysed onlookers. Flakes of cindered parchment floated up to the stars.

'You fool Guilhem! It was the patriarch who gave us the scroll. Even he believed it was too dangerous to be in any other hands but Rome.' Witiza's despairing cry rang out across the desert.

CHAPTER THIRTY

807 AD

– Whispers –

It was the smell that penetrated the pain. The smell of burnt flesh that picked its way through the confusion of nightmare and memories and brought him back to painful consciousness. He expected darkness and the cold night air of the desert.

'You fool! It was the Patriarch who gave us the scroll.' The memory of those words spat in fury by Witiza overwhelmed him again, as they did every time he remembered them.

Guilhem tried to shake his head. Something was not right. He was lying on something soft. The smell was not the same; it was the smell of venison! Suddenly he felt hungry. His eyes opened against the light. The pain concentrated itself across his shoulders and arms. Breathing was difficult.

Brother Jonathen, his face a picture of concern and love, was gently holding his shoulder.

'My lord abbot you were calling out and trying to move. You shouldn't, not yet.'

The confused mixture of dream and the reality of now gradually resolved itself into the steady ache between his shoulders. Guilhem came back to the present.

'Brother Jonathen – you are always close – who cut me down?'

'The constable Arnulf of Bezier. The Emperor had given orders for your protection.'

'Ah!' There was a pause. Guilhem found that gathering breath was not easy.

'You were right my friend. The church will not give up. I am indeed fortunate to have the protection of the Emperor Charles. Maybe that is also part of the Lord's plan.' A pause, 'is there some water? I am very thirsty; and that smell. Is it long since I ate?'

Water was held to his lips. Jonathen set the wracked body to a semi-upright position, and food was given and swallowed with difficulty.

'Now drink this. It is a draft of vervain to ease the pain and help the wounds to heal.'

As the drug took effect Guilhem's body visibly relaxed into the pile of skins on the litter.

'Carolus M M Magnus,' he murmured, a smile spreading across his marred features. 'You have repaid your debt, but this old carcass will never be the same again.'

It took his escort three days to make the return journey to Gellone carrying the racked body gently home. On the last day Guilhem insisted on rising from the makeshift bed and trying to walk. Jonathen, as ever, was at his side encouraging and supporting the figure which had lost its upright stance and the powerful stride of the warrior priest who had joined them five years ago.

Slowly they made their way alongside the rushing tumbling river called Herault and as the track climbed away from the torrent the sound faded into the background and the abbot's heavy breaths became audible above the river sound. Jonathen looked anxiously at the struggling figure.

'My Lord abbot, you have done enough. Please take the bed again. The men are pleased to carry you.'

Guilhem shook his head with the stubbornness that often accompanies the failing power of the strong. Eventually the guard post that protected the river road came into sight. At the gates there was the usual melee of traders, small farmers, travelling musicians, knife grinders, shoemakers, all trying to gain access to the small prosperous village that had grown up around the abbey. Guilhem had decreed that a limited number of traders should be allowed inside the fortifications at any one time. There was always competition for the places.

As the labouring group made its painful way up the slope some of the throng, spotting a new opportunity, detached themselves from the rest and ran towards the abbot and his escort. He was instantly surrounded by a sea of outstretched hands holding their irresistible offerings. The soldiers formed a guard round Guilhem and Jonathen, but a lithe wiry figure wormed its way under the cordon only to find a large arm locked round its neck. The small figure struggled against the restraint, looking beseechingly at Guilhem from under a crop of dirty curly locks and holding up a hare for inspection.

Guilhem stopped, thankful for an excuse to break his painful progress. Suddenly a memory of a small boy skipping goatlike over the grass and rocks of the Cirque de Navacelles came to him. It was Arnaud. The same boy who had led him through the rain to the dying hermit Paul. He gestured to the soldier to let the struggling boy go.

'It is Arnaud, is'nt it? You have something to sell? Let's see. Brother Jonathen have we need of a hare for the pot tonight?'

Jonathen was quick to take his cue. 'My lord abbot the hare looks well fleshed and healthy. It would be a welcome addition.' A pause, 'of course if the price...'

'Masters such a hare will grace your table and surely your Christian duty will mean that you will give a fair exchange.' The young lad was grinning as he spoke, well aware of the temerity of his speech. 'Let me see, perhaps my lord abbot could find some salt or a small bag of flour made from your fine wheat....'

He tailed off and looked into the smiling eyes of the abbot leaning heavily on his stick. Suddenly he was aware that all was not well with his old acquaintance.

'My lord,' he knelt. 'I have been foolish. I did not know'..... He gestured helplessly at the staff which supported Guilhem.

'Come my son, help me b..b..back to my bed. This,' he shook the staff, 'is but a temporary trial the good Lord has set me. All will be well.'

As Arnaud supported him back to the litter Guilhem felt his hand being taken and something being pressed into the palm. The young boy closed his hand around the object to prevent it being shown.

'Now my lord what will it be? Salt or flour.' He held Guilhem's hand closed while he tenderly arranged the skins over him.

'From farmer Peret at Usclas.' A low quick whisper.

When satisfied that Guilhem had got the message he released him with a quick wink.

'Jonathen what say you to our importunate friend here? Maybe a small bag of salt.?'

The exchange was quickly completed. 'Well my lord you certainly did not drive a hard bargain did you!'

'I have my reasons brother Jonathen. I have my reasons. I trust the good Lord does too.'

With that he turned away and opened the closed fist. In it lay a small golden bee. A fierce joy filled him. This was a sign that the secret lived on. The scrolls that he had sent after the fight at the hermit's refuge had been safely gathered in. The church was not all triumphant.

CHAPTER THIRTY ONE

779AD

– Heredity –

The prior from the Northern isles was a man who did not draw attaention to himself. His robes were of coarse wool and of an undistinguished dun colour. When he was in a group he was usually quiet. Alcuin seldom raised his voice but had a skill in finding the gap in a babel of speech; when he did speak there was always a brief silence afterwards as if the substance of his words were worth reflection.

The log fire sparked and fizzed as an aroma of fresh pine filled the ante-room. The walls were hung with tapestries which depicted stories of legendary battles among the ancient gods. The palace at Aachen was well appointed.

Guilhem leaned forward and poked the fire unnecessarily. Close up he found that the prior from the North had hazel eyes and an expressive left eyebrow that penetrated further than his words and left a feeling of discomfort as though he always knew what was behind the speech of another.

The fire crackled and spat filling the silence. Guilhem knew that silence was not an advantage that he could use in the way that he had so often used it. This was not a question of settling a dispute between warlords or dictating the terms of a surrender. He had come to this priest seeking advice and resolution, but now he was here he was not sure that he wanted to hear what this formidable theologian would have to say.

'Prior Alcuin, I was told by my grandmother, the old d..d..dowager Queen Nanthilda, that my heritage would be important in my life, and that the church – the church in Rome – would not approve. Indeed that the church would consider me a danger to its teaching.'

'So Seigneur are you a danger?' The tone was quiet but insistent.

'My story would appear to contradict some of what we have been taught.'

'Where do you think the truth lies, my son?' The voice had a slight unfamiliar lilt to it and the Latin accent was suffused with richer 'rr' sounds.

'Could our Lord Jesus have had a family?' the words were blurted out before he had meant to utter them.

The eyebrow shot up as the hazel eyes examined Guilhem's face. No longer the face of a youth it had acquired lines that ran from the side of his nose to the corner of his mouth. The skin had tightened over the cleft chin and its colour had darkened through exposure to the elements. Years of campaigning under the tireless king had given an assured air to the man before him. Yet at this moment it was as though his confidence had evaporated and he had entered terrain which could engulf him.

Alcuin looked with respect at this soldier with a stammer who was so trusted by his friend the king.

This was no fool. This was the trusted henchman of King Charles who had been recently created Count of Toulouse and who had ridden tirelessly, criss-crossing the ever expanding kingdom in his service. Furthermore this was one of the men who carried the insistent message of the great ruler that the church was the foundation on which all men relied for salvation and that the Pope in Rome was the fountain of the revealed truth.

That truth did not include a family for the Lord Jesus, at least not in the way that the count had meant.

'Did you know that there was a gospel of Mary? No I am sure siegneur Count that you did not. There is one quotation I remember; something like this I think, 'Do not lay down any rules beyond what I appointed you, and do not give a law like the lawgiver lest you be constrained by it.' Yet it is true that the church has sometimes made doctrines that have not come directly from our Lord.'

The slight figure paused in the action of picking up a log as though waiting for a response. 'Odd,' thought the prior, 'we are both using the fire as an intermediary and yet I should have no need of one.' There was something about the young soldier that said 'handle with care.' This was a precious soul that was in need of more than a ritual reply stating the church's teaching.

'You see my son there are certain things that may be presented to the church and to avoid chaos choices have to be made. Irenaeus bishop of Lyon was one the early fathers to propose that only our four gospels should be part of the Holy Book and he lived one hundred and fifty years after our Lord. Later at the Council of Nicea it was confirmed that the Gospel of Mary and others should not form part of the Holy Book. Prayers were said and the guidance of the good Lord sought and we believe the decision was taken with his blessing.'

'But in the end it was a decision made by men,' said Guilhem.

'Men of the church who had sought the guidance of our Lord,' emphasised Alciun.

'As to a family... as to a family there is little evidence to support such an idea. Of course we in the church know that this idea has arisen from time to time but..'

'But the church has always turned its face against such a possibility.'

The tonsured pate caught the light from the fire as Alcuin nodded agreement, the mobile eyebrow acknowledged the quick conclusion.

'Even in my far off home there have been such ideas concerning Mary Magdalene and Joseph of Aramethea. There was a letter from a priest in Alexandria which stated that Mary had other children, but this was regarded as heresy as far back as 150 AD by those such as Bishop Clement of Alexandria.'

'If you know these things how can you believe in all that Rome teaches?'

'I follow the church in good conscience because I know that the Lord Jesus and God the Father have guided our holy Church and our bishops since Peter in Rome. For the salvation of man I believe that these choices are made under the hand of God and we can best seek salvation by following the route shown to the Holy Fathers and his councils in Rome.'

Prior Alcuin does a man go against the wishes of the Lord if in his actions he obeys the commands of the church and his king and yet even so does not reveal all that, that they would wish?'

Guilhem delved in the folds of his fine wool tunic and his hand emerged holding a small finely worked leather pouch. Loosening the drawstring he shook something into the palm of his hand and held it out to the prior. Alcuin examined it for a moment before taking the golden bee and letting it sit in his own palm.

'Ah! My son you carry a heavy burden. Maybe you are nailed on the cross of doubt. Pray that the Lord God will give you a sign. The House of Meroveus has this as its treasured symbol I believe and I know that this has led you to far-away places in search of the truth my friend. The priest Witiza has told me of your adventures and warned me that you carry heresy deep within your soul. I expect you have your own story of heredity.' Alcuin looked him in the eye.

'And Jesse begat David the king and David begat Soloman; and Soloman begat Roboam; and Roboam begat Abia; and Abia begat Asa ... and from David to the carrying away into Babylon are fourteen generations; and from the carrying away into Babylon unto Christ are fourteen generations.' A pause to take in the astounded expression on Guilhem's face; the fire crackled. 'As I am sure you know Count Guilhem according to the Gospel of St Matthew.'

Guilhem stopped, his hand falling to his side. He had not expected the wiry figure before him to have any knowledge of his story or for him to get to the heart of his story so quickly. This was a different account of history to that handed to him by his grandmother.

'Well my lord, do you? Carry heresy in your heart? Do you believe you are the one to destroy the church?' The eyebrow was in full motion but the hazel eyes were firmly fixed on Guilhem. Yet there was no aggression in the gaze. Instead there was compassionate enquiry.

'It is possible Prior Alcuin, that priests of the church may have destroyed the written word of our Lord Jesus.' Guilhem spoke without emphasis, paused for a moment to see if this last piece of knowledge had come as a surprise. He held out his hand for the bee and then turned quietly away.

'Seigneur, seigneur Guilhem. Remember the words of our Lord at the sermon on the mount ....' by the fruits of their labours ye shall know them."

'Thank you Prior Alcuin. I will hope that my labours will be blessed by our Lord.' For the newly created Count of Toulouse there had been no resolution of the dilemma that he carried with him, but maybe a clue how to live his life with God's blessing.

CHAPTER THIRTY TWO

780 AD
– The Siege –

The standard of the king flapped desultorily in the occasional breath of sea breeze. On a slight rise about five hundred paces from the northern defensive wall of Barcelona the great figure stood beside his emblem. The newly created Count of Toulouse stood by his side. Circles of fatigue underlined his brown eyes. His leg ached as it did when tired. Wearily he thought 'it was not that far away from this place that an Arab sword slashed my calf'. It seemed a lifetime ago although twelve years had passed. The seige had been in place for eight months and there was still little sign of capitulation. Suleyman al-Arabi was proving to be a stubborn and brave opponent.

'You are weary, cousin Guilhem.'

'It has been a long siege sire. I had not thought that they could hold for so long. I am wondering if...'

'If there is something you could have done better,' the king interrupted, pacing in measured strides to and fro. Contained energy radiated from Charles as he walked. This was not the restless pacing of indecision but the movement of one who wasted little time, 'but I see no fault in your campaign thus far. However my sense is that this heat of summer will have taken its toll. There must be sickness inside those walls and I am not disposed to offer terms. This border has been a running sore for over fifty years. I will stop it.' The latter statement was made unemphatically which underlined the growing confidence of King Charles and his place in his expanding kingdom. They stood, the king and his henchman, plainly dressed, their loose cotton shirts covered by chain mail hauberks; trousers of plain light wool and leggings that laced to knee height. The only items that betrayed their rank were the worked leather belts and the inlaid handles of the straight swords that protruded from their scabbards. Yet that authority lay with these two men was not in doubt. The group of captains, constables, and seigneurs that stood waiting a few paces off showed it in the hushed tones in which they spoke among themselves and in the distance that they kept.

A messenger came and knelt.

'Mining?'

'There are two places where the earth will allow us to undermine, sire, but we have not been able to withstand the attacks on the testudos.'

'Ah!' Charles grinned, 'I thought I was about to teach you something cousin. The testudo is not a well known aid to the mining method of siege.'

'The Romans....'

'Yes, as usual the Romans. We have lost much since that time Guilhem, yet the knowledge is there if we look – as you have done.' He turned to the still waiting messenger. 'Where from?'

'Lombardy, your majesty.'

'And?' The monosyllable did not belittle the kneeling man but summarised the atmosphere of disciplined urgency that accompanied Charles on his ceaseless movement across his expanding territories.

'Your majesty the Duke of Spoleto has raised an army and the Holy Father is concerned that another attack is imminent. General Obelario asks whether he should move to proect the Holy Father at the risk of weakening protection of Pavia?'

There was a pause while Charles paced his ten step route. 'Tell Obelario to defend Rome if he deems it essential. I will reinforce Pavia from Lyon. Bring me another messenger. And you soldier, make sure you are rested and have a new horse to return.' A silver coin spun through the air and a great smile transformed the weary face of the messenger.

'Thank you Sire.'

The breeze stirred the banners again and a faint smell of rottenness and ordure reached their nostrils. Black buzzards circled greedily over the walled city.

'I am sure there is pestilence there. The latrines cannot cope. How much food are they getting?' The king instantly turned his attention back to the scene in front.

'Some via the sea. We have not been able to close the sea routes completely sire.'

The two men whose lives had been so entwined over the past sixteen years stood silently contemplating the problem. Behind them and spread to their right stood the lines of tents in shades of cream, brown and grey. Each stood foursquare in the sun unadorned save for the occasional banner that a count or lord had errected. The lines were straight and the spaces between clean and tidy.

'You have kept discipline well Count Guilhem.'

'There was some sickness early on sire. I had new latrines d..d..dug well away from the living area and insisted that all rubbish and waste should be taken away and burned. It seems that there is a connection between sickness and bad smells and waste.'

'What will be your next move Guilhem? There is trouble again on the North East frontiers with those damned Saxons whose treaty word is twisted like ivy on a tree. Twisted round the trunk of truth till it knows not which way to face. I will have to go back soon.'

'Your Majesty if we bring the mangoles to bear on the section of wall near the north end of that redoubt,' Guilhem pointed to the spot, 'I think there is a weakness there. Meanwhile during the next storm I plan a diversionary attack on the far side of the city. At the same time we will employ the t..t..testudoes again and try to undermine the wall where the mangoles have been pounding. Maybe the combination will be enough to create a gap in the defence.'

'If you are right and there is sickness they will find it hard to defend both sides of the city. Let it be so. We need to end this defiance of the Saracen. It has gone on too long. We have enough to do to ensure a stable peace within our boundaries and to make God's word secure in the hearts of all my people.' The great king clasped the Count of Toulouse round the shoulders and turned away. The decision made, Charles's thoughts were already on his trek across his kingdom which was part of his ceaseless pursuit of control of the warring nobles and the dispensation of the true 'word'.

'Guilhem,' he had turned back from ten paces away, 'remember it is important that we all stick to the one true path. Only then can we be united enough to defeat our enemies. Oh! And I've found a wife for you.'

Four days later a small dark cloud appeared on the western horizon. Guilhem was examing the beleaguered city walls where the mangoles had concentrated their missiles. Three great catapults had been dragged up to this vantage point. Wooden screens had been erected in front to provide protection from the arrows that sometimes whirred through the air and thudded into the defences. It was hive of activity behind the screens. Each catapult had its own team. Slaves brought a never ending supply of rocks on creaking wooden carts pulled by hand in the fierce sun. The air was full of the sounds of barked orders from the sergeants. The creaking of the great ropes made from animal tendons or horsehair twisted together and tied to the shafts which held the leather pouch at the end of the long arm of the siege engine; the groan of the great arms as they were winched back down to be reloaded.. Timbers cracked, men heaved, all under straining tension; their backs glistened with sweat as they forced the great arm back. The ratchets clicked as the pawls bit into the teeth to prevent accidental release. The chosen rock was then loaded and at a command from the artilleryman the pawl knocked free. A great shudder and whirring of ropes as the arm flung itself skywards and a 'whoosh' as the rock flew through the air. Seconds later a great thud as it crashed into the defensive walls. This had been going on through the hours of daylight for four days now.

Although the attack had been concentrated on one small part of the wall the catapults were not accurate. Though some of the masonary had been dislodged it was not possible to be sure how much the wall had been weakened.

Guilhem looked at the cloud again. The small fist had become an iron bar on the horizon. The small breeze had dropped. The signs were that this would be a major storm. It was time to put his plan to the test.

'Sergeant, tell the men to stop the bombardment. Make a show of dismantling the shields and let them see our retreat.'

The first moves to haul the mangoles away were greeted with a derisive cheer from the defenders who lined the battlements.

The iron bar in the sky had changed into full bellied tumbling rumbling clouds that were tinged with purple at their bases. Overhead the sun still shone as the armies in the sky churned their way towards the city.

With every appearance of dejection they retreated as planned. Hidden in a gulley some three hundred paces behind their lines two great battering rams were ready to be hauled forward. Separately steep sided testudoes designed to shelter the ramming crews from rocks arrows and boiling oils were also ready.

'Not much resemblance to the tortoises after which these structures had been named,' thought Guilhem as he checked the readiness of the crews.

A vivid streak splintered its way through the purple mass now overhead with the edge of the sun just about to be engulfed by the churning, towering clouds. Then the deafening crash which made even the bravest recoil. Suddenly it was dark. They waited in the gloom for the water to pour from the sky.

It was actually sometime later before the water began to flow. For hours the troops had flinched under the jagged streaks of blue white which flashed and sizzled aound them, accompanied by the rumble of rolling barrels and breaking skies. But now the fading light was intensified by the approach of nightfall. This was the time when the gods let loose their anger and there were many who made signs that the one true church would not have recognized.

The Count of Toulouse gave the signal soon after the torrents began their ceaseless drowning of the world. Messengers left for the other side of the city to instruct the diversionary force to start their attack with arrows tied with rags and dipped in oil and set alight before being fired into the city. Fire would divert even more attention. They would have to wait till the night sky had leaked its last.

Meanwhile the rams were being brought up silently in the squelching mud through the still falling torrent. Water streamed off the leather helmets into the wool or coarse hemp tunics. Rain streamed off the points of lances; the rounded iron helmets; the menacing nose guards dripped their separate rivers of water; it soaked through the tent roofs and ran into dishes; fires were extinguished. Leather boots soaked up the water and became weights that dragged at every muscle. The temperature fell and cold seeped into tired bones. It was just another night in the life of a siege soldier.

It was in the dark mid of the night that the rain stopped. Within moments Guilhem and the main body of the siege force could see the arrows flaming their way into the heavy air. It was time to begin the attack.

The great rams moved forward pulled and pushed by slaves mostly captured from the surrounding area of the Spanish march. In the thick night, thunder continued to rumble, sometimes far, sometimes closer as the thunder gods fought their own sky battle. The heavy air and dark night and grumbling skies were the perfect disguise for the approach. The long heavy iron tipped rams were carried separately from the stout oak timber frames carrying the rope and leather cradles which were wheeled into positon below the stone ramparts. It was as the rams were being fastened into the cradles that the alarm was sounded from above. Moments later the attackers were subject to a hail of spears, stones and flaming arrows. Men reeled away clutching arms or shoulders or subsiding into the mud with puzzled gasps. Reinforcements took their place instantly.

The testudoes were rushed into position and the hail of missiles on the wooden shields merged with the thunder from the warring skies. Within minutes the rams were ready and the sergeants were giving the orders. Like rowers in a galley the soldiers began to rock the great horizontal poles to and fro until sufficient momentum was reached that the tips began their task; crashing into the huge stone walls towering above the ramming crews.

Ignoring the missiles the rams quickly established a crashing rhythm whose power made the earth shake under the feet of Guilhem's men. The engineers scrutinised the great walls for any sign that the attack would succeed. Suddenly a block shifted slighty; the following crash showed a splintering crack appearing. Another crashing blow; another slight shift. The catapults had done their work well. This was a weakened wall.

A cheer went up from the crews. They knew that the defenders could not prevent a breach. A messenger came through the dark to the Count of Toulouse.

Guilhem motioned to his sergeants to prepare. He donned his helmet the golden bee just visible in the gloom.

Then a rumble of thunder that did not come from the skies: it came from the cascade of stone as a section of the great wall of Barcelona crumbled into a heap. Guilhem took his men in a tight disciplined phalanx to the base of the wall. Shields were held high to protect against the archers who were shooting down into the huddled invaders below.

Finally a narrow gap in the rubble was cleared.

At first the breach was filled by two soldiers with body length shields to protect them from the hail of arrows. Then two more. A small bridgehead. The trickle of men became a stream. Guilhem was everywhere exhorting, gesturing, trying to prevent an early disintegration of the phalanx. Swords glimmering in the gloom; spears thudding into shields and torn flesh. Guilhem waited till sufficient numbers had forced their way into the small square behind the breached wall. Then raising his sword and shouting 'for Christendom and the king!' they charged into the grunting, heaving mass of fighters. Crouching behind his round shield; weaving, ducking, leaping over fallen bodies, his sword cutting and stabbing, the count led his men over a thickening carpet of broken bodies and spilt blood.

Suddenly the opposition seemed to melt away. The attackers stood, breasts heaving, looking at the alleyways and arches barely visible in the gloom. Guilhem motioned the troops to re-form. Shields held high the army filed into the square and began infiltrating the buildings and alleyways. Still no sign of a counter attack. Guilhem knew he would not be able to hold his men for long. Eight months of boredom amd frustration was pent up in this body of soldiers.

Then from under the main arch facing the attackers came the sound of jingling harness and the clopping of hooves on the paved street. But this was not the sound of an attack; these horses were walking. Out of the dark came two horses carrying figures dressed in ornate durra'as. Gold and silver thread gradually becoming apparent in the glimmering light of flame torches which a few men now carried. The horses stood skeletal like, bones protruding as if to burst through their patchy encrusted coats. The two men dismounted and stood side by side in front of the invading army. Then as one they drew their swords and knelt, offering the weapons on outstretched arms. One of them was the vizier and commander of the defending army, Suleyman al-Arabi. The siege was over.

In the momentary silence the smells of victory and defeat permeated the nostrils. The warm smell of recent blood; the undertones of sickening decay of untended corpses; the foul smells of disease and excrement which filled the throats of victors and vanquished alike.

'For Christendom and the king?' wondered Guilhem as he raised the kneeling figures to their feet.

CHAPTER THIRTY TWO

780 AD
– The Fountain –

During the three days it took for the victors to be escorted to Cordoba to finalise the treaty details with the caliph Abd-al-Rahman Guilhem found his thoughts becoming increasingly difficult to marshall into proper soldierly order. The king's last words so casually uttered as he had departed, 'by the way I have found a wife for you' clashed with his increasing inner turmoil at the possibility of seeing Nihal again. Nihal whose name meant 'drink' and with whose love he had indeed slaked his thirst. Nihal whose face floated before him as they rode, but in a way that prevented a complete recollection. The inability to solidify the image intensified his emotions.

The memories of those breathtaking weeks with her spilled uncontrollably into his unfinished search for the truth of his heritage. The warring thoughts then refused commands to concentrate on the details of the treaty negotiations. How should he best serve God and his king? One thing was sure Charles had no doubts about the importance of solidifying the rule of the king with the teachings of the church of Rome. The one would strengthen the other.

But if the church picked this teaching at the expense of that; this record in place of one that did not fit the politics of the time; suppression of one document, even whole gospels, at the expense of another....

Was Alcuin right?

All was justified because the good Lord himself guided these seemingly arbitrary decisions.

Nihal's laughing eyes and sweet breath interupted these musings. Nihal who had disappeared with the avowed intent of never seeing him again.

And now sometime he was to be married! This news casually imparted at the very time he might see her again.

A faint flutter of air alerted his wondering thought – then the soldier ahead; a strange stick protruding from an angle of the man's neck. The fluttering hand grasping jerkily.

'Ambush!' he shouted. Immediately his soldier's instincts took over as he wheeled his horse into the direction of the arrow and simultaneously hunched low to minimse the target. Sword drawn, Guilhem charged into the thicket of oak and ash that bordered the road. It was an unexpected tactic and three bandits broke cover.

His sword flashed in the bright sun as it slashed into the neck of the first fleeing archer. It was then that two mounted men appeared from under the trees. Leather helmets; close fitting brocaded jackets; inlaid handles to their curved swords; these were not bandits. Guilhem glanced behind him. His own men, used to the tactic, had drawn up behind him in file formation. Shields raised; offering little target to the attackers.

Then other horsemen appeared from under the trees. There were about twelve such mounted warriors. The outcome would depend on the courage of the escort sent by the Caliph to protect his conqueror. His own embassy of men of Francia were eight in number, all mounted. Their escort numbered twenty, of whom two were on horse. The two Saracen captains spoke Latin

Instinctively the Count of Toulouse took charge. Three of their number were already dead or wounded. Disrupting the archers was the priority. Wheeling his mount back to the road, he gave the orders. Good discipline and understanding and two enfilades were formed mixing horse and foot soldiers.

Thrrrrp the next volley of arrows split the air; this time they were ready. Only a narrow target which was well shielded. Even so two more men were down.

Now was the time to attack. The two lines charged up the slope to the trees; the horses keeping close to the foot soldiers. Now the odds had been evened. In moments the battle had broken into a melee of individual fights among the trees.

Guilhem saw the two richly mounted warriors keeping back out of the skirmish.

'Cut off the head and the body will whither.' His sword slashed down at a thrusting spear and whirling his mount round, rearing up on its hind legs he scattered the men in front and made for the two leaders.

They responded with a yell and swords held high in the Arab manner they galloped straight at Guilhem. At the moment of impact Guilhem threw himself sideways wheeling his horse to the left. Taking the blow on his shield, he slashed at the exposed right thigh of the Saracen. The soft impact of steel on flesh and his blade drew red. Then the other was on him. Blades flashed in the dappled sun sending blinding light through the dark green of the forest. Horses neighed; men shouted and cursed as iron wreaked its bloody fate.

It was one of the streams of blinding light that changed Guilhem's life. Swords locked together with one adversary, Guilhem felt the movement of his wounded companion coming up behind. He glanced behind and at that moment the sun blinded him. His sword dropped. With a yell the Saracen slashed down and across his face. A keen stinging followed a spurt of blood down the left side of his face. His opponent thought he had dealt a death blow and drew back to deliver another thrust. Guilhem wheeled his horse again knocking him off balance. The Saracens arms went up to regain control. Guilhem thrust his blood soaked blade into the unprotected flank and watched as the figure lost his posture and collapsed onto the earth. Blood pouring through his other hand which he held to his face, Guilhem watched him grow still.

The fight dwindled into a dimenuendo of muttered curses and heaving breaths. Guilhem sat dazed on his horse as blood continued to carve a red river over his side to the ground.

****

The faint scent of jasmine touched the air with memory. There was no-one in the room but she had been there recently. Her scent hid amongst the smell of cedar wood and lilies that fringed the trickling fountain. Carved wood pillars supported the heavy oak coffered ceiling and the floor was scattered with fine carpets and a low black wood table inlaid with tortoiseshell took centre stage. It was a reception chamber that bore the feminine imprint of its owner.

How had he come to be in the mansion of the special envoy to the court of Abd-al Rahman? It was as though a thread had wound itself into his will and he had no choice but to be here in this place at this time. She had sent a message to the palace while his wounds were being tended and his resolutions had unravelled.

Guilhem paced the side of the chamber that bordered on the courtyard. All the feelings that had lain buried for seven years came flooding to the surface again. His hand went to his face, still bandaged across his nose. It was a week after the skirmish. It had taken two days to fully stop the bleeding and the ugly wound had begun to crust and fester, leaving him feverish and sometimes dizzy from the loss of blood and high temperatures that came and went. They had carried him to the Palace of the Caliph; the very one with red and white pillars tucked under the Sierra Nevada hills that he had seen under construction all those years ago.

Abd-al- Rahman was still plump. His voice still a note above those who surrounded him. His eyes still cold but the little chilling giggle that Guilhem remembered seemed to have vanished. The Caliph's conqueror was weakened and completely in his power yet he had done everything possible to aid the Count of Toulouse to recover. Doctors had been brought to the bedside and eventually the fever had been brought under control and the disfiguring scar began to heal.

Arnaud, the ever faithful lieutenant, stayed close sniffing suspiciously at the herbs and insisting on tasting the food before his lord could eat. The seigneur of Capestang started the negotiations with the Arab generals and the treaty was quickly signed when Guilhem had sufficiently recovered, Abd-al Rahman making little ceremony and even less obstruction. It was as though he knew that the tide had turned against his people and that he had lost interest in the proceedings. There remained only the perennial question of adherence to the terms. In particular the promises to deal harshly with bands of brigands in the marches who were sometimes employed by the local Arab viziers as mercenaries and whose allegiances changed with the rising of the sun and the direction of the wind.

'My lord,' the low tones froze his thoughts. His hand went to his face to cover the wound. He could not turn to see her; he could not move.

There was no sound but her scent drifted over him. He could sense the warmth of her body so close that he could not breathe. Suddenly she moved in front of him seizing his hand from his face and placing it on her breast. Eyes exchanged feelings. He noticed fine lines at the corners of the dark brown eyes and at edges of her mouth where none had been before.

Keeping his hand on her breast she went on her toes to kiss him. Involuntarily he flinched but her mouth followed his averted head and brushed the unwounded side of his mouth. The touch released him and he crushed her to him.

'It seems my lord that I can only see you in my country when you have bled for yours.'

Seven years of loss took his power of speech and he could only hold her with his one arm drinking the perfume from her hair and feeling the swell of her breast as she held his hand imprisoned between them. That imprisoned hand expressed perfectly both the urgency of feeling and the barrier of their situation. It told him that she still loved him and yet that nothing had changed.

'Does my lord come to me each time bleeding that my feelings may be stirred?' She released his hand, lightly kissed him again, and slipped out of his grasp smiling as she did so. Head on one side looking up at him in the gesture that bridged the years.

'Come Guilhem. Sit. We have time.'

And so it proved. For ten days the concerns of the world outside the mansion in Cordoba receded. Their days were filled with each other. Even the torn face proved to be a source of deepened intimacy and heightened sensuality as Nihal tended the wound and in her inimitable style made fun of his restricted abilities in the use of his mouth.

Even in that time of special closeness and emotional intensity there was a mystery about Nihal. At odd times she would stop whatever they were doing and draw breath as if to speak. Then there would be a little shake of her head and she would pick up where they had left off. Sometimes she would disappear fror half a morning or afternoon and return breathless avoiding his unspoken question.

'My life did not stop when you came Guilhem. I have duties, responsibilities. I am with you as much as I can.' The mystery was never resolved.

There was one moment that he never forgot and that was when

she allowed him to see his own face for the first time. They were lying on cushions spread out by the side of the courtyard pool in the warm aftermath of love, Nihal's head on his chest, her hand trailing in the still water. Suddenly she stopped talking and her hand stilled in the water.

'My love, look at us in the water. We are so beautiful!'

Guilhem turned and looked down. The disfigured nose with its missing piece and the long livid scar gave back its image. There was silence.

'Your's must be a great love indeed,' he squeezed her hand so hard that she gasped. 'I have been made a monster.'

'But not to me my dear,' she replied quietly.

'At least the king will find it difficult to marry me off now!'

The laughter that filled that private space was the greatest proof of all.

CHAPTER THIRTY THREE

806 AD
– The School –

The reflection of the scarred face looked back at him. After all these years it was still a shock. 'Court nez' thay called him after his return to the court in Aachen. Her face swam up through the water distorted by the ripples made by the feeding carp. The back of his hand brushed the disfigured nose in a reflexive gesture that had become a protective habit soon after his wound had healed.

That day by the pool in Cordoba had been their last but one. The memories of the last days were very clear as their destinies played out to the inevitable parting.

'My love, there is someone you should go and see,' Nihal had stretched out a closed hand and slowly uncurled it. In her palm lay a golden bee.

Guilhem had looked at her in shocked silence. Surely she was not still using him as a pawn in some intricate international plot.

'No my dear, those days are gone. I am not acting in any role for our Umayyadh people. It is true that when we were in Axum there was a hope that your discoveries might divide the Christians further and that we might be able to exploit that weakness. The time for that is no more. We are too weak. Your king, they call him Charles the Great now, is too strong to need us. But you may have your own truth to find. This was given to me by a Jew who has provided me with much help in my journeys over the years. He is a trader with many connections.'

'Nihal,' Guilhem interrupted, 'Nihal, what c..c..can I believe? How have you come by this symbol of my family? What interest can it be to you?' In his agitation his stutter became very pronounced. Guilhem was suddenly aware that he might still be a pawn in a game that he did not understand.

'Guilhem I can only tell you that this came into my possession at the request of the Jew Samuel ibn Negrela. But I do know that it is a symbol of importance to you. Wait!' She had rushed off and quickly returned.

'Look my love it is here for all to see.' She was holding his helmet with the emblem at its centre. 'When you first came to us sick, all those years ago, we repaired this helmet. This symbol is in my heart. It is part of you. When Samuel ibn Negrela came to me I knew I had to give his message. You may do what you like.' Tears sprung from her eyes. 'Do not let this come between us. Not after the years could not. I can throw it in the pool!'

He had reached out and caught her hand folding it to him and pulling her close. So he had gone to see the Jew Samuel ibn Negrela in his small shaded house just two hundred paces from the great mosque that was beginning to dominate the city.

The Jew was tall and stooped whether from disability or habit it was difficult to tell. His face was striking, being composed of deep furrows that ran from the side of a large nose and permanent horizontal lines that creased the broad forehead. He put his hands together and deepened his stoop fractionally.

'Ah Count, you are the Count. Yes that's right the Count. The Count of Toulouse. So my lord you got my message. Of course you received my message. You have it with you? Must always be careful. Yes always careful.' The repetition made it difficult to answer.

Guilhem had held out the gold bee in the palm of his hand. 'So it is you that are descended from the House of David. So you are one of us. Do you think you are a Jew my lord? Mind I see that you have taken measures to deny your... inheritance. She is a wonderful woman!' He tapped the side of his own nose and roared wirh laughter.

It was infectious and Guilhem had laughed with him. Just as suddenly Ibn Negrela's mood had changed.

'Do you know who attacked you on the road from Cordoba?'

'I have made enquiries from the Caliph himself and he s..s..said they must have been robbers, but I think they were too well organised and their leaders...'

'Were richly dressed and well armed,' interrupted Samuel.

'Exactly so.'

'The leader was Seigneur Angilbert who had bribed certain of your hosts to be allowed to make the attack. It was to prevent you getting this message. Who do you think has such interest in preventing messages reaching you Count Guilhem?'

'That would depend on the contents of any such message Samuel ibn Negrela.'

'Open your hand my friend. Yes your hand. See what lies therein. In your hand. That's right,' as Guilhem opened his hand where the little gold bee still lay.

'The church?'

A silence filled the cool courtyard as the implications of the Jew's tale filtered through Guilhem's mind

'Documents. Documents my friend. Axum. The prophet sent copies did he not?'

'But how do...?'

'How do Jews know about documents from the prophet Jesus? Let us just say that our scholars have a great interest in the teachings of the prophet. Indeed a great interest ...' His voice had tailed uncharacteristically away.

'So the message Senor Samuel?'

'Ah! Yes of course the message. There is a town on the marshes on the coast of your country. Go to the church of the Lady, Sous Sainte Marie- that is the message my friend. There are many people with differing beliefs who have an interest in protecting the will of the prophet... though our motives may differ. Indeed they may. Jehovah may speak to us all in different ways. Yes indeed in different ways.'

Guilhem eased his shoulders as he trailed his fingers among the gasping carp. His shoulders ached all the time now. He too had a permanent stoop much like the Jew in Cordoba. Had the good Lord decided to give him a physical burden to add to the doubts that he had carried for most of his life? Anyway that was one message that he had decided to ignore. He had never gone to Sous Sainte Marie.

Yet this was the place he wanted to end his days. It was right that he should be here. Only the good Lord could have given him such guidance; such an opportunity for all faiths to work together for all men in the school at Gellone. The school was already gaining a reputation for quiet scholarship and they had requests from all over the world to come and work alongside brother Jonathen, Rabbi Solomon Chalafta and

Iman Ubada Rushd. He had been given the means and the inspiration to create this haven and he had been given Jonathen Annias of the flying halo to provide wisdom and scholarship. There could be no doubt but that this was the will of God even if Rome looked on this unique experiment with hostility and suspicion.

Yet this was indeed a fruit of which to be proud. A place where the Lord could speak to many nations.

It always eased his mind and gave him peace to see the scholars at work. There was time before Nones. He heaved himself straighter with the aid of a stout stick.

'My lord abbot, walk with me.' It was Leo the priest, he of the earlier wavering mind and weakness of the flesh. Now only his eyes of an indeterminate grey still slid away from meeting Gullhem's enquiring gaze.

'Thank you brother Leo, thank you. It is true that movement becomes a little harder each day. Thank you.' He looked at the stout figure beside him as he hooked his arm through the priest's. Weakness there might be, but then which of us is free of weakness, Guilhem thought.

'And Maria, she does well? How many do you have now Leo?'

'Six my lord. The good Lord has blessed us with six, all thriving. We thought...' there was a hesitation.... 'we wondered if this last we might name after you my lord. To call him Guilhem, that is if you would bless such a name we would be..'

Guilhem held up his hand to stem the flow. 'Of course brother Leo, of course it shall be so. I would be proud to have the little one named after me.'

It was true too. Of all the small band of priests who had nervously welcomed him to Gellone those six years previously it was Leo who had grown in authority and confidence. Even his belly protruded somewhat less and he was neat and clean, gown unstained though nothing could be done about the missing teeth, and those that were left were still stained. Although Guilhem had not officially appointed him to the post it was Leo who acted as second in command of the religious community, in effect the prior.

A wave of giddiness swept over him as they walked slowly towards the school. He staggered slightly trying to hide the weakness from his helper.

'My lord you are not well.'

'Age my son. 'Tis the passing years. I am well enough to continue.' Indeed the spell passed and they walked on quicker. But, reflected Guilhem as they reached the door of the school, these dizzy spells were more frequent. Perhaps he would see the infirmarian.

The smells of the scriptorium underpinned by the drying skins for vellum and parchment; the odours of inks; verdigris, indigo, iron gall from hazel twigs and the soft crunch of pestle and mortar grinding the ink pastes quickly served to make him forget his physical problems. He passed through the busy scene and on to the librarium where Jonathen and his colleagues were often to be found in civilised disputation.

It was so today. Tables were arranged round the room. Each was piled high with scrolls and books. The abott was familiar with the method they had evolved to aid their discussions. One table had Arabic scrolls and books; another Greek scripts, and a third parchments scrolls and books of Jewish origin. Two scribes sat in attendance and made notes of further researches needed. They also fetched and carried scrolls and books to the centre table as required by the participants.

Ubada Rushd was taking his turn to make a point. His Latin was very correct and gave force to the logic of his arguments. Somehow his measured speech was at odds with the small rotund figure which was a fountain of suppressed energy. Sitting and standing in simultaneous agitation while his argument flowed sonorously on. He was difficult to interrupt.

As Guilhem watched in quiet satisfaction at this perfect demonstration of civilised difference the tall unco-ordinated figure of Rabbi Soloman Chalafta, all black beard and high colour under the bushy hair held up his hand and pointed to a line in the script under discussion.

'But my friend Ubada I think there may be a... mistranslation here,' the slight hesitation in the thick accented Latin took all offence from the interruption.

'My friends,' interrupted Guilhem, 'my friends, my mother once told me 'not everyone sees the same truths even if they are reading the same words.' I think there was wisdom there.'

The disputing scholars looked up at the unusual interruption. Indeed there was wisdom there!

'My lord abbott,' it was Leo who had accompanied him to the librarium. Guilhem had forgotten his presence and he was obviously out of his depth here.

'I'm sorry brother Leo. Thank you it was kind of you. Yes of course you must go to prepare for nones. I am quite well now. Thank you my friend.'

He turned back to the disputing scholars only to find them looking anxiously at him.

'My lord welcome to our disputation, but if you do not mind my saying you do not look at all well. You are very pale.'

'Brother Jonathen you always...'

'My lord please excuse me but you really look quite ill. I think I should escort you to your cell.'

Guilhem looked at the concerned faces who were nodding agreement.

'Very well, very well,' he grumbled and with unchristian like bad grace allowed himself to be led gently out.

'Rabbi would you fetch the infirmarian to attend on the abbot?' Jonathen asked as they went.

And so Guilhem abbot of Gellone learned that he was being poisoned.

CHAPTER THIRTY FOUR

783 AD
– Marriage and Whispers –

It had taken the king three years to bring his plan to fruition and now the Count of Toulouse was finally to be married.

He was thirty five years old and high in the estimation of his king. The wedding was to be held in Aachen as a symbol of his importance to the king.

He had met his bride once before when he had been created Count of Toulouse to replace the disgraced Chorso who had been taken prisoner by the rebellious Gascons. He had helped in the campaign to reassert Charles' authority. His reward was to be the vehicle to cement the loyalty of the rebel Gascon lord Sanche by marriage. Giselda was seventeen years old at that time. He remembered a slim figure with startling hair the colour of ash and large eyes which for the most part were demurely hidden. She had not spoken during the swearing of the oath of fealty to the king. Their second meeting was to be in the church of Saint Mary at Aachen.

The great palace and basilica were far from complete at the time of Guilhem's wedding although much progress had been made since his meeting with Alcuin. The outer wall now completely surrounded the palace and the basilica of St Mary which was under construction. The palace was a simple two storey structure, thick walled with defensible window slots. The upper floor contained the great reception chamber with an apsidal west end. In the chamber a raised dias supported the simple throne carved from a single block of light grey limestone with a low elliptical back and shaped arm rests. Great frescoes coloured the walls depicting the heroic deads of Roman and Frankish kings and generals; Caesar in Gaul; Clovis in Alimania. They always showed the defeat of the barbarian hordes. It was here that the wedding feast would be held.

Guilhem wandered slowly down the slope to the building site that was the church of the Virgin Mary. On either side of the enclosure storerooms, stables, armouries, forges, administrative offices, scriptoria and a library had already been competed. This was the centre of the king's burgeoning empire.

Otto of Metz hurried with his distinctive limp in which one leg lagged and dragged slightly behind him, to meet the guest of honour. The limp was the result of his leg being crushed by a falling block of granite many years previously. Otto was the mason architect in the permanent employ of Charles and considered one of the greatest builders of his time.

'Seigneur, seigneur Count, welcome to Aachen,' and he knelt before the young Count, his great uncut beard which swamped his face almost touching the ground.

'I am so sorry seigneur that the work is not finished for this great occasion but perhaps this chapel may please.'

He led Guilhem through the melee of chipping and grinding, drilling and boring, around wooden ladders to where the great sixteen sided basilica grew out of the ground in a solid demonstration of power and faith. It already looked as though it had been rooted there for many centuries.

'Otto I see your imagination has not deserted you. This is magnificent.'

In truth Guilhem felt for the first time that here was a contemporary construction that matched the giants of old.

'The bishop feels that we can use this space for the ceremony. The chapel was consecrated some weeks ago. The weather is fair and in this early summertime we should be fortunate.' Otto sounded proud that his building, still unfinished, was to be used for its first big occasion.

'I think the bishop is right Seigneur Count,' The voice came from behind one of the massive pillars. The tones were instantly recognisable. The tall gaunt black bearded figure stepped forward. It was Witiza.

He gave a half mocking bow the grey eyes looking straight at Guilhem as he bent from the waist. Then the familiar dazzling smile that Guilhem remembered from their childhood days and which had always softened the severity of his address. But now he noticed that the smile did not reach the cold grey eyes.

'Of course I could not miss the wedding of my childhood companion and I hope still my friend?' A slight emphasis on the word 'still' made the statement into a question.

'If you are here as my f..f..friend, Witiza of old, you are more than welcome,' Guilhem grasped the taller man's shoulders and tried to dispel the smell of burning flesh that had suddenly sullied the warm summer sun. The memory of their last meeting in the desert flooded his senses.

'I am the Witiza who serves the Lord God and my king and you know as well as anyone Guilhem that the king believes in the one true doctrine as do I.'

The immediate reference to the king's belief in Rome warned Guilhem that the events in the desert had changed little in Rome. He suddenly wondered how much of the truth had reached the Holy Father.

'Great things have been said about your conduct of the siege of Barcelona my friend.'

The sudden change of topic threw Guilhem off balance for a moment, and his hand brushed his disfigured nose unconsciously.

'And I understand that the scar you bear was inflicted there. Robbers attacked you?' Witiza continued.

'The truth was never discovered. No-one was brought to justice. At least not so far as I am aware,' replied Guilhem

'Ah! The truth. We are all searching for the truth my friend, sometimes so difficult.....'

There was something in the tone of Witiza's voice that alerted Guilhem. Had this been an attack planned by the church. Perhaps by Witiza himself?

'But you were there when the truth was destroyed in front of your eyes Witiza. You allowed it to happen; there in the desert. The word..'

'Enough! Count Guilhem, you have no knowledge to say what was destroyed. There are forgeries placed to lead us astray. What is certain is that you would have misused that letter against mother church.'

'I have never done anything against the t..t..teachings of the church and you know that well Witiza. But this is not the place for this discussion. Otto is waiting for my comments about the wedding.'

The instinctive gesture with the back of his hand to the disfiguring scar showed that Guilhem had decided that the conversation was at an end.

Otto was indeed waiting for the incomprehensible exchange to finish but the antagonism between the deacon and the count hung heavy in the air as the tour continued. The feeling of disquiet never left Guilhem.

The day of the wedding dawned fair. The congregation stood closely packed in the apse of the unfinished chapel a gently moving mass of changing colours as the brocaded tunics in black, dark blue and reds threaded with gold and silver of the men stood out against the long robes of the ladies in mauves and greens and pinks; the head-dresses and veils adding to the sumptuousness of the scene. Many of the most important nobles in Francia were there.

The king Charles sat to one side of the altar resplendent in cloth of dark blue silk embroidered with gold and his crown of gold embellished with four crosses. The bishop of Aachen, Angilbert, a man of small stature but with an exaggerated sense of status to compensate, officiated and was assisted by the deacon Alcuin.

When Giselda entered from a side chapel with four ladies of the court supporting her train there was a murmur of appreciation as the veiled figure approached the altar in a fine silk gown of emerald with white flowers delicately embroidered thereon. The startling flaxen hair could be seen through the veil as though hinting at the beauty that lay hidden beneath. Her uncle the Seigneur of Prades accompanied her down the aisle. It was he who had negotiated the dowry and was the senior member of her family there to give her away. But the Count of Toulouse saw the sudden stiffening of the veiled figure as she saw the disfigured nose and the jagged scar that ran from the left of his nose just past his mouth to the side of his chin. He admired her composure when that proved the only indication of shock that showed.

The great round chapel filled with sound of the monks' choir raising their voices in the gentle sound of the Gregorian chants. The sound that filled every corner of the rounded space and left trailing echoes that kept the congregation silent till the last whisper died away.

It was not until the wedding feast in the great hall that Guilhem realised that King Charles had used the occasion to demonstrate the power of his position. Princes, dukes, ambassadors and envoys thronged the great hall. From Rome the bishop Leo representing the Holy

Father Adrian, from Benevento the fractious Duke, from Brittany his old acquaintance Gersvind, from Lombardy the count Obelario, from Saxony the nimble figure of Luitgarde who had sworn fealty at least three times! However he took his place in the throng unabashed. There were many others from across the expanding reaches of the empire.

But as Guilhem and Giselda stood to the left of the throne to greet the guests after they had made obeisance to the king he realised that also present were many of those who lives had influenced his own over the years. Father Bedier of the bald pate and now permanently bowed, supported by a large staff on one side and a young lay brother on the other. His light blue eyes twinkled with life only diminished by the tears that filled them. As they embraced Guilhem was filled with remorse that that he had been so neglectful of his early friends and mentors.

'Your father would have been so proud had he lived to see you here in the favour of the king. Your mother...' he paused, 'I know you sent for her to come but she has not stirred from the convent these many years. She has shut herself away from the world....' He was shaking his head as his voice trailed away.

'Father Bedier it is enough that you have come. We are so pleased that your health was strong enough for the journey. Giselda this was the priest who taught me to read and write.'

'And with that thought in mind and to help you and your lady stay near to word of God I have brought this gift from our church and monastery at Narbonne.'

He handed to Guilhem a small book bound in the new fashion with leather bindings. The count handed it to his new wife who opened it and gasped with pleasure. On the first page an angel in russet gold and red floated in the air holding a dragon in an enchanted circle which surrounded a decorated O. This was the first letter of the first prayer in the small book of prayers.

'Oh seigneur what a treasure!' She looked anxiously at Guilhem. Should she have spoken uninvited? Guilhem took her hand smiling. 'We are indeed lucky to have so precious a gift.'

In that moment Guilhem had conquered the fears of his young bride. It seemed as though she saw him as a person and not as a damaged soldier for the first time.

But turning to the next guest Guilhem all but forgot the small precious gift in the flurry of greetings and other gifts that filled the day.

There also was Adelchis the ambassador who had run through his life as a thread sometimes visible at others stitching some mysterious pattern which was never quite apparent. The suave envoy greeted Guilhem with evident pleasure and seemed to make an instant favourable judgement of his new bride. They arranged to meet in the days following. Beside him was the most exotic guest, Habtu Gabre the vizier to the king of Ethiopia resplendent in the most exqisite durra'a in silk and brocaded tunic.

'The king the most honoured Abuna Yemata Selassie sends greetings and says that you are welcome to hunt lion any time. It appears that my lord count may have already encountered a beast of another kind.' The gaunt face broke into a full gleaming smile revealing the still blackened teeth after all the years.

Giselda again kept her composure well. This was the first black man she had ever seen. And she accepted with evident pleasure the gift of a filigree gold necklace with a central ruby mounted on gold lion claws.

Then as though all those from Ethiopia had planned to pay their homage together there stood in front of them the patriarch of the Church of Ethiopia Abba Wolde-Mikhail. Guilhem did his best to show appropriate surprise and delight.

'The manuscript my lord; the great scroll that remained. What have your scholars made of it? Did we discover something to shake the world?'

Guilhem thought that it would be most normal to enquire about the letter as well. "And the letter, the letter that may have been..', he paused, 'but which was so sadly stolen...'

The patriarch interrupted hastily.

'My son seigneur count, first we must congratulate you on your great good fortune to have have the lady Giselda as your bride. We will have time later to discuss these matters of dry scholarship. Now is a time of rejoicing. But I am sorry to say that there was little left that could be deciphered. The damp and mould had been very destructive.'

The line moved on as did the day, which turned to evening and the great feast which the king had organised. The tables were groaning under weight of gold and silver platters. Great gold goblets studded with jewels for the major guests; silver and pewter for the lesser. This was a display very uncharacteristic of the king well known for his down to earth attitude to display, but Charles knew well how to use the burgeoning wealth of his kingdom to good effect. Deer, wild boar, ducks and geese, great mottled carp were served in a never ending flow.

Yet all the while Gulhem felt that there was another event taking place hidden from those not in an inner circle. This event was invisibly stitched together by the black robed crows that shadowed the gaiety of the lay throng. The church was here in force with an especially large contingent from Rome. Their presence only increased Guilhem's feeling of unease that had remained with him since the unexpected appearance of Witiza.

The next day there were more surprises. There was a delegation from Cordoba sent with the blessing of Abd al Rahman. They had come to celebrate his wedding but more importantly the Caliph was asking for assistance from Charles to subdue rebels in the Arab ranks. Charles called Guilhem early in the morning straight from the wedding chamber to take part in the meeting.

'You know them best cousin. Should we be involved? Is there any benefit to the kingdom in giving this help?'

In the delegation was the vizier Ibn Abjar the father of Nihal. Seeing him unexpectedly the day after his wedding night created turmoil in Guilhem's mind. He felt that somehow his wedding night was a form of betrayal and he could not really concentrate on the matters in hand.

'Cousin you have not responded to his honour the vizier.'

'I am sorry your majesty. F..f..forgive me. Yesterday was so overwhelming. Your generosity so great. So many people and then last night..'

'Ah! Last night. Of course your mind might well be elsewhere, but I need to give reply to his honour the Caliph.' A great grin spread across the large distinctive face that he loved so well; the bright blue eyes twinkled. But Guilhem knew that this was a short-lived reprieve. The king expected his lieutenants to be ready to serve the kingdom at all times.

'Well Sire I think it would all depend on the control that his honour the Caliph can exercise on our borders. There may be some advantage if he can place more troops near Barcelona to control the incursions. This has been promised many times but...

Ibn Abdar held up his hand. 'I understand what the seigneur count means. I can assure your majesty that any border trouble that has occurred since our treaty three years ago would have been much worse were it not for our constant vigilance, but the border is long and the mountains wild...'

'Very well Ibn Abjar, very well. I understand that trouble cannot be completely stopped. Perhaps some payment in gold or silk?'

The discussions went on for some time before Charles called a halt and said he would send a letter with his answer with the vizier. Guilhem and Ibn Abdar left together.

'Nihal wishes you to have this for your bride,' he produced a small sandalwood box inlaid with mother of pearl and held up his hand to forestall Guilhem's protest. 'She said to tell you that things are as they have to be. Nothing has changed.'

Later that day Guilhem took the little box to his new bride with a mixture of emotions. It was certainly a strange feeling to be giving a gift from his lover to his wife but he felt that it would be a betrayal of a different kind not to give the gift.

'Giselda here is yet another gift. This t..t..time from the Vizier of the Caliph of Spain. You will remember that I have had some dealings with that country.' There was a slight hesitation and the back of his hand touched the scarred face unconsciously.

As she took the box with unfeigned pleasure he felt a surge of affection for this young beauty as she examined the box commenting on the craftmanship of the intricate inlay. She gave it back to him.

'You open it my lord.'

It was as he was examining the box to see where the hinge lay that he realised that the scene so cleverly made showed marsh grasses, a walled city and a boat on the sea. Hidden in the grass was the tiny picture of a bee in flight. This was a reminder that he had not yet followed the lead to Sous Sainte Marie given him by the Jew Samuel ibn Negrela in Cordoba three years ago; that he had not made a special effort to visit the church of Saint Mary had hardly been a conscious decision, more a feeling that this was an imposition because of an accident of birth. In fact doubt had taken the place of action and he had immersed himself in the life of the court and the service of his king and to tell the truth had managed to forget all about the strange Jew in Cordoba. The destruction of the Word in the desert and the way that Witiza refused to acknowledge the shattering event had left him empty. The discoveries in Ethiopia had not changed his life nor resolved the doubts he carried. He had always doubted that this coded message would lead to anything more definite.

As the reminder created the familiar mixture of resentment and anger in Guilhem's mind Giselda was exclaiming in pleasure at the sight of a pair of emerald earrings set in a basket of filigree silver. They were very beautiful. Nihal had chosen well. But Guilhem could only feel frustration as once again he was being asked to make decisions that did not spring from his heart. Even on his wedding day both sides were circling the court. Guilhem had no doubt that Witiza still hoped to extract something from him in the name of the church.

Absentmindedly he stroked the blonde hair of his new bride who was looking at him. Suddenly he realised that she was asking something.

'My dear I am sorry. What were you asking?'

'This gift; it does not please you my husband?'

He was surprised at her ability to read his feelings so soon. Their wedding night had brought them closer together as he had dealt gently with her inexperience and he sensed that her first sexual encounter had not been as bad as her wise women had warned her. Nevertheless he had to stop himself comparing the experience with his first night with Nihal and her determined sensuality.

'It comes from a time in my life which was not easy Giselda, and it reminds me that my actions are not always able to follow my inclinations.'

At that moment there was a loud knock on the door and his squire Arnaud called out,

'My lord the king asks that you attend him in the chapter house.'

He should have realised that this was no ordinary summons for a matter of state because of the location, but he was completely unprepared to see both Witiza and the spare figure of Alcuin of York along with the king.

'Sire,' he bowed and knelt.

'Cousin approach. We will all be seated.' Charles did not have his customary cheerful look. 'My friend the church, that is Witiza here whom you know well, has brought certain things to my...' His voice died away. This diffidence was not the Charles that was normally presented to the world; the king that was building an empire; the scourge of the barbarians.

The pause gave Guilhem a moment to collect his thoughts. At least now he knew what the summons was all about. It was Alcuin who filled the uneasy silence.

'Your Majesty, if I may,' Charles gestured his assent. 'Seigneur Count the church is worried that you may be working against the one true faith and aiding heresy to survive in our kingdom.'

'The church has good reason to so believe,' it was the sonorous voice of Witiza who had risen from his seat propelled by the righteousness of his cause, his grey eyes alight with fervour.

Guilhem looked at him speculatively. It had suddenly occurred to him that there was no way that the story of the scrolls found in the monastery of Abba Salama could be the story that was being promulgated by the church. Rome could not admit that its priests had dared to destroy the Word of God to keep it from the possession of a young adventurer from France. Even more that such an action could have been taken against the king's cousin.

'What have I done that the church believes that I have worked against their teaching?'

'We know of the heresy that exists linked to your family seigneur Count. We know there is a belief, a heresy, that there is a bloodline descended from Our Lord Jesus,' the words came faster as Witiza struggled to keep his composure, his voice rising uncharacteristically. 'We know that this is a blasphemy that cannot be countenanced by any believer in the true faith and we know that it is your line from the Merovingians that keeps this heresy alive. And you could destroy this evil if you wanted to help keep the true faith.' The words tumbled to halt as Witiza, chest heaving with emotion ended with an accusatory finger in Guilhem's chest.

'Is it so cousin?' the king spoke quietly.

'Sire it is has been told to me that there is such a belief extant. And attempts have been made to involve my interest'

'And you cousin Guilhem what do you think about such a heresy?'

Once again it was on this answer that his future, maybe even his life depended. More than that the whole future of the church itself could be turned upside down. If it was known that the word of Jesus had been destroyed to protect the teachings of the church..... yet what proof had he? Ranged against him were many of his wedding guests. Witiza, the Patriarch of the church of Ethiopia, and the clerics from Rome. Even Alcuin and Charles would support their cherished beliefs unless he had tangible proof. And that had floated into the cold night sky in the Egyptian desert ten years ago.

'Sire I am who I am. The good Lord gave me life and it is said that my bloodline is indeed ancient. You know that it was your g..g.. grandfather who took the throne of Francia from my line, yet I have been your faithful servant all my years. I have never allowed siren words to sway me from your service.

'So it is with my faith. I serve the Lord and the church to the best of my ability. I have never taken action against the teachings of the church, but you know yourself Sire that there are d..d..disputes that rage among the members of the church itself. For instance the question of icons.'

'But concealment can be action as harmful as action. The Count prevents us finding these heretics and the evil source of their beliefs.' Witiza again who had recovered his composure and whose voice resumed its normal sonorous tones that brooked no dispute.

'Your majesty there are many paths to the truth. The church itself has had to make choices between one p..p..path and another, is that not so Alcuin?'

The spare wiry figure in his plain black wool robe folded one hand over the other as though the next words would carry more weight than usual. As he was a man of few words which were always respected, this was obviously of particular importance.

'Sire it is my belief that the father in Rome is the true conduit for our beliefs and that for the church to win souls to our Lord we should speak with one voice. This has been our work together for some years now. But even we, my king, have been known to disagree with Rome on occasion and as our young friend has said the true path is not always clear. It is also true that such paths may alter with new revelations to great men of holy spirit such as when Bernard came to us to teach poverty and abstinence among the servants of the church and so founded his monastic movement.

Sometimes truths have their own time in history to be revealed and there could be danger in destruction for its own sake. Even the church may have been mistaken in destroying things it did not fully understand.' He looked up at Witiza and the mobile eyebrow did its work of appearing to penetrate disguises.

Witiza shifted uneasily. It was not at all clear that the destruction of a letter supposedly by the hand of the Lord Jesus would be sanctioned by the church, even if it had been done in the true belief that such a forgery would lead the faithful into evil.

Airing the existence of such a letter would cause such turmoil unless the whole story could be suppressed completely...

'Sire if the count can truly swear that he has never, and will never act against the interests of the church...'

Witiza had retreated. The ground on which he stood was not as firm as he had hoped.

The king sensed that there was insufficient proof to harry his cousin further. It appeared that this was more a matter of internal church politics than cause to bring down one of his most effective lieutenants.

'Cousin you understand that I believe that the church and the kingdom stand as one. Betrayal of one is betrayal of both. Kneel down before us now and swear anew your oath of allegiance.'

Guilhem knelt. This was an oath that he was happy to renew with a clear conscience. It was at this moment that he realised that if he lived long enough his path to heaven would come through service to the church of Rome even though it might be flawed.

'Sire, I swear that I will give my service, even unto my life, to you my seigneur the king of all Francia and to the glory of God.'

It was the warm hand of Alcuin on his bent head that lifted the cloud that had hung over the preceding days. Even so Guilhem feared that the pursuit by the church was not ended.

CHAPTER THIRTY FIVE

807AD
– Reflections and Plots –

Father Leo led the abbot gently along the path behind Gellone. Guilhem leant heavily on his long staff as they made the familiar journey to the head of the valley where the sheepfold still stood. Leo eased the frail figure to his regular seat on a large fallen tree.

A black bumble bee hummed low among the buttercups. Daisies thin-stemmed and compliant to every move of an indecisive breeze bent their white heads.

'Father I shall leave you now?' The statement combined deference, concern and affection.

'I think the ravening wolves will l..l..leave me in peace for a time brother Leo.' The dark eyes looked up at Leo and his hand flicked his nose. The unconscious habit showed that the abbot was relaxed and ready for his meditation before prime.

'Send Pierre Clergue to collect me. I want to talk to him about the next phase of building.' Guilhem never took his gaze from the face of the traitor who had been attempting to poison him a few short months previously. Careful investigations by Adalung and Jonathen had established that Leo was the most likely culprit. It was as though he was deliberately putting himself into the hands of the priest who had been ordered to kill him.

Leo walked away carrying his somewhat reduced belly before him totally unconscious of the thoughts that followed him. 'Of course knowledge was not the same as proof' thought Guilhem as he watched the heavy figure disappear.

So here he was some twenty-five years later carrying out his promise to serve the church and his king. Yet there were still factions within the far-off hierarchy that saw him as a threat to the future of Rome as ordained by the good Lord. Guilhem heaved a sigh of resignation and tried to turn his thoughts to the progression of local matters and the care of the souls under his domain. Slowly he relaxed and pushed his cowl back to let the mild sun play on his tonsured pate. At his side, where the brush bordered the meadow, hazy clouds of forget-me-nots echoed the blue of the sky. Hiding lower down in the tall grasses speedwells showed tiny stars of darker blue and the occasional stems of columbines hung their quiet bells in benediction. Above two brown eagles soared in lazy circles.

It was that special time of year when the good Lord worked his annual miracle. But somehow it was the promise of the new growth and renewal, the shades of vibrant spring greens and the flags of yellow broom on the hillside opposite, and the anxious bleating of the young lambs that turned his thoughts perversely to melancholy.

Giselda had died in childbirth after having given him four children. He had never gone to Sous Sainte Marie to follow the mysterious hints that suggested that there was still a different destiny available to him if he chose to take it. The warm hand of Alcuin and his resolution to serve his king had never left him until the extraordinary incidents in Rome at the coronation of Charles had forced him once again into actions that neither church nor king would have approved...

In truth he had never had time to really know his young slender flaxen haired wife or his three surviving children Bertrada, Lothar and Bernard. Charles had kept him continually on the move defending the growing empire which had defined him as Carolus Magnus in Rome and Charlemagne in Francia.

In fact it was in the service of the king that he had accidentally stumbled on Gellone now some eighteen years ago. He had been returning to Narbonne from Toulouse and had received orders from the king to escort a baggage train as far as Narbonne. The ten wagons were piled high with armour, helmets, chain mail tunics, piles of lances and newly forged straight swords each carefully wrapped in oiled hemp; the whole load topped with bundles of the finest iron tipped arrows. A tempting haul for brigands and so it had proved.

'It's iron that builds empires cousin, iron: the law and the one true faith,' the king was pointing with pride to the heavily armoured troops that were returning from a successful raid in Saxony. It was certainly true that Charles had sought the best in weaponry wherever he found it. Arab and Saxon blacksmiths had been captured and had been forced to work alongside Frankish craftsmen. In time the armour produced was the best tempered; the lightest and the sharpest. It lent the cutting edge to the expansion of the empire.

The baggage train had been attacked between St Pons de Thomieres and Aniane and the chase had led Guilhem to the wild scrubland bordering the river Herault. Eventually he had trapped the remnants of the band of robbers in a limestone cul de sac just above where he now sat. It was after the skirmish was over and he was leading his small troop back to join the baggage train that he had seen this peaceful haven from the cliffs above. He had never forgotten the perfection of the green grassed bowl that lay hidden from the world with its clear stream running down the middle, and even in the aftermath of the chase, a picture of a place of worship and reflection had come to his mind. Now the dream had been realised.

'My lord abbot!' The cry brought his musings to a close. It was Pierre coming up the path from Gellone. It was then that it dawned upon him why he had not been attacked again. The speed at which the square muscled figure of the mason Pierre had responded to his call suddenly called to mind the slowness of response to his letters sent on church business. Suddenly he realised that messages to the world outside Gellone had received little or very slow replies over the past few months. His messages were being intercepted.

The plan of attack had changed with the death of the bishop Benoit and the interrupted attempt to torture his secrets out of him. They had realised that the old man eeking out his days in this secluded corner was not the enemy. The enemy of the faith lay in the proof of the heresy. But much of that had been sent to the Count of Razes in the Pyrenees after the fight at the hermit's hut two years ago.

Pierre knelt before him. 'Thank you my son for your haste.' He made the sign of the cross and raised the grizzled figure to his feet. Close-up the years of his trade were clearly visible on the saturnine lined face. Hollows, scars and red pocks marked the cheeks nose and forehead where years of flying stone chips had scarred the mason for life. Yet it was a face content in its work and in the knowledge that his skills had added to the world.

Guilhem felt a surge of affection for the old stone warrior. Here in front of him stood a man of God in another mould. Pierre supported Guilhem on his left side, the side that had never properly healed since his own agony on the cross two years ago.

'Now my son the work on the chapter house is slow and you had promised it would be finished by the end of the summer. But I must tell you that the craftsmanship on the pillars is exquisite. The twisting columns are beautiful.'

'Thank you father, but it is they that are causing much of the delay. So much of the marble is faulted and some do not reveal the fault till much work has been done. Then it must be made again. These are supporting columns and cannot be faulty.'

The abbot paused on the grassy path. He looked at the mason searchingly. Here right next to him was surely the man who could be trusted; moreover a man who would not ask to know more than he was being told. Guilhem laid his arm across the muscled shoulders.

'I think you should send a man to the quarry to supervise the extraction of the blocks. There is someone who you could trust?'

'Indeed father, Raymond, Raymond Belot. You know the lad with a birthmark here,' Pierre rubbed the area between collar and ear. Guilhem nodded. Raymond had earned praises before. Fearless on the high scaffolds and with an innate understanding of stone.

'Good my friend. Let it be he. Now near the quarry is the village of Minervois. I may wish to send vellum for the making of scrolls from time to time to the village.'

And so it was arranged that Raymond would travel between Gellone and Minervois to supervise the quarrying and to deliver small quantities of vellum sheets to the priest in charge of the church of Saint Mark. Although a priest like himself, he too did not want the ancient truth to die.

Guilhem sent a verbal message to the priest Cerdan to examine the vellum with care. Nestled between the soft blank sheets there would lie on rare occasion a letter which should reach its destination unhindered. There was certain information that would have to pass on before he died if he was to keep his promise.

Strangely the trail to yet another part of the puzzle had started deep in the Saxon forests.

CHAPTER THIRTY SIX

792AD
– A Message in the Forest –

The bridge had been the idea of Theodo a young lieutenant in Charlemagne's latest campaign against the Avars. The mobile enemy had lead them a merry dance for much of the summer of 791AD, crossing and re-crossing the river Enns and never engaging the army in full combat. Every crossing necessitated the construction of large rafts so that the supply wagons could be carried across.

'We should make rafts that we can carry on barges and then tie them together to make a bridge when its needed,' the young lieutenant suggested somewhat diffidently in the presence of King Charles and other senior generals.

Of course the boatmen laughed at the suggestion pointing to the already difficult navigation in the fast flowing river with its shallows, eddies and rocks. It would be impossible to steer the barges with great unbalancing structures taking up all the deck space. Apparently the king had said nothing at the time but during the winter he had the engineers and boatmen working together and experimenting with different constructions. In typical fashion the king himself would go out on the fast flowing icy river waters to test the feasibility of the latest idea. By the spring of 792AD the first mobile pontoon bridge was ready to confound the Avar general Neuenahr.

Guilhem had been summoned to aid his king in yet another 'final subjugation' of the warrior tribe. Theodo had been rewarded for his idea and the enthusiasm with which he had seen the first clumsy attempts evolve into a sophisticated and relatively safe method of crossing a river. He was a short man with a shock of nearly white hair that sprouted round his face from chin to crown. He cut a somewhat comic figure among the dark Franks and the tall Saxons that had joined the king. Some had tested him and found to their surprise that the little man moved with surprising agility allied with great strength. The young lieutenant was now a captain and had been seconded to Guilhem on his arrival from Toulouse.

'Some of our main problems were the bindings needed to lash the small raft lengths to each other when ready to launch. Coir was too expensive and not readily available; hemp stretched too much in the water; leather shrank which was excellent till the rafts were to be dismantled...'

'Captain, can I presume that you have been able to overcome the problem?' Guilhem's quiet voice held just a touch of impatience. The little man blushed. He understood that the details of their winter travails were not of primary interest to the Count of Toulouse; the man who had been responsible for the fall of Barcelona; the very same who had opened the trade routes to the edge of the world and who was held in such high regard by the king.

'Sorry seigneur count. Of course.' He changed tack immediately. 'Our scouts report a larger than usual gathering of the enemy on the east bank of the Danube about two days march from here. His majesty has suggested that if he crosses with the main army here you could take a smaller force by river past their encampment to cut off their retreat here.' He had rapidly scratched the geography into the soft earth, showing the river and its winding trail and the reported positions of the Avar army and their own position.

They were standing on the shore of the Danube, the Avars having retreated from the Enns to the much bigger obstacle of the wider river. Sounds of swaying crashing trees punctuated by axe, saw and hammer punctuated the tactical discussion. Guilhem had taken an instant liking to the little man with the spiky white hair.

The scent of cut pine filled the air.

'Captain Theodo that will mean two b..b..bridges at the same time. Have we enough rafts and barges to carry them?'

Theodo was impressed with the Count's instant grasp of the main logistical problem. This wiry figure with half a face and the unlikely stutter was no fool. He waved his hand at the frantic activity around them.

'I need ten days. The king has given me seven.'

'Where is the main army?' asked Guilhem, 'There is little sign of them here.'

'Ah! The king has taken them three days march up river. They will mass on the banks and make some attempts to cross by boat to divert Neuenahr. I have another group of raft builders further downstream where we are to cross.'

It was the news that the new monastery of St Aloyaisus had been attacked that had forced the king to act. The monastery had been constructed two years previously with the agreement of the then king of the Avars after he had been defeated by Pepin, Charles' second son. The king always used a combination of merciless slaughter of heathens followed by the opportunity for salvation through Christ. Monastery outposts to 'encourage' conversion to the true faith had sometimes proved remarkably successful. But they were always vulnerable to the broken treaty. Neuenahr had found the easy target irresistible.

Seven days later Guilhem found himself swinging out across the dark dawn water on the lead raft pontoon. A low mist shrouded the far bank. Silence apart from the occasional jingle of harness and scrape of chain mail on scabbard. The black water chuckled against the pine logs as the rafts linked one to another were pushed into the water on the west bank and the expanding snake was led by a single boat to the east. The crossing went without a hitch and Guilhem, still not at ease on water, led his bay thankfully onto the bank and settled his helmet firmly on his head. Theodo glanced up at his leader, his gaze lingering on the burnished helm with its unique symbol of a golden bee. Scouts disappeared into the black forest. Guilhem formed his troop of two hundred horse and foot soldiers into three columns. The black turned to grey as light streaked the eastern sky. Wagons started to roll across the pontoon. They waited in disciplined silence for the scouts to return.

The first reports indicated that the monastery had already been laid waste and there were few enemy troops left at the scene. Guilhem sent Theodo off toward the southwest to find a position to ambush any of Neuenahr's retreating army. He himself led his column to the devastated monastery. There would be clearing up to do. The smell of charred wood and wandering tendrils of smoke announced the site. Two half naked women huddled dull eyed at the side of the track to the fenced clearing. Dirt and ash streaked their faces. Blood soaked the hair of one and had dried in rivulets across an exposed breast. The women made no effort to hide themselves or even to beg for help.

Inside the gateway lay the body of a monk, his torso curled in useless protection around the sharp stake that had been driven right through him; blank eyes stared at the sun. He had bitten through his tongue in agony. There were more dead. Guilhem turned away in disgust though such sights were part of the life of a soldier.

Quickly he gave orders; the dead to be buried, the frightened and wounded to be tended and sufficient food left for a few days. Two drunken Avar soldiers were discovered in a cellar. They were taken swaying and stinking into the light.

'Behead them,' ordered the Count of Toulouse. He did not stay to watch the execution.

As they were getting ready to follow Theodo's column and to make ready their ambush, the captain galloped into the clearing where once the monastery and its small village had stood.

'Seigneur I have found an excellent place to cut off the retreat and our scouts say that the king has indeed won a victory but that many of the enemy are retreating in some semblance of order. We have till this evening.' He stopped but Guilhem could see that there was more.

'Well Theodo. What else? I can see you have more to say.'

'My lord if you would not mind I have something for your ear only.' He glanced round at the assembled lieutenants and sergeants at arms.

They walked some distance apart from the soldiers and there in full view of his men and in the heat of the early afternoon sun Guilhem's chosen path in life was disturbed once again.

'Count Guilhem I know something of your history. I too believe that the church has led us astray. There is another truth that will bring us closer to God..'

'Captain go no further. You do not know what I believe but you should know that I serve my king and the church as best I can.'

With that Theodo put his hand inside his tunic and put into Guilhem's hand a small part of a scroll. The words were in Latin but they followed the pattern that Adelchis had left for him in Axum.

FOR THOSE WITH
Those who would follow me to my father's mansion....

....the teachings of the Son of Man. If ye abide in me and my words abide in you,

ye shall be saved..........................

Therefore I have causd to be written..........

Guilhem's breath stopped and he bent slightly as though receiving a physical blow. Theodo moved to him and gently supported him till they could find a fallen tree to sit on. He realised that this scrap was in Latin and therefore must be a copy. But what was the source of this translation?

'There is a monk who escaped the slaughter. We found him wandering and gave him help. We talked and it became clear that he too is of our belief. Even as he serves God inside the church he works to protect the truth.'

Guilhem found it difficult to hear the words. He was staring at the small torn scroll and the words brought him back to the mansion in Axum and the emptiness in his heart as he had read Nihal's farewell followed by Adelchis' translation of the letter from the Lord Jesus Christ. The few words on the scroll echoed those he had read all those years ago. His past had found him once again.

There was little time to gather his thoughts. A few hours later he was kneeling in greeting to the king, his sword streaked with blood but eyes shining in the exhilaration of victory. Charles raised him to his feet.

'Count it was well done. The plan worked to perfection and we have Neuenahr as prisoner. And so our thanks to you also my son,' his high clear voice carried to those around as he had to Theodo kneeling still. 'Rise. Your idea of the bridges worked also as we had hoped and saved many a long march in pursuit of the Avar army. There will be land as reward.' Theodo flushed with pleasure at praise from the great man.

'But now my cousin I have decided that our borders should stop here. We need an ally to prevent attacks from the south and east. We need an alliance with Byzantium and that witch queen of theirs, Irene.'

'B..b..but my lord I had hoped to return to the west. My family has missed...'

'Guilhem I know it is a hard task I set but I need someone I can trust and who can stand the wiles of that bitch. Such an alliance will be difficult to negotiate. Even marriage may be necessary with my son Pepin. It is a great trust I place in you... as always my friend.'

So Guilhem with Theodo as his captain and twenty men set off on the long journey to the east.

CHAPTER THIRTY SEVEN

793 AD
– Byzantium –

Spring found the Count of Toulouse entering the fantastical city of Constantinople. His embassy now numbered only seventeen, brigands and sickness had taken their toll. He came with a dual purpose. One to serve his king; the other to put substance to the story behind the torn scroll that he now carried next his skin.

Light and colour and shape and smell, all compounded into a heady mix designed to bewilder the senses. The sun glowed out of a cloudless sky and its rays darted and ricocheted off every surface. Occasional blue and gold onion shaped domes threw the light to flags and buntings of emerald, yellow, red and purple. Thick glass windows in tall buildings gathered colour to each pane and reflected it. Tesselated walls in black, terracotta and white distracted the eye yet again. It was as though the heavy Roman palaces and churches were being overwhelmed. The narrow streets were a never-ending river of clashing colours; turbans, veils, wimpled head-dresses; cottons, damasks, silks and leathers. Black or brown clad monks priests and nuns, often cowled, mingled in the human rivers making a statement against the vanity of man. Pushing against the streams of humanity, creating their own islands round which the pedestrian flows magically parted were the carts, barrel wagons, horses, donkeys, herds of goats and even the occasional stately camel.

Constantinople was the centre of the Eastern Christian church which had split from the rule of Rome. This was the centre of another empire and another variant of the faith. The Archbishop Nikephoros was every bit as convinced that he was carrying out God's will as was Pope Adrian I.

But in spite of all the magnificence and glowing colour Guilhem could sense that all was not well with this empire of the east. Look closely and part of the outer defensive walls were in poor repair. Look beneath the dazzle and one could see tiles missing from the grand buildings. The streets were poorly paved and then there were the drains. More accurately where were the drains? The stench of excrement underlay the atmosphere of the city and in places almost made the small party, used to the clean air of the northern forests, want to vomit. Sometimes the stench was made worse by the overlay of roasting wild fowl or sucking pig on street braziers. Mix this with the occasional hint of musk or attar of rose or thyme and the whole melange could excite or disgust in the same breath.

Stoically Guilhem led his party through the crowds stopping occasionally to ask directions because although the Great Palace of the queen could be seen from afar getting to the main gates through the maze of narrow streets and small squares was not so easy. Churches with square towers mingled the Roman heavier style with the new building styles of the Middle East. Monasteries and convents presented their closed façades one upon another. Christ was everywhere.

The party made a strong contrast to wild clashes of colour that surrounded them save for the equally sober clothes of the monks, nuns and priests which seemed at times to outnumber the laity. Their horses were soberly saddled and reined. Their clothes of grey and brown hemp or rough wool; chain mail glinting at their chests and helms of leather or beaten iron were dulled with use and travel. All were covered in the dust of many weeks. There was little to show that this was an embassy from the most powerful king that Western Europe had ever known.

At the closed gateway to the main palace square they dismounted and waited patiently for their group to be admitted. Of course messengers had preceded them but the ritual of admittance served to place the embassy in its proper rank.

Eventually the gates swung open and the Household Chamberlain Ionnes and a small troop of guards welcomed the weary travellers with much bowing and speech making. The brilliant colours of the welcome party; the gleaming lances; the ceremonial swords; the fluttering pennants all served to remind the visitors that they were in the court of what still claimed to be the greatest power of the known world.

Guilhem went through the routine with minimal courtesy and tired appreciation of the display being presented.

The Empress Irene continued to demonstrate her superiority in the time honoured way by using time itself. She and her court were very busy with matters of moment, but moments were things of which Charlemagne's embassy had an infinite supply. So they waited. In truth they were treated well. Their quarters were generous. They dined with the captain of the guard; with the keeper of the treasury; even with the bishop Petrus of Constantinople. They were allowed to go where they wished though Guilhem and Theodo would compare notes on the skill of those assigned to follow their movements. However the time was not wasted because such freedom gave them opportunities to discover the matters of state that were truly important.

On the northern and eastern borders the Asiatic Hun continued to harass and despoil the rich farmlands. This had a resultant effect on tax income. The treasury was empty, a fact that the Empress refused to acknowledge, and therefore her extravagances went unchecked. On the Mediterranean the galleys of Muslim pirates, or the navy of Harun al-Raschid – they were interchangeable – created havoc with the trade on which the city relied so heavily. It appeared that Irene's navy was fighting a losing battle.

It seemed to the Count of Toulouse that the Empress would be very amenable to an alliance to prop up her ailing empire.

It was on the fourth day of waiting that another surprise shook the Count. The embassy of seventeen had been invited to a feast at which the silk merchants were the hosts. Ostensibly it was to celebrate the safe arrival of three dhows laden with silks and jewels from across the far seas.

Nikephorus was the prince among merchants and the palace of Chalke showed his status. The large hall had grey white marble floors. Tall cedar wood doors panelled and carved created an imposing entrance. Long tables gleamed with silver and gold and pewter platters. Bowls of ebony and ivory and crystal piled with sweet cakes, fruits, and breads assaulted the senses with competing spices.

Guilhem and Theodo were led to the top table; the remainder of his party were scattered about the lower tables. The sombre tunics of grey and brown of his embassy made a sharp contrast with the wild mix of silks, cottons, damasks and gleaming jewels that swirled about the hall. The effect was to make the embassy from Charlemagne the most noticeable in the room. Guilhem smiled wryly to himself. 'Lilies of the field...'

From the gallery above the musicians announced the hosts (for this was a joint party) with a trumpeted fanfare. Leontius with his lady Patricia, Tartinnus and his sister Leodacia, another Leontius, Attalus and his wife Agnes and finally Nikephorus and his guest Nihal-al – Sawba an emissary from Spain.

Guilhem already bored by the proceedings was not really paying attention but then he saw her. He stared blankly at the tall imposing figure of Nikephorus and noticed the deepset eyes, the grey hair swept back and the trimmed beard which was black in contrast. The figure obstinately refused to stay in focus. Somehow he could not move his eyes to the figure next in line. The noise of two hundred guests faded and he gripped the back of his chair.

'I must not know her. . if it is her' even as he tried to control his thoughts his eyes finally came into focus on the face that was the meaning of love.

Nihal's gaze swept passed him indifferently except for the slightest twitch that told him he was right not to show any recognition. As the noise of the feast reasserted itself the shock faded and Guilhem was able to pay attention to Leontius on his left who was bald with a sprouting mole beside his ear. His commerce was in cotton about which he knew too much to be interesting, even if Guilhem's mind had not been elsewhere. He realised that Nihal must have known that he was in Constantinople and that he would be at the feast. The fact that there had been no message from her indicated that she was not a free agent.

Empires whose power is in decline often compensate by excess and this feast was no exception. Flavours and colours assaulted the senses; quantities invited admiration but only succeeded in invoking disgust, at least to those used to the more Spartan court of Charlemagne and the life of a soldier.

The Count of Toulouse made his excuses as soon as politeness allowed and fled into the night air that was, as ever, tainted with smell of unemptied cesspits and overflowing drains.

Nihal was here. The thought overwhelmed all others. And was she here in her role as courtesan spy? Was she the lover of Nikephorus? How could he bear to stay in the same city and carry out his mission?

His thoughts swam like shoals of small fish changing direction without cause or reason. When the attack came out of the black shadows Guilhem could not have been worse prepared and for the second time that night he lost his senses, this time to a heavy blow to the back of his head.

A sharp acrid smell and foul taste of a burning feather brought Guilhem spluttering to his senses. The sensations combined ill with the thudding ache over his temples. He groaned and tried to sit up. Somebody was holding a cup to his lips and as he drank the face holding it swam hazily into focus. It was Theodo!

'Seigneur, please! I am sorry but we have so little time.'

'Theodo did you find me? I was attacked.'

'My lord it was us. We could think of no other way to get you out of sight. There is someone here you know. She will try to explain. I will leave you and keep watch. There is little time...' His rushed voice repeated the warning.

A figure ghosted in the gloom of a spluttering oil lamp. Guilhem rubbed his throbbing head trying to shake the taste and smell away but then came that unforgettable hint of jasmine. He held out his hand to the gloom and felt Nihal take it gently to her lips and hold it; then a playful nip on his index finger.

'In bed again seigneur?' the teasing smile in her voice did more than anything to clear his mind. His body responded and he tried to draw her close.

'My love we have no time, though I am glad you still...' she pulled away. Her voice became urgent, 'I will be missed and they will searching for you too. Listen my love. Listen carefully. We have made a son, you and I, a son born of our love. He is nineteen years old.'

'A son! Our son,' Nihal placed her fingers across Guilhem's mouth. 'I am so sorry, my heart that you must learn in this way. It is hard but there is more you must hear and time runs so...' Guilhem struggling for control of his pounding heart and throbbing head nodded.

'I have called him Mahwab al-Axum. You remember the Jew in Cordoba Samuel ibn Negrela. He gave you a message.'

Guilhem nodded and suddenly felt guilty that he had so steadfastly ignored the cryptic message.

'Two years ago he came to me with this,' she pulled from her bodice a small scroll and began to unroll it. In the guttering light it was hard to make out the letters but suddenly Guilhem knew.

'It is part of a copy of the letter from the Christ Jesus?'

She nodded. 'Theodo says you have a fragment too. We do not understand exactly what is happening but it might be that one of the keepers of the true scrolls or someone who knows the story has decided to discredit the heresy by making false copies and distributing parts of the script around till nobody can distinguish truth from falsehood. Or that such traces will lead to the discovery of the original scrolls and they can be destroyed along with those who believe.'

'But Nihal why are you d..d..drawn into this Christian struggle? Why are you here?'

'Because of our son. I have learned what I can about your heritage my love. Our son carries the blood of your holy line, at least such is the belief of those who know. Already he has been attacked,' she reached out and traced the line of his scar tenderly. 'So far he has only a mark here,' she indicated her left shoulder, 'and one of the assassins lies with your God or mine. He is a warrior like his father. Of course it may have been a robber or other enemy but.....' A tremor in her voice told him that she was close to tears.

'But why here in Constantinople? Does the t..t..trail lead here?'

'According to your Christian scholars the style of script and the Latin used in the torn scroll pieces is to be found only in Byzantium. And I am here my love, in my other guise, to negotiate the trade of spice and silk for leather and weapons and olive oil.'

'You hope that if we can find the source of these s..s..scripts the hunt for heretics may slacken or stop.'

'We hope that it may help. Remember I am not part of the innermost secrets so there may be other motives. Your son hopes that you will take up the call of your line and fight for the truth.'

'The truth? Yes my love but I fear that the truth has been lost in ages past and even this that is said about us, the Merovingians, has been discarded by those with much greater faith and scholarship than I.'

'I must go Guilhem. It may be that we can meet on the long journey back to the west. Here we must be strangers. Help our son.' The warmth of her lips on his hand remained for along time after Nihal vanished into the gloom.

CHAPTER THIRTY EIGHT

793AD

– Faith and Death –

The queen Irene said 'maybe' to Charlemagne's suit and sent the Count of Toulouse back to Aachen with a long letter sealed, in a leather pouch also sealed, in a cedar box which was twice sealed. It appeared that the queen did not want Guilhem to see the contents.

Meanwhile Theodo had set about tracing the origins of the scripts. The small spare figure with pale hair, spiky beard and intense blue eyes turned out to be a true enemy of the Church of Rome. His father Alaric had held seigneurial estates in Neustria which had been granted by Charles Martel to his grandfather. The abbot of Rouen had manufactured a dispute about taxes due to the one true church and those due to the new king Pepin. Alaric lost the judgement and his lands which were acquired by the abbey.

This injustice inspired Theodo into becoming a scourge of the abbot Hugo and an expert in examining church transactions as far as was possible. Since nearly all the records were in the hands of the church the only way to examine them meant some form of bribery of the sacrist. This proved to be relatively simple when he found the sacrist peeping through the wattle and daub at the herdsman's wife washing herself. A silver coin to Rusilla ensured that the sacrist was indebted enough to allow Theodo access to the abbey records.

However this proof proved insufficient to force the wily Hugo to make reparation to Theodo's family as 'other' records were found to contradict those that Theodo had seen and copied. As a result Theodo and his squire had offered their services to Charlemagne on the northern frontier and Theodo acquired a deep distrust of the church.

Theodo was the rare combination of a soldier who could read and write and one who had a hound's persistence in following a trail, especially if it could embarrass the Church of Rome. While serving on the Pyrenean frontier he had become friendly with the Count of Razes and had learned something of the hidden truth and Rome's determination to suppress the heresy. He became a convert. And now he was the servant of the man who was of the true line!

The boat glided softly on the black water of the sea. There was no moon and no star pricked the sky with light.

'There you can just see the cliffs.' Theodo flung an invisible hand over the bow. It was true, even in this dark the faint bulk of a lighter shade towered above them as the little craft moved toward the limestone cliffs that formed a small bay.

The two oarsmen shipped oars and all that could be heard was the faintest slap of water against the wooden hull. Then the grating of the stem as it nosed onto the stony shingle.

'Now! Lets go.' Theodo levered himself over the side carrying unlit torches high and Guilhem followed reluctantly. He hoped it was not deep. He still distrusted the water. The salt tang of the sea intensified in the small bay as they splashed to shore. Theodo led the way to a small crevice and they started to climb stairs cut into the rock. Every surface sweated the sea in the clammy air and the steps slid underfoot as they climbed the narrow twisting stairway.

Theodo led the way in a feverish excitement which propelled him up the slippery steps careless of the danger. Then a cleft appeared in the rock face. Guilhem could hear Theodo fumbling for the tinderbox and suddenly the space was revealed in the smoky light of the oil torch. In front of them was a heavy wooden door with strong iron hinges and iron banding. Theodo ran his hand up and down the left side of the door, pulled a square block aside and revealed a bronze ring. He pulled it and turned to Guilhem. 'Seigneur this is the home of Alfinius. He is a revered scholar of their church but has for a number of years lived a hermit's life. It is said he has one of the largest collection of scrolls and books outside the monasteries.'

'Well my friend let us hope that he can help us find the origin of our scrolls. Keep calm Theodo you are trembling,' Guilhem looked closely at the young soldier. 'Do not put too much faith in a solution to our mystery. Besides which, why is a man of...'

With no sound the heavy door opened and revealed a tall spare figure whose beard came down past his waist. He was dressed in the traditional monk's gown but Guilhem noticed that his tonsure had been allowed to grow back. He stood silent in the doorway as though deciding whether to let them enter. After a pause he waved them ahead then turned to lock the door behind them. A narrow passage led to a hanging curtain which transformed into a large vaulted chamber which had been cut into the rock. The whole atmosphere of damp sea had vanished and was replaced by dry air that held on its current the hint of pine. Parts of the space were lined with wood panels. Good oil torches lit the room with little smell and strong light. And everywhere were books and scrolls; lining the walls; covering two large tables; even on the floor. It was such a transformation that the two men at arms stood astonished in silence. Their strange host, still silent, motioned them to a table and chairs and then disappeared to return moments later with a silver jug and pewter goblets. He poured the wine and gave them a cup each. Then he drew up a chair close to Guilhem and looked at him closely. His eyes were grey in colour and very clear.

'So you are the one they call the son of David,' his voice was penetrating and pitched unexpectedly high. Guilhem was immediately reminded of Charlemagne.

'So it is said,' answered Guilhem.

'But you are not sure? Tell me the..' he paused. 'I am sorry Theodo but I must ask you to leave us for a moment. Through there you will find food or more wine if you desire.' Guilhem waited till Theodo had left the chamber.

'Meroveus, Clovis, Faradon, that's what you wanted is it not?'

'Ah! Yes of course that would have to come. Who taught you the roll of names?' The grey eyes never left Guilhem's face. There was no formal address.

'My grandmother.'

'So your father…?' The words trailed away

'Never mentioned my lineage except to say that his brother had the throne of Francia taken from him by the mayors of the palace and that we should be careful of strangers with offers.'

'With offers of power that rightfully belonged to you and your line.' The clear voice sounded weary as though expecting disappointment.

'Tell me more of the names of the line. There are few left who know the full roll. The names that lead back to our Lord. Especially those of the earliest times.'

Guilhem's hand touched his face as he decided whether to comply. He had never liked this recital of proof. The last time he had had to prove himself had been in the strange land of Ethiopia. Even there proof, if it was such, had been snatched away by time and the church itself. He was weary of having his life interrupted.

'Clodion, Farmund who married Argotta, Frotmund, Boaz, Titurai...'

'Enough. You have been well taught my Seigneur Count. Yet you are well thought of by the great king Charlemagne. Is he not afraid that you will use your knowledge to usurp the throne?'

'I gave him my oath. To s..s..serve him and the church,' Guilhem interrupted harshly losing patience with the game being played out yet again.

'So you are bound to destroy a different truth. A thread that might prove more valuable to man than the teachings of Paul.' The high clear voice was insistant..

'I have born the conflict all my life. Have you heard of Alcuin, of P..P..Paul the Deacon, of father Bedier, an obscure priest in Narbonne? These are all men who carry the conflict within them too.'

The tall monk with grey eyes put his hands on Guilhem's shoulders. The touch felt good. It was a touch full of compassion.

'You carry a heavy burden my son. May the true Lord give you the strength to reach the end of your journey. I think you do not understand what has been happening, nor why so many pursue you for their own ends. I will try to explain.

From the earliest times some were entrusted with the knowledge that our Lord had left summaries of his teachings for the benefit of man. However many did not believe in the existence of such writings. Among those were St Paul and St Peter. They believed that they carried the truth within themselves and had been blessed by our Lord to show mankind the true way to salvation. The writings disappeared. Rumours abounded that some may have been found. Copies purported to come from original sources were made. The church itself forged more to cause confusion. Yet even today there are many that are convinced that we will find the truth and be able to correct the manifest errors of mother church. But it is a dangerous path and some such as your friend Theodo may have been blinded because of hatred and their fanticism is not to be trusted either.'

The curtain was brushed aside suddenly. As if on cue Theodo appeared.

'Alcinus this is not the man we seek. From what I have heard and seen the Count is not committed to OUR journey! This man, even so a descendant of the true line will not lead us. If he will not lead us he will betray us.' He took a step towards Guilhem. 'I hoped that you might be the one to take us from under the yoke of the false church; to lead us but...' his voice shook with anger.

He took another step forward then turned away as if he had changed his mind. Then suddenly whirling back, his sword showing fire along its length as it caught the light of the torches, he sprang at Guilhem who recoiled and ducked under the leaping figure. The straight blade shot over his shoulder and he sensed it finding a target. The soft slicing sound of iron in flesh. Guilhem straightened turning and drawing his dagger from his belt he saw Alcinus doubled over the errant blade, his clutching hands already streaming red.

It was then that the years of frustration created by doubt boiled into consuming rage. All his life he had been pursued by the story of the blood that ran in his veins. Now it had led to the unnecessary slaughter of a wise man by a madman. This same man was now determined to kill him. He felt his rage fuel his strength and speed. He was not ready to die.

Theodo was a man possessed. He seemed to hardly notice the dying monk. He was already turning to attack once more. Guilhem stepped close behind the raging soldier and seizing Theodo round his neck he twisted his head up and slashed across the exposed throat. Then he dropped to his knees beside Alcinus.

'The copies,' the grey eyes showed no fear at approaching death. 'The copies come from Rome. There are some of us there, in Rome itself. A guardian, a guardian of the scrolls. He.....' his voice was fading. 'He was a traitor. A traitor to our beliefs. He made false copies so our story would be discredited.' The grey eyes filled with joy. 'Now I will know who was right. But I know that somewhere the original letter and the summary of our Lord's teachings will be found…It is there to found. Maybe it is your destiny!'' The eyes wandered round the books and scrolls. 'There will be no more…copies. The traitior died. We found him.'

His eyes focused on Guilhem. 'Doubt can be a good thing in the search for truth. Take these,' Alcinus tried to raise his hand to indicate the contents of the room.

'I think you are a good man. Use these. Find scholars… all beliefs. We should all work together to find…….' His voice trailed away and his soul left through the grey eyes; their light dimming, as the force that rooted him to the world broke.

CHAPTER THIRTY NINE

806AD
– The School –

Jonathen sat on the high stool, his head framed in the east window. The hair was sparser now but still provided a halo against the early morning sun. On the sloped desk in front of him lay an ancient scroll. He was seated at a scribe's desk taking advantage of the strong clear light. Along with the loss of hair had come difficulty in making out the detail of the script before him. The light helped.

Guilhem stood in the doorway looking at his old friend and felt a great love well up inside him. He glanced round the scriptorium. The foundation of the library was the collection of books, scrolls and bound quires that Alcinius had bequeathed him as he died in the midst of his own life's work in Byzantium.

His thoughts drifted through the bright window back to the scene where the life of another man of God had been lost to this world. This centre of scholarship was the result of that loss. Suddenly his heart clutched at his breath. His son! Where was he now? Was he even alive? And Nihal....

'My lord abbot,' Jonathen had caught sight of the figure standing silently in the doorway. 'My lord look at these. Here on the desk I have a very early copy of Paul's letter to the Hebrews.' Guilhem drew closer.

'Papyrus from Egypt?' The pale beige tint and slight texture allowed him to make the guess.

'Yes my lord, exactly. Papyrus from Egypt but the lettering is Greek.' As usual the words tumbled out and Jonathen was grinning. He was always pleased when his abbot showed understanding. 'And here, here on the table is a real treasure. This came from the Holy land.' A heavy leather bound volume lay on the table open at Paul's letter to the Hebrews. The lettering had been made with meticulous care. Two exact columns to each page exactly aligned. The paper smooth and creamy. 'Leather bound, g..g..good quality vellum, also Greek lettering,' ventured the abbot.

'Right again my lord abbot. But this one, the scroll, has been made in haste. See the lines are not straight and letters have been missed.' It was true the Egyptian scroll was indeed haphazard and gave every indication of haste. 'The scholar who brought this to us said it came from a monastery in Ethiopia and claimed it to be very old. Made not long after the death of our Lord. Of course such claims...' Jonathen shrugged his bony shoulders, 'but what is wonderful is that the words in both correspond virtually exactly.' The words were now rushing like a stream in torrent.

Guilhem clasped his shoulder. 'And brother what does that mean for us? Should not the words of the chosen books be the same through the ages?'

'It is true both are in Greek script but written so far apart in place and time? Maybe the Lord is guiding our hands that the truth may not be lost. And this from the Holy land so beautiful, so careful, so correct in form and line. This scribe had time and place and was in a safe place. But this written in so much haste...' he pointed to the uneven lines that sped across the small scroll. 'This seems to have been written in fear. Yet the scribe knew his Greek. There are few mistakes, but why the haste?'

Guilhem picked up the scroll and let it hang in front of the bright sunlit window. He looked closer.

'Brother Jonathen could this be overwritten? It seems that there is a faded script beneath this. I cannot make it out. We need stronger, younger eyes to see.'

Jonathen joined him at the window. 'It does seem there is something. It is not uncommon to reuse parchment if the previous writing has faded. But it is not usual to reuse parchment to copy the Word.'

'T..t..t trying to hide something,' suggested Guilhem.

'It is possible my lord abbot. Leave it with me. There are things that can be done to help clarify the older words.'

The abbot went into the reading room where Ubada Rushd and Soloman Chalafta and two monks were engaged in earnest discourse. He greeted them and waved away their formal greetings.

'You are engaged in the work for the one true God even if we approach him in different ways. May your discourse be free from rancour and your minds open so that all may learn.' It always gladdened his heart to see his dream in action although these days it was difficult to translate the feeling to a spring in his step.

There was no doubt that his health had improved since Leo had been sent to Fontfroide as cellarer. For nearly a year there had been no further attacks on him or the library. However Guilhem was under no illusion that he had escaped the watchful eye of mother church.

It was two days later that Jonathen approached him after Nones and whispered that he had something to show.

'The script is unknown to me but I have made it clearer. It is not Greek or Latin nor Arabic..'

'Have you shown it to anyone else yet?'

'Not yet my Lord.' Jonathen's deep voice had raised an octave in supressed excitement.

'Who has knowledge of such scripts from the desert?'

'The most learned is Rabbi Soloman Chalafta my lord abbot.'

'Let us send for him. If he can translate we may learn something but brother Jonathen do not spend too much time on such a script. You have more important work.'

'True, true my lord yet sometimes the most interesting revelations are hidden in small packages. So you never know.' Jonathen left nodding to himself at the wisdom of his words.

The next day the tall ungainly figure of Rabbi Chalafta stood in the open door of the small room Guilhem used for administration and meetings with individuals who sought his advice and counsel. It was his practice to leave the door open.

'My lord abbot I have made a translation of those words that could be distinguished. The script is Aramaic, the language of the prophet Jesus and does seem to be of ancient origin. There are words and ways of forming letters that have not been used for many years.'

'Rabbi Chalafta have you discussed this scroll with brother Jonathen, or any of the others?'

'No indeed my lord since Jonathen said the request came from you.' The tall spare figure with trailing beard was trying to contain his excitement. He held the small faded scroll out to Guilhem who received it gravely.

'Well my friend since you are here, what have you found? T..t..tell me,' some of Soloman's surpressed excitement had transmitted itself to the wiry figure of the abbot.

'It starts thus. Ah! but first I should explain that this scroll seems to have been cut from a much larger one which had probably been spoiled by damp and mould. You can see here traces of mould. They probably tried to re-use pieces that could be saved.'

'Yes, yes I see, but what is the content? What is the faded script about?'

'It appears to be written on the instruction of the prophet himself. It begins thus. You will have to excuse me but not all the words could be deciphered... but it starts

This is.. help those who would follow the true path. I have seen that man .... by interpretation, yet my teaching is simple. First, love the one true G... Second love thy neighbour as thyself. I .... best to follow the path to eternal life and I have dis.....

The rest is even more spoiled my lord abbot. Perhaps with work we may...'

As Soloman spoke the smell of dust and mould transported him to the monastery of Abba Salama. The room full of robed figures all bent forward, taught as a bow string, straining to see the long unfolding scroll so cruelly damaged by time.

Then the voice of Adelchis in his clear dispassionate way. 'It appears my lord abbot that we are listening to the words of Jesus in his own hand.'

The vision wavered and Guilhem returned to the present. There was no doubt in his mind. This was part of the great damaged scroll that they had found with the letter from Jesus. He had never heard any other reference to this scroll since that far-off time. He came to a decision and the back of his hand touched his face.

'My friend,' he spoke to the Rabbi holding up his hand to stop the flow of words. 'I would be grateful if you would remain silent about this. Please call brother Jonathen and I will tell you both a story. I need time to think and to pray for guidance.'

Soloman Chalafta left without a word and Guilhem sat heavily in the carved oak chair. He stared blindly round the small bare room as if trying to see through the walls.

The honey grey limestone buildings sitting in perfect peace, soaking up the rays of the sun, centered on the solid outline of the church, attesting to all the faith that that had created. The small band of scholars working to find harmony in knowledge surrounded by the smell of parchments and inks. The beauty of the pages coming to life under the skilled hands of dedicated scribes, colours glowing like jewels as the Word was recreated again and again. Then there was the gathering of monks and priests immersed in the daily rhythm of prayer for saving of their souls and those of all men. In all of this there was no room for doubt.

Yet once again God had thrown a stone against the carapace of belief, as if to remind him that there was another truth that must not be allowed to die. Was this a sign that he had taken the wrong path? The last time had been in Rome during the coronation of the Emperor seven years ago. In the dank sweaty confines of the labyrinth of catacombs, among the Christian dead, a box had been stuffed into his hands.

'Take this. Protect it. Here is your inheritance. Here is the truth the Church will kill to prevent being spread.' It had been a hermit monk, Grimald, who had pushed the small box at him with pleading eyes.

It had been the time he had seen his son; the last time he had heard news of his lover. Rome...

CHAPTER FORTY

800 AD
– Emperor –

Cloud covered the great city in an unrelenting, deadening, colourless cold. Snowflakes drifted out of the leaden belly. A small army clattered across the Ponte Saint Angelo. It was led by an imposing figure sitting erect on a large white charger. His dress reflected the sky; iron helmet, broad shoulders encased in grey chain mail, lance tip again of iron. At his side rode Guilhem Count of Toulouse and behind the two leaders rode three hundred mounted and armed men sworn to the service of Charlemagne king of Francia.

Crowds lined the broad paved avenue that led to the huge piazza in front of the basilica of Saint Peter. Charlemagne was making a statement to the populace of Rome on Christmas day 800AD. It was he and his army who had once again saved the institution of the papacy. Pope Leo III owed his survival to the great king. The hooves of the chosen guard clattered on the paving, the sound hollowed out by the cold. Clouds of steam rose from the horses' flanks as they approached the arcades roofed by red tiles and supported in a series of harmonious arches by slender carved stone columns which surrounded the great square. In front of the west door to the basilica they dismounted. Slaves ran to take reins.

Sonorous chanting drifted out of the great church and across the vast paved piazza to mingle with the dismounted soldiers and the crowds making their way to the Christmas service. The great fountain in the centre of the square was still. The pool surrounding it was frozen.

'Take them in Guilhem. Line the nave. There are still those who wish to usurp those who God has appointed. I will wait for the Holy Father and his retinue.' The king's distinctive high pitch carried clearly above the hubbub.

'Sire.' Guilhem bowed and then gave his orders to the sergeant, 'Fifty men up by the altar. Fifty by this door. One hundred down each aisle. Keep watch for any disturbance during the service. Arrest anyone causing trouble. Remember you are greatly honoured. Today on this special Christmas day you have been chosen to protect the Holy Father and his majesty the king. But be always aware that we are in another country. Our behaviour must set the standard.' He seldom stammered when giving orders.

A short time later Guilhem followed the troops into the great nave which was nearly one hundred paces in length. Double aisles on each side supported by rows of shaped columns with decorated capitols meant that the width of the greatest church in the world was nearly seventy paces.

His eye was drawn down the length of the magnificent space to the pergola placed at the crossing of the transept and nave. The simple shape with rounded and curved roof was lifted by four slender red marble columns carved with spiralling vines. Under this lay the sacred bones of St Peter himself. In front of the monument to St Peter was the plain stone altar installed by Gregory the Great some two hundred years before. Above the altar suspended from the great wooden beams hung the Imperial crown of gold which symbolised the power of the Holy Father.

'But', thought Guilhem as he paced the great nave inspecting his troops, 'but the Imperial power was saved only by my liege lord king Charles so where does power really lie? Why does the Lord God not protect his one true church without such a man-made intervention?'

The troops stood in between the columns; round shields held down on the left and spears planted and straight on each soldiers right side. All were in chain mail hauberks. Even here in the great church on the very day of the birth of Christ who brought his message of peace on earth it was the iron army of Charlemagne who had made the celebration of the Christ mass possible.

'In the shadow of your wings I sing for joy.' The words of the Sixty Third Psalm died away into the great rafters and the cantor signalled for silence. The choir of black robed monks moved to the left aisle behind the altar. The silence in the great house of God was only broken by the shuffle of boots and shoes as the laity gradually filled the huge nave.

Then the monks knelt, as passing through their midst from the Chapter house, came a small group led by the archdeacon. Behind him came the Holy Father Pope Leo III, and behind him, dwarfing the leader of the Christian peoples strode the imposing figure of the king of Francia, Charlemagne with a surcoat over his armour emblazoned with a plain red cross on gleaming white silk.

He held his great helmet under his left arm, his famous red gold hair and trimmed beard fully revealed under the lantern.

The pope turned to the congregation, arms outstretched, and led by the king the huge throng of worshippers prostrated themselves at full length to the representative of God on earth.

The Count of Toulouse knelt in the side aisle as did the soldiers under his command. They had rehearsed this beforehand and obtained the blessing of the Holy Father when Guilhem had pointed out that if an attack took place during the prostration his men would be at somewhat of a disadvantage.

The service proceeded in what was just becoming a recognised and repeated form throughout the empire. The Holy Father assisted by the archdeacon Paul intoned the petitionary prayers and the monks chanted the responses. At their conclusion the congregation rose to their feet once more. It was then Pope Leo III stepped forward and placed a circlet of gold on the head of the great king declaring 'Carolo piisimo augusto, a Deo coronato magno et pacifico imperatore, vita et victoria !' Long life and victory to Charles, the most pious Augustus, the great peace loving emperor, crowned by God!

There was a stunned silence among the vast assembly. Here during one of the most important religious services of the year a huge political statement had been made. This was a final break with the Holy Roman Emperor of the east based in Constantinople. Here the Pope himself acknowledged the debt of the church of God to Carolus Magnus. A new empire had been acknowledged.

It was at this point that Guilhem was aware of a figure standing close behind him on his left shoulder.

'So my friend you have just witnessed history being made, but I noticed that you did not prostrate yourself before God. Perhaps you still march to a different drum?'

Guilhem did not have to turn to know his old tormentor. The deep tones were those of Witiza, now bishop of Aniane.

'Bishop I believe we have not met since your preferment to the bishopric. Please accept my congratulations. Perhaps it was a just reward for your assiduous persecution of heresy.'

'In some small part no doubt. In some small part. But our work is never done. There are always those who seem to believe that they know better than Mother Church. Would you dine with me tomorrow? Just a small group. Some from our native country. We are quartered in the east wing of the Lateran Palace. There is something I should like to show you my friend.' The deep set grey eyes brooked no dissension and Guilhem nodded.

Witiza disappeared into the now dispersing throng. It looked as though the danger of attack had passed. Guilhem busied himself with dismissing the guard and ensuring that their quarters were adequate and that provisions had been provided.

'Sergeant remember the great honour that has just been done to our king. Ensure that every man lives up to this honour.'

The count left his men satisfied that they had fulfilled their task. There were still considerable crowds oozing their haphazard way through the great gates away from the basilica. He wandered slowly down the wide avenue and across the Ponte Saint Angelo. It was on the bridge that he first became aware that he might be being followed. It seemed unlikely but then it occurred to him that Witiza might just be keeping him under surveillance in case he could find real evidence of his continuing apostasy. Ever since Ethiopia the newly created Bishop of Aniane was sure that his old childhood friend was a dangerous source of heresy. Or maybe he was afraid that Guilhem could prove that he had been guilty of the gravest of errors in allowing the destruction of the Word of God in the desert.

On the other side of the bridge a Christmas market had formed to attract the crowds ready to breakfast after the Nativity service. Great cauldrons of mulled wine steamed; the smell of dried rosemary and thyme perfumed the air. Pastries filled with honey and nuts tempted the palate. Jewels glinted and seduced in the dim light for the clouds still hung heavy trying to dull the rising merriment of people released from their religious duty. Heaps of dried fruits competed with salted fish, leather jerkins, strings of beads, piles of apples, bunches of chickens squawking and kicking, while dogs ran squealing from casual boots.

Guilhem wandered aimlessly amongst the stalls but now his soldier's senses had almost blanked the smells and tastes and shouts. His senses were tuned to the sudden movement, the glimpse of a fine leather boot with a silver buckle for it was that that first seemed to confirm his suspicions. There were not many feet so clad and this buckle had shown itself three times now.

He paused and leaned forward to feel the thickness of a wolf skin being offered. He looked under the cart piled high with skins. And there was the buckle paused also on the other side of the stall. He straightened and suddenly strode away at great pace right to the edge of the market and into a narrow lane where a tavern sign hung. He turned into the doorway, waited a short moment, then burst out of the door he had just entered. His hand was on his dagger.

Guilhem walked straight into a black robed and cowled monk who recoiled in confusion. There indeed was the silver buckle, not normal footwear for a monk.

Unceremoniously Guilhem flicked the cowl away from the lowered face and forced the follower's chin up. He looked into the eyes of Nihal! His mind blanked as he dropped the cowl and his hand left his dagger. Then two things simultaneously; his brain registered that the bearded face was not that of his lover and he felt his right wrist seized. In the same movement the stranger placed his leg behind Guilhem's left knee while twisting and turning his wrist. In a moment the Count of Toulouse, henchman of Carolus Magnus, was forced against the wall, pain shooting up the captured arm. This was no ordinary monk.

'Seigneur,' the voice was accented but somehow familiar, 'Seigneur I hope I may be forgiven for such an inauspicious introduction.' This was a man of education, a fighting man and one whose intonation still registered in his memory.

Guilhem went limp against the wall. The voice continued, 'I had not planned it so I assure you but..'

Guilhem twisted to ease the pressure on his arm and then slid down the wall apparently in a faint. As he slid he used the leverage of the wall at his back to lurch forward and upwards into the face of his attacker. His head made contact. A strange expletive as his hand was released. In a moment his dagger was pressing against the groin of the black robed figure.

'Well brother stranger,' he gasped, 'you may start your introduction again if you wish.' The monk threw back his cowl and revealed a copious flow of blood from his nose. He shook his head but at the same time managed a smile.

'Count Guilhem, my apologies once again but I am your son Mahwab-al-Axum. My mother...excuse me Seigneur but..' The young man turned aside to deal with flowing blood from his nose, 'my mother Nihal said to tell you of the Jew from Cordoba.'

'Perhaps we should indeed start again,' said Guilhem, 'let us take a cup of wine while you recover.' His thoughts tumbled over each other caught in a surge of emotion. He did his best to remain calm. As yet there was no certainty that the warrior monk was who he claimed to be.

So they found themselves in a corner of the tavern, father and son, strangers, across a plain wooden table in a land strange to both.

'I am glad I did not overcome you Seigneur. I have heard so many tales of your prowess as a warrior, even against my own people.'

Guilhem looked again at the eyes which had won his love so many years ago. This young man had quality, humour and generosity of spirit. Every instinct told him that he was who he said. He was a son to be proud of. Guilhem's eyes filled with tears as the realisation of the lost years overwhelmed his emotions.

'I truly loved your m..m..mother,' he said looking through his tears at the face that had stirred him so deeply.

'And she you,' came the quiet reply in that strange intonation that created yet another wave of feeling.

Guilhem felt his hand being taken, 'I have been told your story. My mother said that you would have given all to be with her and that it was she that left you before you knew she was with child.'

'And now my father we are drawn together as strangers because of our family heritage.' Mahwab removed his hand and felt within his robe and then placed a golden bee gently on the back of his father's outstretched hand which lay between them.

'I am told that this may yet be a cause to split the strength of the Christian empire and if our caliphate in Spain is now too weak to take advantage of such a split, I myself may be seen as a threat to your church's beliefs as I carry your blood.'

There was no doubt now. This was the son that Nihal had told him of seven years ago in Constantinople.

A silence fell between them as though the chasm of years was too big to bridge with words. And yet words were all they had. In truth they were strangers and displays of feeling or grand gestures could so easily ring false.

Guilhem searched the face opposite memorising every line and shape. The nose had stronger traces of the slight hook that distinguished Nihal's face. The eyes shaped like almonds dark brown with bushy eyebrows. Those were hers too. Hair straight and black, just an auburn hint, with neatly trimmed beard. That was more similar to his own.

'Your life my son?'

'I could not have wished it other, save the lack of my father.' A simple answer that covered a lifetime.

'Your Latin is very good,' said Guilhem, 'so you can explain, no doubt, how we c..c..c..come to meet thus,' his glance covered the monk's robes.

'My mother said that after a few moments I would not see your scar. She said that my father showed his soul so brightly that you could not see the scar. She was right my lord, but I would like to touch it?'

The question in the quiet voice nearly undid all Guilhem's remaining self-control. This was the most intimate question that he had ever faced. Here was a test to bridge the years. Only Nihal had ever shown her love in that way. His hand flicked his face reflexively as he decided and his face tilted fractionally, an offering to this son he had never known.

The touch when it came was so delicate that he was not sure that it had taken place. But in that moment his life felt richer.

'My life?' Mahwab removed his hand, 'there is one other problem. This absent father has a story attached to him which seems to be important to the Christian. This story has attached itself to me without my permission and is trying to change my life. Maybe even to end it! I think I should understand while I have time.'

'I think you should Mahwab, but you should understand now that there is no certain truth to this story. At least not for me. Others have found certainty on one side or the other and have died or killed to further their belief. But since you have been drawn into this tale you have a right to know what there is to know, or at least what little I know.'

'I am glad for in the telling we will spend time together. Now I can say that the guardians, that is what they call themselves, have asked me to bring you to a secret place. If I am with you they will accept that I will not betray them for you have tested me. If not....'

'Why you?'

'Because I am not known to many in Rome. Because they think that I will not excite the interest of the spies of the Mother Church. Because they think that you will be followed and a stranger may help to throw them off your track.'

'I was not followed here except by you my son.'

'No you were not, otherwise I should not have been so close!' Mahwab laughed out loud and drew Guilhem into his merriment. It felt right to be laughing with his son.

'We had better part before the spies of one side or another find us,' said Guilhem.

'Yes Seigneur, I will find a way to pass a message when I hear next from the followers.'

The monk rose easily and quickly disappeared. Once again Guilhem felt the vice-like grip of opposing beliefs closing round him.

Tomorrow he was to dine with the Bishop of Aniane. He was under no illusion that this would be purely a social dinner to exchange reminiscences.

CHAPTER FORTY TWO

800 AD
– The Catacombs –

'By the way Seigneur Count I have taken the name Benoit now I am a bishop. Benoit of Aniane; I like the ring of it.' Witiza laughed but there was not much humour in the sound, just as there was little respect in the words 'Seigneur Count.'

Guilhem felt that he had completely lost touch with this tall gaunt man of the church.

'This way my friend. The main audience chamber has been redecorated and the Holy Father was to show it to you tomorrow. I have persuaded his Holiness that I might usurp that privilege.' The deep rumble betrayed a certain amount of self satisfaction.

'Witiza, your p..p..pardon please, Bishop Benoit I had not thought you had an interest in decoration,' said Guilhem trying to make conversation, an art which was not foremost in his accomplishments. He was nervous about this meeting and he was annoyed with himself for being so.

'True, very true Seigneur. I do not think God's work is much taken in that direction, but for this work I make an exception.'

The tall gaunt figure stepped forward and flung open the double doors to the chamber. It was unmissable. Behind the papal throne was a huge mosaic. Three figures dominated the wall panels. In the centre sat Saint Peter in deep blue robes. To his right, kneeling was the figure of Pope Leo III hands outstretched to receive the stole of office and to the left was the unmistakable figure of Carolus Magnus being handed a battle standard. At the very least this work showed that the crowning of Charles had long been in preparation.

'But this is magnificent Bishop Benoit. I had not known that the Holy Father had prepared so long for the coronation. It makes me proud to be the servant of King Charles and the church.'

'I have shown you this before our discussions Count Guilhem.' His cloaked arm swept characteristically over the scene, 'I have shown you this because our king of Francia is a brother to the Holy Father and you are a brother, albeit in fact a cousin, to King Charles.'

So saying but without further elaboration the bishop guided Guilhem into a small chamber where a feast had been laid out. Thrusting a silver cup into his hand he said, 'no formalities please. Paul the Deacon you know I think. In Aachen was it not? Yes. And here is the archdeacon of Saint Peter's, you may recognise him from the service yesterday? Archdeacon Felix, Guilhem the Count of Toulouse. And last but of course not least the theologian to His Holiness, Father Angilbert.'

It was this last introduction that showed the way the meeting was likely to go and Guilhem resigned himself to another assault on his propensity for heresy.

'Are we to rehearse my family history yet again?' Guilhem took the initiative.

'We cannot change your history Seigneur but we can question the use to which it is being put.' This from Angilbert whose name and accent confirmed his origin from the misty northern isles. His high domed forehead dominated a ruddy face from which protruded very blue eyes. His hair and lashes were so fair that he seemed almost hairless. His eyes avoided Guilhem.

'You will remember Seigneur an oath that you swore in front of King Charles, Prior Alcuin and myself on the occasion of your wedding,' Benoit in his deep voice.

'Indeed and I can kneel before my judge without fear. At least as far as any man can so do. I have served the king, encouraged learning and followed the teachings of the church.'

'But have you used every opportunity to discourage those who believe in the heresy of a bloodline from our Lord himself?' Angilbert's eyes wandered to the ceiling.

'With respect you are in the presence of someone who stood by while one of the mother church burned a letter that might have been in the hand of our Lord Jesus himself. Is it part of the teaching of the church to discourage an independent search for the truth? You Benoit, you are the least suited to find heresy.' Guilhem waited for the reaction he knew must come.

There was a shocked silence. 'There lies the proof!' Shouted Benoit.

'There is a man who protects the most serious heresy against the teaching of Saint Peter by accusing me and Father Joseph, may God rest his soul, of destroying the Word of God. A letter my friends that was a forgery and which could have done untold harm to Mother Church.' The grey eyes glinted with passion and his deep tones filled the room.

From the reaction of the others it was clear to Guilhem that the story had been told beforehand. Somehow Benoit had persuaded his seniors that there was no possibility that such a heinous crime had been committed.

'But bishop you never allowed true scholars to examine the document. You never allowed the church to reflect and pray for guidance. You ...

'My friends we are forgetting the objective of our meeting,' it was the even tone of Paul the Deacon. A scholar whose speciality was the interpretation of ancient scripts and whose work with Hebrew and Greek was renowned. 'I myself believe that the destruction of any document is a tragedy. Even forgeries may reveal a truth of their own. We rely on the will of God to help us find the truth.'

'A fine priest and scholar of Constantinople died because a fanatic wanted me to lead a rebellion against our church. I killed my own constable Theodo because he tried to force me to act against the church. I think I have shown many times that my allegiance lies with Rome. But I also believe that the search for truth ...'

'There cannot be many truths but only one.' Benoit again in angry certainty.

'My lord bishop I am not sure that is so. I think there may be truths for their time. New discoveries may lead to new truths. For instance the great councils of the church have in the past decided on new doctrines which we believe are revealed with the help of prayer and Almighty God.' Paul spoke with the air of a scholar removed from the politics of the moment, his eyes gathering each one present; so different from Angilbert.

'I have heard enough!' This time it was the archdeacon who entered the fray. He was of mid-size but betrayed the signs of too many Papal feasts. A square face of florid complexion topped by a grizzled tonsure and short greying beard.

'The Count has been a faithful servant to Charles and to the church. There is no evidence that he wishes to lead a faction against the established teachings.'

'Thank you Archdeacon. I have much to attend to so if...'

'I warned you that it would come to this. We will not pursue this man because of his relationship to the new emperor Charles. I tell you the Church will regret this moment.' Bishop Benoit threw open his arms in a hopeless gesture.

Guilhem left the room to the continued rumble of Benoit's dissatisfaction.

'Maybe if I joined the church they would leave me alone and I could pursue the truth wherever it might lead. Surely that must be the will of God.' That thought was not the first time that idea had come to Guilhem. The meeting designed to discredit, even destroy him, had given him the idea to join his persecutors.

Two days passed in frantic activity ensuring alliances that would hold fast in support of Pope Leo; in deciding who to leave behind to build an army to protect His Holiness; to ensure the payment of tithes which had fallen behind in the rebellion against the Pope, and finally the capture of those who had held him against his will and threatened to put out his eyes.

All through this activity his mind turned again and again to his son Mahwab who was nearby in some sort of disguise. But when the contact came it took him by surprise.

'The Seigneur should pay particular attention to the boots that have been laid out today. He would do well not to change them, if it should please him.' The rather embarrassed instruction came from the young girl who was one of the retinue employed to keep his quarters in good order. It slipped his mind till he was pulling on the left boot. His foot encountered a pebble which turned out to be a small pouch. Inside a small parchment scrap 'Catacombs dusk Saturday M.'

So the other side of his life announced itself in cryptic style. Here in Rome, the seat of his beliefs, he was being called once again to keep faith with opposing views of the truth, and with his conscience.

It had been with some difficulty that he had made excuses to slip away.

'I have to meet someone. He's a troop commander to the Duke of Benevento. I think he will turn to our side but wishes to see only me.'

Promising to be back in time for a feast hosted by Duke Winigis of Spoleto, a long time supporter of Charles, Guilhem slipped out of the back door. Under an anonymous cloak he wore his armour but had left the famous helmet behind.

Light was fading as he left the great mansion by the old Temple of Venus along past the Trajan baths, down the hill along past the towering walls of the Colosseum to the Circus Maximus. Under the tiered seats of the long oval stadium stables had now taken root where he rented an underfed stiff jointed mare with a propensity to curl its upper lip and display yellow broken teeth. The catacombs were well to the south west of the city along the Via Appia Antica but from time to time he diverted from the main road, riding his reluctant mare up tracks that bordered the paved route to the necropolis. At one stage he dismounted and waited to see who followed. It seemed that his subterfuge was working. The darkening hills were empty.

A steep sided valley led to the grove where he had been told to turn right. It was at this point that another figure appeared out of the gloom at his side. Guilhem reached for his sword.

'Father, my lord count, it is I, Mahwab.' Guilhem relaxed,

'So my son you have kept safely hidden these days. Are you still in monkish robes. There is d..d..danger there for you if your cowl is removed I presume you have not taken the tonsure.' He spoke too fast and too much. Seeing his son again had loosened both tension and his tongue.

'But you are mistaken father. My disguise is thorough.' So saying Mahwab threw back his cowl and even in the gloom his bare scalp glinted.

This young man was impressive. Nihal and his teachers had done well.

'Very good my son. So now you have only to learn that an enemy down may not be an enemy defeated.' There was a smile in his voice.

'I have learned my lesson well father. I will never let a man turn towards me when I have him in an arm lock.' Once again the young warrior had understood the reference to their first meeting. He was quick.

'Here! We should dismount here.'

They tethered their horses and climbed a few paces to an insignificant stone hut. Inside were two men dressed in poor cloth and somewhat wild bearded. Hurried introductions followed. One said he was a priest who lived as a hermit in the swampy wilderness near the coast. He seemed to be particularly uneasy and kept pulling his unkempt hair across his face.

'My name is Grimald,' he mumbled obviously troubled by so many people so close.

At their feet a trapdoor was open. A faint light flickered at the base of wooden stairs. Stale air that bore an unpleasant odour drifted up into their faces. At the bottom of the steep stairs the space widened to a small chamber and three more men greeted them. Evidently the tufa rock was quite soft and easy to tunnel. Two appeared to be soldiers in leather armour and leggings laced with leather straps. Each carried a short sword. In between stood a tall thin figure in a fine wool tunic, deep brown in colour, it was belted in fine leather studded with jewels and his scabbard was also decorated. Guilhem took in the scene with a swift glance and then waited.

'Seigneur Count of Toulouse my name is Otto. I am a member of the council of the city of Rome. I have long waited to meet the man who bears the true blood.' He turned to Mahwab, 'and this 'monk,' a slight smile laid gentle emphasis on the word, 'this monk, I am told is your son. So he also carries the line but,' he paused.

'Councillor Otto, your name is familiar. I believe you did your best to support His Holiness Father Leo in his time of trouble. I am pleased to make your acquaintance. This is indeed my son who has been drawn into my story through his accident of birth, as indeed am I.'

Otto beckoned Guilhem and Mahwab to follow him a little way down the narrow tunnel that led away from the antechamber. The soldiers made to follow, but a gesture held them back.

'I am aware Seigneur Count that you have taken an ambivalent line in your life. You have not been convinced of the truth of the claim your line is descended from our Lord?'

'I know that many holy men who have sincerely studied the evidence believe that the teaching of the church is right.' Guilhem sounded as though he had rehearsed the arguments many many times.

'If I may speak, father, councillor Otto, you know that I have been brought up in the faith of Islam. We do not believe that Jesus was the son of God anymore than we are all sons of Allah. Our peoples have been at war over our beliefs, but my mother taught me that different beliefs may be held sincerely and we condemn such differences at peril of our own souls. Yet I have evidence that because of my birth your church may have ordered my death.'

'It may be so,' said Otto. 'There are parts of the church charged with eliminating heresy or those who may allow heresy to take root. I think they must be careful with your father because of his service and kinship to Carolus Magnus.'

'I can never myself be a leader in your struggle councillor, but if I am to be killed for my birth I would like to help preserve the possibilities of a different truth for future generations. So I am here.'

Guilhem looked at his son with amazement. A young man in danger, among strangers any of whom could betray him, he stood calmly certain of his position and his reasons for being in Rome and seemingly unfazed at finding himself confined below ground in a strange necropolis close to the heart of Christianity.

'It may be so. We who protect the line decided that through you we might persuade the Seigneur to help us. For the church is everywhere and we have been warned that this place which has hidden parts of the so called for many, many years may be betrayed. But Mahwab-al-Axum we must ask you to go no further here tonight. The guardians have said that we may take only the lord Guilhem the final steps. What he chooses to share with you will be for him to decide. The more that is known, the greater the peril.'

'But I...'

'No my son. I must take these steps on my own,' said Guilhem. 'You have done enough.'

Guilhem looked round and by his side stood the old hermit Grimald exuding an odour of unwashed skin and troubled breath. The three of them set off down the narrow rock tunnel lit only by the wavering light of the torches they were handed. Guilhem noticed that Grimald walked, or rather scuttled in eccentric bursts, and with a heavy limp on his left side. The unwashed hermit added his own smell to the cloying air. He would scuttle ahead, then pause, wait to see that they made the right turn, for now they were in a maze of tunnels.

'He has suffered much for his beliefs,' said Otto. 'Many years ago he was suspected of heresy. He was tortured but confessed to nothing. When they let him go he was a broken man. Now they think he is a crazy old hermit but he is one of very few who can lead us.'

Guilhem suddenly realised that they were passing shelves cut into both sides of the tunnel. There were about six recesses on each side and he realised that each held a coffin or the bare remains of a skeleton. Most were closed off with a small slab of marble.

'Stop. Who are these poor creatures thus buried in such anonymity?'

'These are the remains of the Christian martyrs slaughtered by the will of the emperors of Rome up to the reign of Diocletian. Some have been brought here from the gladiator circuses. Some were slaughtered in their homes or in the street. They carry no name.' Otto sounded weary, 'and now Christians slaughter each other in the pursuit of truth. Maybe my own remains will lie here one day.'

Grimald scuttled back to them gesturing to make haste.

'In some tunnels important Roman families are buried but their tombs are marked by carved statues in marble. There are some even earlier tombs in stone but we do not know where those people came from.'

'Could you find your way out if Grimald left us?' asked Guilhem, suddenly feeling oppressed by this citadel of death.

'Mmmm it would be difficult. The torches would burn out but there are air shafts cut into the rock. It would be a slow death among the dead.' Otto laughed.

Eventually Grimald stopped in front of a set of grave shelves that looked no different from those he had scuttled past in the flickering light of their torches. Showing little respect for the occupants he scrambled up to the top recess and disappeared head first alongside the bony remains. A moment later he re-emerged covered in dust and coughing. He had with him two cedar boxes, one larger that the other. Both were inlaid with silver and reinforced on the corners. Staring with wild eyes he held the boxes with outstretched arms so they could take them. Otto moved forward but the unkempt head shook and he looked to Guilhem.

'Here take these. They are at least part of the treasure the church would kill to find...'

Feeling strangely moved by this gesture of trust, Guilhem moved forward and took the boxes carefully from the filthy hands whose nails were torn and dirty. Grimald scrambled down from his shelf. Then he seized Guilhem by the shoulders and tears streaming down his wasted face he knelt before him.

'We who live alone in search of God. Some of us have knowledge of those who would keep the faith. I know of the old school that once was at Gellone. I knew the man of God who lives nearby – Paul, that is his name! I remember him well. A good man. And my lord you have the library of Alcinius that he bequeathed you as he lay dying. Use them my lord, use them to find the truth!'

Guilhem was astonished. Those who sacrificed so much to protect this strange imperfect story certainly knew how to keep the tale alive in far flung places.

CHAPTER FORTY THREE

800 AD
– The Secret –

But Guilhem was wrong in his assumption of the contents of the larger scroll box. The two days previous to the meeting scheduled at the church of Saint John Lateran had been hectic. Charlemagne the Holy Roman Emperor was preparing to return to Aachen. There were still rebels to be hunted and alliances to be strengthened. The new emperor could not spend his time coming to the rescue of weak popes.

In between all this business Guilhem seized every possible moment to be with the strange monk from the Pyranees. Mahwab and he had concocted a tale to account for his presence and his strange accent. Purportedly he had brought messages from his mother who was now near the end of her life in the convent of Molesnes.

The time passed in a flash as they tried to cover twenty years of absence in four days. They became close, much closer than Guilhem had ever been to his sons of his marriage to Giselda.

'But they share the bloodline too. They must be in equal danger if not more so,' said Mahwab on the second day.

'I think it may be felt by the church that they are visible in their p..p..posts within Francia and so pose little threat. They are good boys but have shown no interest in the story of their heritage so..'

'But fath..., Seigneur, you cannot share this just with me, moreover an infidel!'

'If you wish to call me father I would be happy. My son!' Guilhem was smiling and crying at the same time. The two men, strangers but a few days before, clasped each other.

'But father,' said Mahwab also smiling, 'they must be warned for even if they have no knowledge it may be assumed by the church that they have. And like me it may threaten their lives.'

Guilhem thought about that conversation as they made their way down the Esquiline hill through a part of the city needing repair and renewal. Cracked and broken paving; gaping windows; gateways with missing blocks of stone; then down into the forum flanked on either side by great palaces, storehouses, temples no longer used and some converted to churches. In between the great buildings of the past a huddle of wooden houses and huts that were the source of the frequent fires that were a regular part of city life. At the foot of the temple to Saturn still stood a tall column; the Milarum Aureum. It stood as a reminder of the great Roman empire. Inscribed on it in gilt bronze letters were the distances to the main cities of the empire at its height. Many of the letters now missing, it was a rather forlorn reminder of a different world. Rome itself was now a city with missing letters.

Mahwab was fascinated and kept stopping and asking his father about a history of which Guilhem knew little.

'Power no longer resides here. Something changed father. Maybe the secret you have been entrusted with could cause another such shift in the world.'

They started the steep climb to the top of the Capitoline hill. Mahwab climbing effortlessly while Guilhem struggled to keep up. He did his best to show that he was in no discomfort by keeping up the conversation.

Mahwab paused ostensibly to take in the view which was indeed astounding, but Guilhem knew that it was to allow him time to catch his breath. Once again he was overcome with affection for this young adventurer who had come into his life so recently.

'We feel as we do because of my mother,' said Mahwab quietly. 'She said that I was to give you this if love grew between us.' He fished beneath his monk's gown and gave Guilhem a small decorated scroll.

'Read it later father. Now is not the time.'

Guilhem nodded. They had reached the top of the hill and the church was right in front of them. Two extended porches fronted the west door supported by Corinthian columns. It was built in a plain style with red clay roof tiles covering the nave and two side aisles. On the left stood the chapter house and a small palace for the bishop of the church. It was from the palace that Otto the councillor emerged accompanied by Paul the Deacon.

Guilhem thought there had been a problem which meant that Paul was there in error and fell to discussing the architecture of the church with the priest from the Pyranees. He was pointing to the work on the capitols of the columns as Otto and Paul approached.

'Seigneur Count you need not stray from our matter, the deacon here is one of us.'

'Seigneur,' Paul bent his head, 'I know I was part of Bishop Benoit's group that questioned you. It is true that I am also part of the church. But years ago I heard of the belief in the continuing bloodline and that somewhere there was proof of the story that lay hidden. Some time ago I was allowed by the guardians to examine the scrolls. The ones that are now moved, with your help, to a safer place. I think that it is God's will that they should be preserved. Let me show you something in the church my lord count.' With that he strode off under the portico and disappeared into the church.

He was a square man. Strong shoulders moved under his robe. Large hands scarred and roughened by manual work gestured as he spoke. His skin was darkened by the sun but the dark brown eyes under heavy black mobile eyebrows looked with confidence at the world.

'Deacon Paul you have studied them and you can interpret them?' asked Guilhem following him.

'Yes Seigneur I can translate the letter from Aramaic. I have spent many years learning the ancient scripts. Arabic, Aramaic, Greek..' he broke off.

'I see Count Guilhem that you were looking at my hands - not the hands of a scholar, that's true. When not with my scrolls I like to work in the gardens of the abbey. I believe that God's work is best done with mind and body.'

'Deacon Paul why have you not shown your findings to the Holy Father the Pope?' It was Mahwab.

'Because my son I think the church is not ready to believe. I think the Holy Father and the all the body of the mother church are frightened. If the complete scrolls were found they might show that the teachings of the church are wrong. They are afraid that the whole structure of the church would split under such new ideas. Maybe the whole of Christendom would collapse. Maybe then the tide of Islam would indeed sweep the world. And, my son, I think they are right.'

Paul sounded as though this was a conclusion that he had reached very reluctantly.

There was silence as the both Guilhem and Mahwab thought over what they had just heard.

Paul the Deacon turned into a small side chapel. It was dimly lit by only one small window. He stood aside and waited. Guilhem and Mahwab knew they had been brought to this spot for a reason. It was Mahwab who saw it first.

The source of the dim light was a small square window of thick crude glass. The colours of the sand in the glass obscured the light. In the centre of the little square was a crudely painted golden bee. The three men gazed up in silence at this strange message from the past.

'This window is very old my friends. It seems that even in the early days of the church in Rome there were those who carried a different story in their hearts,' said Paul.

'But the s..s..scrolls...?'

'The scrolls. Yes those precious links to the past and to knowledge. I have studied them closely my lord count. But we have a problem. The guardians over the centuries have had to take measures to protect them and their message. Some have been cut into parts. Some copies were made. Some translations also. To tell the truth I think parts of the Word have been spread so that we may never recover all the texts. We can only do what we can to protect that which is in our care.'

Guilhem and Mahwab waited expectantly but the scholar with the roughened hands of a farmer did not continue. As they walked Guilhem thought over the words of Paul. His own experience had borne them out. Of course he would be a focus for those trying to continue the search, but he had come across scripts small and large in Cordoba, in Axum, even in the wild forest of Saxony and now here in Rome. Could the pieces ever be made into a coherent whole?

They continued back to a small refectory next to the chapter house. Otto rejoined them and wine was served in pewter mugs.

'You my son, wish to know if you are protecting the word of God,' said Paul.

Otto interrupted. 'Paul is a scholar, Seigneur, and a scholar who is touched by the grace of God. He is troubled by the attitude of the church to the pursuit of truth.'

'That is so but I also understand that there would be a huge risk to Christ's church here on earth if.....' Paul paused again, 'there may be a time in the future where man is better prepared to see another way, perhaps even without bloodshed....' his voice tailed away.

'Father Paul, I too have spent my life in the service of his m..m.. majesty the king, unable to reveal everything to him or indeed the church. We are b..b..both men who must live with the burden of doubt.' Guilhem's stammer was more pronounced than usual.

Paul looked at the Count of Toulouse with sympathy. 'There is more you should understand Seigneur. Scholars do not always agree. There is conflict about the truth of the origin of parchments. Are they forged to cause dissension? Then there is the question of interpretation of the words... it is not an easy path.' He sounded suddenly weary.

He reached over and took the larger scroll box and opened it. Guilhem had still not seen the contents because he was sure that he would not be able to understand them. Surely the contents would be a section of the instructions similar to those spoiled by mould at Abba Salama.

He was wrong. Paul unfolded the scroll carefully.

It was a map with place names and even names of buildings carefully written.

'The guardians created this many years ago. It shows the part of the story that we in Rome were entrusted with. It is an attempt to show the places where the trail lies. This is what some of us think took place near the end of His life here on earth. Our Lord sent a summary of his teaching to different parts of the world. Perhaps with Paul to Damascus, with Peter to Rome, with Mark to Alexandria and possibly with Mary to Francia to the small port of Sous Sainte Marie.'

'Sous Sainte Marie! So that is why the Jew from Cordoba wanted me to go there,' exclaimed Guilhem.

'This map was made later but no-one knows by whom, but it does accord with the stories that have reached us through the ages. The problem is that the Word has had to be hidden many times from those who would persecute men of our persuasion through the ages. And now....' The deacon's voice trailed away.

'And now it is very hard to be certain of what is true and what is false. But if someone of the true blood put his faith in these few scraps then he could cause...'

'Trouble for the church,' said Otto who had been silent for a long time.

'But the actual summary of the teachings. Was that the large scroll that was so spoilt which we discovered in Axum? Has anyone seen the full text? Would it prove the church has followed the wrong path?'

'If writings were discovered in the hand of Mohammed that showed the Imams were in error with even a portion of their interpretations of our Holy Book there would be great disruption among our people.' Mahwab interrupted. 'I think our teachers would try to hide such from the world at least until they could rconcile the new discovery with their teaching.'

All heads turned to Guilhem's son.

'Indeed the young man speaks the truth. No seigneur Guilhem we have not found the teachings that were sent. You may have been the closest to seeing what all have sought for so long, but these ancient scraps may yet help us find them. But Mother Church wishes to find them first,' said Paul

'I was wrong d..d..deacon. I thought that that was what lay in the second box...'

'You should know what you are protecting Seigneur,' said Paul.

'You should come to Gellone deacon. There I will try to found a school whose sole task is the search for the truth.'

'And will they find it my son?'

It was then that Guilhem realised that the search for truth would never finish. Truth was not a finite destination but maybe the search itself was God's task for man. It was not a realisation that sat well with a soldier and a man who preferred destinations to journeys.

That night Guilhem read the letter from Nihal.

My love this is who we made together. You are reading this so I know that Mahwab loves you as I do. Absent you have been but I have tried to bring our son up so that you would be proud. You are reading this so I know that I succeeded in your eyes.

I pray that our blood may not cause him suffering or even death. That

would be harder even than your absence.

I know that he too will feel that his life is enriched by knowing you. I know because you are reading this.

Our lives are as they are. It is the will of Allah
Nihal

Two days later having made arrangements for the safe passage of certain small packages, Guilhem embraced Mahwab and said goodbye to his son.

CHAPTER FORTY FOUR

809AD

– Relics –

'O God, you are my God, I seek you,

My soul thirsts for you

My flesh faints for you...'

The familiar chant filled the abbey church at the service of Prime. The morning psalm that set the rhythm of the day. The early sun sent shafts of light from the small high windows striping the sturdy pillars and setting the dust motes dancing.

'Maybe they dance all night but we cannot see them' thought Guilhem as his attention wondered. It often did these days.

'And the Lord said ' Listen to what the unjust Judge says. And will not God grant justice to his chosen ones who cry to him day and night? Will he delay long in helping them?" This week it was Steven who was the lector. The large square head bent in concentration as he read the familiar lesson. In truth they were nearly all there, the monks and priests who had looked at him uncertainly when he had arrived unheralded five years ago.

Steven who had fulfilled his promise and Guilhem thought, would be the choice of the monks to succeed him.

There was Simon, the former night watchman, who had taken the tonsure last year and who was proving to be very able in the scriptorium. Adalung still excitable and full of opinion but whose faith burned bright in the little community, and of course Jonathen whose wisdom and scholarship combined with scarce bridled enthusiasms made him his closest friend. They were a good group thought Guilhem as he let the comfort of the Word sweep over him.

'And will not God grant justice to his chosen ones who cry to him day and night?' The words penetrated his musings. Was this life of prayer what God had wanted for him all these years? Was this sense of fulfilment and achievement God's reward for the life that had been besieged by doubt? Was this the seal of approval that he had chosen the right course? But then if it was so why did the kernel of doubt remain with him like a pebble in his sandal? He shook his head. Always more questions than answers.

The small group moved out to the cloister. As yet there was only the fountain placed in the southwest corner of the little square that was made of stone. The simple basin raised on two fluted pillars to waist height gurgled happily in the sun. The ambulatory that marked the cloister was a simple wooden structure with a tiled roof. The floor as yet just beaten earth. It was the abbot's next project – to build a cloister of stone to complement the sturdy abbey church.

'Steven take Fulrad with you to the forest people. Take two sacks of grain. See if they will join you in prayer and listen to the scriptures.'

It was part of the ongoing struggle to bring the forest people into the fold.

'But my lord abbot...' Steven exclaimed.

'Yes I know my son. It seems that we make little progress. But there is progress. Last Sunday there were four from the forest at our service. The Word will prevail if we are patient.' Guilhem gave his blessing to the kneeling figure.

It was on the way back from his walk up the valley that he began to feel strange. It was as though something was squeezing his heart. He leaned heavily on his staff. The sky tilted. The sun blazed across his vision as he sat heavily on a large rock. A strange sensation, not quite a pain, ran down his left arm. There was something very powerful about this feeling. After a time the sensation abated and soon he felt strong enough to continue back to the abbey. But Guilhem sensed that something had changed. Perhaps time was short.

'Brother Jonathen, what do you think of our relic?' he had called for Jonathen on his return. He had a sudden urge to see again the famous relic donated by Charlemagne four years previously. It was this relic that brought a steady trickle of pilgrims to the growing abbey.

It was a piece of the 'one true cross'.

'In truth, my lord abbot?' the wispy hair still flew wildly in the candlelight although in the last five years he had lost much of it.

'In truth, my friend.'

'In truth I cannot find solace in this small piece of wood and yet if it is true that our Lord's suffering body lay against such fragments it should help give substance to our prayers and ......'

'If it is true...' repeated Guilhem.

They were in the small crypt beneath the altar which served as a chapel. The relic was above the plain altar in a silver box fastened with thin silver straps. The oil torches flared and crackled in the dim light throwing the shadows of the two monks against the low arched ceiling.

'Many people including our king and even the Holy Father value this small scrap highly my friend.'

'Indeed my lord abbot they do. Many would die for it. And yet...' Jonathen was unaccustomedly hesitant. The wispy hair was like a halo in the shadows; the long thin face with prominent nose, the flesh worn thin by a life of prayer, looked up doubtfully at the silver box.

'So if men would die for this poor scrap what would they d..d..do for a scroll in the hand of our Lord that told us the church had made errors in its teaching. And what if this truth was produced to the world by a man of the true blood?' Guilhem flicked the back of his hand across his nose in that familiar gesture.

'If the story caught fire my lord abbot the world would never be the same. Christendom could tear itself apart.'

'And yet could such a scroll ever be an uncontestable truth of itself? Look at that piece of the true cross. Why has man valued that scrap of wood over eight hundred years? Many would choose to die for that little splinter because they believe His body touched it at His end.'

'A scroll would be the same my lord. Such a thing could tear the world apart because of what each man believed about it.'

Jonathen had been told a lot of Guilhem's life story. He had known for many years that his master had hidden certain things from the church. Of course it was but three years ago that he had found that scrap of ancient writing that the Jew Soloman Chalafta had translated for them.

'That is what I think too. My friend you know that I have been the subject of much scrutiny because of my birth. You know of some of the things with which I have been entrusted. I would not burden you with all the story, but you also know that I have served our Lord and the church to the best of my ability. You know too that I was put upon a cross because some feared I was hiding the seeds of d..d..destruction of our mother church. I was rescued by the agents of the emperor and I am still here because of his protection. At least so I think.'

'My Lord abbot, I have always thought of you as a truly Christian man. I have been so lucky to serve God with your help and guidance. We both believe that scholarship will help man to learn to live with other men and our work is done with his blessing. We may not be able to know all truths now but one day knowledge will be granted to men to distinguish between truth and falsehood.' Jonathen's words were coming in spate as they always did at times of stress.

Guilhem clasped the tall figure to him. 'Brother Jonathen you know I have not been strong since the trial on the cross. From time to time I have a pain here which seems to me to be a warning,' he gestured to the area of his heart. 'I may not have long before the good Lord calls this servant.. I can only pray that 'the fruits of my labours' will be sufficient to commend my soul to our Lord. A wise prior told me to pray so, many years ago. I can only commend my efforts to His mercy.' He held up his hand in the flickering light to forestall the inevitable protest.

'I must send messages but I will make arrangements for those. But in addition I need someone to know the last hiding place for certain,' he hesitated, 'items. Will you t..t..take that burden my friend? Perhaps we should pray together for God's guidance. You should be very certain before..'

'Of course my lord I will.'

'Would you like to see the few scraps that are in my care? '

Jonathen shook his head and turned back to the altar. The two old men knelt painfully on the cold stone paving. As they knelt together in prayer the torch flickered and went out.

CHAPTER FORTY FIVE

809AD

– Trace –

It was a kind summer at Gellone. The sun shone. There was sufficient rain to make a good harvest. The great brown eagles soared indifferently in their world, while the grasshoppers flew with great whirring leaps in the heat and cicadas competed with the birdsong.

But as the weeks spent their days toward autumn, the abbot became weaker. His favourite walk to the end of the valley became less frequent and could only be accomplished with help from Fulrad or Steven, or sometimes the Rabbi Chalafta. The pain became more frequent, and brother Steven gradually took some of the duties from his much loved abbot.

Guilhem seemed particularly interested in his own internment, which the brothers thought was somewhat out of character. He could be seen with Pierre Clergue, poring over sketches in the sand which were obliterated if any of the brothers came too close.

As always, the pace of the days were dictated by the timetable laid down by Saint Benedict. Lauds, Prime, Teree, Sext, and so on through the day and night.

When he was not occupied with administrative matters, Guilhem would be found in the scriptorium watching his school of mixed faiths at work. There were now two Jewish scholars and two Arabs. Ubada Rushd had taken on a young scholar from Alexandria who was extremely shy and would rarely look at the person he was talking to. Ubada explained that he was his cousin, who had been recommended to him, and that in spite of his awkward manner, he was exceptionally quick at translating the old scripts.

Guilhem would watch them at work, usually led by brother Jonathen. When a new scroll was being translated, or a new book opened, he would lean forward on his staff, mouth slightly parted and gaze fixed on the scholars, as if waiting for some great revelation that might ease his passage from this world to the next.

And in fact this was exactly right. Although part of him had settled in the knowledge that the good Lord had decided to take him into His arms with his doubts unresolved, there was always the hope that something irrefutable would guide his last actions.

It was Arnaud, the young boy from the forest people, the very same who had led him to the hermit Paul and had witnessed that poor man's slow death, who broke the rhythm of the days.

'My Lord, there are messengers from the king!' The small lad with the quick brown eyes had developed into a neat, wiry young man with a light footed walk that covered the ground with amazing speed. He had converted wholeheartedly to the faith and was one of the most enthusiastic of the lay monks.

'How distant Arnaud? How much time do we have?'

'They will be here at nightfall.'

'Very well. You be the messenger to the village. We must be ready to make them welcome.' They were in the study room next to the scriptorium and already the scribes and everyone nearby had gathered to hear the news.

'I think they will bring more rules.' It was the voice of brother Alsom, the small sacrist, whose function it was to keep the papers in order and to promulgate the voice of both king and church. Charlemagne had become famous for a continuous stream of capitularies which encapsulated the way that he wished the kingdom to be run. It was the responsibility of every lord, count, constable and abbot to ensure obedience to the latest instructions from the court.

'No doubt, brother Alsom, but the king seeks unity and justice in his kingdom. There is much g..g..good in the guidance he sends.'

'But there is so much guidance my lord. And all have to be copied and sent to the constables and priors and abbots. We have not the scribes to do so much and to keep the Word available.'

Guilhem held up his hand. 'You do very well, brother Alsom. Our scriptorium is one of the most respected for its quality. The good Lord will reward you in heaven.'

The small sacrist knelt and left the room, beaming with pleasure.

In the late afternoon, the jingle of harness and the soft percussion of hooves on turf announced that the royal emissaries were at the gate.

Leading them, dressed in full armour, was Constable Arnulf of Bezier with a troop of six armed men. This was the noble who had rescued Guilhem from the cross two years before. Behind them were two monks from Aachen and a senior member of the constable's establishment.

The greetings were almost completed and Arnulf himself was receiving the blessing from the hands of the abbot, when he noticed a late addition to the royal party. The slab like figure and rounded belly of Leo the priest had appeared.

'My lord abbot.' A slight grunt as the belly followed the protesting knees.

'May the Lord be with you brother Leo.'

'You are surprised my lord abbot?'

'Of course it is always a pleasure to see one of the original flock at Gellone again, but yes, I am somewhat surprised.' Guilhem was not only surprised but also apprehensive.

'Perhaps, my lord abbot, you would like to read this message from Archbishop Joseph who is newly appointed by the king and with the approval of the Holy Father.'

Guilhem received the small scroll with some foreboding. He had never met Joseph, who had been sent from the north of Francia, but he had heard that he was another who looked to root out heresy wherever it might be found.

There was something slightly smug in Leo's expression as he heaved his bulk upright.

'Thank you, my son. I will read it later, when all our guests have been settled and we have eaten.' Guilhem tucked the scroll away and forgot about it.

Arnulf was always a welcome guest. Big, bluff and loud, with a way of finding sexual innuendoes in unlikely places, he kept the company in laughter and at the same time was a source of news about the kingdom. The bluff exterior hid a brave heart and a shrewd mind. It was a good evening, only interrupted by Compline. At the service Guilhem suddenly felt very tired and was supported to his small chamber by an anxious Steven as soon as it was over.

He lay in the low light emitted by two small oil lamps feeling his heart labouring under his robe. As the thumping gradually quieted, he reviewed the last few months. He had sent messages to all who needed to hear. Two of his three remaining children in Francia had visited. Bertrada was comfortably married and seemed content. Lothar was carrying out his duties as constable of his region with diligence. Bernard was engaged in warfare on the borders of the Pyrenees and wanted more money to fund his battles. That was as it ever was. It was strange, thought Guilhem, as he lay in the dim light, these were his heirs, yet there was little emotional bond. Suddenly he realised that this was exactly the same as the relationship with his own father. They had just grown apart. None of them wanted to be involved with their heritage, or to know about the burdens he had carried all his life.

Except Mahwab. He had grown closer to Mahwab in those few days nine years ago than any of the offspring that had come from his marriage to the fair Giselda. Perhaps if she had lived....

He struggled upright and poured some water into his wooden mug. He would sleep a little before the night service of Matins. It was as he shrugged off the coarse wool robe that he felt the scroll bar and remembered he had not yet read the message from Archbishop Joseph.

To the abbot of Gellone, my brother in faith

We are not known to one another but I have heard good things of the work you are doing at Gellone. Mother church is especially pleased that some of the forest people are being led away from their lives outside God's will to the true way for the salvation of souls.

We are equally pleased with the quality and diligence of the work of your scriptorium. Please ensure that brother Jonathen and chief scribe Fulrad are aware of our satisfaction.

We have not heard much in the way of detail of the work of your school and can only hope that the ways of the Lord our God are being observed. It would be unfortunate should scholarship lead us away from the one true path.

This message is brought to you by brother Leo who was under your tuition. He has worked hard at improving his scholarship and has shown great commitment to the church. We have also heard that sadly your own strength is failing and that it may be that the good Lord will call you to him.

You should know that in this event we are minded to appoint brother Leo as abbot of Gellone. It may help his early days if you could prepare your community for such an eventuality.
In Christ
Archbishop Joseph

Guilhem held the script closer to wavering light and re-read the letter. It looked no better the second time. Here, in the carefully coded words, lay the seeds of destruction of much of his work of the last five years. '...should scholarship lead us away from the one true path...' meant that they would close the school. He thought that the words also were a reminder about the church's continuing doubts regarding his own faith. And to ensure that there was little he could do little to avert the catastrophe, they had sent Leo to watch over him. Maybe he had been instructed to finish the task he had not completed two years previously.

A combination of rage and despair swept over him. He felt betrayed by the church to which he had devoted so much of his last years. He would salvage what he could. He had levered himself upright and had the quill in his hand before the pain swept up his left side and he was overtaken by a singing blackness.

Steven found his lord abbot before Matins and raised the alarm. He was slumped over the small table holding the letter from the Archbishop. Drops of black iron gall ink scattered from quill point to the parchment. He was still breathing and some colour remained on his face. The infirmarian and the tall ungainly Arab Ubada Rushd took over the care of the much loved leader. The Arab soon showed that the rumours surrounding his people's superior knowledge of medicine were well founded. Guilhem was made comfortable and he seemed to sleep quietly.

'We must let him rest my friends. He is in the hands of Allah.'

'Better in the care of our Lord Jesus...' a barely audible mutter from the doorway. Jonathen turned to see who had uttered such an unwarranted comment. It was Leo.

The days passed as the year moved in sympathy to its end along with the weakening abbot. Guilhem could not move anything on his right side, but he was lucid and unfailingly encouraging to those around him. He put up with the indignities of his weakened state as if they were unimportant. He insisted on being carried to the church for all services, save the early Matins.

The news of Leo's likely appointment had spread because the letter had been seen by Steven and others. Guilhem did as he had been asked and spent time with Leo to advise him as best he could. He ensured that the sacrist Alsom, the almoner, and the cellarer all spent time with Leo.

But on another level, other things were being organised. Guilhem dictated two identical letters and sent them by different routes to Emperor Charlemagne, protesting at the choice of Leo. Secretly, he put Jonathen in charge of removing some of the scrolls, books and other written works to a monastery in the foothills of the Pyrenees. This was done with the enthusiastic practical help of Arnaud. His knowledge of the hidden routes in and out of Gellone allowed the boxes to leave unobserved.

'Brother Jonathen, we will save what we can,' he said one sunny afternoon as he lay in the cloister. 'I am sure the Archbishop will close the school when I am gone. But I do not want you to act against your conscience. You may feel that this is a betrayal of the wishes of the church.'

Jonathen knelt beside his old friend and placed his hand on that of the abbot. 'Give me your blessing father.' The subject was never mentioned again.

The failing abbot did not abandon his strange obsession. He frequently asked to be taken to the mason's workshop and took great interest in the progress of his own tomb. He lay on the bed that had been carried to the spot, quietly giving instructions to Pierre Clergue, the trusted mason. As the figures on the side of the marble slab emerged, chipped, chiselled and rubbed, it became apparent that the dying man had commissioned a depiction of a pilgrimage. This was not a pilgrimage of nobles and churchmen, rather the figures that were slowly revealed were of the common man and woman carrying the tools of the farm through the countryside. Trees and flowers grew out of the stone, all delicately executed, each detail lovingly rendered.

The abbot seemed pleased and anxious as the work progressed. It was as though he needed to see it finished before he could release his fading grip on life.

The last detail was a flight of bees disappearing into the bole of an oak tree. It was a miracle of craftsmanship, and Guilhem's face lit up with quiet satisfaction.

As the news of the impending death of the abbot spread, the number of visitors grew. In only five years, the little abbey tucked away in the remote hills of the Cevennes had grown in reputation. Scholars came to marvel at the collection of books and scrolls and to beg the opportunity to read and learn. Priors and abbots and bishops came to examine the work of the scriptorium and to elicit the secrets of the consistently high quality of its output. A few of the churchmen came as well to learn of the spiritual life of the abbey and its success in converting the forest people. Then there were nobles and soldiers with whom Guilhem had fought against the infidel, or even fought against in the name of the king. Paul the Deacon came from Rome with other members of the church, with a blessing from the Holy Father himself.

And of course they all wanted to pray in front of the fragment of the one true cross. Many of the pilgrims asked to be blessed by the abbot before departing. Under the watchful eyes of Steven and Jonathen, he became used to placing his one good hand on the kneeling figures in benediction.

Guilhem was bemused by all this attention. His small gift to God of service and labour had spread far beyond his imagination. It was clear that the internal struggle which had been so integral to his life had not dimmed the effects of his life of service to crown and church. 'By their works ye shall know them.' Indeed; but had it been enough?

'It would seem, my lord abbot, that you have lit a beacon for the church in your small corner of the world.'

Paul the Deacon, who had travelled from Rome, had found a rare moment to be alone with Guilhem in his cell. The dark hair and beard were now flecked with grey, but the mobile eyebrows and level gaze were unchanged. The strong scarred hands lay folded on his lap.

'It is somewhat of an embarrassment for mother church, or at least those who suspect a link with heresy,' he smiled. 'And may I ask that, if there were any such links, my lord abbot, have they been suitably treated?' The two men looked at each other and smiles grew to chuckles which turned into stomach wrenching laughter.

'I do not think, Paul, that this is r..r..recommended for a man in my weakened...' Laughter broke out again. Guilhem felt a weight lift from his soul. There could be no serious sin if the good Lord allowed such joy.

He beckoned the grizzled head closer, and for some moments whispered in his ear. Paul looked at him in amazement.

'It would appear that the secrets are well hidden my lord abbot. And scattered. In future times will they ever piece it all together?'

'From what I have seen in my life, Paul, there are traces both false and true in many parts of our world. But if God wills it, he will make his truth known when the time is right.'

Paul left Gellone that same day bearing with him part of the knowledge.

The next day Guilhem called for Jonathen. His breathing was more laboured.

'My time is near, old friend. I will not go to the church for the services any more. But if it please any of our brethren, perhaps they would come from time to time and read the Word or pray with me.'

Jonathen left the bedside with tears in his eyes.

But Guilhem did not die. It was as though he was waiting. A few days later, a message came from the court at Aachen. It was dictated and sealed by Charlemagne himself. Guilhem asked for more light to be brought to his spartan cell, and with Jonathen holding him upright on his bed, he read;

'The abbot of Gellone
Cousin Guilhem
I am sorry to hear that you think that your time on earth is now short. I have given much thought to your request. You have been a great servant to my kingdom. It appears that many in the church feel that your work at Gellone has been blessed by God. Others still worry that your heritage carries within it the seed of heresy.
Nevertheless I grant your request and hearby confirm the appointment

of the monk Steven as your successor as abbot.
    Carolus Magnus'

A smile spread over the face of the dying man. He looked at Jonathen. 'Our work will be spared for a time my friend, but I fear that it will be a short respite. Tell the others.'

Late that night another monk asked to be blessed by the abbot. He was just another pilgrim, come, he said, from the far Pyrenees. There had been many such over the past weeks. He had prayed in front of the fragment of the true cross along with others. Although it was very late, Guilhem slept very little these days and had given instructions that those who wished to receive his blessing should be allowed to visit.

'Father, bless me.' The hooded figure knelt as countless others had done beside his bed. The oil lamps flickered their weak light on the kneeling monk and the pale drawn face of Guilhem, abbot of Gellone. The scar now dominated the fleshless face. Only the eyes showed the warmth and strength of the spirit behind the wasting flesh.

'Father!' The voice more urgent, as though he feared he might miss the touch of this man of God.

'Bless...' Something in the monk's voice caught Guilhem's full attention and he looked into the kneeling monk's eyes.

'My son. It is you?' He was looking into the eyes of Mahwab, or were they the eyes of Nihal? He couldn't really separate the two.

'The bees, my son. The bees...' It was obvious that the old man's mind had wandered.

'Father, I just had to see you once more.'

'I am so glad you came Mahwab. I can let my life here go now. The Lord has truly blessed me. But you are in danger in this land. You must go. May you be blessed.'

The old man seemed in full possession of his senses now. His hand flicked feebly in the direction of the old scar. A decision had been reached.

'But should you be compelled to follow our mystery, follow the bees my son. I shall be resting on them after I have gone from this earth. In the church; that's the funny thing. In the church...'

'Father I don't ......,'

'Kiss me my son. Hold me close. I shall rest upon p..p..part of our mystery when I am gone. The last two bees and...' his voice faded again. There was a long pause. The ragged breath rasping as life ebbed from the old man.

'I truly loved your mother.'

Jonathen found the strange monk holding Guilhem. Tears were streaming down his face. The abbot was still breathing as the monk rose from his knees and disappeared into the night. Jonathen cradled the person dearest to him on earth. He was the second man alive who knew that the body of his beloved abbot would rest on more than just marble.

The abbot of Gellone never spoke again, but was there a hint of a smile on the disfigured face of the dead man? It was difficult to tell because of the scar.